GUIDED BY INSTINCT...

"Don't think you can lie to me."

Cadence forced herself to meet a pair of eyes that were suddenly as cold as the depths of space. "I am not lying."

He studied her features as though by sight alone he could discern the veracity of her statement. He appeared on the verge of releasing her when inexplicably his expression began to alter subtly. His eyes left her face to skim down her body, and Cadence realized that, during their confrontation, the blanket had slipped from her grasp. Only the sheer, shimmering fabric of her spiderweb-woven nightshift remained.

Slowly, warily, she raised her eyes from the thick bronzed column of his neck. It was a mistake. The sheer male hunger reflected in his storm-hued irises paralyzed her. Like a wild beast responding to a distant howl of need in the wilderness, her body answered that wordless call.

CHRISTINE MICHELS

IN DESTINY'S ARMS

LOVE SPELL ◆ NEW YORK CITY

LOVE SPELL®

June 1996

Published by

Dorchester Publishing Co., Inc.
276 Fifth Avenue
New York, NY 10001

Copyright © 1996 by S.C. Michels

Printed in the United States of America.

In Destiny's Arms

Chapter One

Sergeant Cadence Barrington gripped the arms of her flight seat with white knuckled fingers. Storms in hyperspace were unheard of. Yet there it was, looming before her like a malevolent ghost intent on her destruction, visible only because its violent cyclonic movement churned the rainbow-hued mists of hyperspace.

"Time to impact?" Cadence demanded of the ship's on-board computer, one of the more advanced C.L.A.I.R.E. models. Claire was an acronym for Comox & Lassiter Artificial Intelligence and Robotics Enterprises.

"Five minutes."

Even as she secured her helmet to the neck of her flight suit, Cadence studied the ship, trying to anticipate stress points. The *Ulysses* was a relatively small, two-seat, Tachyon-class ship with the sleek lines of an oceanic predator. A good little ship, but it didn't have the shielding capabilities of a larger vessel. How would it handle an electromagnetic storm containing mysterious unidentifiable elements? There was no way to know. She had to be prepared to take manual control—something rarely, if ever, done in hyperspace.

To add to that problem, this lane led directly into the black hole known as Cygnus XI. The closest lane exit—the one which had been calculated to deliver the ship into Fortunan space—was located much too near the event horizon of the collapsed star for comfort. Topping off the bad news: According to Claire's calculations, they would reach the event horizon, or gravitational boundary, within mere minutes of contact with the storm. If Claire was off-line, Cadence had to complete the maneuvers for exit from the lane before the ship was caught in the star's gravity. Just a slight miscalculation, an almost insignificant delay in making the turn for the exit, and she could be caught in the clutch of a gravity so intense that not even light escaped, crushed to death by the weight of her own body. And that was only *one* of the possibilities.

Black holes usually affected everything around them, sometimes disrupting time, often warping space, and invariably scrambling communications. Only a computer was capable of making the hundreds of thousands of minute calculations necessary to successfully navigate near the powerful collapsed stars. And *her* computer was already experiencing difficulties: Its guidance systems were off-line.

Cadence felt sweat bead on her upper lip as tension seeped into her shoulders. The awareness that she could end up dead or missing without anyone knowing what had happened to her or where to look for her flared distressingly in her mind. "Claire, can you access a jump satellite?"

There was a brief pause. "Negative."

"All right. I want you to begin sending two messages in an alternating repeat pattern. One will go to Stellar Legion Internal Affairs Headquarters on Space Station Olympus, the other to Fortuna. You will detail our current situation and let them know that I will be trying to take manual control of the course alteration in the event that you are not on-line at the critical time."

"Understood." Claire seemed hesitant. "You do understand that the odds of a message escaping hyperspace without satellite assistance are approximately fifty to one."

"I know, Claire. Just make sure that you send enough of those messages to beat the odds."

"Affirmative."

Cadence stared at the violently churning vortex coming toward her. Somehow, life had never seemed as precious as it did at this moment.

She looked at the ship's clocks. Three-and-a-half minutes to impact with the storm. Her limbs felt leaden. The storm filled her universe, had become the universe. She turned her head for a last look at normal hyperspace from the side window and murmured her brother's name. "Chance." There was a wealth of emotion and meaning behind the single syllable. It was for him that she was here.

I'm sorry to have to tell you this, Cadence, but your brother is missing. Even now, the words resounded in her mind, as stark and disturbing as the echo of stalking footsteps. According to what she'd been able to glean from the written report forwarded to her, her brother had disappeared without a trace, before the very eyes of friends and colleagues on Fortuna.

Impossible, of course! Someone was hiding something. A cover-up of some kind?

She closed her eyes. *Please!* She prayed to whomever or whatever might be out there. *Let me live to find him.*

As her twin, Chance was connected to her in a way that no other person could be. Dammit! What had happened to him? Why hadn't she felt something?

Without hesitation, her superiors at Stellar Legion Internal Affairs had granted her permission to travel to the colony world of Fortuna to investigate his disappearance. Not because of any particular compassion, but because, as an intelligence-gathering agency, they were intrinsically paranoid. The fact that something mysterious had happened to someone connected to one of their employees worried them. The Stellar Legion ruled space. It was the Stellar Legion that provided the Legionnaires, who acted as peacekeepers, explorers, soldiers, prison guards, and in virtually any other capacity deemed necessary by Earth's coalition government. Those who governed the Legion governed space, and they jealously guarded their power and jurisdiction. Anything suspicious that was even remotely connected to the Legion had to be investigated. And, like Cadence, her superiors regarded Chance Barrington's sudden disappearance as suspect.

Upon receiving authorization from her superiors, Cadence had promptly arranged a meeting with the Fortunan Guardian who had inquired into Chance's disappearance. From the little she had been able to learn prior to meeting with him, though, it seemed that the Guardian had already closed the file. That didn't bode well. Yet Cadence was certain her brother was alive. She would have known if it were otherwise.

"Impa . . . act." Claire's voice, unrecognizable and mechanical, jolted her into the present.

Cadence felt the computer losing control of the ship almost immediately. Lights on the computer panel flickered wildly. She grasped the manual controls in preparation for the attempted turn.

"Claire, are you there?" she shouted.

No response.

Damn! So, it was up to her. Hitting the button to trigger the stellar drive, she began to turn the lever that would allow the ship to skirt the event horizon of the massive black hole. As she turned the ship, she fired the rear thrusters to give the ship an extra boost of power in breaking away. Then she checked to see if there were any reliable readings coming through. Nothing. Everything was wavering. Her eyes widened as she noticed the wildly fluctuating digits on the clocks. Including ship and destination time.

"Claire, are you there?"

No response.

She looked defiantly at the storm beyond the viewscreen. "You won't win," she said with quiet determination.

As she continued the turn, Cadence kept one eye on the panels, searching for any sign of a return to normalcy. But there were no readings she could trust. She wanted to scream, to release the pent-up feelings of helplessness and rage. But she fought on in stubborn silence.

A minute later, some innate sense told her that she had completed the turn. This should be the end of the lane. She held her breath. In the next instant, the brilliance of the colors of hyperspace began to fade. So far, so good. Then, a few seconds later, a torrent of lights rushing toward her at tremendous speed signaled her drop into normal space. Cadence exhaled an audible sigh of relief.

Now to check the readings. The scanner cameras appeared to be functioning normally. But was she in the Fortunan system? It was definitely a binary star system. The giant red sun held within its powerful grasp thirteen planets, twenty-seven moons, and— on the outer rim of the system—a smaller yellow sun with its own system of five planets. It certainly appeared to be the correct star system. But where was Fortuna? Not daring to consider the possibility that the space-warping phenomenon of the black hole had caused her to miss her coordinates, she searched again for the planet. There! It wasn't quite where she'd expected it to be, but at least it looked like Fortuna. She used thrusters to adjust her course and headed for the giant Earthlike planet.

Thank the stars! She would never have thought that she'd be so glad to see a world, any world, as she was at that moment. She felt absurdly pleased with herself. I won't even be late for my meeting with the Guardian, she thought, automatically glancing at the clocks.

Wait a minute!

She looked at the clocks again, her gaze arrested by the incomprehensible digits highlighted there. The time read 1900 hours February 15, 1761 A.D. Cadence swallowed. 1761! That wasn't possible! The clock must be malfunctioning. She couldn't have lost 510 years.

Cadence spoke into her helmet microphone. "Claire—" Her voice failed her and she tried again. "Claire, have you . . . have you resumed operation yet?"

"I'm here, Sergeant."

"What is your status?"

"Due to the unique structural shielding of the flight helmets, all the data transferred into them appears to be intact. However, the ship's data banks are distorted and inoperable. I will not be able to resume normal operation. If residual electromagnetism is not too intense, I should be able to assist you in most ship operations by transferring and utilizing the data in the helmets as needed."

"Are the clocks accurate?"

"Checking."

Cadence stared sightlessly at the console as she waited for Claire's assessment. Time travel into the past? All attempts at traveling back in time had been deemed failures because those who had attempted it had never returned. It had naturally been presumed that participants in the experiments had perished. But what if . . . ?

Minutes passed. The giant sphere known as Fortuna grew until it occupied the entire viewscreen. "Claire, have you been able to assess the accuracy of the ship's clocks?"

"Initial calculations would lead me to conclude that they are accurate. I am receiving readings from two stars which definitely do not exist in our time."

Cadence closed her eyes and swallowed. She was suddenly very frightened, and her palms began to sweat uncomfortably in the gloves of the flight suit she'd donned as a precaution against the ship's seals bursting under stress from the storm. "Claire, re-engage automatic cabin pressurization," she directed absently.

"Affirmative. Automatic life-support systems and pressurization are re-engaged now."

Releasing the seals on her flight suit, Cadence pulled off the gloves and then opened the visor on her helmet as she stared at the planet below. Fortuna. She'd never been on the colony world, but it was purported to be a beautiful, if somewhat primitive, planet—in her time. What concerned her now was the memory that the ruins of an alien civilization had been discovered there. An alien civilization that had been gone for scarcely five hundred years.

Five hundred years! And she'd just traveled back in time 510. Oh, quarks! Her stomach churned with anxiety. And then another thought struck her. One that had nothing to do with who or what she might find on the world below. Would she ever go home?

In the next instant, she thrust the question aside. Of course, she would. She refused to consider any other eventuality. She would be the first person to have traveled into the past and returned. However, for the moment she might as well try to figure out how to make the most of this opportunity. Unfortunately, she was not an explorer-type; she had never been trained or prepared for first contact. This was more Chance's style. She could still remember his excitement upon hearing about the ruins. *Just think, Cadence. If we'd found Fortuna just a few hundred years earlier we might actually have had the opportu-*

nity to meet an advanced species of extraterrestrial life.

"Well, Chance," she murmured. "It looks like I just might get to meet those aliens that so fascinated you." Not that she wanted to. As Chance had often accused, her sense of adventure was stuck in neutral. She couldn't help it. All she wanted to do was go home. But she wouldn't be going anywhere without first repairing Claire's system. So . . . it was time to think this through rationally. She tried to remember everything she could concerning the archaeological discovery on Fortuna.

She recalled that the scientific community had been shocked to learn that the vestiges of civilization on Fortuna were almost identical to the Atlantean ruins that had been found deep in Earth's Atlantic Ocean by seismologists in the mid-twenty-first century. Ultimately, they'd arrived at two unmistakable conclusions: One, the Atlanteans had not originated on Earth. And, two, whoever they might have been, they had also settled Fortuna. Yet the ruins on Fortuna had been very young in comparison with those on Earth. What kind of beings had they been? Human in appearance certainly. Legend told them that much. But. . . .

A red light began to flash on the console to her right. "What's that?"

"We will be entering the upper atmosphere within two minutes. You will need to decelerate manually."

Stars! The Legion didn't devote enough time to the study of manual operations. She felt woefully inadequate to the task. Some training suggestions would definitely be in order when she got back. Pulling back the lever, Cadence began to decelerate even as she watched the rapidly growing picture of the planet. Didn't the planet seem to be rising toward her much too quickly?

"What's wrong with deceleration, Claire?"

"The decelerators are functioning at sixty percent

of normal. I cannot detect the problem."

"Great!" Cadence swore. "Is there anything I can do to increase deceleration efficiency?"

"At present, no. When we are deeper into the atmosphere, you may be able to aid deceleration by firing forward thrusters."

"Wonderful. And with guidance systems out, I can't adjust trajectory. Right?"

"That is correct."

"All right, based on our present angle of entry, where will we . . . land?"

"Present trajectory will place us near the northern edge of the continent of Sendiri, approximately 1,700 miles from programmed destination."

Cadence ignored the viewscreen, concentrating on decelerating with more determination than ever. This feeling of impotence was almost more than she could bear. Her body strained against the seat harness. With decelerators working at only 60 percent, it was going to be a crash landing. She frantically adjusted controls on the ship, anything to give her the slightest edge.

"Deceleration is at eighty percent of normal," Claire announced a second later. "Thrusters may be able to increase that by as much as ten percent."

A tight smile curved Cadence's lips. She had a fighting chance.

Abruptly a sensor began to shriek a warning.

"Claire, what's happening?" Cadence cried.

"Sensor readings indicate that the ship has been caught in some type of an energy beam. Classification unknown."

"Origin?" she demanded.

"It appears to be a . . . city located here." A map appeared on one of the console screens, displaying a representation of the continent below. A small green dot flashed in an area north and slightly west of center.

17

"Then there really *is* somebody down there." Her eyes narrowed in thought. "And they obviously don't want me to choose my own landing location. I wonder why." Whatever their reason, she didn't think she liked the idea of having strangers—*alien* strangers—take control of her ship.

"Claire, see if you can help me break free."

"Acknowledged."

Over the next few minutes the small ship bucked and whined as it fought the relentless pull of the invisible beam of energy with little, if any, success. The planet grew steadily larger on the viewscreen.

They were at an altitude of just over 30,000 feet when Claire suddenly announced, "We have broken away." The ship lurched and the angle of descent altered drastically. The ground rose to meet them at an alarming speed.

"Firing forward thrusters!" Cadence noted a slight decrease in speed but it wasn't enough. A large river loomed ahead, and she decided to try to reach it. The water might cushion the impact.

As the Tachyon vessel skimmed over the tops of some tall trees, Cadence fought the instinct to close her eyes. If she was to meet death, then she'd do it with her eyes open. The water lay only a few hundred yards away. Could she make it? She felt a frenzied vibration engulf the ship through the soles of her feet. The noise of crumpling metal reverberated in her ears. She screamed—an insignificant sound that went unheard amid the din. And then everything went dark.

A voice next to her ear kept calling her name, demanding that she wake up. Cadence frowned and tried to move away, but she bumped her mouth on her knee. Why was she sleeping in such an uncomfortable position? The voice screeching in her ear made it difficult to think, to concentrate. She wanted to think, to examine the strange dream. She'd

18

dreamed that she'd been thrown back in time, to a Fortuna that was still inhabited by alien beings.

"Sergeant, are you there? You must wake."

"Go away," she murmured to the annoying voice.

"I am incapable of executing your command. The verb *go* implies physical movement, which is impossible for me in my present configuration."

Cadence grimaced in pain as she moved her left hand. "Claire?"

"Yes?"

The storm. It was beginning to come back to her now. As a safeguard against the dangers presented to the computer by the electromagnetism, she'd told Claire to create a back-up copy of as much of its data as possible by transferring it to the microchips in the helmets. That was why Claire was talking incessantly in her ear. She opened her eyes, but immediately felt nauseous, so she closed them again. "How long have I been unconscious?"

"One hour, twenty-five minutes."

"We crashed?"

"Affirmative. We came down approximately five hundred feet from the river. However, if sensor readings are still accurate, forward momentum seems to have carried us almost into it."

Cadence nodded. "Damage?"

"The ship has sustained extensive damage."

Cadence swallowed, trying to soothe her dry throat. "What do we need in order to repair her?"

"I would suggest a Tachyon scout factory."

Wonderful! A computer with a sense of sarcasm. Just what she needed!

Lying quietly, she tried to assess any possible injury to herself. She was still strapped in her flight seat, but the seat itself appeared to have tipped back. There was a slight bump on her forehead, the only part of her head not protected by the helmet because she'd raised the visor. It was quite painful when she probed it, but she didn't think she had a concussion. Her left wrist burned with pain. Slowly she released the seat-belt fastening and began to move other parts of her body. Her right leg, bent so awkwardly toward her head, ached terribly but did not appear to be broken. As she came to the conclusion that, miraculously, she really was alive and relatively unhurt, she rolled to the side and looked around a bit. That was when she saw him, the most breathtakingly handsome and darkly disturbing male specimen she had ever laid eyes on.

His short hair was blacker than a midnight sky. His eyes were the color of a storm cloud, mysterious and complex. And his features were so perfect as to be almost beautiful. Yet never would anyone mistake this man for anything other than pure, unadulterated male. Very tall and well formed, he had the broadest set of shoulders she had ever seen. He wore dark blue, strangely fitted trousers that hugged his abdomen and hips before ballooning out in an abundance of fabric over his thighs. At knee height the garment disappeared into the tops of snug-fitting, dark brown leather boots. On his torso he wore a loose blouson-sleeved shirt of the same indigo color as the trousers. Trimmed in gold, it had a deep V-neck that displayed a generous sprinkling of silky-looking black chest hair.

He didn't look like any Fortunan that she'd ever seen. Oh, stars! She really had gone back in time. She studied the man nervously, swallowing against the lump of dread in her throat.

Rather than camouflaging his strength, somehow the loose-fitting clothing served to accentuate his muscular build. There were two major problems with this glorious specimen of the male sex: First, he was directing what appeared to be an alien weapon at her. And second, and perhaps most disconcerting, he seemed to be surrounded by a halo of brilliant light.

After a blink and a more thorough inspection, Cadence decided that the aura of bright light surrounding the man could not possibly be celestial unless heaven was a vastly different place than propounded. He simply looked too darkly menacing, despite his incredible handsomeness, to be of angelic origin. That impression was exacerbated by the weapon. It was a straight, spearhead-like object, about eight inches long, that looked as though it had been carved from pure diamond. Only the strangely mobile colors that rippled up and down its surface belied her identification of the substance. Diamond it was not.

Favoring her injured wrist and studiously trying to ignore the pain in her leg, she slowly squirmed into a sitting position and held up her hands in the age-old universal sign of surrender. She would try diplomacy, but if that didn't work, she wasn't about to go down without a fight. Daring a quick glance at her laser holster, she sought to reassure herself with the comforting knowledge of the laser's presence, only to discover that the weapon was no longer in place. Had she been divested of it while unconscious? Or had it been dislodged during the crash? There was no way to know. Was she being apprehended or rescued, she wondered. She decided to give diplomacy a very determined effort.

Stretching her lips into a wooden but, she hoped, nonthreatening smile, Cadence spoke slowly, cautiously. "I'm not dangerous. Honest. You can put your weapon away."

His eyes widened slightly, but he made no other response. The weapon did not waver. The strange brightness that had surrounded him when she'd first opened her eyes seemed to be fading. She could only see it now during that flash of a second when her lids were half-closed during a blink. The phenomenon must have been a result of the accident, she concluded. Maybe the bump on her forehead was more serious than she'd thought.

She tried again. "My name is Cadence. I'm a citizen of the planet Earth." She frowned. She really had been thrown back in time, she realized. Either that, or this planet was not her intended destination. "This is Fortuna, right? So who are you?"

Chapter Two

A shiver of apprehension traversed the length of Gildon's spine as he stared down at the woman he'd been assigned to either greet or capture, depending on which of the foretold arrivals she proved to be. If he didn't hurry, both he and the woman could well be apprehended.

He was on Madaian soil. Enemy territory.

He studied her intently. Her demeanor gave no clue as to who she was. Yet he needed to determine her identity quickly in order to know how to proceed.

Still irritated that he had been appointed counselor to her, he frowned. Another could have monitored her and assessed her presence here more readily than he. However, the Council of Prelates had presented irrefutable reasoning for their faith in him and had given him little choice in the matter. As one of the few citizens who was both a priest of the Order of the Avatar, trained in combatting the arcane, and a Kami warrior, he was one of those best suited to protecting himself and the woman. And he had been the only qualified citizen within easy contact when news of her crash came.

Gildon raked the woman with his gaze again. Was she destined to become an instrument of good, he wondered. Or of evil? Savior or demoness? Neither? Her aura definitely lacked the power he would have expected in either of the foretold arrivals.

In truth, he saw before him merely a foreign female who'd initially appeared more than a little startled at the sight of him. But not afraid, he realized. His eyes narrowed thoughtfully.

Only those who willingly embraced the unknown or those who possessed an understanding of his vocation did not have some fear of him for the arcane capabilities he possessed: the talent of being able to plumb the mysteries of alien and unfamiliar existences; and, on occasion and under rigid conditions, of being able to command alter-realm creatures. Although he was not currently garbed in the raiment of his office, the scope of the power he wielded was present in his aura for all to see. How was it that this foreign woman did not fear him?

Could it be that she felt she had no reason to fear him? As a priest of the Avatar, he was well aware that evil came in many innocuous guises. He did not trust her. Then again, he had never really *trusted* anybody.

She spoke again, her language incomprehensible. Flat. Discordant. A result of pain?

Gildon grimaced. Time was at a premium. Nuisance or not, she was injured and she was his responsibility. And he did not take responsibility lightly. He supposed that, had he been a man given to compassion, he might have felt sympathy for her. Since he was not, he was rather amazed that the idea had even occurred to him. Yet, in the scant moments that he'd studied her, he'd received the distinct impression that she was very self-assured for someone in her position.

Concluding that she did not seem overtly dangerous, he tucked his dislocator into a pocket in his loose-fitting trousers and knelt at her side. The sight of beautiful moss-green eyes momentarily immobilized him. Their eye contact must have startled her as well, for she ceased making the bizarre sounds. As gently and carefully as his sense of urgency would allow, Gildon aided her to a more relaxed sitting position and helped her to remove her strange headdress. Her complexion was warm, sun-kissed. Her gold-highlighted brown hair, shorter than that worn by the women in his culture, curled attractively around her features.

Removing his *falar* stone from his pocket, he placed the chain over his head, centering the near-black jewel over his forehead. Pointing a finger to his temple, he indicated that she should communicate telepathically. *I have been sent to welcome you to my world, kaitana. We must move quickly.* Although telepathy was certainly possible without the garnetine stones, they amplified ability considerably, almost always ensuring success and easing the amount of effort expended. Gildon had thought it a prudent course when initiating his first contact with the alien woman.

However, the woman merely frowned and, pointing at her chest, repeated a flat, discordant sound. The tone was so unpleasant that Gildon felt it must represent pain, or something very negative.

Gildon studied her a moment, wondering if she was trying to tell him something about her chest, which, the male in him noted, was very nicely if not abundantly endowed. She kept repeating the gesture and its accompanying sound. Then with a grimace, she reached out and touched his chest, raising a brow questioningly.

By the One! She wasn't trying to tell him that that disagreeable noise was her name, was she? When she repeated the gesture and then once again pointed to him, Gildon accepted the unthinkable. Since she appeared to be getting frustrated with her attempt to communicate, Gildon did his best to initiate her vocalization of her name. "Cadence," he said. Yet he knew that from his lips the tone had been completely off, the discordance missing.

She seemed content. Smiling and nodding, she once again pointed at him and cocked her head questioningly.

He studied her. "Gildon," he said, the sound clear, elevated, and pleasant. "Gildon of the line of Ksynjan." She merely shook her head in confusion, so he repeated it.

"Gildon?" she murmured.

He reared back. He had never heard his name uttered in such a fashion, not even in anger. Why would this woman use such a disharmonious tone with him?

Another series of sounds rushed at him as the woman, apparently distressed, reached toward him. Not one of the tones was harmonious. They clashed with the natural vibrations of his world as violently as her means of transportation had burned through the atmosphere and torn through the forestation. Suddenly Gildon had a horrible suspicion.

Could these sounds be the woman's only means of communication? She was alien. Perhaps her species had not mastered telepathy. Perhaps their senses were incapable of perceiving the natural harmonies of the universe and living in accordance with them. Perhaps he and his people would have no means of communicating with her or others of her species. If that was so, how would he ever determine her possible role in the battle to save his people? How could she aid them in the war against the insidious evil perpetrated by the Vradir cult if she could not communicate?

Casting courtesy aside, Gildon reached out with his mind, intending to probe her surface thoughts. But in that too he was circumvented. Her mind was shielded! Very strongly shielded. Gently he probed the protection, testing for weaknesses, for a breach large enough to at least access her outer thoughts. It did not exist. Surprise made him blink. He had never encountered anything like it.

And the impasse continued. It seemed he could do no more here. He could not communicate with her either verbally or telepathically. And she could not communicate with him. Replacing his *falar* stone in his pocket, Gildon rose from his kneeling position and took a moment to study the woman's means of conveyance as he let his mind tackle the problem of communication. The vehicle was very . . . strange. It lacked light. No, that was not quite right. It had light, but the illumination was an unusual coloration that made the small chamber in which he stood seem dim and lacking in vitality. Perhaps it was due to the damage the vessel had incurred.

Abruptly another voice sounded, blaring into the silence. This one emerged from the headdress he had just aided the woman, Cadence, in removing. Staring at it in surprise, Gildon noted an eye-like device in the center of the forehead section that seemed to be focused on him. Cadence responded to the voice, and Gildon began to get an idea. The headgear was either some type of a communication device or a data processor. In either case, it might be able to serve as an interpreter if it possessed the ability to learn foreign languages quickly. However, before such a plan could be implemented, he would have to take Cadence back to Jafna, his home city.

But what if she were the woman destined to lead the Vradir to new prominence? Fated to destroy his world with her immoral designs and evil intent?

Despite his skepticism regarding her importance, he could not ignore the foretelling of the Priests of the Lidai Order. He'd been directed to ascertain which of the foretold arrivals she was before returning with her. Yet their communication problem made that difficult in the extreme. He would have to find some means of testing her alignment before taking her into the inner city.

Holding out a hand to her, he beckoned. "Come, Cadence."

Without reticence, she nodded her understanding and reached out to grasp his hand, allowing him to pull her to her feet. Immediately she gasped, her complexion paled, and she muttered something beneath her breath that sounded extremely unpleasant as she gingerly took all weight off of her right leg.

Pointing to her leg, he raised a questioning brow. When she merely shrugged in response, he gestured to the vessel's exit and indicated that he wanted her to follow him. For a moment, he thought that she'd failed to understand him. She stared at him with an unreadable expression, looked at the door and then back at him. Finally, rather hesitantly, she nodded. Then, with a determined set to her jaw and an apparent purpose in mind, she hobbled to a cabinet set into the wall of the craft.

Wary of her motives, Gildon unobtrusively grasped the dislocator in his pocket in preparation for some type of assault. However, she merely removed a box with a large red cross emblazoned on its surface and a large fabric bag. After placing the box in the fabric bag, she slipped the strap over her shoulder. Frowning slightly, Gildon decided he could not allow her to retain the satchel until he knew its entire contents. With a series of gestures, and finally the firm removal of the bag from her shoulder, Gildon conveyed his intent. Although she looked decidedly perturbed as he searched her belongings, she didn't try to interfere. Satisfied that its contents seemed harmless, Gildon returned the satchel to her.

Placing it over her shoulder again with icy dignity, she turned, retrieved the headdress she had worn, and turned to scan the interior of the ship. Her eyes widened. Handing her headgear to Gildon almost absentmindedly, she turned and limped toward the most badly damaged portion of the ship. With a cry of dismay, she sank to her knees and began struggling to remove something from a pile of crumpled metal. Gildon moved up behind her just as she managed to extricate the item, and he saw that it was another headdress like the one he carried, although this one was crushed and useless.

Cadence turned to him and said something he couldn't understand. He was about to attempt some form of response when a voice emerged from the headgear in his hand, and he realized that she'd been communicating with the device, not him. When the voice stopped talking, Cadence sighed and dropped the ruined headdress. Then she rose painfully to her feet, took her headgear from him, and indicated with a gesture that he should lead the way.

Gildon eyed her doubtfully. With her hobbling or hopping along behind him, the time delay would guarantee that one of the Madaian warrior guilds would catch them. He'd been forced to conceal his mount, a kuma he'd dubbed Lofen, in a copse of brush a good distance away to prevent any Madaian arrivals from being immediately alerted to his presence. Still, perhaps she would be capable of more speed once outside the confines of her cramped conveyance. He didn't know her customs and preferred not to initiate a contact that she might view as insulting unless it became necessary.

As soon as they stepped outside the battered little ship, Cadence turned to survey the damage. It was worse than she'd imagined. The belly of the *Ulysses* had been torn open. The gleaming metal of the Tachyon vessel was crumpled like so much paper. Claire was right, the *Ulysses* needed factory repairs. Cadence swallowed and then jumped as her escort grasped her arm. She limped along a couple of steps in response to his insistent guidance, but was unable to take her eyes from her ship, unable to accept the verdict that her vision transmitted to her brain.

In the next instant, she felt herself lifted in strong arms. The horizon tilted crazily as Cadence found herself looking up at her host. She barely remembered to tell Claire to seal the ship, ensuring that no one—without her voice command—would gain access to what was inside without cutting their way in, before rational thought deserted her.

Cadence was not used to being carried by men. At five feet seven inches in height with a medium-boned frame, she was not petite by any means. And the fact that much of her lean physique consisted of solid muscle meant that she was heavier than she looked. The shock of being lifted so easily into this man's arms, of being held against the broad chest she'd admired only moments earlier, rendered her speechless. Now she clutched the precious remaining helmet to her, praying it held enough intact data to somehow get her home, and studiously tried to ignore the unfamiliar barrage of feelings that assaulted her. But the warmth of his body penetrated the left side of her flight suit, raising gooseflesh of awareness. And his uniquely male scent rose to tantalize her olfactory senses. Only by concentrating on the way the strap of her duffel bag cut into her shoulder was she able to catch her breath, calm her racing pulse, and ignore her sweating palms. Then she made the mistake of lifting her eyes to study her escort's face.

His expression distant and his firm jaw set, the man who had introduced himself as Gildon-something examined their surroundings with his storm-colored eyes as he carried her. Cadence found herself admiring his profile. He had a strong patrician nose, full sensual mouth, and, contrary to her initial impression, not all of his midnight-black hair was short. He wore the hair at the nape of his neck long and braided. He was at least six feet three inches tall and well muscled. Very well muscled, Cadence decided, as her thigh pressed against a solid, warm midriff. And once again, she became uncomfortably aware of the heat of his body penetrating the thin fabric of her flight suit.

Enough of this! Cadence determinedly focused her gaze on the world around her.

They were in a grassy valley surrounded by rolling hills. A narrow band of forestation stretched off to the right. Many of the trees showed damage, and Cadence realized it had been these into which the *Ulysses* had crashed. To their right, only an occasional large leafy tree or giant boulder dotted the grassy landscape. Then she heard a peculiar muted roar. It was so much a part of the landscape that at first she'd thought it was only the roar of profound silence in her ears. Looking over her shoulder, she identified it as the sound of the wide, swift-moving river at their backs. It tore through the landscape on its journey to the sea, its white-capped waves proof of nature's violence unleashed. Yet, for all its power, its roar was somehow soothing.

Her eyes moved forward again, and up. The sky overhead, devoid of clouds, looked like a giant inverted mauve-white bowl. The one overwhelming impression Cadence received was of space. More space than she'd ever seen. There were no domed enclosures and no walls. Having been born and raised on a space station, she found the transition a little unnerving. As though without walls to contain it, her body might simply disperse, fly apart.

Gildon sensed Cadence's tension and looked around to see what might have disturbed her. That was when he saw him: A Madaian warrior, his shielding shimmering in the light of the two suns overhead like a heatwave. Almost invisible, but not quite. Trouble! Gildon itched to summon his mount to him, yet such a move would alert the Madaian to Gildon's knowledge of the warrior's presence.

Gildon's eyes narrowed in instinctive mistrust as he once again looked down at the woman in his arms. She was not looking in the direction of the warrior, but then she wouldn't if she wanted to conceal an alliance.

Who was she? The answer to a prophesy or merely an alien traveler? Had she come here by chance or design?

She was very beautiful and seemed more beautiful the more one looked at her, studied her. Yet, because beauty often proclaimed nature's greatest good, it was frequently evil's most effective cloak. Was the fighter on the hill perhaps the contact Cadence had been trying to meet in Madaia? The reason she'd fought against the Prelates' guidance of her ship to land in this accursed territory? Perhaps she was capable of telepathic contact and had only blocked such contact with Gildon. Had communication already taken place between the Madaian and the woman?

Gildon didn't know what to think, but he kept a watchful eye on the shimmering form of the Madaian warrior as he hurried toward the copse of brush concealing his mount. Gildon was, after all, trespassing on Madaian soil. He had no doubt that the Madaian fighter would attempt to claim the woman. The question was, was he a scout? If so, he would wait for reinforcements. Or would he make an attempt for the woman alone?

Without waiting to reach the copse, Gildon uttered a single piercing note, summoning Lofen to him.

Cadence barely had time to jump in response to the unexpected sound before the thicket of brush they'd been approaching began to rustle threateningly. When the shrubs began to shake violently from side to side, her eyes widened apprehensively. And

32

when a huge bear-like creature rose on its hind legs before stepping out of the brush toward them, she almost screamed. Almost, because the sudden paralysis of her throat muscles arrested the sound, reducing it to a frightened squeak.

Gradually, as the creature lowered itself to four legs and trotted toward them with an awkward lumbering gait, she saw that her escort appeared not in the least threatened by its advance. In fact, he began running toward it, meeting it in the open. As Gildon halted at the beast's side, it turned its huge furry head to examine her with small, close-set black eyes. While its large flat teeth proclaimed it most definitely a herbivore, Cadence perceived intelligence in its expression. Awareness and understanding. This was no dumb animal.

Gildon lifted her onto the creature's back, placing her on a large smooth saddle that she'd not noticed in the first flush of panic. Making a determined effort to curb her trepidation and ignore the fact that solid ground seemed distressingly distant, she studied the animal. Upon closer examination she realized that Gildon's mount actually displayed more resemblance to a gigantic dog than a bear, with the exception of its tremendous size and propensity for walking upright. Cadence had always liked dogs; she'd had a miniature shepherd when she was a child. Tentatively she reached a hand toward the animal's inquisitive nose. Turning its head, it sniffed her but made no threatening moves, so she trailed her fingers through the fur on its neck. Mottled in shades of tan, black, and dark brown, it was amazingly soft.

She had just taken her eyes from the animal to look at Gildon when she noticed a flicker on the summit of a nearby hill. Looking at it, she saw a shimmering form, large and bright. The first thing that popped into her mind was the representation of an

angel she'd once seen. In the next instant, the form
shimmered again, and it was nothing more than a
man astride another beast identical to the one beneath her. Cadence blinked. A trick of the brilliant
sunlight? She looked at Gildon to find him observing
her with a curiously intense expression. Was
something wrong?

Before she could interpret his strangely accusatory
and suspicious expression, he took the helmet and
her bag from her. There was an air of urgency about
him as he quickly opened a saddlebag, removed a
piece of rope, and began securing the helmet to the
saddle. Why? Cadence wondered. She looked
around, but could discern no cause. Even the man
on the hill was gone now. Thinking that perhaps
somehow she had simply misread his intensity, Cadence decided that they had to find some means of
communicating. And there was no time like the present . . . or the past. She shook away the thought.
They could start with simple words. Clearing her
throat to draw Gildon's attention, she gestured to the
animal beneath her. "What is it?" she asked.

Although he tensed slightly, he didn't seem to have
any problem understanding her query. "Kuma," he
said with a nod toward the beast.

The word was uniquely accented, almost musical.
Cadence looked down at Gildon questioningly from
her now superior height. "Kuma," he repeated as he
secured her duffel bag by a tether to one side of the
saddle and swept the summits of the surrounding
hills with his perceptive gaze.

Cadence nodded. "Kuma." Her eyes widened when
he visibly winced at her repetition of the word. Why
did he keep doing that? In the next instant, Gildon
vaulted up to take his seat behind her.

Cadence tensed as he slid an arm around her waist
in a manner that could only be termed familiar and
settled her firmly between his thighs. Stars! This was

getting to be a bit much. First he'd picked her up and carried her as though she were a child and had no voice in the matter. And now, with his muscled arm encircling her waist, his rock-solid chest at her back, and his tree-trunk thighs bracketing hers, she felt as though she were engulfed in testosterone. But before she could think of a way to protest, Gildon made a soft sound and the kuma broke into a smooth, loping run.

Cadence gritted her teeth. Although she couldn't make a verbal protest that would be understood, she could definitely make a silent one. After all, when it came right down to it, she didn't even know whether she'd been rescued or captured. So she maintained a ramrod-stiff posture, holding herself away from her escort as much as possible. She soon discovered, however, that the swift pace of the kuma made her rigid posture uncomfortable in the extreme. Finally, defeated by the unfamiliar course of events, she allowed herself to relax against Gildon, although she wasn't quite able to release the wary tension from her muscles. Though she wouldn't admit it to herself, she also had a very personal reason for wanting to maintain her distance: She simply found contact with him . . . unnerving. Her body's reactions to his proximity were unfamiliar and alarming. She hadn't felt this flustered around a man since she was sixteen.

Chapter Three

Gildon fought against the distraction of having a beautiful woman so near; forced himself to remember what greeting her and conducting her to safety had cost him in terms of time. He had so much planning to do, and so little time in which to accomplish it.

His brother, Jakial, had been Prelate of Madaia when the disturbances in the province had begun four years ago. No one outside Madaia had seen Jakial in three years. Communion had revealed that he lived, but no more. Had he been imprisoned? Repeated attempts to locate his brother had failed, yet Gildon refused to give up. He would search the whole of Madaia on foot if he had to . . . if there was enough time. With their power united, he and Jakial could discover the answers to the questions now plaguing his people.

Nothing in the prophecy said that the woman who would be instrumental in saving them must work alone.

A shiver traveled the length of Gildon's spine. Although he, like all others of the priest caste, had sensed the disturbances originating in Madaia almost as soon as they began, today, as he'd journeyed into the province, he'd felt, and seen, the true strength of the encroaching darkness for the first time.

In Destiny's Arms

His people needed a means of escape. Badly. Yet the portals linking this world to others had been destroyed centuries ago in an effort to keep the very evil which threatened them now from finding them. Priests throughout the continent had been working for almost a year on the construction of evacuation portals for removing their people. But the knowledge of how to program them, which had been set aside so long ago, now eluded the portal architects, and the portals remained incomplete. Even now, the architects of the Geduin Order scrambled to complete their research before it was too late.

Yet none of their urgency had brought home to Gildon the truth about the foretelling of his people's eventual obliteration on this world as explicitly as what he perceived today. He could *feel* the evil sweeping the land, sense its insidious advance like the silent approach of a swarm of ravenous insects. And he could see its spread in the parched earth and animal carcasses that already littered the plains.

That awareness left Gildon torn between duty and hope.

It forced him to acknowledge his own more personal and less altruistic motivations for wishing to find his brother: He needed to put an end to the muttered suspicions concerning his brother's alignment with the Vradir cult, which now ruled Madaia. Even less altruistic was Gildon's need to banish his own guilt-inducing doubts about the brother he had always loved—and envied. But regardless of the reason for his plans, this woman's presence, his duty to her, would delay them.

Abruptly he sensed something, a peripheral awareness on the fringes of his mind; the approach of a number of people. Since they were still on Madaian soil, it could mean only one thing: pursuit.

* * *

Cadence couldn't believe the transformation in the landscape beyond the fertile river valley. The lush green carpet gave way to parched brown grass that seemed to disintegrate into choking dust with each stride the kuma took. The cloud of dust seemed to hover immobile over the landscape. Trees and bushes stretched bare, skeletal limbs toward the sky as though in entreaty for life-giving moisture. An occasional bird call broke the stillness and then was quickly silenced as though in fright. There was no visible sign of life. Despite the brightness of the sky overhead, a pall hung over the landscape. Cadence shivered.

They had only been out of the river valley a short time when she sensed a new tension in her escort. Glancing back over her shoulder at him, she saw that his attention was fixed to their left. A dark mass of milling forms descended toward them at lightning speed from the summit of a large, moderately sloped hill. She tried to count the number of riders. At least ten, she thought. And judging by Gildon's ferocious expression, and the increased speed of the already racing kuma, they weren't friendly. In her position, she couldn't be absolutely certain that Gildon was friendly either. However, since he had made no overtly threatening gestures, she quickly decided to side with him. If only she had her laser.

"Gildon," she shouted over the sound of thudding feet and the rush of wind in her ears. He looked down at her with a question and a trace of irritation in his eyes. She gestured to the empty holster where her laser had been secured. "My laser. Do you have it?"

Although he obviously couldn't understand her words, his eyes lit with comprehension. His gaze shifted thoughtfully from the empty holster to her face, to the pursuing riders, and back to her face. For a frozen moment, as their eyes met, the sound of pounding feet and pursuit faded. Cadence had the impression that he could peer into her very soul. He nodded and reached into the voluminous shirt he wore, removing her laser. After placing it carefully in her hand, he turned his attention back to the pursuing riders. They were gaining.

With a grim cast to his mouth, Gildon considered their options. The Madaian warriors were too close for him to safely reach the border of his home province, Shemeir, and the portal he had planned to use in Shemeiran territory. However, it wasn't the nearest portal. There was one nearer. Ancient and often unused, established by the first Tesuvian explorers upon their arrival here, it lay only a short distance away—on Madaian soil. Could they make it in time? The One only knew. But it was their best hope. With a subtle telepathic nudge and change in posture, he prompted the kuma to turn. And as he did, Gildon prayed that the woman would not betray him. She had fought the Prelate's guidance so valiantly in order to reach Madaia that her sudden alliance with him, a Shemeiran, seemed questionable.

They'd gone only another mile before it became obvious that they would not make the Madaian portal either. They had no choice but to fight. And unless Cadence's weapon was something extraordinary— which judging by its appearance it was not—they were drastically outnumbered. Seeing a tumble of large boulders to their left, Gildon veered toward it. They would provide as much protection as he and Cadence were likely to get out here on the river plains.

Stopping Lofen, Gildon leapt from the kuma's back, hastily placed Cadence in the shelter of the largest boulder, and telepathically directed his mount to find shelter too. His responsibilities taken care of as well as possible, Gildon pulled the dislocator from his pocket and, concealing himself behind a boulder, turned to watch the arrival of his enemies.

As soon as his pursuers noticed he'd halted, they drew their dislocators and began firing. They meant to keep him pinned until they were close enough to overwhelm him physically. Thankful that the phase-shifting dislocators had been designed to have little effect on inanimate objects, Gildon crouched behind the boulder and returned their fire without bothering to verify his targets. He had to slow them down, phase enough of them that he'd at least have a chance of winning a physical confrontation. He looked over at Cadence. She seemed to be watching him carefully. Waiting to be guided by his actions? He could only hope.

Quickly he altered his physical vibratory rate, giving his form a shifting, hazelike appearance without color or detail, rather like the surface of a pond shimmering in the sun. Although the warriors would be expecting the maneuver, he hoped it would make him a slightly less obvious target. He sensed more than heard Cadence's gasp of surprise, and looked over to see a shocked expression on her face, but had no time to wonder about it. His attention was on the approach of their pursuers. It was time to launch a more focused attack, to reduce their numbers before they got any closer.

When the inevitable pause in the concentration of fire came, he was prepared. Peering around the boulder just enough to target his enemies, some of whom had also cloaked themselves, he focused on the nearest Madaian fighter and fired. A cascade of minuscule stars radiated outward from the blast point at lightning speed, engulfing the warrior's body in effervescent energy before the phase-shift was complete and his body disappeared. Even before that combatant had vanished, another flash leapt across the space between the cluster of boulders and the

Madaians. An arrow of light struck another Madaian in the chest. With a shout of pain, he fell and did not rise.

Gildon glanced at Cadence. She knelt in the shadow of the neighboring boulder, her weapon at the ready. Noting Gildon's look, she nodded sharply before focusing her attention again on the advancing fighters. So, Gildon thought, her people had harnessed the energy of light into a weapon. Interesting. And not nearly as ineffective as he had feared it might be.

Despite the effectiveness of her weapon in conjunction with his own, however, they were unable to vanquish the Madaians before being overtaken. It was only a matter of moments before the remaining five warriors abandoned their mounts to descend upon them, weapons at the ready. Three men faced Gildon, while two moved to confront Cadence. She met them like a warrior, eyes alert, legs slightly splayed for stability and agility. And, although two dislocators were trained on her unerringly, her own weapon did not waver at all. It was at that moment that Gildon realized that this was a woman trained to face death. Perhaps Cadence was a warrior on her own world. Female fighters were unusual but not unheard of. Whatever she was, she did not betray her fear in the slightest. He could not help feeling a flicker of admiration. She was a strong woman.

With a sharp command and a hand signal, the Madaian fighters demanded that they surrender their weapons. Whether she had understood the command or not, Cadence had definitely grasped the meaning of the gesture. She looked toward Gildon, and the expression in her eyes told him that she would follow his lead.

Gildon's mind raced at light speed. Death was not a desirable option. Neither was surrender. It would only delay death and place them in a position from which escape would be all but impossible. Their only option was to make a stand here. But how?

Their dress proclaimed the Madaian fighters Kami-trained. Despite the fact that they had now abandoned that Order, they would be proficient fighters. Two Kami, Gildon knew he could best. But three? He had rarely surmounted those odds. Five would be almost impossible. Nevertheless, Gildon had not attained the level of High Priest within the Order of the Kami without mastering every aspect of Kami fighting technique. Since none of his opponents wore the gold band of a High Priest on the uniforms they still wore, he could safely assume that none had mastered the fighting disciplines of that station. That at least was in his favor. And although the more recent disciplines and responsibilities of High Priesthood within the Order of the Avatar may have rusted his fighting abilities slightly, Gildon was still among the best Kami on the continent.

Still, the odds were not good. He was infinitely thankful that, as ex-Kami, they would be unable to draw on *halal*, the death touch. Proficient Kami were trained in the ability to place their psychic power behind physical contact, often killing an enemy with a touch by disrupting the flow of the life within his body. To draw on that particular ability, however, a warrior's motivations must be honorable. Since the dawn of their creation, the Kami had been warriors of and for the One. Protectors of the righteous. Warrior priests. The Madaian warriors, seduced by Vradir promises and personal greed, had abandoned that purpose.

Since Gildon could not hope to aid Cadence until he had defeated the three men now opposing him, he sent a hasty entreaty to the One that, as the priests of the Lidai had foretold, the Madaians' intent was to capture rather than to kill her. Even as he concluded the prayer, Gildon allowed a defeated slump to round his shoulders as he prepared to drop his dislocator to the ground, feigning compliance with their directive. Then in an explosion of movement he fired the weapon at one of his combatants and simultaneously leapt to fight his remaining enemies before they could aim their weapons. The blinding swiftness of his sudden action surprised everyone, as he had meant it to.

Cadence had already weighed the situation. Her always powerful sixth sense had warned her that Gildon had no intention of remaining as docile as he'd appeared, and she was ready to take advantage of the diversion he created. In the split second that her two captors' eyes shifted from her to the battle waged by their counterparts, she lifted her laser, fired, and dove for cover.

The problem was that the laser blast incapacitated only one man. Doing her best to ignore the renewed pain in her strained leg, she landed, rolled, and tried to position herself for a shot at the other man, but it was too late. He came after her with a speed that rivaled the best martial artist she'd ever seen, landed a blow to the side of her head that produced a whole new galaxy of stars, and forcibly divested her of her weapon. Then, glaring malevolently at her, paying no heed to his fallen comrade, he pulled her to her feet and stood back to observe the ongoing battle between Gildon and his opponents. Breathing heavily as much from fury as from the rush of adrenaline caused by her fear and exertion, Cadence blinked to clear her vision and followed his gaze. The combat was still two to one, she observed.

The headache that began to pound behind her eyes, exacerbating the already constant ache of wrist and leg, increased Cadence's initial dislike of her single remaining captor tenfold. She used his preoccupation with the fight to study him, seeking a weakness. He was a tall man, a couple of inches taller than Gildon, with the lean, firm build of an athlete. His hair and his eyes were coffee brown, his complexion swarthy. Although he and his companions wore identical clothing in the same indigo color that Gildon wore, giving the garb the appearance of some type of uniform, they did not wear it with the same aura of pride. In fact, the uniform and the man both exuded an unkempt quality. Nevertheless, his stance and his speed proclaimed him to be a more than capable fighter. And she was injured. Although she could now use her right leg, she still couldn't put her entire weight on it, and her wrist remained swollen and painful. Her advantage lay in the fact that he obviously didn't think she represented a threat. Since divesting her of her weapon, he'd maintained a firm hold on her upper arm, but otherwise ignored her. It would be relatively easy to break free. However, she didn't want to do that until she had decided how to best him. As a Legionnaire, prior to her promotion into Internal Affairs, Cadence had been trained in a number of combat techniques. She simply had to decide which she was capable of using in her present condition and what would be most effective against this man.

She closely watched the battle between Gildon and his two opponents, one of whom was now obviously failing. It was a strange contest. With the exception of an occasional grunt or gasp when a blow landed, the men waged the entire fight in complete silence.

Cadence frowned. Silence?

She remembered Gildon's tendency to wince every time she spoke. She had heard him speak, but there had been a unique accent to it, an almost musical softness that she'd never heard before. No, *softness* wasn't the right word. It was more of a tranquility. She looked at her captor assessingly. Perhaps these people were sensitive to loud or harsh sounds.

Her brow cleared. Karate. It could be loud and

harsh when desired, and very effective. Definitely worth a shot. She wanted to dispatch her remaining opponent and, if possible, retrieve her laser, before she ended up in the position of a hostage to be used against Gildon. And since she still didn't know her escort that well, she didn't want to trust completely in his altruistic nature. He might decide that saving her was not worth the effort after all.

Gildon was tiring. He'd not had even the momentary opportunity it took to concentrate and focus the psychic power of the *halal*. The battle had been entirely physical. He leapt, adroitly avoiding a tandem effort to conquer him, and turned to deliver a lethal blow to the neck of one of the Madaians. Then only one remained. More wary now, he squared off, facing Gildon.

Suddenly a horrible scream rent the air. It was loud, discordant, and paralyzing. Gildon's heart nearly stopped as alarm receptors discharged in his brain. Instinctively, both the Madaian and he swung in the direction of the sound, braced to witness the result of some unspeakable torture. Knowing that the cacophonous sound could only have come from his alien charge, Gildon's eyes sought her out, wondering what injury she suffered. What he saw was completely incompatible with his expectations.

Her green eyes blazing, Cadence crouched in a half squat, her right foot on the throat of a Madaian warrior who lay supine at her feet as she held his arm up at a painfully awkward angle. The other fighter lay unmoving a short distance away. Somehow, she had bested two Kami! Had she injured herself in the process? Once again, his gaze swept over her. But he could see no reason for her scream.

In the next instant, he sensed an increasing tension in his opponent and knew that the few seconds of reprieve were over. The battle was about to renew. He turned. But fatigue had slowed his reflexes and he was not swift enough. The Madaian landed a crippling blow to his side. Had Gildon not been in the process of turning to meet the assault, the move would have snapped his spine. As it was, the blow was enough to knock him to the ground and leave him gasping for air against the pain of badly bruised or possibly cracked ribs. He tried to rise, to meet the assault he knew was coming, but pain robbed his limbs of strength.

The Madaian's boots came into view. Gildon looked up at cold blue eyes gleaming with triumph and malevolent pleasure. At the approach of death. But if the Madaian thought him beaten, he was wrong. Gildon girded himself to deflect the coming blow and, he hoped, turn it to his advantage.

"Hold it right there, mister!" The incomprehensible alien words rasped along his nerve endings, sparking a discomfort that was close to pain in his skull. Like the accidental shrieking scrape of fingernails on the chalk-stone that the masons used, the sound was impossible to ignore. The Madaian turned to face Cadence, moving away from Gildon. Even as Gildon blessed the woman for the reprieve accorded him by her interruption, he hoped she would try nothing foolish. The Madaians' original intent had not been to kill her, but that could swiftly change.

"Stop right there." Cadence raised the laser threateningly, directing it toward the fighter with unwavering accuracy. The gesture alone should have told him she meant business. Yet he kept advancing. His eyes shone with anticipation. Cadence swallowed and risked a glance at Gildon. He was rising, but obviously in pain. She couldn't count on his help yet. And she dared not release the man at her feet in order to back away or she'd have two of them to contend with. Damn! Maybe this guy needed a little demonstration. She made a hasty adjustment in aim, depressed the button on the laser, and shot a deadly beam within centimeters of his arm.

He stopped. She redirected the laser at his chest and said, "The next time I fire, I won't miss." He frowned at her words and then, with a shake of his head, he took another step toward her. Cadence began to get a strange feeling. He understood her intention, the gleam of intelligence in his eyes told her that. He'd already seen what the laser could do. Why wasn't he more cautious? He acted as though his life had no value.

Cadence glanced at Gildon. He was on his feet, but his movements still looked too painful for him to be of any help. Within another few seconds, the advancing fighter would be close enough to attack. She couldn't take the chance. Somehow she had to stay alive long enough to get off this planet and back to her own time.

The man at her feet squirmed briefly as though trying to distract her. Without taking her eyes from his compatriot, the greater threat at the moment, she automatically increased the pressure on his throat. He quieted. Then, before she had time to think about it and hesitate too long, she depressed the button on the laser and fired. The man stalking her flinched as the cutting beam pierced his thigh, but barely hesitated in his advance. What kind of person was this?

He was close. Too close.

She fired again. The laser pierced his chest. For a moment it looked at though he would ignore that injury too. And then, with a smile and an unholy look in his eyes, he sank to the ground. Some of the tension seeped from Cadence's muscles.

She looked at Gildon. Although he favored his right side, he slowly made his way toward her. "Are you all right?" she asked.

When he looked at her with an expression of puzzled incomprehension, she realized that she'd forgotten for a split second that he couldn't understand a word she said. Still, they had to communicate. With an expansive gesture that encompassed the man at her feet, she asked, "What do you want to do with him?"

He understood her gesture, if not her words, and slowly, painfully, bent to retrieve one of the crystalline weapons that had been lost during the fracas. As he directed it at the fallen fighter, Cadence obligingly backed away, perfectly willing to allow him to take over. In the next instant he fired his weapon at the fighter, and the man disappeared. So much for mercy, she thought. Queasiness began to assail her in belated reaction to the stress of combat, and Cadence wanted nothing more than to find a few moments of privacy behind one of the boulders.

It was not to be.

She had barely taken a step when a strange whisper of sound attracted her attention. She glanced at the body of the man she had just killed and . . . froze. Hell's universe! What kind of world was this?

A bizarre and frightening apparition that looked like nothing so much as thick, oily smoke rose out of the body. Terror and incomprehension froze Cadence in place. What was it? It had a vaguely humanoid shape: upright, with two arms, two legs and a head. But there the similarity ended. With the exception of two glowing yellow eyes, devoid of pupils, its head had no visible features. Five small claw-shaped appendages grew from the end of each limb. And a pair of what appeared to be huge wings lay folded in repose behind its arms.

"Gowjean!"

The alien word jerked Cadence from her horrified trance. For the first time, Gildon had uttered a sound that didn't sound musical. His alarm was almost palpable. Waving frantically at her to move away from the oily apparition, he directed the weapon in his hand at it and began . . . chanting. Chanting? Backing away as directed, Cadence looked from the apparition to her escort and back again. Whatever Gildon thought he was doing didn't seem to be having any effect. The smoky form fixed its yellow eyes on her and began slowly, steadily advancing.

Quarks! She felt as though she'd been plunged into somebody's nightmare.

The spirit or ghost or whatever it was advanced more quickly than she could back away with her injured leg. A scream of fear clawed at her throat. She didn't bother trying to restrain it. It emerged, half scream of terror, half roar of rage, and before the sound had died on her lips, she remembered the laser in her hand. Aiming at the form, she depressed the button. The beam cut through the center of the apparition with no apparent effect. And the creature was less than twelve feet away!

Muttering a curse beneath her breath, Cadence cast a desperate glance at Gildon. He continued to direct his weapon at the smoky form but it was having no effect. His chanting seemed faster, more urgent. What was he doing? Praying?

She cast another glance at the oily, incorporeal figure. "To hell with this!" she muttered. Since Gildon seemed to know what the thing was and how to deal with it, she figured the safest place to be was *behind* him. Limping hastily to the side, she began to move in his direction, trying frantically to stay ahead of the advancing apparition.

She wasn't fast enough.

Chapter Four

Without warning, the oily, smoke-like wraith engulfed her. She could taste its mustiness in her mouth. Sense its invasion of her body. Smell its rank decay in her nose and feel its greasiness in her lungs. She screamed, but she never heard the sound. It was as though her consciousness, her spirit, had been supplanted. Shoved into a tiny corner of her mind. Imprisoned.

Her sight was gone. Blackness surrounded her. Her only remaining sense was of the alien life form battering at her mind, seeking admittance.

No! She wouldn't lose her life to this thing. She wasn't ready to die. Even as her spirit fought, she felt a surge of power, of life, within her.

Gildon watched in horror as the Gou'jiin began its possession of Cadence. He'd known even as he began his attempt to create a vortical dimension gate that there wasn't time, but he'd had to make the attempt. Hoping that Cadence might be able to fight the Gou'jiin's invasion a little longer, he continued his incantation, using the power of sound to call upon and manipulate the forces of nature to do his bidding. The One willing, it could still work.

A dimensional vortex began to form.

He prayed that the alien woman was strong.

Suddenly his eyes widened in surprise. Cadence's insubstantial and powerless aura unexpectedly gained substance and strength. Like a glowing shield, it grew to encompass her body. He had never known any but the three High Priests of the Tridon to be capable of projecting such pure, untainted energy. How was it possible? Who was this woman with the will of steel? He could almost see the battle being waged within her fragile female body.

An incredibly fierce expression unfolded on her countenance. She looked almost savage in her resolve. Yet the purity of her glowing aura continued to grow. Even from several feet away, he could feel its energy. And, a moment later, she accomplished something that no other he knew of had ever done: She triumphed against a Gou'jiin without the assistance of the still incomplete dimensional gate.

With a fiendish scream, the Gou'jiin left her body as though it had been torn out and hurled across the boulder-strewn plain by some invisible force. Fighting for its existence, it fixed its glowing gaze on Gildon. A Gou'jiin could live only a very short time on this plane without a corporeal host, be it human or animal. But it was too late for the Gou'jiin. Even as it began its advance on Gildon, the dimension threshold completed its formation and the intense gravitational pull of the vortex began to draw the Gou'jiin in. It twisted and fought and wailed. It howled its rage. Gildon felt its hate like a palpable blow. The tremendous wind sucked at him, tugging hungrily at his hair and clothing, but he stood fast. And then the Gou'jiin was gone. Its chilling wail slowly faded to silence. With a single sharp tone, Gildon dispersed the threshold. The sudden silence thundered in his ears.

He sighed with relief and immediately thought of Cadence. He must learn how to communicate with her. How had she bested the Gou'jiin? How had she obtained the power that had suddenly flared in her aura? Was it possible that she had always had it and had merely prevented its presence from being betrayed in her aura? So many questions. But when he turned to face her, the woman with the superhuman strength was gone. Crumpled in her place was an ordinary woman who lay curled into a tight knot, her arms around her knees, as she shuddered convulsively and stared blankly at nothing.

A surge of compassion, as foreign to him as the woman herself and perhaps more alien than the Gou'jiin, swelled in his chest. Gildon knew firsthand the horror of contact with the alter-realm beings known as Gou'jiin. When he'd been touched during the performance of an exorcism, it had taken days for him to feel clean and untainted. And he had never suffered as complete an invasion as had Cadence. What she had endured was almost beyond imagination; the rape of the soul. As swiftly as his pain-ridden body would allow, he moved to Cadence's side and lowered himself to the ground.

The unfamiliar urge to offer comfort made him forget for a time all he needed to know and understand about this woman. Laying a tentative hand on her shoulder, he sought to provide solace. Once again, he was frustrated.

By the One! He didn't know what to do.

And then, with a suddenness that nearly knocked him over, Cadence sat up and threw her arms around him. Luckily, she pressed herself against his uninjured side. Slowly, cautiously, he allowed his arms to encircle her. To ease his uncomfortable position, he moved back slightly to lean against a convenient boulder. For endless moments they simply sat together like that. Gildon absorbed her shudders with his body, reassuring her in the only way he knew, with his body heat, his presence, and his understanding. It felt very inadequate.

Cadence returned to awareness slowly. The last thing she remembered clearly was a sudden fierce determination not to die when that . . . thing tried to take over her body. She swallowed against the bile that rose in her throat at the memory and determinedly focused her thoughts on the external.

She felt warm and safe. She recognized the hardness beneath her cheek as a solid pectoral muscle. The rhythmic sound beneath her ear as the steady beat of a human heart. The comforting arms around her as those of her escort, Gildon. And then she had a vague recollection of all but throwing herself into his arms. A flush of embarrassment colored her cheeks. She didn't even know the man. For all she knew, he had a wife and a half dozen children at home. Avoiding his gaze, she sat up and cleared her throat.

"I'm sorry," she murmured, knowing that he wouldn't understand, but needing to say the words anyway.

He said nothing, and a moment later began to move away. The gasp he made as he attempted to rise was unmistakable in any language and it drew Cadence's gaze back to him. He was in severe pain. Remembering the blow he had taken to his side, she concluded that his ribs had to be badly bruised if not broken. Unaware of her frowning assessment, he continued his attempt to rise.

"Wait!" Cadence extended her hand palm out, in a manner she hoped he would interpret as *stop*. He sank back, looking up at her with a question in his eyes. "Just wait there," she said as she turned around, looking for her duffel bag. He'd tied it to the kuma's saddle, hadn't he? Frustrated in her search, she looked back at him. "Kuma?" she asked.

"Kuma?" he repeated, obviously wondering why she wanted the animal. In response, Cadence pantomimed slipping the strap of her duffel off her shoulder and opening the bag. He nodded, although there was still a question in his eyes. Pursing his lips, he made a loud, musical sound, similar to a whistle, but distinctly different. A second later, Cadence saw something move behind a distant boulder and the kuma began loping toward them. When it halted a few feet from Gildon, Cadence quickly retrieved her duffel bag and searched the contents for the first aid kit, then returned to kneel at Gildon's side.

Taking a roll of bandage from the kit, she met Gildon's gaze. It was a mistake. The magnetic quality of his dark sapphire eyes robbed her of her breath. She felt a flush of awareness rise to her cheeks. Quarks! What was the matter with her? Forcing herself to take a deep calming breath, she held up the bandage. "I'll need you to take off your shirt."

Although he seemed to tense slightly at her words, there was no comprehension in his eyes. Stars, this was harder than she'd imagined. But since she had the distinct impression that he'd been injured while saving her from their attackers, she felt compelled to do what she could to ease his pain. Grasping the sleeve of his shirt, she pantomimed its removal and said, "Off. I need you to take the shirt *off*."

Comprehension dawned in his eyes. Lifting his back away from the boulder, he slowly, painfully removed his shirt. Cadence had meant to help him do so, but by the time she remembered that intent, the task was done.

Cadence's mouth had gone dry. Hell's universe! And she'd thought the man was handsome with his shirt *on*. His broad bronzed chest with its clearly defined pectoral muscles was so perfectly developed it could have been sculpted from marble. A triangle of silky-looking ebony hair shadowed the center of his chest before arrowing down over a flat abdomen ridged with corded muscle. And the magnificence of his upper body did not end there. His arms were so smoothly muscled, the biceps so firm, that Cadence had the unfamiliar impulse to simply run her hand over the bronzed flesh in admiration. She squelched the inclination ruthlessly.

Stars! You'd think she'd never seen a handsome man before. She'd not only seen handsome men, she'd dated a few. Gildon was just another handsome man.

Liar! An inner voice taunted even as her eyes once again moved to his chest as though drawn by a magnet. Her fingers itched to tangle themselves in the light sprinkling of soft black hair there, and she curled them into fists around the bandage.

The bandage!

Flushing in embarrassment, she raised her eyes to meet Gildon's and, for the first time, saw a hint of amusement in their depths. He knew, damn him! He knew how he affected her.

Damn all men to hell! Twice she had been taken in completely by a broad chest and a nice behind. When was she going to learn? The first time had resulted in a disastrous attempt at marriage. The second time she had discovered that she was simply one more in a long string of conquests, some of which her so-called lover had yet to end. After that, she had focused on her career with a grim and single-minded determination that had left no room in her life for men. She'd done very well for over four years without a male in her life. She'd thought she'd finally conquered her treacherous hormones. But it seemed that she had merely been lulled into complacency. Damn! She simply couldn't allow it to happen again.

Unrolling the bandage in her hand, she focused her mind on her desire to get off this planet and back home, on anything other than the man. Then, with her purpose firmly in focus, she began to bind his ribs.

She studiously attempted to ignore the tantalizing sensation of soft chest hair brushing lightly against her fingers. The texture of smooth, warm, bronzed skin beneath her hands. The unique musky scent of his body that was a combination of perspiration and something indefinably, sensuously male. It didn't work. Sparks of awareness, impossible to disregard, flared in her body and raced over her flesh. Her breasts swelled and tingled. Her pulse raced. And she couldn't seem to catch her breath. Cursing in an undertone, she finished tying off the bandage with an enthusiasm that made Gildon gasp as she inadvertently applied pressure to his injured side.

"Sorry," she muttered. She felt his eyes on her face, but refused to look at him.

Then, before she could move away, he placed a gentle finger beneath her chin and lifted her head, forcing her to meet his gaze. The expression she saw in his eyes made her breath catch in her throat all over again. It was a heady mixture of compassion, admiration, approval and . . . desire. She hadn't expected to see that. All of his contact with her had seemed so matter-of-fact, so impersonal. The power of his gaze immobilized her even as it increased her awareness of him to an almost mystical level. She saw the tiny streaks of azure that starred the stormy indigo of his eyes. She could have counted each of the thick dark lashes that framed them, darkening their hue. In those few arrested seconds, she saw the bold blade of his nose, the fullness of his lips, and the sexy blue-gray shadow of what would have been a full beard lurking beneath the flesh of his jawline. As he slowly lowered his head to touch her lips with his, she stared in hypnotic fascination, incapable of doing otherwise. The contact was a mere whisper of a kiss. Yet the electricity that arced between them assured her that she had not imagined the contact. And then, it was over.

Gildon looked away, giving the impression that it was now he avoiding her gaze. Sanity returned, and she hastily rose and moved away.

Gildon stared after her. He should not have kissed her. He could not understand from whence the intense motivation had come. How much time had they wasted binding his ribs? How could he have lost all sense of the passage of time? He was not some inexperienced novice to fall for the beauty of a woman. Or was she a mere woman? If the foretelling was correct, and she was the demoness predicted, she could have all the seductive power of a succubus.

Conflicting emotions and warring thoughts tore at him like jagged fingernails. Cadence had stood at his side in the battle; defeated a Gou'jiin with the purity of her power. Or had she? She should not have been able to rout the Gou'jiin alone; they were very powerful entities. Had the entire situation been staged to make her *appear* to be other than she was? In his mind's eye, he saw her beautiful, sun-kissed face turned up for his kiss. He remembered the luminosity of her expressive, moss-green eyes, the softness of her coral lips. And heat rushed to his loins. By the One! He had no answers. Yet he was honest enough to admit that something drew him to her as he had been drawn to no other.

Impossible! He could not become involved with Cadence. The doctrine of the Avatar dictated that, should the time come when he desired a life-mate, a companion, she must come from within the Order. And, until that time, it was strongly advised that any physical desires he might have be met by the members of the Order of Shajati who were trained in the sensual arts. Gildon had not always followed that advisement. However, when he had chosen to ignore it in order to socialize outside the boundaries of his Order with a woman whom he'd found attractive, he'd been astute enough to ensure that there was no danger of his heart becoming involved. Instinct told him that his emotions could well be more difficult to master with this alien woman. No, it would definitely be best not to become involved with her no matter which of the foretold arrivals she proved to be.

As he rose painfully to his feet and awkwardly donned his shirt, Gildon conceded that he no longer doubted she would prove to be one or the other. Demoness or savior. An instrument of good or evil. Her power might be camouflaged, but it was definitely there. His task now lay in determining who she was and how her presence was meant to affect the Tesuvian people living on this settlement world.

Avoiding her eyes and his own thoughts, Gildon examined the landscape around them. Except for the few Madaian bodies still littering the area—a result of Cadence's less thorough armament—the area appeared to be clear. Knowing that there was no time to do anything with the bodies, Gildon ignored them. The Madaians would collect them in any case. A few of the Madaian kuma remained nearby, not yet certain what the loss of physical and psychic contact with their riders meant. Another time it would have been possible for him to ride one of them. However, previously bonded beasts were extremely difficult to master, and his injury precluded such a course today. And although he fervently wished it were otherwise, the idea of harnessing one of the beasts for use by Cadence wasn't feasible either. She would be incapable of controlling the animal.

With a single piercing note, Gildon called Lofen, who had wandered a short distance away. The animal lifted his head and began to lope toward him.

Turning, Gildon sought Cadence. She was bending to retrieve her weapon. He swallowed. The double ride aboard his mount was going to be pure torture. His lips still burned with the soft contact of the kiss they had shared. As she straightened, her eyes suddenly met his. He saw the uncertainty in the depths of her eyes and steeled himself against it. He could not trust her.

Lofen padded to a halt before him, tongue lolling sideways out of his mouth, eager to go. Knowing that he could not lift Cadence onto the animal with his ribs in the condition they were, Gildon led the kuma to a boulder and beckoned to Cadence. With a series of gestures, he indicated that he wanted her to use the boulder to help her mount the kuma. Her expression now guarded and closed, she nodded her understanding.

Cadence managed to step up onto the boulder, but when she tried to get onto the kuma's back, she found that the slope of the boulder made the task difficult. Normally she could have leapt the distance onto the kuma's broad back, but her sore leg affected her agility. Leaning forward, she threaded her fingers through the thick fur on the kuma's neck. Then she jumped as well as she could manage, but fell short. She ended up straddling the kuma's side rather than its back, and found herself slipping toward the ground.

Her fall halted abruptly, and she felt the imprint of Gildon's hand burn through the thin cloth of her flight suit as he braced her thigh in support. Sensation shot through her, and she quickly used his support to scramble aboard the animal so that she could break the contact. A lot of good it would do. Within seconds, her back would again be pressed against his magnificent chest, her thighs to his. Magnificent? She had to stop thinking that way. Gildon's chest was nice, but ordinary, she assured herself. Somehow, she wasn't convinced. How was she going to endure the prolonged contact of riding with him?

As soon as she was secure, Gildon used the boulder himself to clamber up with painful deliberation behind her. After he settled her comfortably between his thighs, they were off at a swift, smooth lope.

Although the actual time that passed until they reached Gildon's destination wasn't long—less than an hour by her estimate—to Cadence the ride seemed interminable. Despite the distraction of aching limbs, she had found her physical awareness of Gildon growing with each stride the kuma took. And since he had obviously instantly regretted whatever impulse had prompted him to kiss her—in fact, she'd had the impression that he somehow blamed her for it—she refused to embarrass herself by betraying her awareness of him in any way. When Gildon finally drew the kuma to a halt alongside a strange circle of monolithic stones, Cadence's first thought was, *Thank the stars!* She was so grateful for the end of the journey that, had Gildon not prevented her, she would have leapt from the kuma's back, forgetting her injured leg. But since Gildon himself slid from the kuma's back immediately upon their arrival, she was content to remain where she was for a while longer.

Then she looked at their location. *Really* looked— and realized that this could not possibly be Gildon's final destination. They were in the middle of nowhere. There was nothing here. Nothing except a circle of huge stones. Cadence studied the gray monoliths. They looked vaguely familiar, but for the life of her, she couldn't understand why. She was still frowning in perplexity over her strange sense of cognizance when Gildon returned to the kuma's side to aid her in dismounting.

On her own two feet once again, Cadence hobbled slowly around the stones, studying them. Those that rested on the ground seemed almost to have thrust their huge bulk through the surface of soil, perhaps during some cataclysmic planetary disruption. She could even write the precise circular shape of the formation off to coincidence. But how in the universe had the enormous stones that appeared to balance precariously on the summits of the base stones gotten into place? The more she stared at it, the more she realized that this could not possibly be a natural formation. Yet what purpose could it have? Not shelter, certainly.

Hearing a football behind her, she turned to face her escort. "What is it?"

Gildon merely tensed slightly and shook his head while indicating that she should join him in entering the circle of stones. Cadence studied his features warily, but saw no threat. When he stepped into the circle and beckoned, she followed. The kuma was already within the circle. She was suddenly aware of the cessation of sound. There was no breeze. There were no bird calls. No rustling grasses. Nothing. Absolute silence. How strange!

Gildon studied Cadence closely as they moved toward the center of the circle. He had noticed that her aura had flared more brightly as they had approached the portal. And now, within the circle, her aura was positively brilliant, as though it drew upon the energies centered there. The bands of energy within the circle, although unweakened, pulsed with a strange rhythm. Who was this woman, he wondered. Or, perhaps more to the point, *what* was she? Friend or foe? He must know the answer to that question before he took her into the inner city. But how?

He grasped her arm and drew her nearer himself and the kuma. How could he learn for certain where her allegiance lay? And then, even as he asked the question, he knew the answer. The gates to the city of Jafna themselves could very well provide the most comprehensive test.

Just as all things in nature possess a unique vibratory rate or harmony, so each person possessed a personal vibratory rate governed by his alignment with the outside forces of good and evil. The souls of those who walked closest to the One or whose intent was most righteous, regardless of their individual beliefs, would resonate at a much different frequency than someone who dealt in corruption. Yet there were so many gradations of good, and of evil, that no definitive test of alignment had ever been found. Therefore, city gates had been designed to detect alignments according to a precise variance and could be programmed to present barriers to those who did not conform to the specific range of resonance.

All of the cities on the continent of Tumar—the only continent inhabited by Gidon's people on this world—had been constructed according to the same plan. A plan that utilized individual vibratory rates to protect or, when necessary, control its citizens. This was done by creating three distinct cities within a city, each dependent on the others for trade, yet separate: an outer city, a central city, and an inner city. The gates to the outer city had always been open to all, even those who walked on the dark side farthest away from the Light of the One. The gates to the central city originally had been programmed to a vibratory rate in the range of those who walked closer to the One; those whose intent was pure but whose will was weak. And the gates to the inner city had been styled to resonate in the range of those whose purity of purpose was clear. The inner cities had always been the home of the moral and the ethical.

Over time, the Tesuvian people who'd immigrated here had gradually come to know to which section of the city they belonged and where they would be welcomed, and the gates had fallen into disuse. Gildon frowned. Since the gates had only recently been reactivated due to the difficulties facing his people, the problem he faced was that all three city gates had been set to accommodate a very wide range of vibratory resonance. They would prevent anyone of purely evil intent from entering the inner city, but that was the only certainty.

Still, they could work for his purpose. He would simply have to make some minor adjustments to the gate's settings. As an inner-city High Priest, he was one of the few capable of making the required alteration. And it was the most precise test he could perform. After her contact with the barrier, he should know which of the foretold arrivals she was, for surely someone of good intent could not be destined to lead the Vradir.

With his purpose clearly in mind, he keyed his thoughts to a portal near the north entrance to the central ring of the city. Then, closing his eyes, he reached for the energy centered and magnified within the stone circle and . . . thrust. But the force was not enough to complete the transfer. Something was wrong. He looked at Cadence's brilliant aura and wondered. Was she drawing the energy of the portal into herself?

Removing his *falar* stone from the folds of his clothing, Gildon centered it over his forehead and closed his eyes once more. Frowning in intense concentration, he again drew on the energies within the ancient circle. The power seemed changed in some indefinable way, but it was there. Intoning a brief augmenting chant, he drew upon the force and . . . pushed, propelling himself and Cadence—and Lofen too—through the fold in space. For a brief moment in time, nothingness surrounded them; like a dense gray fog, it obliterated all perceptions. And then they were within a domed portal near the gate to the central city.

The first thing Gildon heard was a torrent of strident, incomprehensible sound from Cadence. She gestured frantically to the sealed structure that surrounded them with its white stone walls and looked at him demandingly. Gildon tried to reassure her telepathically, but his attempt at even that much communication was again useless. Grimacing, he wished for the hundredth time that he had not drawn this duty. Obviously her culture did not use or understand the technology of transference portals and he had no means to explain their operation to her.

Trying to ignore the grating annoyance of her continued attempt at communication, Gildon grasped her arm and urged her toward the exit. As they emerged into the bright sunlight, surprise accomplished what Gildon had been on the verge of strangling her to achieve: It stilled Cadence's tongue. Sighing in relief, Gildon remembered Lofen and turned. He divested the animal of Cadence's headgear and bag, and tried to forget the pain of his ribs. Just a few more minutes and he would have them cared for.

He sent the kuma a brief telepathic vision of his stable, and after a snort of satisfaction, the beast trotted off. As Gildon turned back, Cadence gestured to his injured side and held out her hand toward her bag. He was about to refuse to give it to her, but her obstinate expression changed his mind. It was only a few yards to the gate . . . and the test.

They had gone only a step when a flash to his right attracted his attention. Before his eyes, one of the random dimension thresholds that had begun to plague their land flashed open. No province had been immune to their threat. Although the priests of the Avatar had found a means to protect the central and inner cities, the outer cities remained vulnerable.

Gildon glanced down at the woman walking on his left to see what her reaction to the threshold might be, but she was looking the other way. He hoped she continued to do so.

The threshold hung in midair for a second, an egg-shaped gateway ringed by a coruscation of yellowish light. A container of flowering plants very near it began to wither, succumbing to a virulent disease. Unfortunately, his people had never found a means of fortifying plants against such pestilence, and only a few domestic animals were thus protected. Their genetic shielding against contagion did not make the people near it complacent, however, for it posed a different kind of threat to them. Everyone hastily moved away from the poisonous rupture, giving it a wide berth as they continued on their way.

And then, as abruptly as it had appeared, the threshold closed in on itself and disappeared. Gildon heaved a sigh of relief. The gateway had been a short-lived, unstable one. He didn't think an entity had come through. The last thing he needed at the moment was to run into another Gou'jiin.

Blissfully unaware of the tension in her host, or its cause, Cadence stared around in undisguised awe as they walked the short distance to the center-city access. All the buildings, most of which appeared to be a mere two or three stories, were constructed of a white plastery substance. Each was slightly different in design from the others and quite beautiful, with rounded corners, arched doorways, and ornately carved pillars supporting elaborate porticos. The streets were clean and paved with a hard yellow-gold stone that she didn't recognize. Pots of brightly blooming flowers abounded. A number of small birds with brilliant plumage flitted in and around the buildings and their occupants. People milled everywhere, some carrying burdens, some leading children, some merely walking swiftly, intent on some private business.

Cadence noted that they were an unusually tall race. Gildon, whom Cadence had thought tall at an estimated height of six feet three inches, was actually average in height when compared with the other men she saw—some of whom appeared to be over seven feet! The women were tall as well. Most were almost six feet and a couple neared Gildon's height. In fact, with the exception of a few children, Cadence was the shortest person in evidence. And she had never before considered herself lacking in stature.

Her observation of Gildon's people switched to their clothing. It was fascinating. The women wore sleeveless gowns constructed of softly draped, pleated fabric that fell to mid-calf length. The garments were predominately backless while the fabric in front crossed over the breasts, forming a daring V. Their footwear consisted of flat, ornately decorated sandals. Those who had apparently felt a chill in the air covered their gowns and bare arms with cloaks.

The men's clothing was more diversified. Some wore ankle-length tunics. Some wore clothing styled similarly to Gildon's but in varying colors. And still others wore a trouser style more familiar to Cadence, which was complemented by a short hip-length tunic. The men hurried to and fro as inhabitants of any city did. Yet, despite all the hustle and bustle of a normal populace, the atmosphere seemed eerily subdued and tense.

There was conversation: that musical intonation of syllables she'd heard Gildon use. So, although the city had a much lower noise level than what she was accustomed to, the impression of tension did not arise from silence. What was it? Curiously, Cadence studied the people she and Gildon passed.

A woman holding a young boy by the hand walked by. Even though neither the woman nor the child could completely contain their curiosity about Cadence, they certainly couldn't have been accused of staring. And neither smiled. Cadence was not used to seeing children with such serious demeanors. The next person they passed was a man. He too gave Cadence a quick, thorough perusal, without any alteration of his solemn expression. Cadence made a swift study of all the faces she could see. Everyone was somber. Not one person had the slightest hint of a smile.

She looked at the man walking next to her and realized she had not seen a smile from Gildon either. She wished she could speak with him. Were his people naturally so lacking in gaiety? Or was something wrong?

Cadence shivered. What could be bad enough to keep a whole city from smiling?

A moment later, they approached a wall that seemed to stretch off endlessly in either direction. A large arched gateway was the only opening. Cadence began moving toward it, but Gildon's hand on her arm halted her. The electricity of the contact seared her arm as he drew her to one side. Even after he'd released her, she felt the imprint of his hand burning through the cloth of her flight suit and surreptitiously rubbed at the spot to alleviate the sensation. What was the matter with her?

Determined to somehow ignore the perplexing phenomenon, she watched him curiously as he brushed his hand lightly over a series of raised motifs carved into the stone at the edge of the gate. Each movement of his hand prompted a faint musical note or series of notes. Interesting. How did it work? She saw nothing present that should have been capable of producing music. And *why* was Gildon doing it? She frowned in puzzlement. She was certain the sounds were not meant to be entertaining, so what was the purpose?

Although he sensed her curiosity, Gildon paid no attention to it. Cautiously ensuring that he made no errors, he completed realigning the gate. He was altering its frequency to that of someone whose vibratory rate resonated in harmony with the forces of darkness. If Cadence's alignment was pure, when she came into contact with the invisible barrier, she would be stunned, but otherwise unharmed. If her alignment was corrupt, she would walk through the restriction with no sign of discomfort.

Yet, even as he completed the realignment of the gate, Gildon hesitated without knowing why. He had no choice but to proceed. He needed to know which of the two foretold Cadence represented. His people needed to know. And if she was the one destined to cause the destruction of his world through her alliance with the Vradir, then—as instructed—he would need to find some means of preventing any interaction with others before he took her into the inner city for incarceration.

Cadence was looking at him with a question in her eyes, and he could delay no longer. With an expansive gesture, he indicated that she should precede him through the gate. As Cadence nodded and took a step toward it, his breath hitched in his throat. Remaining a step behind her, ready to catch her if she fell, he followed.

She didn't even pause as she neared the invisible force field. Did she sense nothing? Even from behind her, he could feel the radiant power of the barrier. Yet she stepped into the force field without hesitation. Her aura flared more brightly than he'd yet seen, flashing prismatic colors with kaleidoscopic speed. The effect was unlike any he'd yet seen. She paused, as though perhaps sensing something strange, and then . . . stepped through.

No! The word was a silent wail of denial in his mind.

Chapter Five

Gildon stared in bewilderment as Cadence paused on the other side of the gate and waited for him. He didn't want to believe what his eyes were telling him. Had the gate malfunctioned? Although he could feel the power emanating from the barrier, he did not have in his possession the instruments necessary for testing the accuracy of its alignment. After all these years of disuse, was its test unreliable? He had to know.

Ignoring Cadence's curious gaze, he extended his right hand toward the barrier. The tingling sensation caused by the energy there increased. His fingers came into contact with it, and the repercussions were immediate. He felt blinding pain. Pain radiating down his arm and into his body. Pain flashing through his mind like cutting shards of ice. Pain . . . because now he knew that Cadence was not the person he subconsciously had wanted her to be.

Jerking his hand away from the tentative contact before he lost consciousness, he hastily moved to the side and realigned the barrier. Then, stepping through the gate, he joined Cadence. The sudden tightness in Gildon's chest told him why he had hesitated earlier. Told him how badly he had wanted the outcome to be different. He met her lucid green-eyed gaze and wished . . . What did he wish? He didn't know. He didn't even know why it mattered. This woman should mean nothing to him.

What he did know was that Cadence was of corrupt intent, her alignment harmonious with the forces of evil. And her presence on this world, according to the priests of the Lidai Order, would bring about the destruction of his people and, possibly, this world unless her influence was countered.

But that, at least, was not up to him. His duty was almost over. That much had worked in his favor. Had she proved to be the other arrival, he would have been assigned to continue as her counselor for the duration of her stay or until she had joined their society. Now he had only to deliver her into the Prelates' hands and allow them to decide her fate.

More stunned by the turn of events than he would have believed possible after knowing her such a short time, Gildon avoided Cadence's eyes as he led her to the next portal. Why did he feel such a strong attraction to her? It wasn't like him. Or was the attraction a result of her power? Some attempt to cloud his senses? He would know, if it began to fade when he was no longer in her presence. Suddenly he could scarcely contain his desire to be quit of the beautiful alien female and all the questions concerning her.

He would take her to the gate of the inner city, where he would realign the force field to resonate in harmony with the purest of those who followed the one. When she came into contact with such an extreme opposing force, she would be rendered insensible, thus preventing any and all interaction, as demanded. And she'd be incarcerated for a time.

Cadence followed Gildon along the street. Her escort's expression had gone from solemn to downright gloomy in the space of moments. In fact, he glowered like a thunder cloud at the entire world. She looked around for a clue as to the cause of his sudden temper and could find none. Finally she concluded that his expression must be the result of pain.

When he approached another of those small round buildings very like the one they'd just left, her scowl echoed his. Whatever means of locomotion these transporters used, she hadn't liked the sensation at all. She really, *really* didn't want to travel that way again. She wasn't certain she could handle it without losing everything in her stomach—which probably wasn't much, because she was starving. Gildon stepped through the doorway and she peered past his shoulder. The place was indeed identical to the building they'd just left. Damn!

"Gildon—"

He turned and looked down at her with a hard, remote gaze. Hostility radiated from him in palpable waves. Cadence took a hasty step back. What the hell had happened? What had she done? Deciding that she didn't want to compound whatever mistake she'd committed, she choked back the protest on her lips and stared up at him. When he raised an aloof, questioning brow, she shook her head slightly. "Forget it," she murmured.

After a brief second when a hint of confusion registered in his eyes, he entered the building. It was brilliantly illuminated by some indefinable source, as had been the previous transporter. Inside, a white stone pillar marked with innumerable carvings and exhibiting a small winged statuette on its crown graced the center of the single room. Other than that, the chamber was empty. Cadence swallowed and looked to Gildon for guidance. Impersonally grasping her upper arm, he led her to the center of the chamber, where he quickly ran his hand over a couple of the motifs there.

A moment later, the bottom dropped out of Cadence's stomach. The sensation of falling, of spiraling down at the speed of light through a gray fog, robbed her of all equilibrium. Suddenly it was over. The transporter chamber came back into focus. Had something gone wrong?

And then she noted some dissimilarity. This place had sets of wings carved into the outer wall at regular intervals. Its central pillar was taller, although it had an identical winged figurine on its crown. Definitely another chamber. Swallowing as her stomach regained its steadiness, she followed Gildon from the transporter.

The city outside the transporter appeared much the same as the area they'd just left. Still, there were enough subtle changes for Cadence to know that they were no longer in the same area of the city, if indeed they were in the same city at all. The buildings were of a corresponding architectural style, but layouts differed. The identities of the people had changed. And the potted flowers and song birds, too, seemed to be more abundant.

She followed Gildon for about half a block to another gate set into a stone wall that appeared identical to the last one. She hadn't particularly liked the sensation of stepping through that either. Although she hadn't seen anything, at one point it had had a distinctly sticky feel to it, as though she'd walked through a wall of gelatin. But it hadn't been painful or induced vertigo like the transporter, and the stickiness had vanished instantly, so she supposed she could live with the sensation.

She knew absolutely nothing about these people. Even though she hadn't been treated like a captive by Earth standards, she really didn't know whether she'd been captured or rescued. Were she to refuse to do something required of her, she might receive entirely different treatment. Who knew? She didn't want to anger these people without reason. She had nowhere to go until she found means of repairing her ship and returning to her own time.

She refused to contemplate the possibility that she

might not get home. Just because nobody else who'd traveled into the past had returned didn't mean it couldn't be done.

Immersed in her thoughts, Cadence barely noticed as Gildon stepped to one side of the gate and stopped. She would have walked on had his hand on her shoulder not halted her. Wishing irrationally that he would stop touching her, she rubbed surreptitiously at the spot and watched as he ran his deft, long-fingered hands over the ornate carvings, once again producing a strange series of notes. She frowned thoughtfully.

Since he did not want her to try to walk through the gate until he'd done whatever he did to produce the musical notes, he must be releasing some kind of locking mechanism. She stared hard at the open-arched gate, but try as she might, she could see no barrier. A force field? Slowly, hand out cautiously, she advanced on the gate. Would she be able to feel it?

When he completed his realignment of the gate, which accessed the inner city, Gildon turned to Cadence only to find that she was no longer beside him. For an instant panic assailed him. She was his responsibility. Had she somehow sensed his intent and escaped? And then he caught sight of her. She stood examining the gate with a puzzled expression on her face. The problem was, she was already on the other side. How had she managed that? Had she moved through it before he'd begun reprogramming it? He was certain she had not, for he had felt her next to him as he'd begun the realignment. So how?

However she had accomplished it, he supposed it didn't matter much as long as she came into contact with the alignment field now that it was at full force. The opposing polarity of the field should still work to incapacitate her physically and psychically, allowing him to safely bring her into the inner city.

He felt almost absurd doing things this way, when—if the Lidai Order was so concerned about her possible interaction with inner city citizens—he could simply bind her, blindfold her, and escort her in. He felt certain that were she to try anything untoward he could have handled the situation physically even with his bruised ribs. But, as he'd been accused many times, perhaps that was simply his warrior mentality surfacing. Regardless of his feelings in the matter, the priests of the Lidai Order had been adamant: If there was any doubt whatsoever as to which of the foretold arrivals she was, the woman must not be allowed to interact with anyone in the inner city. If he simply escorted her in, interaction would take place, even if it was merely eye contact. With all that was at stake, he could not afford to disregard the beliefs and instructions of his brethren.

He observed her frowning with ferocious curiosity at the gate and would have smiled had she been another woman and the situation not so grave. "Cadence," he called. When she looked at him, he beckoned to her.

She immediately stepped forward and began talking to him in that strangely discordant language of hers as she waved one hand expansively at the gate. He had no doubt that she was asking questions about its purpose. However, since he had no idea what questions she asked and would not have revealed the information even if he had, he did not attempt a response. He merely waited for her to come into contact with the barrier, anxious for this distasteful assignment to be over.

But it seemed that fate did not want to make his life easy.

As Cadence stepped through the gate, her aura flared briefly, but unremarkably. Then she stood before him looking up at him expectantly.

Rational thought abandoned him. He could only stare.

By the One! How was this possible? No one could move through two diametrically opposed alignment gates without the field having some effect on them. And he had aligned this gate to the resonance of a saint. Not even *he*, an inner-city resident, could have walked through it without feeling some discomfort.

He had no answers for this. No idea what to do. Leading Cadence to a stone bench, he invited her to sit. She sat gingerly on the edge of the bench and looked at him inquiringly. Gildon did his best to block her bright green questioning gaze from his mind as he tried to assess the situation. Nothing particularly illuminating came to him. In desperation he closed his eyes for a moment, concentrated, and sent a telepathic knock winging its way to his mentor, the Prelate of Shemeir, Tailen of the line of Goryne. *Counselor, may I speak?*

When contact was made, there was a hint of surprise at the unexpected communication, a trace of anxiety. Telepathic conversation of any duration was mentally taxing for both the transmitter and the receiver and—because it lacked the powerful resonance of vocalized speech, which conveyed so much more than mere words—was used primarily in emergencies or circumstances where verbal communication was dangerous, undesirable, or not possible. *Speak, my friend.*

I require guidance, Tailen. With as much detail as he was able, Gildon related his dilemma, visualizing the incredible phenomenon he'd witnessed as Cadence walked through the first gate and the less spectacular display at the second.

Tailen hesitated only a moment after Gildon completed his narration. *She may yet establish her identity as the deliverer mentioned in the prophecy. In that event, we don't want to risk insulting her by treating her badly. Take her to the Sadhue Temple,* Tailen directed, referring to the Healing Order. *There, you can have your ribs and her leg cared for. Have the physicians ensure that she does not carry disease. When you leave the temple, deliver her directly to me. To appease our Lidai brethren, avoid as much interaction with others as is possible.*

Gildon opened his eyes. *It will be done, Counselor.*

Feeling confused, isolated, lonely, and—though she didn't want to admit it—very much afraid, Cadence followed Gildon through the city streets. Once again Gildon's mood had changed, and again she didn't know what she'd done to cause it, if anything. Rather than appearing angry with her, he now wore an expression of intense wariness spiced with suspicion. What did he think she was going to do? Steal some state secret or something? She sneaked a glance at the man walking at her side and skipped a step to match his long stride.

She couldn't wait to get wherever they were going, retrieve her helmet from Gildon, and see how much of Claire's data remained intact. Hopefully, it would be enough to try to work out some course of action. Thank the stars, she'd had the foresight to have the computer transfer itself into the helmets. Even with all the data Claire had possessed intact, however, Cadence knew her chances of getting home were minimal. The loss of one of the helmets, containing half of Claire's data, could prove catastrophic. But she refused to acknowledge that. Not yet. It would be tantamount to giving up, and that she wouldn't do. With a rueful shake of her head, she decided she would accomplish nothing by worrying about the future. She would probably be better served by paying attention to the world and the people around her.

She and Gildon were entering a huge square that looked large enough to accommodate a small moon without difficulty. A number of equally enormous buildings bordered the vast stone-paved space. Ten crystalline towers or pillars rose high into the sky from the roof of the edifice that appeared to be the focus of the square. Smaller but similar towers speared the sky from the tops of most of the other buildings as well.

Grasping her upper arm in a way that irked her both for its proprietary manner and its devastating effect on her senses, Gildon led Cadence to one side. Their destination appeared to be a less imposing structure sporting five much smaller crystal towers.

After ascending a column of stairs, they approached a pair of ornately carved arched doors. The doors did not open at their approach, so there was no pressure plate or electronic eye at work as there might have been on Station Apollo, yet neither did the barriers have handles or any recognizable means of opening them. Cadence stared in puzzlement as Gildon stepped forward and gently touched the barriers. In response to his contact, the doors swung inward.

They walked into a wide corridor bathed in a light as bright as the sunny day outside. Yet there were no discernable skylights or light sources of any kind. Peaceful, lilting music filled the air, so subtly that one was almost unaware of it. Cadence sensed a definite change in the atmosphere, an unusual serenity, a lightness of being.

She and Gildon had only taken a few steps when a woman wearing a deep forest green robe entered the corridor from a room ahead and on their right and came forward to meet them. She was very beautiful, Cadence noted. Slim and pale, she had long golden-blond hair, much of it woven into an elaborate coronet on the crown of her head. Her eyes were a bright golden-topaz color. A frown creased her forehead as she took in Gildon's rigid bearing and Cadence's limp. She immediately looked at Gildon and half sang, half chanted some alien phraseology. He responded in kind, while Cadence stood at his side wondering how she would ever manage to learn such an exotic language well enough to communicate her need for their aid. The woman nodded, the deep green stone suspended over her forehead flickered briefly with an inner light, and then a young man stepped into the hall to join them.

The man, also wearing forest green clothing, led Gildon down the corridor and into a chamber on the left, while the woman courteously guided Cadence into a chamber on the right. The room was totally vacant. Then the woman opened her mouth, sang a short, high note, and a platform slid out of the wall at waist height. Cadence stared at it.

The woman smiled at her reassuringly and, pointing to herself, intoned a few indecipherable syllables. A name? Cadence wondered.

She, too, indicated herself. "Cadence," she said. She immediately received the same pained expression with which Gildon consistently favored her. "Cadence," she repeated, persevering in her effort.

"Caydynz," the woman intoned.

Cadence smiled. "Close enough. And you?" She gestured to the woman. "What is your name again?"

"Kahlayne," she said, pointing to herself. "Kahlayne."

"Kahlayne," Cadence repeated with a nod.

Although the woman winced slightly, she nodded and smiled encouragingly. Then, with a series of gestures that indicated Cadence's leg a number of times, she explained that she wanted Cadence to disrobe for an examination. When she was certain that Cadence understood, she handed her a white gown styled like those worn by the women on the streets and left the chamber. A solid-looking white door, devoid of ornamentation and again lacking a handle of any kind, materialized in her wake.

Cadence sighed in relief at finally having a moment alone and allowed her gaze to roam the room in a thorough inspection. Was she imprisoned, she wondered. Curiosity prompted her to approach the door. Nothing happened. She reached out to touch it, and her hand went through it at the same instant that the unique obstruction disappeared.

Astonished, she jerked her hand back, and the barrier re-materialized. A holographic door! It worked like a curtain, simply giving privacy without blocking access or exit. Very unusual!

Well, it might take her a while to become accustomed to these things, but at least she wasn't a prisoner. Yet.

Remembering the task she'd been set, Cadence turned back to the room. Setting her duffel bag on the floor, she began to disrobe, taking off everything except her underwear and the anti-grav cups she used to support her breasts. She folded her discarded clothing and carefully placed it in her bag. One never knew how long it might have to last. She had just donned the long white gown and was silently lamenting its daring style when a slight hiss sounded and she turned to see Kahlayne reenter the chamber.

With a pat of her hand on the waist-high platform, Kahlayne indicated that she wanted Cadence to lie upon the examination table. From its hard, shiny appearance, Cadence expected the sterile white table to be very uncomfortable, but she discovered when she climbed onto it that it was not only restfully flexible, but soothingly warm. Rubbing Cadence's hand in a comforting gesture, Kahlayne smiled and sang something that Cadence interpreted as *Relax, everything will be fine*. At least that was what she hoped it was. She knew that she was placing an inordinate amount of trust in the belief that these were basically good people. But when it came right down to it, what choice did she have?

Trying to relax, she watched Kahlayne place her hands about two inches over her prone body. Then, closing her eyes, the nurse or doctor or whatever-she-was began moving her hands in small concentric circles over Cadence's entire body. What was she doing? Kahlayne began to hum, and as though in response, the light in the room changed color, going from daylight white to bright rosy blue. Before Cadence could get over her surprise, Kahlayne's tone changed, and a device slid out of the opposite wall. It was a white rectangular box supported at a height slightly higher than the examination table by a set of four legs on wheels. The contraption rolled forward and, at another sound from Kahlayne, began to slowly fit itself over the platform on which Cadence lay. She stared at it nervously.

As it moved forward, it directed a bright light down at her body. The intensity of the beam seemed slightly stronger over her injured leg. When it reached her waist, the dull aching pain in her leg was gone. Although she was no stranger to accelerated healing, Cadence had never seen it performed in quite this way or quite this quickly. What exactly had the thing done? Flicking a glance at Kahlayne, who continued to stand at her side with her eyes closed, Cadence lifted her head higher in order to watch the machine as it continued to move up her body. A second later, it halted and directed a strong beam of light at her sore and slightly swollen wrist. In the next instant the pain and the swelling were gone. The machine continued up her body until it was directly over her head. Almost immediately, the tenderness of her forehead and the dull, nagging ache in her temples—a remnant of the blow she had taken—disappeared. Then the healing device slid back down her body.

Kahlayne hummed another couple of notes. The machine withdrew into the wall and the light returned to normal coloration. Opening her eyes, she looked down at Cadence, smiled, and raised a brow in a manner that seemed to say, *Feeling better?* Cadence nodded and, although her answering smile felt a little shaky on her lips, she returned Kahlayne's courtesy.

As soon as the conveyor had completed the healing process on his ribs, Gildon looked at the young physician he knew as Beldon. Beldon had not yet attained High Priesthood within the Sadhue Order, but he was very good at his craft. "I thank you," Gildon said automatically. "Has my clothing been brought yet?"

Beldon nodded. "It is just outside the door. I will bring it in as I leave."

Gildon nodded. Immediately upon arriving here, he had asked that a novice be summoned to bring him his priestly robes from his quarters in the Temple of the Avatar. It would not be seemly for him to walk the corridors of the Temple of the Eidan, to meet with the Prelate of Shemeir, in his grimy warrior's garb.

Until five years ago he'd worn the indigo color symbolic of his chosen order, the Kami Warriors, on a daily basis. Then, due to his brother's relocation to the country of Madaia, the time had come to continue the study dictated by his bloodline. At the time of Jakial's move, Gildon had railed against the fates that required him to fill his brother's position within the Order of the Avatar. For of all the Orders, only the Order of the Avatar required that posts be passed to members of blood relationship. It was believed that only those related by blood to the first successful founders of the Order would have the strength to withstand the subtle allure of Darkness Arcane. Yet there were those who murmured that even that was not enough protection for some. *Like your brother,*

Jakial? an insidious voice asked. No! He refused to believe such evil of his brother.

Pulling his mind firmly away from such useless musing, Gildon turned his thoughts to Cadence. "The woman and I must leave immediately. Where is she?"

"She is being healed in a chamber across the hall and up two." Placing Gildon's stark white robes on the foot of the healing table, he nodded in a slight bow of deference just as he turned to leave. "I will see you again, kaitan."

Gildon nodded without comment, his thoughts and his entire being already focused beyond the healing temple. He must get Cadence to Tailen as quickly as possible. After hastily donning his clothing and picking up the headdress he still carried for Cadence, he left the chamber without a backward glance. He didn't worry about his discarded Kami clothing; Beldon or another novice would ensure that it was sent to a launderer and then returned to him.

A half dozen long strides carried him to the entrance of Cadence's healing chamber. At a touch, the barrier disappeared and he stepped into the room. The sight that met his eyes stopped him dead in his tracks and wiped all thought of things beyond the here-and-now from his mind.

Cadence, her back to the door, stood alone in the chamber, looking into something he could not see that sat on the examination table. She wore one of the backless, softly draped gowns commonly worn by women of his culture. Yet he could not remember ever seeing a woman's back displayed so attractively in one of the gowns. The brilliant white of this particular gown deepened her golden-tan skin tone to the color of wild honey. The lines and curves of her back were subtly sculpted, the indentation of her backbone as seductive as a lumina-flower-scented night. It induced images of moonlight stealing through diaphanous curtains to bathe her sun-kissed woman's body as she lay upon a silken bed. Of her welcoming arms reaching up to him as moss-green eyes glowed with love and passion. Of Cadence. By the One! He wanted to touch her. Needed to touch her.

Chapter Six

Without quite knowing how he got there, Gildon found himself standing directly behind Cadence. So close that he could smell the warm female scent that clung to her beautiful skin. He reached out, needing to know the texture of her flesh, its temperature. At the slight touch of his hand, Cadence spoke, startling him into jerking his hand away guiltily.

"Kahlayne, I—oh!" Her voice registered shock as she turned and saw who it was. She met his gaze without fear. And that, too, was an aphrodisiac to him. "Gildon." His name emerged in a murmur on a warm breath, as though she'd been stunned, immobilized by what she saw in his eyes. And what did she see, he wondered. Desire? Passion? It raged through his blood like a drug.

She licked her lips in unconscious invitation. Her full lips were as ripe and inviting as the peach-colored fruit of the *prieka* tree. The need to kiss her, to hold her, became as urgent as the need to draw breath. Placing one hand gently beneath her chin, he slowly lowered her mouth to hers. The contact was like oxygen to a drowning man. He wanted more. *Needed* more. Wrapping his arms around her, he caressed the silken skin of her beautiful back, drank in the sensation of her soft breasts crushed against his chest, and plunged his tongue between her teeth to taste the sweet elixir of her.

Ah, she was so good. Holding her was like returning home after an eternity away. Like finding a part of himself he had never known was missing.

Suddenly Cadence began struggling in his embrace. He lifted his head, looked into her eyes, and recognized the passion and the anger warring there. That she reciprocated his desire he knew. Yet obviously she was not willing to act on it. She hissed something at him that sounded very discordant and unpleasant despite its softness. Immediately the memory of his purpose here, the possibility of Cadence's identity, returned to the fore. He released her and stepped back.

What had he done? It was not like him to succumb to lust in this way. All of his adult life, women had accused him of being cold, emotionless, devoid of compassion, consumed by his work. And yet, since coming into contact with Cadence he had not only found himself capable of emotion and compassion, but he'd been unable to suppress the urges to express them. Something was wrong. Dreadfully wrong.

Was Cadence in some way beguiling him? His only knowledge of the powers of beguilement came through tales, and he scoffed inwardly, his male pride swelling indignantly at the idea. He would not have succumbed to such a thing . . . even if it were possible. Besides, it had been Cadence who had stopped the embrace.

Cadence forced herself to break the mesmerizing hold that his storm-cloud eyes had on her. Her gaze swept his bold nose, high cheekbones, and firm whisker-shadowed jaw, looking anywhere but into his smoldering eyes or at his sensual mouth. He had changed his indigo clothing for a pair of white trousers and an equally white robe that hung to his knees in the back while coming only to his waist in front. The flaps of the robe formed a deep V over his chest that revealed too much of his wide, muscled torso.

Somehow the stark white cloth against his dark hair and tanned complexion only accentuated his handsomeness.

It had been more than a little pleasant being in his arms. Much more! That frightened her. It would be so easy to have an affair with him. The problem was that Cadence couldn't seem to have an affair without getting her heart involved. And getting involved with a man like Gildon would ultimately only bring her more heartache. She couldn't lose sight of the fact that she was only on this world—in this time—temporarily. Once she found a means to leave, there would be no coming back. She didn't want her affections tearing her heart in two when it came time to leave. Besides, she'd already promised herself that she would not fall for another gorgeous male with a shallow personality and the inability to feel anything for anybody other than himself.

Drawing a deep breath, she met Gildon's gaze again. The heat was dissipating. However, once again the shadow of suspicion flickered in the depths of his eyes. Hell's universe! She wished they could converse. She would have given a month's pay credit to know what was going on in his head.

Abruptly turning away, he picked up her duffel bag and indicated that it was time for them to leave.

"Like this?" Cadence asked incredulously, looking down at the gown she wore. During their walk through the city she had seen countless women wearing the gowns, but it just felt too . . . revealing. "I was just going to change when you came in. I'd rather wear something of my own," she said, holding out her hand for her bag.

Although he hadn't understood her words, he grasped her intent. With a shuttered look on his face, he shook his head and again indicated the door, showing no signs of relinquishing her bag. Cadence studied his expression for a moment, trying to understand. Perhaps he didn't want her drawing too much attention, she mused. That must be it. Knowing that she would not get her way without a battle—which she was not prepared to do over something as inconsequential as her attire and a bit of modesty—Cadence acquiesced and headed for the door.

Upon leaving the hospital, or clinic, or whatever it was, Gildon guided her across the square toward the enormous building with the ten crystal towers. Reaching the entrance involved climbing a set of steps unlike any Cadence had ever seen: one step up, three steps forward, one up, three forward, until they had climbed at least thirty steps. At the summit, she turned to look back and was shocked that she could see the entire city laid out before her. The steps hadn't seemed *that* high. Perhaps the building had been constructed on a hill, she thought. They approached a pair of ornately carved doors. The barriers, like the others she'd seen, had no handles or recognizable means of opening them, yet neither did they open at Gildon's touch. Rather, he gently traced a pattern on the designs of the door. In response to his strokes, a sweet sweeping series of notes drifted on the air, and the doors disappeared.

Before they entered, Cadence turned back for a look at the city spread out, all white and gold. So clean. She noted that the walls she'd seen earlier divided the metropolis into three distinct areas and she wondered about their purpose. Then Gildon grasped her arm to lead her forward.

The wide corridors within the Temple of the Eidan were never crowded, but they were always busy. A group of young novices stopped talking in mid-conversation, following with their eyes the tall, dark man clad in the stark, unadorned white raiment of a priest of the Avatar. *A Darkling walked in their midst!* Gildon could almost feel them recoil at the realization. Yet, let one of them become possessed or tormented by an alter-realm entity, and they would turn to him without a qualm, expecting him to perform miracles.

He sighed. People rarely understood the nature of the work of the priests of the Avatar, and that lack of comprehension bread fear. It was natural. He, like his brother before him, was an adept, a master manipulator of the darker aspects of existence. He'd spent years learning the Dark Arts in order to thwart practitioners of them. Or, when necessary . . . and possible, to reverse the damage generated by their malevolence. Yet, even before he'd joined the Order of the Avatar, his darkly intense appearance had induced nervousness in others. Since he'd become a priest of the dark arts—a Darkling, as the young people called the priests and priestesses of the Avatar—the instinctive inclination of others to avoid him had merely intensified.

Novices and young priests alike continued to move silently aside, making way for the priest with the fluid warrior's stride. Few if any of them noted the strangeness of the beautiful woman who walked at his side. And those who noticed would not have dared comment.

Gildon's footsteps slowed as he neared the wide double doors of the Prelate's judicial chamber. He looked at Cadence. Since her true alignment remained undetermined, responsibility for her should now pass to the Prelate. Considering his own inexplicable behavior with her, it was probably a good thing. Still, he couldn't help but feel a twinge of regret. Before the strange sentiment clouded his senses, he reminded himself of his own plans. Plans that would have to be put on hold should he be burdened with the woman. With his purpose fixed firmly in mind, he touched the door. It shimmered and disappeared almost instantly. Guiding Cadence with a hand on her shoulder, he stepped into Tailen's office.

Having apparently dismissed his transcriber, Tailen was seated on a cushion at a low table laden with delicacies. Two empty cushions flanked the table. Gildon smiled. He could always count on his friend to remember a guest's stomach—even an official guest. After bowing courteously to the Prelate of Shemeir, left arm behind his back, right arm across his waist as was customary, Gildon ushered Cadence to the cushion on Tailen's right and set her duffel bag and the headdress on the floor at the end of the table. Deciding that he could not expect Cadence to address Tailen by his official title with her limited grasp of their vocabulary, Gildon indicated his friend with a sweeping gesture of his hand and supplied his name.

Cadence looked at the older man clad in his scarlet robes of office and nodded. "Tailen."

Tailen, true to his nature, dipped his chin and smiled without giving any indication that her pronunciation was anything less than perfect. Cadence returned his smile and pointed to herself. "Cadence."

Tailen repeated her name easily and then turned to observe as Gildon seated himself on the remaining cushion. He offered his right arm to his friend, and they clasped forearms. "I am glad to see you, my friend."

"And I you." Gildon flashed a glance at Cadence. "So what do you think?" he asked the Prelate.

Tailen hesitated. "I don't want to make the mistake of judging her too quickly, Gildon. I concur that her ability to alter her personal vibratory rate to the extent of camouflaging her alignment is unsettling, to say the least. However, we must not overlook the fact that, above all, she is *alien* to our world. Perhaps the alteration in vibratory rates is an instinctive thing unique to the humans of her home."

Gildon frowned thoughtfully. "I hadn't thought of that."

Tailen smiled and waved the discussion aside. "Come. We will eat first. Then we have much to discuss."

Although none of the food that Tailen and Gildon placed before her was familiar, surprisingly, Cadence liked most of it. Judging by the feast, her hosts were predominately vegetarian. There were plates upon plates of colorful fruits and vegetables arrayed in designs that were as pleasing to the eye as the taste was to the palate. One bowl contained a flat, bread-like food that reminded Cadence of crepes, while another held a creamy substance that looked like whipped cream but tasted more like honeyed cream cheese. Having finally appeased her rumbling stomach, Cadence found that she'd relaxed enough to actually enjoy a second cup of the steaming green beverage Tailen called *cai*. It had a bit of a bite to it that reminded her of coffee. Sipping it, she listened to the musical language of her hosts as they casually conversed.

She had half finished the beverage when she detected a subtle change in the tone of the conversation, or perhaps it was in the atmosphere itself. She watched as Gildon retrieved her helmet and presented it to Tailen. He seemed to be talking about the camera eye in the forehead. She took advantage of a break in the conversation. "Claire—"

Surprised by her unexpected speech, both Tailen and Gildon pinned her with their eyes. She ignored them as the helmet responded, "Yes, Sergeant?"

Tailen, startled by the talking helmet in his hands, quickly set it down on a table.

"Can you understand any of what they're saying, Claire?" Cadence asked.

"Their language does seem to have a few almost familiar sounds or syllables," the helmet said. "However, I am unable to interpret it."

Cadence sighed. "All right. Keep trying."

In Destiny's Arms

Gildon observed the slump of Cadence's shoulders and felt the need to communicate even more keenly. "What do you think, Tailen? Is there some way we can reach her?"

Tailen shrugged. "There is certainly no harm in trying. Since neither you nor I can penetrate her shields, telepathy is not possible. That leaves us with only two options. Either we learn her language or she learns ours. Since she is on *our* world, it makes more sense for her to learn ours."

"Thank the One for that!" Gildon said with heart-felt relief.

Tailen smiled. "Her language is a bit . . . flat, isn't it?" he asked rhetorically. "Then again, I imagine she finds ours equally disagreeable, if for different reasons."

Picking up the helmet again, Tailen reexamined it. "I agree with you, Gildon. This device must either have been designed for communication or data processing. In either case, it *might* be able to learn a language. If so, at the very least it should be able to provide the services of a translator. Unfortunately, I don't see any way that it could be compatible with our data processors. Compatibility would have saved considerable time." Setting the headdress on the table between them, he delved in the folds of his robe and withdrew a gold chain from which his *falar* stone dangled.

"I'll summon Delan," he said, referring to his transcriber, "and ask him to bring a written copy of our language." Placing the gold chain over his head, Tailen ensured that the deep red stone hung precisely in the center of his forehead and closed his eyes. Like most of the *falar* stones, which were prized for their ability to amplify telepathic talent, Tailen's stone was a garnetine. The stones came in many colors, but coincidentally, Tailen's matched the robes of his office. The stone flashed briefly with inner light while the communication took place, and then Tailen opened his eyes. "He comes," he said simply.

Conversation had relaxed again, and Cadence, waiting for some signal that the visit was over, had poured herself a third cup of *cai* when the door shimmered and another man entered. He was young, with bright, friendly blue eyes and dark blond hair. In his arms he carried a huge stack of books. Books! Cadence watched him curiously as he came forward and deposited the volumes on the floor between herself and Tailen. She watched Tailen anxiously, hardly daring to hope. The thought that through some effort of her hosts—picture books perhaps?—they might be able to carry on a rudimentary conversation was exhilarating.

Tailen picked up Cadence's helmet from the table and passed it to her, indicating that the lens should be directed toward him. Then, sorting through the stack of books at his side, he extracted one from the pile and opened it. Cadence saw nothing but row upon row of differently sequenced, vertical bands of color. Her heart sank. What was this?

Turning to the first page, Tailen pointed to the first color. No sequence here. Just plain yellow. Then he surprised her by opening his mouth and intoning a sound. Not a word; it contained no syllables. Simply a sound. He pointed to the next color, also yellow, but of a slightly different tone. And as he did, he intoned a slightly varied sound. Cadence frowned in confusion and looked down at the helmet in her lap.

"Claire, are you getting this?"

"Yes, Sergeant."

"What's going on? Is this a music lesson? Or is it what I think it is?"

"Since I do not know what you think it is, I cannot answer that question. However, I do not believe it is a music lesson. If I am not mistaken, Sergeant, we are being instructed in their alphabet."

"That's what I thought." Cadence stared at the confusing display of colors on the page. All yellow! "If they have a sound for every shade of every color . . ." Her voice trailed off as her mind grappled to understand such a complex language system. "That means their alphabet alone consists of thousands of sounds. Quarks! I'll never learn it."

"It is possible that you'll be able to learn the language from me through subliminal instruction while you sleep. You will, however, have to retrain both your hearing and your voice to hear and interpret many more variations in sound than you are accustomed to."

"And if I can't do that?" Cadence asked.

"Then I believe I will have to serve the role of interpreter."

Great! Just what she'd always wanted. She could think of a number of instances where it would be damned inconvenient to be forced to communicate through a computer. All right. So she'd just have to do her absolute best to learn this language. "Claire, record every nuance of this language. I will learn it subliminally."

"Yes, Sergeant Barrington."

Looking at Tailen, Cadence smiled and nodded to indicate that she understood what he was trying to do. He went back to the first color and intoned the sound. Although she found herself extremely self-conscious beneath Gildon's watchful gaze, Cadence did her best to imitate Tailen's intonation. He corrected her. She tried again. After a smile of encouragement, he moved on to the next shade.

After going over one entire page, he nodded and closed the book, returning it to the stack. Apparently he'd just wanted to illustrate how their language worked. So who would instruct her, she wondered.

She yawned unexpectedly. She needed rest. She'd been running on pure adrenaline for hours, but fatigue was catching up with her. Stifling another yawn, she observed the interchange between Tailen and Gildon, wishing she could understand more. Judging by the frown on Gildon's face, he wasn't particularly happy about something.

"You can't be serious, Tailen. We still haven't verified who she is, and you want *me* to counsel her?"

Tailen lowered his head in acknowledgment. "I do. *We* do. My colleagues and I arrived at the decision during a consultation. Technically, of course, she will not be your student, nor you her mentor. You will not instruct her in the doctrines of the Avatar. We merely want you to introduce her to our ways. We will assign a very circumspect and trustworthy scribe to teach her the language, but beyond that she is your responsibility. However, none of the usual strictures between student and mentor will apply. We will rely on your judgment."

"But why?" Gildon demanded. He'd been so certain he'd escaped this duty. Although he had long been qualified to instruct, he had never done so. He liked his privacy. The thought of someone living with him, even someone who would serve him and maintain his quarters in return for the knowledge he imparted, never had appealed to him. And Cadence would not even fall into that role. She would merely be a burden, a disruption to his ordered life. *And a danger to your senses*, another voice reminded him. *A constant temptation.* He met Tailen's gaze. "I would prefer that you choose another, Tailen."

His friend shook his head. "I'm sorry, Gildon. That is not possible. There is no one else suitable as both instructor and protector."

Gildon stared at him. "You believe she requires protection?"

"If Cadence is destined to lead the Vradir, I have no doubt that they will attempt to recover her. Conversely, if she is the foretold savior, do you not think it possible that our enemies will seek to destroy her?"

"So either way we can expect an attempt at contact."

Tailen nodded. "We believe so, yes."

Gildon thoughtfully sipped his *cai*. "How am I to instruct her in our ways, when I am to keep her sequestered until we know which of those foretold she is?"

"Conversation alone will have to suffice for a time."

Gildon nodded. "I see." He burned with impatience. He wanted only to escape his duties for a time. To infiltrate Madaia and find his brother, Jakial, before it was too late. To save Jakial from the evil that permeated the province that had been under his administration until his disappearance. Was that too much to ask? The entire province of Madaia was now under the dominion of the Vradir cult. Those who'd fought its domination had long since died, been enslaved, or fled to other provinces. If he didn't find his brother soon, it would be too late.

Then, as quickly as the thoughts had occurred to him, he felt remorse. What kind of priest was he? Tailen and his colleagues, the Prelates of the other provinces, sought to preserve their race and save a world from the annihilation that came from constant infiltration by alter-realm beings. Yet *he* found it difficult to think of anything but the saving of one man. He must look beyond his own desires. If he did not aid in preserving this planet, saving his brother would be meaningless. Finally, he looked at Tailen. "So be it."

"Good." Tailen smiled. "Then I will allow you to escort our guest to your apartment and show her to her quarters. She is fatigued. I will arrange for a guard to ensure that she does not leave your quarters unescorted until we ascertain her identity. Bring her to me in a few days so that I may see what progress she has made."

Far away in Madaia, in the bowels of an ancient temple, a man lifted his head at the soft sound of a footfall across the room. He frowned at the intrusion, eager to return to his study of the ancient tome before him. "What is it, Raulen?"

"My lord, the fighters were unable to catch the Shemeiran and the woman."

He rose from his seat at the table, his displeasure evident in every line of his body. "What you are telling me is that they escaped. Isn't that so, Raulen?"

"Yes, my lord."

"Curse the One! Such incompetence will not go unpunished. How can I achieve anything when my only tools are imbeciles?" Raulen did not respond. "Go!" he barked. "Get out of my sight before I decide to punish you for the failure of your brothers."

The fighter bowed and left the room.

Oblivious to the blackness of the walls that hungrily absorbed the little light provided by the phosphorescent light crystals, he paced the chamber without seeing it as his vision turned inward. Was this the woman? The savior foretold in the prophecy? The defender who would threaten their plans? Or did the Shemeiran rescue her because he was unsure of her identity?

Skirting the large, unadorned wooden table upon which sat the now forgotten tome, he walked across the uneven stones of the ancient cobbling to some dusty shelving. Old bowls and vials and mallets clattered and fell as he hastily searched the shelves. Then, triumphantly, he removed a large wooden bowl and a stoppered flask containing a dark, oily-looking liquid.

Blowing the dust from the bowl, he took it to the table and emptied the flask into it. After settling him-

self comfortably into a chair, he took a deep breath
to collect his thoughts, placed his deep yellow-brown
falar stone over his forehead, and began the incantation.

Utilizing the power of sound, an adept could manipulate the forces of nature to do his bidding. By
adding to that force the power of the mind, there was
little that could not be accomplished—with the right
training. Slowly he felt a piece of his consciousness
take flight, leaving the city of Eston. Within minutes
he saw below the gleaming white Madaian city of
Rabar, resting in its emerald valley. As his mind's eye
began to traverse the miles between Rabar and
Jafna, scenes unfolded on the black shiny surface in
the bowl. Visions of the endless fields and rolling
hills of the Madaian countryside, of a mauve-white
sky and fluffy white clouds, of grazing gray-elk and
hunting dragators. Gradually the scenes came faster
and faster until they became nothing more than a
blur of half-formed images. He sensed more than
saw his passage over the border between Madaia and
Shemeir. And then the city of Jafna was below him.

He slowed and headed for the inner city. Now to
find the woman, to observe her. To determine her
status and her importance. She would be accom-
modated within one of the smaller temples under the
dominion of the Temple of the Eidan, he was certain.

Methodically, carefully avoiding any wardings
that would alert temple occupants to his presence,
he began to search. But his hunt proved fruitless.
She was not in any of the expected temples.

Where was she? There was no place left that she
could be.

Wait! There was *one* place. But surely they would
not have put her in the Temple of the Avatar. Would
they?

His consciousness winged its way to a smaller,
though scarcely less imposing, building in the

shadow of the larger Temple of the Eidan. There were fewer quarters to search here. It wouldn't take long to confirm or deny his suspicion.

Nothing caught his attention in the first few apartments. He moved on to the next, entering through a balcony door left open to catch the night breeze. Carefully avoiding contact with the High Priest, whose senses would discern his presence, he moved into one of the two chambers reserved for novices.

Ah! A woman. He studied her briefly in the shadowy illumination of the night. Was it she? She seemed a bit unusual, but there was certainly nothing extraordinary about her. Her aura was a bit muted, but that was not unheard of. He would have to check more closely, read the surface thoughts of her dreams. He would know if he touched a powerful mind.

Slowly, cautiously, he moved closer and tentatively reached out. Touched her.

Pain! It was the only message his body received. Pain as something hurled his consciousness forcefully back across the miles and into his body in mere seconds. Pain manifesting itself as blinding light as something short-circuited the synapses in his brain. Pain that clutched his head in an iron grip, threatening to crush his skull. Ripping the *falar* stone from his forehead, he flung it across the room and found a small measure of relief.

As the torment slowly receded, he stared across the room at the *falar* stone where it winked in the light of the phosphorescent crystals. He was aware that scrys could be blocked. He had done it himself for a number of years. But normally the result was simply that the scryer received nothing when passing over a location, like a blank spot. Never had he known that a scry could be blocked in this way.

His eyes narrowed with anger and the desire for vengeance. She was almost certainly the alien woman who was destined to meddle in his plans. Yet he needed to know for certain. How could he learn that? Astral projection?

"Are you certain, Claire?"

It was Cadence's second evening on Fortuna. The day had been spent in her first marathon session in language education. After sharing a quiet evening meal with an enigmatic and taciturn Gildon—during which an inexplicable tension had worn on her nerves—she'd returned to her chamber to begin working with Claire on finding a means of returning home. So far the news was not good.

"Quite certain, Sergeant. All files pertaining to the design and repair of the Tachyon vessels were stored in the destroyed helmet."

Cadence raked her fingers through her hair in dismay. "What files *do* you have intact?"

"All language files are complete and available. I also have numerous star charts, information on the survival techniques necessary on inhospitable alien worlds, a number of complete libraries, both fiction and nonfiction, and—"

"All right, I get the picture. Just answer this: Do you have any undamaged files which can help me get home? Specifically, information on time travel?"

There was a pause. "I have no information on time travel other than references available in the libraries I mentioned. However, instructions on utilizing time travel seem to be lacking. In reference to your first question, I do not believe that I am in possession of any files that might aid you in returning to Earth space."

"Wonderful!"

Grabbing the virtually useless computer, Cadence replaced it on the shelf she'd designated for it. Then, biting back her frustration, Cadence stepped out of Gildon's spacious three-story apartment to stand on the narrow stone balcony that opened off of her room. Life had suddenly become very confusing, and for the first time in a very long while she longed desperately to succumb to tears.

If possible, Gildon had seemed more coldly remote than ever after leaving Tailen's chambers. Were it not for the friendly presence of the young woman named Shahra who was teaching her the language, Cadence would have felt as imprisoned as the guard outside the apartment door suggested she was. Shahra had hinted that the man was there for Cadence's protection. However when Cadence had demanded to know whom she needed to be protected from, Shahra had been unable to answer. That naturally left Cadence uncertain as to the veracity of her claim.

About all she had learned about her hosts so far was that the Tesuvians were not from this world, but from a distant planet in another system. Yet Shahra had been unable to tell her where their home world was, or how her people had arrived. Did the Tesuvians have ships somewhere? Some means of travel that might allow Cadence to return home? Shahra hadn't appeared to understand the question, or, if she had, she'd pretended she had not.

Cadence sighed. It wasn't that she had been treated badly in any way. In fact, Gildon's apartment was nothing short of opulent, and her quarters were no exception. Her bed chamber was enormous, with a large raised platform or dais that served as a bed. The dais was high enough to require three steps to gain access, and the bedding that graced it could only be described as luxurious. She had a private bathing chamber—easily the size of her entire stateroom back on Space Station Apollo—complete with sunken tub, colorful mosaic tiling, and enough foliage to classify it a greenhouse. A personal dressing room, equipped with ample closet space that just happened to be overflowing with clothing in her size, opened off of the bathing chamber. At the far end, a dressing table that appeared to be carved from pure crystal flaunted scores of crystalline cosmetic pots and perfume vials.

No, all things considered, the lifestyle here certainly seemed far better than the spartan and functional existence to which Cadence was accustomed. Yet it felt like nothing so much as a gilded cage. However, since Gildon had not left the apartment either, she'd had no opportunity to test her status.

Was she guest or captive?

In addition to that uncertainty, there was Gildon himself. He never smiled. When he deigned to look at her, his gaze held nothing more than condescending patience. He never spoke. Never touched her by so much as a brush of fingers when he passed her a dish at a meal. And Cadence admitted silently, hopelessly, that—against her better judgment—a part of her desperately wanted him to touch her.

Standing on the balcony, she looked up at the stars in an unfamiliar night sky and tried to analyze her reaction to Gildon. She'd always been a bit more emotional than was desirable for a career Legionnaire, but she thought she'd conquered the tendency. Now here she was alone on an alien world with no one to talk to and she was dreaming about the embrace of an ill-tempered, testosterone-overdosed, handsome rogue instead of dreaming about home, and friends, and . . . Chance.

Oh, stars, would she ever see her brother again?

Tears started in her eyes and she angrily brushed them away. Tears never solved anything. She knew that better than most. Tears hadn't brought her parents back from the dead after a burglar had broken into their labs and killed them. Tears hadn't rescued Cadence or Chance from the government-operated orphanage, or found them a new family. And tears certainly hadn't changed the nature of either of the two men she'd had the misfortune to care for.

She absently examined the bright yellow gibbous moon overhead and its larger silver-blue counterpart while she considered her dilemma. Five hundred years from now, Chance had disappeared somewhere on this very world. If only she could find some way to move through time, perhaps she might find her brother. Even if it meant that she might never leave this world, she could be satisfied with that. There was no one else in the universe that meant anything to her anyway. And her job was just that: a job. She had never felt a *calling* toward a certain type of career as had so many of her colleagues. Perhaps she was destined always to feel just a little unsatisfied. To know that there was something more out there, but never to know what it was. Well, she certainly couldn't say that life had been boring lately. Anything but!

She looked out over the city and marveled at the way it glowed with an almost fluorescent luminosity beneath the lunar light. Suddenly she noticed something shimmering at the corner of her vision. Turning, she perceived a strange rippling effect at the other end of the balcony. The rippling slowly took on shape—in the form of a man's body. The figure grew more distinct. His eyes were closed.

She stared open-mouthed. What the hell was happening now?

Whoever he was, he hadn't been completely transported, because she could see through him to the wall behind and he was not solidifying any more. But why would he be appearing on the balcony outside *her* bedchamber? Abruptly, he opened his eyes and looked right at her.

Cadence's mouth snapped closed as her heart sped up. She didn't like those eyes one bit. Much more substantial than the rest of the phantom, they glowed with an inner luminosity, pinning her. She felt like a nocturnal creature paralyzed by a beam of light. Suddenly very afraid, she swallowed. There was something odd about those eyes. She felt their intrusive perusal like the caress of a snake's slithering body. The apparition smiled, coldly, maliciously, and she sensed a wealth of sinister intent behind the simple gesture.

"Who are you?" she demanded, forgetting for a moment that even an apparition would probably not understand her language. When the man merely studied her, she decided to try her limited Tesuvian vocabulary. "Who are you?" she repeated, the alien intonation of the sounds cumbersome on her tongue.

His smile widened, this time with a trace of mockery, but he made no sound. Slowly he began to advance toward her. Since he blocked the access back into her room from the balcony, Cadence found herself trapped against the stone railing, unable to do anything but watch the phantom advance. The thought that it might be similar to the Gou'jiin she'd already encountered terrified her. She couldn't bear to feel that abhorrent invasion of her body or mind again. Putting her hands to her temples as though she could protect her intellect that way, she shook her head at the thing.

"No!" she cried, aware of the equal measure of anger and fright in her tone. "You won't have me. I'll kill you first. I swear I will." It didn't matter that the threat was empty, it was the only phrase that came near to expressing her hate, her fear, and her revulsion.

The apparition reached a spectral hand toward her. She screamed and edged sideways, the only direction in which it was possible for her to move short of tumbling over the balcony rail. It moved with her. Reached toward her. There was nowhere left to go. She screamed again.

Chapter Seven

Seconds later, Gildon raced onto the balcony. His gaze barely had time to swing from a terrified Cadence to the object of her terror when the apparition disappeared. He looked back at Cadence, his eyes dark with concern. Then, to her dismay, the tears she'd been fighting all evening burst the dam.

"Oh, hell!" She turned her back to him and wiped at the embarrassing moisture on her cheeks. A moment later, she felt his hands on her shoulders, his chest so near her back that she could feel his heat, warm and comforting. Oh, no! She'd never been able to hold back tears in the face of sympathy. Where was his anger, his coldness, when she needed it to add a little steel to her backbone?

She resisted the gentle pressure of his hands as he tried to turn her around. Her undoing came when he said her name in that softly accented sing-song way of his. There was a wealth of compassion, of gentleness in those two small syllables. With a half-stifled sob, she turned around and burrowed her head against his powerful chest. His strong, warm arms encircled her, comforted her. The solid, rhythmic beat of his heart beneath her ear soothed her. And all the pent-up tears flowed unchecked. Tears for herself, her untenable situation, and for the beloved brother she feared she might never see again.

The outpouring of emotion finally ceased, and

with a few what she hoped were discreet sniffles, she lifted a hand to dry her face. A small white cloth hung suspended before her eyes in the grasp of two large, sun-browned fingers. Mournfully she accepted it. Oh, stars, how could she ever look Gildon in the eye again after such a display of weakness? He didn't even like her. But then she remembered the devastating kiss they'd shared at the healing complex. Well, most of the time he didn't like her, she qualified.

Drawing a deep breath, she stiffened her spine. Though she did not want to face him, she knew she had no choice. She hadn't made it as an Internal Affairs investigator for the Stellar Legion by being a coward, and she would not become one now.

She tilted her head back away from his chest until she could see his shadowed face above hers. His teeth flashed briefly in the moonlight and he said something that she interpreted as, "Better now?"

She nodded and then, as blue flame flared in his midnight eyes, wondered if her interpretation had been a bit precipitous. She hadn't agreed to something she shouldn't have, had she?

Taking her hand, he led her back into her bedchamber. When he released her a moment later, Cadence held her breath, watching him warily. But he merely turned to secure the doors to the balcony. He chanted a brief phrase that Cadence didn't understand, and for a fraction of a second, Cadence thought she saw a diamond-shaped grid of blue-white lines appear over the doors. In the next instant, however, Gildon reached to pull the curtains closed, and the doors appeared as mundane as ever.

Turning back to her, he pointed to the raised dais in the center of the room with its soft mattress and silky bed coverings. "Sleep, Cadence." He looked as if he wanted to say more, but merely frowned in frustration. Obviously her vocabulary had not yet progressed to a point that would allow her to understand whatever he wanted to say. She stared at his handsome face, at his full-lipped mouth, and suddenly wanted very badly for him to kiss her again. He merely lifted a large, warm hand to cup her cheek, and said, "Sleep," again in his deep, sexy, accented voice.

As he left her room without a backward glance, his tenderness and compassion stayed with her, bringing a lump to her throat. How could one man be so mystifying? He was hard and cold and unfriendly, until . . . until she needed him. And then he was there. Why? What was it about her that he disliked so much when she was not in need of his strength or comfort? Why, if he had such an aversion to her presence, was he always there for her? It didn't make sense.

Well, she thought, thank the stars that at least one of them had retained enough sense not to be overcome by hormones.

As she mulled over her problematic nonrelationship with her host, Cadence readied herself for bed. She needed to learn to speak his language, that's all there was to it. She hated guessing games. Since Claire's schooling in the Tesuvian language had been completed today, Cadence decided she'd start her own subliminal training tonight.

Cadence sat in her bedchamber with her young tutor, the transcriber named Shahra. For a week she had immersed herself in the Tesuvian language. And for a week both Shahra and Gildon had managed to put off most of her questions in one way or another. The answers she *had* received had only left her with more questions.

She frowned remembering one such instance. She'd asked Gildon about the method he and his opponents had used to camouflage themselves during the battle. According to Gildon, the effect was induced by thought. How was that possible, she wanted to know. Her own explanation had leaned more in the direction of a mechanically generated force field. And when she considered the phenomenon again, she was not entirely prepared to abandon her theory.

In general, this seemed to be pretty much her standard response to the answers she'd received to her queries. Disbelief.

From Shahra she'd learned that much of Tesuvian life and philosophy centered around the existence of an all-powerful being they referred to as *the One.* To Cadence's way of thinking, this classified the Tesuvians as a strongly religious people. However, their beliefs were so much a part of their lives that they were not viewed by the Tesuvians themselves as religious in any way. They did not believe in gods or devils. According to Shahra, their entire society was structured on achieving oneness or closeness to the Universal Consciousness that they referred to as the One. Even their cities were constructed with this closeness in mind. But who was this *One?* God? A non-corporeal being? Or something else?

Through it all—the questions, the newness, the learning, the uncertainty—the need to find Chance was a constant nagging pressure in the back of Cadence's mind. She had done her best to put it aside, knowing that she must first concentrate on surviving and escaping this planet. Once she had accomplished that, she would find Chance. She hoped.

At the moment, though, it was more important that she focus on less far-reaching goals. She needed to understand all she could about these people in order to persuade them to help her. And she did not doubt that they could help her. Although their technology was very different—in some ways less advanced than Earth's—in other ways it was much more advanced. The Tesuvian technology seemed to be based almost entirely on the power of sound and the capabilities of crystals. A concept that she found difficult to understand, although she was beginning to grasp it. The *portals* that comprised their transportation system were a prime example of the capabilities of their technology.

An exasperated sound from her young tutor drew her attention. "I'm sorry, Shahra. My mind was wandering."

Shahra's raven-dark brows drew together over her ebony eyes. "You should not leave without proper preparation. Where did you go?"

Cadence merely shook her head, assuming that her pronunciation had been off again and Shahra had misunderstood her. "Never mind. Please continue."

"I was saying that your education in our language is almost complete. You should now spend time reading, learning, and discussing what you have learned. I have brought a number of books which will be useful to you. Kaitan Gildon will take over your instruction."

Conflicting emotions assailed Cadence at the knowledge that she would see Gildon more often. The idea both excited and dismayed her. She wouldn't think about that now. Rather, she focused on the bewildering realization that these people expected her to learn more. Why? "Instruct me in what?"

"In the ways of our society, our people."

"For what purpose?" Cadence asked, frowning in perplexity. "I won't be here that long."

It was Shahra's turn to frown in confusion. "Where will you go?"

"Home."

Shahra shook her head slowly, disbelievingly. "You do not wish to stay with us?" Her tone was incredulous. "To fulfill—" She broke off suddenly. "This is very unexpected."

"Why? I didn't plan to come here. My ship crashed here. I have friends, and a brother whom I very much want to see again."

Again Shahra shook her head. "This is something you must discuss with kaitan Gildon. I am sorry, but I know not how to help you."

"All right." Seeing that she had distressed the girl, Cadence changed the subject. "So, now that you have finished instructing me, where do you go from here?"

"I move into the Shido Temple. I am very excited."

Cadence smiled. "And what is the Shido Temple?"

"The Shido Order is dedicated to the recording and preserving of history. They interpret ancient writings and study other civilizations. It is very interesting, but there is much to learn."

"Will you be there long?"

"Yes." Shahra smiled. "If I do well. I hope to be there a very, very long time, for I plan to become a Shido Priestess."

"Then, I wish you well, Shahra. But I'm going to miss our daily talks."

Shahra lowered her eyes modestly. "That is kind of you to say, kaitana."

Cadence had learned that the words *kaitan* and *kaitana* meant *learned one*. Although the titles were seldom used between priests and high priests or others of relatively equal standing, novices of Shahra's tender years, and diplomats, tended to use the designation as a sign of respect. Cadence smiled. "It's not kindness. It's the truth. How can I repay you for the time you have spent with me?"

"I do not understand."

Cadence realized that once again she'd thrown in an English word, *repay*, when no appropriate Tesuvian word had come to mind.

"I would like to give you something to thank you

for the time you have spent instructing me."

To Cadence's dismay, the girl appeared insulted. "We do not do such things here. That you've learned, that you appreciate the learning, that is thanks enough."

Cadence laid a comforting hand on Shahra's arm. "I meant no insult, Shahra. I didn't know that your culture doesn't allow gifts."

Shahra shook her head. "You misunderstand. Gifts given for no reason other than personal affection or caring are welcomed. It is a gift given as compensation for a service that is frowned upon. Only those who walk far from the One—some of those who live in the outer city—trade for goods in this way, for personal gain. In our society, all people give of their services freely for the welfare of others."

Cadence frowned thoughtfully as Shahra broke off. *Freely?* "If no one is compensated for their services, how do you pay for food, for housing and clothing?"

Shahra stared at her. "Pay? This is one of your words?"

Cadence nodded. "Yes. It means to compensate for goods or services. Here, let me show you." Using the pink grapelike fruit that sat in a basket as hypothetical funds, she launched into a detailed description of a monetary system.

When she concluded, Shahra studied her face. "So this *pay* is a means of determining how many goods or services you are entitled to. If you have no pay left, you are not entitled to more food or clothing?"

"Well, that's a bit simplistic but, yes, that's basically the concept."

"Our way is better. No one ever goes without food or clothing or shelter, because necessities are divided equally. Only luxuries, like a new or larger home, require an accumulation of services that have been performed."

Cadence leapt on the last phrase. "So how does one begin to accumulate a reserve?" Perhaps she'd be able to earn the Tesuvian's aid in returning home. "How are extra services accounted for?"

Shahra reached into the folds of her gown and extended her hand toward Cadence. In her palm rested a pyramid-shaped crystal stone, absolutely clear. Taking the stone from Shahra's hand, Cadence examined it. How did such a thing represent an accumulation of services if they had no monetary system? She returned the stone to Shahra. "I don't understand."

"It is a data crystal, kaitana. It records and transmits entries of all transfers of services or goods to the data processor in the temple."

"And how are these entries made to the crystal?"

"Verbally. This type of crystal is sensitive to sound. It hears and transmits."

"I see." Cadence's brow cleared. Although she still didn't quite comprehend the workings of the crystal, she thought she finally understood the workings of their system of exchange. The Tesuvians merely used a rather complicated barter system. Such systems had, on occasion, been used by Earth civilizations too, but they'd never managed to eradicate poverty. In the Tesuvian system, impoverishment was not a factor because, by dividing the necessities of life evenly, the system allowed for the old and the infirm. Actually, when she thought about it, it made good sense, although she had doubts about whether such a system would ever be practical in her society.

"You understand now?" Shahra asked.

Cadence smiled. "Yes. I think so. Thank you."

Shahra bowed her head in acknowledgment of the courtesy. "I will go now." She rose and headed for the door with an abruptness that still surprised Cadence even after she'd had a week to get used to it.

"Good-bye," Cadence called after her just in time. "Come again, all right?"

Shahra paused only long enough to turn and nod in response to Cadence's invitation, and then she was gone. Whether Shahra would ever come for a visit, Cadence didn't know. The culture here was still a mystery to her. Rising from the cushion at the low table where she'd done most of her studying with Shahra, Cadence scooped up the helmet containing Claire, which she continued to use as a learning aid, and placed it on a shelf in her bedchamber.

It was almost time for the midday meal. If today followed true to every other, Gildon would soon be coming up from his office to join her. They would sit and eat in tense silence. Whenever she would look up and happen to catch his gaze, it would slide hastily away. Walking into the kitchen, Cadence looked toward the staircase.

Not for the first time, she wondered what he did down there. Perhaps one day soon she would be able to convince Gildon to actually talk to her like . . . a friend. Nothing more, she assured herself.

She was not blind to the fact that, for some reason she couldn't fathom, Gildon and his people distrusted her immensely. She would have to overcome that if she wanted their help. But to overcome it she needed to comprehend it. Now that she knew enough of their language to make herself understood, it was time to actively seek that comprehension. Whether he liked it or not, she intended to engage Gildon in conversation.

Gildon frowned at the indistinct sound of Cadence's footsteps overhead. In the week that she'd shared his apartment, she had upset his life without even trying. Not only had she invaded his lodgings, destroying his privacy, but she invaded his mind, surfacing in his thoughts at every turn. Fantasy images of her appeared in his mind at the most disconcerting times. Especially when he slept. He didn't understand it.

She was stunningly attractive and seemed to grow more beautiful with each day that passed. But he'd seen beautiful women before, some more breathtakingly captivating than Cadence, and none of them had affected him in this way. Such emotions toward her were completely unacceptable. Not only did he and his people still not fully understand her purpose here, but he was now her counselor. Sexual relationships between counselors and their students were strongly discouraged. So much so that when such a relationship was suspected, the counselor often lost his or her right to instruct until the situation had been reviewed by the Tridon.

But Cadence is not an ordinary student, a part of his mind reminded him. *She is a grown woman.* His mind provided him with a haunting fantasy image of just how womanly she was. *And I am not truly her counselor.* Tailen had stated when giving him the assignment that the usual strictures would not apply where she was concerned.

Yet that knowledge only exacerbated his agony. Had he been certain that such an alliance would be casual, there would be no problem. But he felt more drawn to Cadence than he'd ever been to another woman. His instincts warned him that that was dangerous. As a priest of the Avatar he could not take as companion a woman from outside the temple. Not unless he wanted to abandon entirely the vocation dictated by his bloodlines.

If he had desired a companion, he would have sought a woman like Cadence within the Order. However, he had never desired, nor even considered taking a companion, and he had made the decision long ago that he would never do so. He certainly had no intention of abandoning his profession for any woman.

Perhaps I could return to the Kami.

The irreverent thought jarred him.

True, he had always felt more at home within the Order of the Kami than within that of the Avatar. Yet he had always known it was not to be. *Never* would he consider abandoning his post. It simply wasn't done.

By the One! Was there no way to escape the persecution of his own thoughts? What was the matter with him?

He shook his head. Enough! The direction of his thoughts disgusted him. He should be investigating Cadence's purpose here, nothing more. Until her role was known, a relationship with her was out of the question for *anyone* among his people. It was too dangerous.

Thinking of the danger that might be associated with her reminded him of the astral projection that had appeared on the balcony her second night here. It had faded too quickly for him to identify the person, or even to retain a memory of any identifiable features. And since he'd intensified the warding on the apartment, there had been no more visitations. Had the projection been an attempt to harm Cadence? Or to make contact with her?

He raked his fingers through his hair in frustration. Always there were more questions. Why did nothing have an answer?

Perhaps today he would be able to begin gleaning some of those answers. Shahra had informed him that Cadence's language lessons were complete. It was time now for him to begin instructing her. He intended to learn all he could about her. Cadence herself was an enigma. And, by nature and calling, Gildon decoded the unknown. It was time to solve the mystery surrounding her defeat of the Gou'jiin and the perplexing manner in which she'd been capable of moving through the city gates without difficulty.

As Cadence had expected, their midday meal was tense and silent. The fruit, vegetables, bread, and cheese which appeared fresh daily in a strange circular cabinet in the center of the kitchen—a device called a *fabricator* by her hosts—although usually delicious, tasted like sawdust today. Shahra's assertion that Cadence's desire to return home was unexpected worried her, and she resolved to broach the subject at lunch. But first she had to establish a conversation. She was just about to make the attempt when Gildon startled her by speaking.

"Cadence . . ."

She saw the hesitation written on his face. "Yes?"

"I must ask you some questions." He seemed to be avoiding her eyes.

She considered warily. "All right," she said and nibbled a slice of cheese without really tasting it.

Suddenly his gaze was on her face, sharp and penetrating. "How did you defeat the Gou'jiin?"

Cadence frowned. "I don't understand."

He sighed. "How was it that you were able to expel the Gou'jiin from your body?"

She swallowed. "I thought you did that."

He shook his head. "No, Cadence. I merely used my dislocator as a channel to open the threshold that removed the creature. The one-way gravitational thresholds, like the one I created, are one of the most effective means of defeating a Gou'jiin when they are in their natural form. And it was the only means of combat I had at hand. However, the thresholds can do little once the Gou'jiin is in possession of a corporeal body." He paused and studied her before concluding. "In fact, such an . . . expulsion as you accomplished is quite unusual."

"But . . . I didn't do anything." She stared thoughtfully across the room. "At least I don't think I did. The last thing I remember is a powerful feeling of . . . determination, almost a conviction that the Gou'jiin would not win. Then everything is blank until . . ." She hesitated, trying to pinpoint the exact moment of returning awareness. "Until the creature was gone, and you were on the ground beside me."

It was Gildon's turn to frown, and Cadence received the distinct impression that his expression was one of dissatisfaction rather than puzzlement. He didn't believe her. She was almost certain of it. Yet she didn't know what she could say to convince him. "I'm sorry I can't be of more help," she said. "What else did you want to ask me?"

He looked at her. "What else?"

She nodded. "You said earlier that you had *questions*."

"Yes. That's so. However, there are some things I must explain before I can ask my next question."

"Such as?"

"Such as how the gates of our cities work. And the alterations I made to their settings on the day of your arrival."

Cadence studied his face warily. She had a feeling that he was maintaining a carefully blank expression. Why? "All right," she said finally and popped into her mouth a slice of crisp pink fruit that she had come to favor for its refreshing, almost effervescent, quality.

Although Shahra had explained something about the segregating of the city, she had mentioned nothing about the gates, or the purpose behind them. Cadence listened with interest and no small amazement as Gildon explained the function of the gates accessing each section of the city. Surely these people did not truly believe that good or evil could be detected in a person by deciphering a vibratory signature?

Yet she'd heard the theory that all things in the universe had a unique vibratory rate. If you carried that theory one step further, perhaps such a thing was possible. To accept that, however, presupposed a belief in absolute good or evil. That she couldn't accept. People were people. Some better than others, and some much worse. But that was all; flawed humanity.

Gildon concluded his explanation and pinned her with his assessing gaze. "We need to know how you penetrated the gates without feeling anything, without experiencing any adverse reactions."

Cadence stared at him, beginning to get angry. So this was the reason behind the mistrust. This . . . this groundless absurdity. "I don't believe this!" She wiped her mouth and threw her napkin on the table. "You and"—she waved an expansive hand that encompassed the city—"your people cannot possibly believe that I'm a bad person, an *evil* person, simply because I walked through a gate. I've never heard anything so ridiculous!"

Gildon considered her silently with his penetrating, storm-cloud eyes. "It may seem ridiculous to you," he conceded. "Although I find myself wondering why my question has made you so upset."

Cadence stared at him. "I am upset . . . no, more than upset. I'm angry because I have done nothing, in word or deed, to warrant your mistrust. You're basing your reaction on a very primitive tendency to fear anything you do not understand."

He stared at her thoughtfully. Finally he nodded. "That may be true. However, if you explain how you managed to move through the barriers, we *will* understand and there will be no more reason to fear your presence here."

Cadence sighed and felt her anger drain away. "I

can't explain what I don't know," she said. "But you're wrong in believing that I felt *nothing*. When I walked through the first gate I did feel something." She closed her eyes, trying to remember the exact sensation. "Some kind of resistance. It was like pushing my way through a thick cold soup."

Gildon's eyes clung to her features. "And at the second gate?" he prompted. "Did you feel the same thing?"

Cadence shook her head. "No. When I walked through that barrier, I felt . . . a warm, tingling sensation. It wasn't unpleasant, really. Not like the first gate. Just . . . noticeable." She met his eyes. "The gates were set differently, weren't they? Which one was which?"

He considered her. "I cannot tell you that at this time."

"I see." Cadence cleared her throat and watched Gildon fold a thick chunk of cheese into a piece of brown bread. "I understand from Shahra that you are to instruct me now?"

He lifted his eyes to hers for a fraction of a second. "Yes."

She decided to plunge in and ask a few questions of her own. "I asked Shahra why I am to be instructed in the ways of your society when I do not intend to be here any longer than it takes to find a way home." Ah, that got his attention. His eyes drilled into hers with disconcerting directness. "She said I should discuss it with you. So, what do you have to say?"

His eyes slipped away from hers and he resumed chewing. When he'd swallowed, he wiped his mouth and then looked at her again. "You do not intend to stay with us?"

Cadence frowned. Why had everyone assumed that she would intend to stay? This was ludicrous. "No. Why would I? I intend to try every means I can think of to find a way home."

"You think this will be difficult? Is your home world very distant?" He waited for her response with undivided attention.

"Yes and no. My world is not so very far from here and it is easily reachable if I can repair my ship, or . . . with the right technology. But there is a problem."

He waited silently for her to continue.

"I encountered a storm in . . . in *hyperspace*," she said, forced to throw in an English word, "that damaged my ship. I was thrown back in time by more than five hundred years. No one who has gone back in time has ever returned to their own time. I . . . I don't know if it can be done." She swallowed.

For the first time she looked beyond her own fears to realize the full extent of what the existence of Fortuna in her time meant for the future of the Tesuvians here. She prayed that Gildon would not ask her about it. How did you tell somebody that their entire civilization was going to disappear?

At the moment, though, Gildon was looking at her as if she'd undergone some horrific metamorphosis.

"Why are you looking at me like that? Everything I've said is true."

"I believe you." He shook his head. "However, I don't understand how your people could have come so far without . . ." He groped for words. "Without *understanding* anything."

"What do you mean?"

He looked away from her, picked up a pitcher of mild wine, and poured them each a glass. After taking a deep swallow, he looked back at her. "You will not like what I am about to tell you."

Chapter Eight

Cadence eyed him warily. "All right, I've been warned. Go on."

"It is not possible to travel *forward* in time. Ever. The future is unwritten. It is the One's way of protecting the universe from those who would profit by such a capability."

Cadence stared at him. "You're mistaken. My people frequently travel forward in time. Our method of traveling from one world to another is dependent on it."

It was Gildon's turn to be wary. "Explain this function."

Cadence did. She explained how, when she left Space Station Apollo or Olympus, she programmed her ship's clocks for her arrival time at her destination to approximate only the amount of elapsed ship time in hyperspace, thus cutting years off her journey. That the lanes in hyperspace were actually folds in the fabric of space-time. How, when necessary, they could even compress time, arriving at their destination mere minutes after they'd left another part of space—although, to be truthful, the result of time compression was often a migraine headache the size of Saturn. Still, it was possible. And, to *really* illustrate forward time travel, she told him how on occasion they could actually program their ship's time of arrival for days in the future, days beyond the actual elapsed ship time in hyperspace. When she'd concluded, Gildon sipped his drink silently and thoughtfully.

Finally he spoke. "Have any of your people ever gone months or years into the future?"

Cadence hedged. "Well . . . no," she admitted. "Not yet."

"Why? Have you tried?"

"Yes. But . . . well, it just hasn't worked. We invariably emerge into normal space at our destination to find that we've come only a few days into the future."

Gildon nodded. "Hmmm. I believe I understand now." He suddenly seemed very sure of himself.

Cadence eyed him suspiciously. "Understand what?"

"What you have described to me is what I would call linear time travel. It is more a case of *stopping* the progression of time while your journey is accomplished than it is a case of traveling into the future."

Cadence shook her head adamantly. "But I told you that we've gone days into the future."

His gaze met hers with unnerving frankness. "Are you certain of that? Could it not be that it is a case of more time having passed than you realize while you are in . . . *hyperspace?*" He raised a brow to ascertain whether he'd used the term correctly. When she nodded, he continued. "When you are in hyperspace, you yourself have no conception of time or space. Correct?"

"Yes. But our instruments measure the passage of time precisely."

He shrugged. "Possibly. However, even instruments can be fooled. I think it likely that, while you yourself only measure the passing of hours in hyperspace, the universe outside the fold measures the passing of days. That would account for your ability to program your ship to arrive at a place *days* in the future from your time of departure, but not months or years."

Cadence shook her head. "This is all supposition based on your theory that time travel into the future is *not* possible."

"It is not a theory, Cadence. My people have known for millennia that traveling *back* in time is possible. Those who did so left carefully worded messages to be found in the future. But once the journey is accomplished, you can never go forward again."

"Why?" Cadence asked, unable to disguise the desperation in her voice. She leaned toward him slightly, terrified as the magnitude of what he was telling her struck her like a blow. "Why can't you go forward?"

He sighed. "Because to go back in time, even for a moment, is to completely alter the time line. The second you move back in time, the future is changed. A bird sees you and changes its flight path, no longer becoming food for the hungry kuma who sometime in the future might have carried a man safely home to his family. The kuma hunts elsewhere, the man dies, never fathering the child he was meant to, and the future is transformed.

"Because it no longer unfolds as you expect, the future—any time forward from the place and time where you now exist—is unknown and unpredictable. You cannot travel to a place, or a time, that does not exist." There was compassion in his eyes as he met her anxious gaze. "Do you understand now, Cadence?"

She shook her head vehemently. Focusing the irrational anger within her into movement, she rose from her cushion and began to pace the room. "No! I can't believe you, Gildon. I have to go home."

He rose to face her. "It is true, Cadence."

"You're just saying that because for some reason you want to keep me here. Well, it won't work. I won't believe you. Do you hear me?" Stars! She hated this place with all of its alien customs and beliefs. She hated this language that wouldn't let you sound angry even when you wanted nothing more than to shriek your rage from the rooftops. She hated Gildon for trying to keep her here.

"Of course I hear you. But why are you so desperate to return to your world? Surely our home is not so terrible?"

She pivoted to face him. "I did not live in a vacuum, Gildon. I have a career, friends, and a brother . . ." Her voice broke on the word as the idea that she might never see Chance again clogged her throat. She swallowed. "A brother who is missing and whom I need to find."

"I am sorry, Cadence. The proph—We did not think beyond your . . . possible function here. We . . . didn't think of what you had left behind."

Cadence stared at him. *Possible function?* What an interesting way to achieve assimilation—by giving a function or employment to strangers. Quarks! She was beginning to get a headache.

Gildon opened his mouth and she waved a hand at him to forestall further conversation. "Apology accepted. Forget it." Folding her arms across her body to ward off the sudden chill that seemed to emanate from deep within her, she walked to the balcony window and looked out at the beautiful, white city below. Jafna. Was she going to have to make it her city? Her home?

Gildon cleared his throat behind her. "Cadence—"

She sighed. "Yes?"

"May I ask how your brother became . . . missing?"

Cadence's throat closed. Oh, stars! How could she answer that question without revealing the future that Gildon's people faced? Or by revealing it, would she allow them to undo it, to prepare for it? Indecision sawed at her. Finally she turned to face him.

"I . . . I don't know much. Chance was working with an archaeological group on another world, exploring an ancient abandoned city. And, according to the report, he simply faded away right before the eyes of his companions." She shrugged. "I didn't believe it, of course. People don't simply disappear. At least not that way. But before I could investigate, I ended up here."

Gildon raised a brow. "Archaeological? What does this mean?"

"Archaeologists are people who study and learn about ancient peoples by examining the remains of their civilizations. I believe Shahra said you call them Shido."

"Ah, yes. The historians." He nodded, but the frown that drew his brows together and the distant look in his eyes told her that his thoughts had already moved on. "Cadence, where was this abandoned city they were exploring?"

Cadence swallowed. This was it. She was afraid to tell the truth, yet her instincts told her it would be a mistake to lie. "It . . . was a world we called Fortuna." She held her breath. Would he be satisfied?

"And where exactly was this world?"

I guess not, she thought. Damn! A lie hovered on the tip of her tongue, but it clung there unvocalized. "Actually," she said, "it was pretty much where this one is."

His brow cleared. "That is what I thought."

"That's what you *thought*?" she asked a little indignantly. He certainly didn't seem overly upset by the idea of extinction.

"Yes." Gildon began pacing the room.

Too concerned with her own plight to wonder at Gildon's reaction, Cadence turned back to the balcony view. Was he right, she wondered. Was it impossible for her to go home? A moment later Gildon called her name, drawing her back from her dark musings. He'd stopped pacing. "Yes?"

"Do you know *exactly* what your brother was doing when he disappeared?"

She tried to remember the details of the communiqué she'd received. "I believe the report said that he'd been trying to determine the nature of some carvings on a small pedestal."

Gildon's expression was suddenly so intent it was almost frightening. "What kind of pedestal? Did your report mention anything else?"

Cadence slowly shook her head. "No. Not that I can think of. Why?"

He grimaced in frustration. "You're sure? There was no allusion to wings or anything like that?"

"Wait! Yes, now that you mention it, the report did refer to a winged figurine he was holding when he disappeared. The figurine itself did not disappear."

He smiled. "I thought it must be so. Wings are our symbol for portal travel." Walking to her, he grasped her shoulders in a gentle grip. "Cadence, you can do more to find your brother from *here* than you could in your time."

"I don't understand."

"Your brother inadvertently activated one of our portals. He was *transported* somewhere."

She stared up at him. "Can you help me find him?"

Releasing her shoulders, he stepped away. "It is possible, yes, because often our portals are keyed to not only a specific place, but a specific time. If your brother activated such a portal, it is possible that he too traveled back in time, sent to the settings last used on that particular portal. But there are no assurances that we will be successful. There are thousands of communal portals on this continent. We have to determine which one he used and try to calculate its possible settings."

"*Will* you help me?"

He avoided her eyes. "Perhaps," he said. "But I think there is something you must do for us as well."

"Like what?"

Gildon merely shook his head. "Tailen wants to meet with you today to discuss your progress. We will address the problem with him. Please prepare yourself, we will leave soon." Before she could say another word, he left the room.

Cadence stared at the empty doorway. Was she about to be bribed? Blackmailed?

A half hour later, they traversed the wide corridors of the Temple of the Eidan. "We're early for our meeting with Tailen," Gildon said. "Come." Placing his hand lightly on Cadence's shoulder, he guided her to the left. "We will visit the planetarium and you may show me which world is your home."

Cadence fought the urge to step away from his touch, to rub at the tingling awareness it left in its wake. "All right."

Halfway down the corridor, he halted at a pair of double doors that disappeared on contact. At his invitation, Cadence preceded him into an enormous circular room with a domed ceiling. Walls, ceiling, and floor were a brilliant white. Although there was no discernable light source, the room was brightly lit. A large cluster of oblong-shaped clear crystals of differing lengths and circumferences protruded from a round platform in the center of the chamber. Other than that, the room was empty. Cadence looked at Gildon in confusion. "Is this it?"

Not bothering to answer, Gildon sang a single note. The entire chamber plunged into a darkness deeper than anything Cadence had ever encountered. She was afraid to move. Gildon hummed another note. Pinpoints of light—stars and their satellites, entire constellations—immediately popped into view. No longer frightened, she examined the chamber in fascination. There were stars everywhere—in front of her, behind her, beneath her feet, and over her head. She felt she could reach out and touch them.

"This is a representation of our galaxy," Gildon explained. "Is your system in this galaxy?"

"Yes," Cadence murmured in response, still awed by the three-dimensional demonstration. "We call this galaxy the Milky Way."

"Can you show me which star system is your home?"

Frowning slightly, Cadence scrutinized the profusion of stars. "I'm not sure. Which one is Fortuna?"

"Fortuna?" There was a brief confusion-laden pause. "That is what you said your people call this world?"

Cadence nodded. "Yes."

Gildon hummed a note and pointed to a binary star system. The large red sun and its smaller yellow companion suddenly began to glow more brightly, standing out from the others. "There," he said unnecessarily a second later.

"Then Earth should be over there." She turned her eyes to the other side of the room. "That's it," she cried a moment later.

"Where?"

"The yellow sun. There." She pointed.

Gildon sang a note and a single star shone more brightly. "That one?" he asked.

"Yes." Even though she'd lived her early childhood and her entire adult life aboard a space station, nostalgia for a world she might never see again suddenly misted her eyes.

"Ah, yes. I recognize it. We once had a colony there as well."

Cadence nodded. "Atlantis. We discovered its ruins

deep in the ocean over two hundred years ago. What happened to it?"

Gildon was silent for so long that finally she pulled her eyes from the representation of her home star system to look at him in the dim starlight. Seeming to sense her gaze, he sighed and turned to look at her. "It was destroyed."

Her lips twisted with dissatisfaction at his ambiguous answer. "That's obvious. But how?"

For another moment, he remained silent. Then he began to speak. "More than ten millennia ago, science—or rather scientists and a branch of researchers which later formed themselves into a cult which we now call the Vradir—all but destroyed my ancestral home world. The power of genetic manipulation grew faster than moral guidelines could be adopted to restrain it, and most of the populace divided into two factions, those who sought the improvement of their own lives at any cost, and those who could not stand by and watch the sins against nature and the One take place. Those with conscience fled, taking up residence on distant worlds." He nodded in the direction of the Earth star system. "Like yours."

"What happened?"

He shrugged. "At first, nothing. They made new lives for themselves, living in harmony with the planetary resonance of their new homes." He silently perused the galaxy of stars. "But it didn't last. The Vradir followed. No one quite knew why. Perhaps they ran out of candidates for their experimentation, or needed new genetic pools from which to draw. Or perhaps, as some have said, it is that those who choose to walk the path of immorality are forever compelled to propagate their corruption." He shook his head.

"Regardless of their motivation, many dark priests, Vradiran researchers with great scientific knowledge, sought out the Tesuvian colonies to continue their work. They approached the colonies in the guise of refugees, and by the time their true purpose was uncovered, it was most often too late. They had infected many, particularly the young people, with their greed and ambition. As the cult grew in strength, the conflict began anew."

Cadence stared at him. "Some of the ancient myths say that Atlantis was destroyed by the gods because of its evil. Did the Vradir destroy it through their experimentation?"

Gildon shook his head. "No. Many colonies were destroyed, but they were exterminated in order to stop the Vradir."

"My stars! Why?" What horror could possibly prompt an entire people to commit suicide?

Gildon closed his eyes in mental anguish as visions gleaned from the crystal recordings replayed in his mind. Animals, whose souls were untainted by greed, had been experimented on without care for their suffering. Even worse, soulless abominations against nature had been created in laboratories: Docile beasts of burden had been genetically programmed with evil temperaments and wings or horns. Reptilian DNA had been altered, creating beasts of gigantic proportions. Some of these, too, had been given wings, allowing them to prey on humans and animals alike. Nor did humans escape the genetic laboratories. Giants with low intelligence and deformed features had resulted from failed experiments. They had often been used as slaves by their creators, until they escaped.

The only thing to be thankful for in all the horror was that all the creations had been sterile. The scientists could create life, program it and manipulate it, but they could not create a life capable of procreation. And that, too, had brought pain to some of their more human creations—creations capable of feeling, capable of love and laughter, desirous of off-spring of their own.

And despite it all, despite all the pain, the genetic manipulators had never found what they sought: the secret of eternal life. The agony and the atrocities had benefited no one.

Having seen the entire library of the original war and the succeeding infiltrations, Gildon knew the initial signs of the encroachment better than most. In the name of genetic advancement, all of these things had been done—and would be done again, here on this world, if he and his brethren did not halt it. For the search for eternal physical life was the only purpose behind the Vradir.

Yet this time the taint of evil was very advanced. The First Avatar, he who'd founded the Temple of the Avatars, was gone now, along with many of the other powerful righteous leaders who'd fought the evil successfully in the past. And, unfortunately, much of their knowledge and ability had gone with them. Gildon didn't know how to stop the alter-realm encroachment initiated by the Vradir without the destruction of the very world and creatures he wanted to save. Even were they to capture and incarcerate the woman destined to lead the Vradir, there were no guarantees of success. He knew no certain means.

No one did. That was why his people now pinned their hopes on an ambiguous prophecy, on one alien woman, and . . . escape.

How was he to explain all of this to Cadence? And yet she needed to know. More than that, she needed to understand. And so he told her of scientific experimentation gone awry. Of human greed and excess without bounds. Of egocentric madness in which the members of a powerful cult set themselves up as gods demanding the obeisance of the more primitive inhabitants of her world.

A shiver traveled up Cadence's spine as she listened. She could visualize that time so clearly: the gaudy temples of gold and silver and chalcedony, constructed to please and impress man. Marble statues and the likenesses of the Vradir Priests stood everywhere so that they might order themselves worshiped by those they ruled . . . or enslaved. An old man, a slave, who moved too slowly was whipped to death on a city street, yet no one lifted a hand to halt the atrocity. She shook her head, trying to dispel the images.

It was merely her imagination running away with her, giving substance to Gildon's narration.

"Not everybody followed the path of corruption," he continued. "Those who still walked in the light of the One knew that only one course could save the world." Pausing, he turned to stare at the representation of the distant sun. "They destroyed the colony."

Cadence tore her gaze away from Gildon's profile in confusion. It didn't help. The visions, the sensations, continued their inexorable march through her brain. How could she see these things in her mind so clearly? She closed her eyes and felt the rumbling from deep within the earth as the explosion that destroyed a civilization rent the planet's crust. She could hear the screams of the dying, feel their terror as the hungry waves of an angry sea swallowed an entire continent in less than 30 minutes.

No! She couldn't know these things! Impossible!

"Come. It is time to go." Gildon's voice drew her back. She opened her eyes. The stars were gone. The chamber was once again just a plain white room. Slowly she studied it, seeking an explanation for the mysterious visions and sensations. None was forthcoming.

She assured herself that it had to have been pure imagination. But a sense of unease stayed with her. Quarks! She wanted to go home, to escape the disorientation she'd felt ever since landing on this alien world. Thinking of home reminded her that she needed to discover how Gildon's people had come to *this* world. But how could she broach the subject tactfully?

She looked at Gildon. "Before we go, could you show me where your home world is? Is it near?"

Gildon hesitated. "Tesuvia is on the outer rim of the galaxy." He hummed a note and the room darkened. Another series of notes sounded, and the room was filled with the representations of stars and distant worlds. He sang a note and a single star grew amazingly bright. "That is Tesuvia's home system."

Cadence stared in disbelief. "How is that possible? If your people don't use the folds in space-time to travel in hyperspace the way we do, it would have taken . . . centuries for your ships to make the trip from there to here."

She could feel Gildon's eyes on her. "We no longer use *ships*, Cadence."

Now it was Cadence's turn to stare at him. "You don't use ships?" she echoed incredulously.

He shook his head. "No. They are very . . . disharmonious. Dangerous. And not very efficient."

"What do you mean, *dangerous*? And what could be more efficient than a ship? How could you travel that distance without one?"

He sighed. "Ships are a risky and uncertain means of travel. We set aside that technology thousands of years ago and concentrated instead on the development of portals. Once constructed and programmed, they are an error-free and extremely efficient means of transport."

Cadence stared at him open-mouthed as her mind whirled with a maelstrom of questions which refused to solidify into one coherent thought. Apparently thinking her curiosity had been satisfied, Gildon hummed a note and the portrayal of the universe disappeared. Once again, they stood in a very ordinary-looking chamber.

"Come, Cadence," he said, guiding her toward the door. "It is time we met with Tailen."

"I still don't understand," Cadence said, finally finding her tongue. "Are you telling me that you arrived here via portal?"

"I didn't, but my ancestors did. Yes."

"But how could your people construct a portal destination in a place millions of miles away? I mean, planets are always moving in orbit, not to mention revolving on an axis. How could your scientists possibly calculate all those variables? And how could they know that the planet was capable of supporting life?"

They were moving down the corridor now, and Cadence noted that a number of people they encountered seemed to give them a wide berth. She frowned curiously, but she was too intrigued by this portal idea and the possibilities it represented for her to be sidetracked.

Gildon cleared his throat and answered in a manner that suggested he did not want their conversation overheard. "There are many ways, Cadence, most of which you would not understand at this point. Much of what is involved merely requires detailed mathematical calculation. Other variable solutions come from communion with the One. There are no true mysteries in the universe, Cadence. There are only events and details we do not yet understand. The One knows all things."

"I see," said Cadence. But she didn't. The cryptic quality of this conversation, the dogmatic atmosphere surrounding this entire civilization, made her very nervous. *There are no true mysteries in the universe.* What kind of nonsense was that?

She'd never seen any evidence of a Universal Consciousness . . . or a God, for that matter. She'd always had a tendency to believe there was *something* out there, simply because there were so many things that science couldn't explain. But her religious beliefs had been more indifferent than consuming. To now be confronted with an entire race of people who not only believed in a God-like Consciousness, but apparently communed with it on a regular basis left her floundering intellectually to explain it in terms she could accept.

Gildon stopped and she almost ran into him. He looked at her quizzically for a moment before extending his hand to contact the pair of doors she'd seen on her first day. And today, as they had then, the doors shimmered and disappeared.

Chapter Nine

Tailen rose from behind his desk on the left side of the room. Smiling a greeting, he gestured toward the table with its thick comfortable cushions for seating. "Please make yourselves comfortable. I'll join you in a moment." With that, he returned his attention to his transcriber, Dalen, and the business they'd been conducting.

Although the midday meal was over and it was not yet near time for the evening meal, platters of fruits, vegetables, soft cheeses, and crisp breads had been laid out to welcome Gildon and Cadence. These people loved food, Cadence observed. They snacked at least twice a day in addition to their meals, and guests were always the perfect excuse to lay out another repast—needed or not. Since their diet was predominately vegetarian with the exception of eggs and an abundance of seafood served at every evening meal, Cadence decided that their dietary habits had probably arisen out of necessity. Since adopting her hosts' menu, she found that she became hungry much sooner after a meal than was usual for her.

Cadence accepted Gildon's courtesy in seating her in the same position she'd occupied on her initial introduction to Tailen, and watched as he moved around the table to take his own seat. He was again wearing white trousers and the strangely cut white robe with a pair of worn, brown sandals that looked

135

as though they were made of rope. He had attractive feet, she thought. Narrow and refined with long, graceful toes. Catching herself, Cadence hastily raised her eyes to the brilliant white of his sleeves. Why was it that he'd worn nothing but white since their arrival in the city, she wondered.

She had certainly been supplied with a varied wardrobe as far as colors went—bright forest green, ivory, white, pastel peach, and teal blue. It was the lack of variety in styles that exasperated her. For this meeting, she wore the pastel peach gown which was identical in design to the white gown she'd first been given. The back was indecently low, and the folds of the bodice crossed over her breasts forming a V that, had she had any real cleavage to speak of, she would have considered very immodest.

She was used to Legion uniforms and Legion codes. When the sexes had to work side by side in the performance of duty, they had to be able to ignore sexuality. Wearing a gown like this, even for social occasions, would have made that impossible.

She was drawn from her introspection as Tailen came forward to join them. He greeted them both, before turning his smile on Cadence. "I hear you are an excellent student. You were able to learn our language much more quickly than we had anticipated with the aid of your"—he fumbled for the word—"data processor?"

"Computer," Cadence supplied.

"Ah, yes. Computer."

Cadence smiled. "I don't know how much it had to do with me being a good student. Most of my success is probably attributable to our system of subliminal sleep instruction. I don't know what we'd do without it in my society."

Tailen frowned. "Subliminal? I'm not familiar with that word."

Gildon set down the carafe from which he'd been

pouring himself a cup of *cai*. "You'll find that Cadence often simply uses words from her own language when she doesn't know the term in Tesuvian." He smiled across the table at her almost teasingly, and Cadence's heart skipped a beat. "She does it without warning, so it can be a bit disconcerting at times."

"I see." Tailen's gold eyes twinkled. "Well, there's no sense in floundering for a word when another will do quite well, I suppose. And what is *subliminal*, Cadence?" He picked up the carafe and offered her some *cai*.

Cadence extended her cup for him to fill. "It refers to a learning process that takes place in the subconscious mind during sleep."

Tailen nodded and poured himself a cup of the steaming green beverage. "Ah, yes. We have a similar teaching method. Ours, however, hinges on telepathic ability. We will have to speak more on this some time."

"Telepathic?" Cadence stared at him. Had he said telepathic? Perhaps Claire had supplied her with the incorrect translation of a word. Although Cadence knew that a few telepaths existed, true telepaths in her society were rare. She certainly couldn't imagine a teaching method that depended on telepathic ability. Then again, this was a completely alien culture. Who knew what was possible here?

"Yes," Tailen responded. "Silent mind-to-mind communication. Our abilities aren't as strong as we would like at times, necessitating enhancement through our *falar* stones." He extracted a deep red stone on a gold chain from the folds of his scarlet robe. Cadence recalled having seen him wear it for a short time on her first visit. "But we use our talents extensively, nonetheless. Has no one explained this to you?"

Cadence shook her head, still feeling stunned.

"No." She gave Gildon a reproachful glance.

Gildon cleared his throat. "There hasn't been time to explain everything as yet, Tailen. In fact, beyond the language itself, her education is just beginning."

Tailen nodded, and they fell into a brief discussion about the course that Cadence's instruction should take. Cadence found her mind still clinging to the idea of telepathy. She wondered if she'd be able to learn it.

Gildon's next words wiped the question from her mind. "Cadence would like our help with a matter, Tailen. I told her that we would put it before you."

Tailen's astute golden-brown gaze swung to Cadence. "What is this matter?"

And so, with Gildon interjecting occasional comments, Cadence recounted the particulars of Chance's disappearance, her determination to find him, and the possibility that she might be able to do so from here. When she'd concluded her story, Tailen merely sighed, leaned back slightly, and closed his eyes. Confused, Cadence looked at Gildon. He shook his head and began choosing a few pieces of fruit for his plate. Her eyes returned to Tailen. So, this trance-like silence must be a normal occurrence. Despite her anxiety over Tailen's response, she forced herself to follow Gildon's lead and began placing a few small pieces of fruit and vegetables on her plate.

A moment later Tailen stirred, but only long enough to extract his red jewel from his robes. Using its gold chain to secure it on his head, he centered the stone over his forehead and closed his eyes again. Almost immediately the stone began to glow slightly. Cadence frowned, wondering how the stone worked to enhance his abilities and to whom he was speaking. It didn't appear to be Gildon. Cadence had asked Shahra about the purpose of the stones and had been delicately put off. Now she knew their purpose, but not how they worked. Why did each new discovery here only prompt more questions?

She lifted her eyes to Gildon's with the intention of asking if it would be permissible for them to converse in low tones. The query never left her tongue. Gildon's storm-hued blue eyes locked on her own iridescent green ones with an almost audible connection. In that suspended moment in time, the blazing hunger reflected in his blue-flame irises was enough to spark an inferno of need in her own body. Her pulse leapt in a chaotic tempo that made it difficult to breathe. Her nipples grew taut. Her nether regions flooded with traitorous molten heat. Then she blinked, and Gildon's expression was as dispassionate as always. Had she imagined it?

Gildon watched Cadence slide a dripping piece of *prieka* fruit between her lush coral lips and felt his loins tighten in instant response. By the One! How could any woman look so sensuous while eating? He tore his eyes from her to study Tailen's familiar office, examine the star chart on the wall, and look toward the window to see if the sky was still cloudless. Anything to avoid looking at Cadence for a few moments. But it was an ineffectual ploy; her image was engraved upon his mind's eye. He could sense each subtle movement she made. Smell the spicy scent of the perfume she'd chosen. It was exhilarating torture.

Tailen opened his eyes and sipped his cooling *cai*. Gildon resisted the urge to heave a sigh of relief. Finally he would be able to occupy his thoughts with the business at hand. He felt his friend's touch in his mind, heard his voice. *My brother Prelates have decided,* Tailen said. *We cannot help her until we know which of the two she is.*

Gildon swallowed. *Understood.* It was no less than he'd expected. But how were they to determine the answer to that question? He munched a crisp vegetable and waited for Tailen to impart the decision to

Cadence, who was now watching him expectantly.

We have decided to tell her of the prophecy.

Gildon jerked his head up, inadvertently betraying the shock that statement induced, and met Tailen's watchful gaze. *Why?*

It has been deemed necessary.

Although he didn't understand it, he could do nothing but accede to the decision of his superiors. With a wordless mental nod, he transmitted his acceptance.

Tailen cleared his throat—something he rarely did—and met Cadence's anxious gaze. "Cadence, I am going to tell you some things which, initially, you may feel have nothing to do with you, but I would appreciate it if you would listen carefully. When I am through, you will have your answer. Agreed?"

She frowned in confusion and glanced at Gildon for a hint of what was to come. He merely nodded slightly in encouragement. Cadence, looking back at Tailen, echoed the gesture. "All right."

"Good." He replaced his *falar* stone in the folds of his crimson robe and sipped his *cai* before he began. "For many years now, my people have lived beneath the shadow of a prophecy. It is an extremely lengthy, cryptic, and convoluted prognostication, subject to much individual interpretation and continual augmentation." He shrugged. "Such is the way of a prophecy. However, one thing has always been clear, and that is that our civilization on this world will not survive. At best, we will be afforded the time and the means to evacuate. At worst, we and all life on this planet will perish."

So that was why Gildon had not seemed surprised by her revelation about the ruins on Fortuna, Cadence mused.

Tailen launched into a detailed description of the prophecy, pointing out a few of the areas that remained subject to interpretation, intoning one particularly pertinent verse:

"And great evil will fall upon the land.
The instrument will appear a righteous hand.
Two female strangers there will come,
Though to each other they be none.

One will be she who will open wide evil's door.
For life's promise, she is his eager whore.
The other will be she who can seal the gates
With love's strength, if she accepts the fates.

The fates' acceptance will preserve the world.
But not even they can save the whole.
Lives will be lost. Many? Few?
The choices of two will influence the view."

He stopped, served himself some fruit, and appeared to consider Cadence. "As you can see, there is one other thing about the prophecy that has always been apparent. That is that the two women I mentioned who figure so prominently as savior and destroyer will both be strangers to this world. Aliens, we believe." He paused and studied Cadence watchfully.

She stared at him, her face gradually taking on a look of incredulity. "Wait a minute. You don't think that I'm—" She broke off. "You think that I'm one of these women?"

Tailen nodded. "Yes."

Flabbergasted, Cadence could only stare as her mind clung to that incredible disclosure for endless seconds before once again providing her with the capacity of speech. "Well, that explains a lot of things, I guess," she muttered to herself in English.

"Pardon me?"

Cadence met his eyes, trying to impress upon him

the sincerity of her next words. "You can't honestly believe that I figure into this. Until my ship crashed here, I didn't even know who you were. My only desire is to leave." Neither Tailen's nor Gildon's expressions changed one iota. "Look. You said that you're telepathic. Can't you look into my mind and *see* that I'm telling the truth?"

Gildon responded. "We've tried. We were not successful."

"Why?" Cadence looked at him in desperation. She wanted to go home, not fulfill a prophecy.

"Your mind is very strongly shielded. Unlike anything we've encountered before."

Cadence looked from Gildon to Tailen and back again, seeking a hint of duplicity. Anything to understand why they were imparting this nonsense. They could perceive absolutely nothing from her mind to verify their beliefs, yet had an answer for everything. And she was supposed to accept all of this on faith?

Unable to sit still any longer, not caring at the moment if she flaunted some foreign courtesy, Cadence rose to pace the room. "This is ridiculous. I am *not* prophetic material. I'm not religious. I don't even understand this *One Universal Consciousness* of yours. And this prophecy you're spouting presupposes a belief in absolute good and absolute evil. I don't believe in either one. Next thing you'll be trying to tell me that *demons* and *angels* are real." She substituted two English words for Tesuvian terminology she didn't know.

Tailen and Gildon observed her agitation with unruffled calm. It made her want to throw something. "Absolute good and evil *do* exist," Gildon asserted. "What are *demons* and *angels*?"

"What?" Cadence looked at him in distraction and then, as the sense behind his query penetrated her numbed mind, described the two types of beings to the best of her ability based on religious portrayals she'd seen.

"Ah." He nodded and provided her with the appropriate Tesuvian terminology.

"I suppose you have an explanation for them as well?"

"There are many species of alter-realm beings, Cadence. Entities who do not even exist on this plane. Some exist on alternate physical planes, while others are non-corporeal beings. The Gou'jiin you encountered was one of these." He paused, considering her thoughtfully. "If you were a slightly less educated or more primitive person, what might you have called that creature?"

Cadence stared at him. "A demon?"

"I think so, yes. Although in our language, a demon or demoness is merely a being that is profoundly evil."

She considered his response. It was possible, she conceded silently, though she wasn't willing to admit it yet. "So how do you explain angels?" she demanded. "I suppose you think they're real too?"

"From your description, I believe they are probably the Empyrean guardians. The spirits of those who have achieved oneness with the One and need no longer return to a physical existence. When we commune it is the Empyrean guardians with whom we most often make contact. They are part of the One."

Cadence stared at him incredulously, pouncing on the aspects of his explanation that she found inconceivable. "Spirits?" Cadence echoed. "Return to a physical existence? That means you people believe in reincarnation, too!" She raked her fingers through her hair. Hell's universe! How could they expect her to accept all of this?

She walked over to the table and looked down at Tailen and Gildon. "All right, tell me this. If good and evil, demons and angels, really exist, why hasn't there been a verifiable sighting of such a thing on Earth? All we have are legends."

Tailen observed her almost sadly. "Your legends arose as a result of the work of the Vradir priests on your world. It was they who weakened the shields between the planes and opened gates allowing access to the beings your people would have called demons. The Empyrean guardians sometimes found it necessary to intervene on behalf of those threatened. They might have been termed angels by your people."

Cadence considered him. If she didn't know better, he'd almost have her believing him. "So who closed the gates?"

"After the destruction of the colony, when the planet regained stability, volunteer priests of the Avatar traveled to your world to undo the damage. It took many, many years, and several lives, but eventually the shielding between the planes was reenforced. Now only those with specialized knowledge can reopen the thresholds. I believe that much of that knowledge has been lost to your world. This is probably a fortunate thing."

Cadence sighed. She was no closer to accepting this than before, but she was running out of arguments. "Look!" She pinned them both with an adamant expression. "I am *not* evil. Neither am I particularly good. Certainly not devoutly so. I simply do not qualify as either of the women in your prophecy."

Tailen observed her solemnly. "At this point in time, we still don't know if the destroyer is evil, or will merely be a tool of evil, Cadence. Likewise, the savior may only be an instrument of the One. Even now, the Lidai Order continues to commune with the One, seeking answers."

Oh, stars! There was no getting through to them.

Cadence's indignation began to fade. They were as desperate as she was, just in a different way. "Don't you think if I was one of the women in your prophecy, I'd have an understanding of my purpose here?" As both men stared at her blankly, Cadence shook her head in exasperation. "All right, suppose for an outrageous instant that I *am* this protector you're awaiting. Just what is it you expect me to do to help you? Who or what are you afraid of?"

Tailen frowned slightly. "I thought you understood. Our greatest enemy is the cult of Vradir. It is they we must fight."

"But. . . ." Cadence looked at Gildon in confusion. "I thought they were defeated forever when Atlantis and the other colonies were destroyed."

Gildon shook his head. "The Vradir cult represents not only a people, but a way of thinking, a system of belief. Such things cannot be destroyed forever. There is always something remaining, some remnant of written records to seduce and lure people back into the doctrine. It requires only a charismatic leader and the human desire for life and power."

"I don't understand. Life and power? Does the cult threaten people's lives if they don't become part of it?"

"Yes, but that is not what I meant." Gildon's gaze drilled into hers, emphasizing the importance of his next words. "The Vradir have only one purpose: to discover the secret of physical immortality. Life. The power they offer is dominance. Those who follow the tenets of the Vradir are granted authority over all others." He swallowed as though to rid his mouth of something distasteful. "They enslave them."

Cadence could only stare at him. There was an ancient tale which she'd seen on vid-disk many times as a child in the orphanage, *Alice in Wonderland*. Gripped by an uncompromising feeling of unreality, she felt a definite kinship with the child in that tale.

This had to be a joke, didn't it? She looked at Tailen, but he too watched her with solemn eyes. "I still don't understand exactly what you think I can do to help," she murmured in a choked voice.

"According to the prophecy, if you are the protector, then you will battle the ruler of the Vradir, their queen."

"Look, I may be combat trained, but I did not come here to do battle with anybody." She sighed, making a conscious effort to release her frustration. "Please. Won't you just help me to go home? There has to be a means."

Gildon shook his head. "There is no way that we know of, Cadence. Only the One could take you forward in time."

Defeated for the moment, Cadence resumed her seat on the cushion. "But you will help me find my brother. Right?" She looked first at Tailen's compassionate expression and then at Gildon's closed one. "Right?" she pressed.

"When we know which of the foretold women you are . . . if you are the protector . . . then we will help you find your brother. That is the decision that has been made by my brother Prelates who govern the other provinces."

"And if I am neither?"

Tailen sighed. "In that event, we will also help you."

"When will you know?"

Tailen shrugged. "That is uncertain. Soon, we hope. All right?"

Cadence studied his set features, then turned her gaze to the hard planes of Gildon's handsome face, which were even more unyielding. "No," she responded. "But I have the feeling that it's the best I'm going to get. Isn't it?"

Gildon merely nodded.

Tailen replied, "For now, I'm afraid so, yes."

Cadence looked from one to the other. "So . . . how do we find out who I am?"

The men shared a speaking glance. Finally Tailen cleared his throat and looked at her. "We don't know yet, Cadence. For the present, you will continue your education. Within a few days, we believe the One will give us the answer to that question."

Far away in Madaia, in the city of Eston, a score of builders chanted. As their *falar* stones magnified the ability of their minds, their voices manipulated the planetary resonance, and the last huge block of stone lifted into place. The castle was complete. Black and angular, the enormous edifice had been constructed on a point of convergent energy. A non-aligned energy that could be utilized by anybody with the knowledge of how to harness it. The building fairly shimmered with puissance.

Tonight he would usher his bride to her new home.

Rushing back to the privacy of his lower-level study, he began his preparations. Within a few long moments, all of his plans would finally see fruition. Tonight he would transform the link of communication from a window to a door. He would grant access to the physical world to the being whom he had loved in every way but the physical for years.

He checked the body of the beautiful young woman who lay drugged on the table: still breathing. He frowned thoughtfully as for the span of a moment he remembered her identity: a novice within the Madaian Order of the Avatar named Eilena. Then he shoved the memory away and she was once more just a body. A vessel for his bride, herself an ancient Tesuvian.

Excitement permeated his entire being as he continued his preparations. He remembered his first encounter with Ish'Kara. He'd been a bit younger then, still learning about the alter-realms. Fascinated by the possibilities they represented, he'd decided that the best way to learn about something was to explore it firsthand. If he could learn about them this way, he would have done something that no other priest of the Avatar had. The knowledge he could share would grant him . . . prestige. So, after carefully constructing all the safeguards of which he was capable, he'd gone on a spiritual exploration of the alter-realms.

Oh, he'd been frightened. Terrified of the endless darkness and the unseen presences. Afraid of the grasping hands he could feel but never see as he fought them off to continue his journey. Horrified by the twisted psyches of the beings he did encounter. And then, just when he had begun to think it all a very bad idea, he saw Ish'Kara.

She was beautiful.

Well, actually, it had been her spirit's projection of her physical form that had been beautiful, because she, like he, had been in spiritual form. She'd stood in a meadow, brilliant green with new grass. Clad only in a brief undergown, her snow-white limbs looked as though they had been carved from ivory. Her waist-length ebony hair floated around her on the eddies of a wind he could not feel. And her ice-blue eyes had gleamed with warm, teasing laughter at his inept exploration of her plane. Then with a smile she took him by the hand and began to show him all that he'd been so anxious to learn. It took many visits.

When they were through with the sharing of knowledge, they shared themselves. Talking. Sharing experiences. Sharing dreams. Journeying to yet other planes, not to learn, but simply to experience new things together. They touched spiritually in a way few people ever manage to do. And it was not enough.

They began to dream of being together physically . . . forever. And together they arrived at a plan. It had been so detailed, so involved, that he'd feared it might not work. But it had. It had! He smiled in anticipation as he began the chant.

Slowly the unique dimensional gate began to form. Miniature bolts of lightning coruscated over its surface in jagged blue-white spears. A ring of sunrise-colored flame flared on the border of the access, expanding as it grew.

He tensed without breaking the chant. He could sense her. She was near.

And then a nebulous gray-white mist began to emerge between the cracks in the bubble-like surface of the threshold. It stretched. Reaching toward the tranquilized body on the table. Expanding until its snake-like coils were as large as his forearm. Carefully he maintained the chant, holding the threshold open until she was completely through. Ish'Kara. His bride.

Any vestiges of morality or remorse faded into oblivion. *This* was what he wanted.

The mist flowed into the body on the table until it completely disappeared. He ceased chanting. The threshold snapped closed with a muted roar. The body on the table blinked and turned to look at him with loving eyes. The Vradir had their queen.

Cadence was lost in a place of darkness, pursued by something shadowy and frightening that she could not see. She ran . . . and ran. But she couldn't seem to escape it. There was a pinpoint of light in the distance, and she ran toward it.

Suddenly there was a voice behind her—cold and musical. "Ali'yah," it called. "Ali'yah."

Her heart pounded with fear and hatred. Oh, no! *She* had returned. She tossed her head on the pillow, denying the knowledge. No! But the voice continued to follow her, laughing and taunting.

Her breath rasped in her throat and lungs, burning torturously even as it fed her body oxygen. She could run no more. She felt fingers grasp her shoulders, digging in like demonic claws. They'd caught her!

Slowly, relentlessly, they dragged her into a vast, tenebrous hall. She had the impression of a thousand disembodied white faces swimming in the blackness before her. Then gradually they began to move aside, creating a path of blackness between them, and Cadence realized that they were merely people in black robes.

Someone approached her now. A woman. And Cadence screamed her name in startled recognition. "Ish'Kara!"

Cadence bolted upright in bed to face the blackness of the night. Reactionary shudders of remembered terror racked her body. A tear escaped the corner of her eye. Pulling her knees up close to her chest, she hugged them, trying to dispel the chill that emanated from deep within her. The muscles in her legs quivered as though she had indeed been running from some nebulous terror. She didn't remember much about the dream beyond the endless running and the horrible feeling at the end of having been touched by . . . evil. Absolute evil. The kind that earlier in the day she had said she did not believe existed. Somehow, alone here in the darkness its existence seemed much more plausible.

She rubbed her eyes, trying to pierce the shroud of sleep to remember what had frightened her so. "Ish'Kara," she murmured, remembering the name. An alien name, it had a Tesuvian flavor and yet was different in some way. But who was she? Cadence had met no one by that name.

There was a rustle of sound in the doorway. A shadow moved. Irrational fear immobilized her. Her breath strangled in her throat.

"Cadence, I heard you cry out. Are you all right?"

Oh, thank the stars! It was Gildon. Relief made her weak. "Y-yes. Fine." Her voice sounded frightened and uncertain even to her own ears; as alien as this place. She'd never been the type to allow fear to govern her actions. But the absolute terror she'd experienced in this dream was unlike anything she'd endured as a Stellar Legionnaire back home.

"You don't seem fine." He came forward, stepping into a swath of moonlight. His midnight eyes glistened in the lunar illumination as he scrutinized her. For the second time in as many minutes, her breath caught.

His only clothing was a pair of form-fitting white trousers. Without conscious volition her eyes caressed his powerful torso, brushing every highlighted curve of muscle and sinew, investigating every shadowy plane. And she suddenly had a fierce, almost uncontrollable longing to throw herself into the circle of his strong arms. To listen to the sturdy beat of his heart beneath her ear. To feel safe and . . . cared for.

Cadence squelched the yearning ruthlessly. Brushing away the moisture on her cheeks, she drew a breath deep into her lungs and forced her vocal cords into motion. "No, I'm fine. Really."

His brows drew together over his eyes. "You've been crying." She could feel his gaze move over her as palpably as a touch. She sensed a subtle shift in his demeanor. An increase in intensity. Abruptly she remembered her own state of semi-dress. Her only clothing was a diaphanous nightshift that looked as if it had been constructed of spider webs. She pulled the blanket from her waist up to her neck and forced herself to find her voice again. "You needn't concern yourself. It . . . it was just a nightmare."

In an instant he was on his knees next to the dais that formed her bed. "What kind of nightmare?"

Cadence instinctively shrank away from the sudden ferocity in his tone. "A . . . a nightmare. H-how many kinds are there?"

"There are many kinds, Cadence. But sometimes, for those who do not commune with the One regularly, dreams—good and bad—are the guardian's only means of delivering a warning. Please. Tell me what you dreamed."

Prompted by the intensity in Gildon's demeanor, Cadence tried once again to remember. She shuddered, recalling the touch of something sinister and corrupt. "I c-can't." To her horror, a renewed bout of tears began to sting her eyes. Seeking to stem the tide of emotion, she rubbed her face with her hands. "All I remember is running and running, endlessly, from something . . . evil." She looked up. "Remember how you told me earlier that absolute evil did exist and I didn't believe you?"

He nodded. "Yes."

"I think I might believe you now. I felt it in my dream."

Infinitely gentle now, he smoothed a tendril of hair back from her face and caught a rogue tear on the pad of his thumb. "Can you describe it?"

Cadence sniffed discreetly. "It was just a feeling."

Gildon handed her a tissue and she gently blew her nose. "Describe the feeling."

Crumpling the tissue, Cadence shuddered. "It was almost as bad as being touched by the Gou'jiin, worse in one way."

"In what way?"

She compressed her lips in thoughtful frustration as she sought a way of explaining her feelings. "What I sensed from the Gou'jiin was not evil. It had a complete lack of morality, and total self-absorption. It cared only for its own life and was interested only in its own pleasure. It would not have been bothered in the least by killing me. But neither would it have felt

. . . satisfaction. Do you understand what I mean?"

Gildon nodded and she continued. "What I felt in my dream tonight was something that . . . thrives on destruction. It enjoyed my fear, and wanted very badly to kill me."

Gildon rose solemnly to his feet to stand looking down at her. "Do you remember anything else?" There was an underlying thread of concern in his voice that warmed her almost as much as its deep, sensuous tone.

"No. I don't think so," she said, shaking her head. "It *was* just a dream. Wasn't it?"

"I don't know, Cadence. Perhaps. You're sure you remember nothing else?"

She began to shake her head and then stopped. "Wait!" She nodded. "Yes, I do. A name."

His eyes connected with hers with watchful intentness. "A name?" he echoed.

"Yes. It was *Ish'Kara*. Do you know it?"

His demeanor changed so rapidly that Cadence hadn't even had time to absorb the fact when he leaned forward to clutch her shoulders in a vise-like grip. "Where did you hear that name?" he demanded.

Chapter Ten

She stared at the hard set of his features in confusion. Distrust radiated from him in waves. Why? "I . . . I told you. In my dream."

A muscle flexed in his jaw and he pulled her up as though she weighed no more than a child until she hung in his grasp, her face just inches below his. "That is an ancient Tesuvian name. You could not possibly know it unless you'd had contact with someone here. Someone from Madaia perhaps?" When Cadence merely stared at him uncomprehendingly, he shook her slightly.

"Don't think you can lie to me."

Cadence forced herself to meet a pair of eyes that were suddenly as cold as the depths of space. "I am not lying." Although the bottom had fallen out of her stomach, she managed to keep any trace of apprehension out of her voice.

He studied her features as though by sight alone he could discern the veracity of her statement. He appeared on the verge of releasing her and, in fact, had begun to put her away from him when inexplicably his expression began to alter. His eyes left her face to skim down her body, and Cadence realized that, during their confrontation, the blanket had slipped from her grasp. Only the sheer, shimmering fabric of her spider-web woven nightshift remained.

Her lips parted to issue a protest that never found

voice for, in that instant, Gildon made a strange growling noise deep in his throat and lifted her in his grasp again. Slowly, warily, she raised her eyes from the thick bronzed column of his neck. Her gaze skimmed the whisker-shadowed planes of his strong jawline, clung momentarily to his full-lipped, expressive mouth, and moved past the bold blade of his aristocratic nose to his eyes. It was a mistake. The sheer male hunger reflected in his storm-hued irises paralyzed her. Like a wild beast responding to a distant howl of need in the wilderness, her body answered that wordless call. Languor flooded her limbs. Her breasts swelled in anticipation.

And then his mouth closed over hers, hard and demanding as his tongue delved between her lips. Powerless to resist the silent command, she opened to him. He invaded, exploring the soft recesses of her mouth with an erotic skill that left her breathless and dizzy. Her hands crept forward to grip the smooth, warm flesh of his powerful shoulders in an unconscious attempt to restore some of her equilibrium. It was a futile effort.

Gildon allowed her to sink to her knees on the bed and his strong hands began to move up and down her chilled arms as though to warm them. Every friction-laden caress sent frizzles of sensation sparking along her nerve endings. More than anything, at this moment she wanted to be in his arms. Yet she sensed that he was putting her away from him.

She didn't want to be alone. Not tonight. Not now. She looked up at him, met his glittering dark-eyed gaze in the shimmering moonlight. "Don't go. Please?"

Gildon stared down at Cadence. She was beautiful. Her brown hair shimmered with highlights of glittering gold as if it had been sprinkled with moondust. Her eyes shone like precious emeralds, deep and mysterious. And her golden-hued complexion took on the appearance of gilt. The wispy silver gown she wore only added to the impression that she was not a flesh-and-blood woman, but the image of female perfection created by the hand of a master artisan.

Gildon felt as though invisible chains bound his limbs. As though an alter-realm entity had sapped every last ounce of his will. As though nothing in the universe mattered beyond this moment in time. Consequences . . . the implicit threat to his vocation meant nothing. His hunger for Cadence far surpassed any desire he had ever felt. His loins were swollen and heavy with the force of his passion.

"Please, Gildon? I don't want to be alone tonight." Her soft murmur was like the sudden awakening jolt of a clap of thunder.

Cadence had not asked him to stay out of desire, but out of fear. She needed the comfort of having another person near. Though she herself might have translated that requirement into sexual yearning, Gildon knew the difference. His male pride was stung.

No matter how badly he wanted her, he would not, could not, take advantage of her desire for simple closeness. He met her troubled gaze. "I will stay, Cadence," he answered. "But only as your friend."

She reared back from him, confusion furrowing her brow. "Why?"

"Because a friend is what you need at this time."

A multitude of expressions flitted across her features too quickly for him to interpret. "Don't you find me . . . attractive?"

Gildon swallowed and fortified his wavering resolve. "I find you very attractive, Cadence. But . . ."

"But . . . ?" she prompted with a hint of challenge in her tone. Releasing her grip on his arms, she moved back a bit as though she had just now become aware of the contact.

"But tonight you need a friend, not a . . . a lover."

Cadence studied his face to verify the truth of his words. Finally she nodded. "All right. I'm trying desperately not to feel insulted, because I think I understand what you're saying. I'm just not accustomed to encountering such . . . nobility of character." She paused and scanned the room. "Well, since I don't have a couch, which side of the bed do you want?"

"Couch?" He focused on the unfamiliar word, ignoring the image that the rest of her question brought to mind.

She shrugged. "Forget it. It's an English word. So which will it be?"

Gildon stared at her. Despite her carefully controlled tone, something was wrong. There was something about her behavior that was almost too composed. "I will simply sit on one of the cushions." The last thing he wanted to do was test the strength of his resolve by sleeping in the same bed with her.

"Nonsense! This is a huge bed, so there's no need for you to lose sleep by sitting for the remainder of the night." She caught his eyes. "After all, I can trust you implicitly. Correct?"

Was that a challenge he saw in her eyes? "Yes."

"Good. Then it's settled."

Gildon stared down at the woman sleeping in his arms. Almost as soon as she'd fallen asleep, she had gravitated toward him. Toward the physical contact and the comfort she needed. Being here was pure torture. And yet he found himself enjoying it too. For the first time, he found himself able to contemplate her, to admire her, without risk of exposing his own chaotic emotions.

Cadence was everything he admired in a woman: strong, beautiful, passionate, and intelligent. He no longer believed that she could possibly be evil herself. Yet there was still no way to know if she was destined to be an instrument of evil.

By the One! Why must life always be so complicated?

Cadence might have been everything he would have wanted in a companion, had he wanted one. But she was not for him. Not only was she not of the Order of the Avatar, but he had decided long ago that he would not make any woman a good husband, nor any child a good father. It simply wasn't in him to be a demonstrative, caring person.

Neither of his parents had been affectionate. His father, Torak of the line of Shoulka, a High Priest of the Avatar, had devoted his entire life to discipline, to learning the unknowable, to understanding that which defied comprehension. His work had absorbed all of his passion, draining him of emotion, leaving almost nothing for his family. Gildon could count the number of affectionate gestures he'd received from his father before he'd died. He treasured them, just as he treasured all the time spent with his father in learning the basic tenets of the Order of the Avatar. And yet, compared to Gildon's mother, Shaylon of the line of Ksynjan, Torak had been a warm person.

Unlike Torak, Shaylon was not a naturally detached person. Rather, it seemed that she had a limited capacity for love. What love she had to give, she had heaped upon her firstborn child, Jakial, and there simply had been nothing left for Gildon.

Gildon grappled to seal the fissure in the wall in his mind. To block the resurgence of caustic childhood memories . . . and the emotions associated with them. It was too late.

He'd been very young, and Jakial only a couple of years older. The summer suns shone down upon the city with savage brilliance. Yet, typically, the children barely noticed the heat. Seeking a diversion to ease their boredom on a day free from lessons, they placed a wide board on some wheels they borrowed from the Builders Guild. Then, deciding that their newly created toy would be much more practical if one did not have to push while the other rode, they took their makeshift wagon to a nearby street that had a wonderfully daring slope.

The ride down the smoothly paved hill was exhilarating and exciting. The exhilaration came in no small part from the fact that they were partaking in the thrilling danger of the forbidden—though not directly, of course. Neither child would have blatantly disobeyed a directive from an elder. Rather, it was that they knew that, had they sought permission for their actions, they would have been prohibited. So they had not asked.

Everything was fine, wonderfully, dangerously delightful until Jakial decided that, instead of taking turns, they should ride together down the hill. He directed Gildon to sit on the makeshift wagon while he pushed from behind, jumping on at the last moment to share the ride. The small wagon careened down the narrow road at twice the speed. Gildon clung to its sides, frightened.

Abruptly their ride veered off to one side, heading directly for the solid wall of one of the buildings bordering the narrow alley. Jakial stuck his foot over the side in an attempt to slow their speed, but it did no good. The only thing that happened was that the rough stone of the street tore his soft-soled rope sandal from his foot.

Eyes wide with fear, both boys opened their mouths and screamed.

Impact was inevitable.

"Jump!" Jakial urged. "Jump, Gildon!"

But Gildon's fingers were frozen, locked onto the sides of the wagon. He couldn't move. Couldn't even scream anymore. He was paralyzed in an agony of silent anticipation. All he could do was watch the stone wall loom ever closer.

He sensed the moment that Jakial leapt from the wagon. Felt the shift in the weight. Distantly, he heard Jakial's cry of pain. There was a bone-jarring jolt and he felt himself torn from the wagon. A brief sensation of being airborne, of moving above the ground, culminated in painful collision. He smashed into the wall, and then he blacked out.

Slowly, insistently, Jakial's voice penetrated the insular fog of unconsciousness. "Gildon, wake up! Please" Gildon's brother's small hand shook his shoulder. He heard a sniffle. "Come on. You're scaring me. Wake up!"

Gildon opened his eyes to Jakial's tear-streaked face. His whole body hurt, but it was the pain in his nose that brought instant tears to his eyes. He lifted a scraped hand to his face and it came away red with blood.

"My nose hurts," he muttered.

Jakial tried to smile through his own tears. "If you think that hurts, you should see my leg. Come on."

Leaving the offending wagon where it lay, the two boys supported each other and slowly began making their way home. Gildon's nose throbbed terribly and he couldn't seem to stop crying.

Jakial studied him thoughtfully. "If your nose doesn't work anymore, maybe you can use that bump on your forehead instead. It's bigger than your nose anyway."

Despite his tears and pain, Gildon managed a small smile. Jakial could always make him see the humor in things. And he had felt a little better . . . until they reached home. Until they faced their mother.

The instant she saw them, she began raving. Her

words came so quickly that neither child could understand them.

Leaving Gildon standing just inside the door, hurting and afraid, she grabbed Jakial and carried him to the nearest cushion. Brushing his hair back from his face, she examined him for injuries. It seemed that she kissed him a hundred times. And then, assured that his injuries were superficial, she turned to Gildon.

Gildon watched her with a sense of anticipation. Now she would turn to him and brush his hair back. Soothe his hurts as she had Jakial's. Now she would love him. He was so certain that this time would be different that he actually took a step toward her. But the words she spoke weren't those he expected.

"This is your fault, isn't it, Gildon? You led him into danger?" His mother's eyes were cold, accusing.

Halting in mid-step, Gildon stared at her, not understanding. Knowing only that he hurt and wanted his mother's love, her sympathy. But she seemed blind to the blood on his face and arms.

"I've hurt my face, Mother," he murmured quietly, suddenly ashamed of the sniffles that he could not seem to control.

She studied him silently for a moment. "Go tell your father I said he should take you to a healer." Her tone was cold, unfeeling. With that, she turned her back on her younger child and administered first aid to Jakial, her firstborn and favorite.

Suddenly hurting more than his injuries could account for, Gildon stared at his mother and brother with a yearning so fierce it was difficult to breathe. Then slowly he turned and left the room.

Gildon blinked and surfaced from the painful memory. Shoving it back behind the wall in his mind, he slammed the door and sealed the chinks. He had never again expected anything from his mother. And, after a time, some of the pain of her rejection had even begun to fade. But it was his relationship with Jakial that he wished could have been different.

He could not remember a time when he had not resented his older brother, had not envied him for the gentle, motherly hands that soothed his hurts or brushed his hair with affection. That jealousy had dogged every step of Gildon's life. And yet, except for their father, there was no one whom Gildon loved more than his brother.

Jakial had shown Gildon more affection than both of their parents combined. Jakial had forestalled the bullying taunts of children who—although they did not yet fear the Order of the Avatar—knew there was something different about those reared within its disciplines. He had taught Gildon the meaning of brotherhood when he had sided with him, arguing against both their parents to allow Gildon to be instructed in the Kami until the time came that he *must* assume his duties within the Temple of the Avatar. And he had introduced Gildon to the esoteric pleasure to be found within the confines of the Order of the Shajati, ensuring that Gildon received an education in the sensuous arts that could not help but enrich his life.

How could one love a brother so much and yet be so consumed with jealousy that the emotion bordered on hate? The two diametrically opposed feelings constantly warred within him. Guilt churned within his gut like the roiling waves of a stormy sea.

But no one had ever guessed at his emotions. He had learned to hide the hurt and the longing for affection beneath a facade of indifference. Gradually, over time, that facade had come to conceal all sentiment, smothering his emotions to the point where he himself began to believe he did not possess feelings . . . except for Jakial.

Until recently.

He frowned thoughtfully, acknowledging that, almost from the moment he'd encountered Cadence, something within him had begun to shift and change. What? And how? It was as though some unrecognized part of himself had awakened. He needed to understand that, to interpret the alteration within himself. Why did she stir things within him that no other ever had?

With a gentle fingertip, he smoothed a tendril of hair from her face.

Cadence sighed in her sleep, drawing his eyes to her lips. He still wanted her with a ferocity that confused him. But thinking of how close he had come to making love to her reminded him of how that occurrence had come about. She'd spoken a name which had not found a home on Tesuvian tongues in centuries, for it had long ago been stricken from the tomes containing the birth names for Tesuvian naming ceremonies. He wished now that he hadn't reacted quite so vehemently to her utterance of the name Ish'Kara, but she'd caught him by surprise and he'd been unable to stifle the renewed surge of distrust. The name, recorded only within the annals of the Temple of the Avatar, echoed in his mind with ubiquitous associations of injustice. But he couldn't remember the exact transcription behind the connotations of wrongdoing. When had he seen the name? Had it been while working with his father? Or perhaps during one of the times when he shared duties with Jakial?

Remember! he ordered himself. But the information eluded him.

He needed to access his family's private library.

He grimaced mentally. Access to Torak's and Jakial's journals could be garnered only by arranging a visit with Shaylon, for she maintained the records of their work within the temple. Visiting the embittered old woman was not something Gildon did any more than was necessary out of courtesy. However, with the question of Ish'Kara preying on his mind, he would have to go.

Perhaps he would take Cadence with him. The presence of a stranger might help to dissipate some of his mother's vituperation long enough for him to accomplish his purpose.

He yawned and realized that he, too, was very tired, but he didn't want to wake Cadence in order to return to his own bed. Surely it wouldn't hurt just to close his eyes and rest for a few moments. Reaching down, he gently drew the blankets over them and lay down to enjoy the simple sensation of holding a beautiful, desirable woman in his arms.

Submerged in the world of dreams, Cadence struggled in her sleep. A cloud of multicolored mist held her suspended and immobile against a backdrop of stars in a midnight sky. Below her, bathed in pale moonlight upon the summit of an ocher cliff, a man stood, his arms outstretched entreatingly toward her as a tremendous wind lashed him. He fought against its force as he called to her, but the words were torn from his lips and whirled away before she could hear them.

The wind molded his white trousers against his legs and billowed his cloak behind him, exposing the strength of the powerful body he used to battle its primal force. His long black hair streamed behind him as he reached for her, calling to her once more. "Ali'Yah." His voice was strong and deep. But as the word escaped, the storm intensified its campaign to compel him back. So mighty was his combat against it that, when the wind lulled for the space of a breath, he almost plunged from the edge of the towering precipice.

Cadence's breath caught in her throat in fear for

him, and in that instant she felt a powerful surge of recognition. It was not the form of the man she recognized, for that had changed, but the essence of him. It had been so long . . . too long. She struggled against the grasping tentacles of the rainbow mist, trying to reach him. But the clutch of the mist only tightened, pulling her further away as it contracted in upon itself.

Her heart felt as though it were being torn from her breast as she gazed upon his form, watching it grow smaller and more distant. Her eyes locked with his. "Kadar," she whispered.

As returning consciousness began to tear and rend the gossamer web of the dream with its cold fingers of reality, Cadence resisted. She tried to seize the threads, to re-pattern the dream for remembrance. She had lost something. . . . something cherished. What was it? But the strands were torn from her grip and she woke.

The first thing she saw was the bronzed flesh of a man's throat. She felt the solid warmth of a male body against hers, the comforting sensation of being held. It felt so right, so perfect, to be in his arms again.

Again?

For an instant, confusion gripped her. Then she remembered the nightmare . . . the reason she was in Gildon's arms. She stirred slightly, easing herself gently away from him. Her brow furrowed with the vague remembrance of a man in her dreams. Had she dreamed of Gildon? She studied him in the red-gold rays of a new day's sunlight.

Even now, her heart raced as she looked upon his handsome countenance. Yet in the bright light of day all her reasons for not becoming involved with him came to the fore. Had Gildon known she would feel that way? Was that why he'd refused her invitation?

See, he is not like the others, a part of her argued.

His noble attitude last night proves that. Cadence frowned, annoyed at the inner voice of temptation. It didn't matter if Gildon was a saint, she had no intention of risking her heart on a man she must soon leave. *If I can leave. What if there's no way to move forward in time?*

Cadence swallowed. It didn't look good, did it? The Tesuvians didn't use ships. They possessed no mechanization at all to aid her in repairing her own ship even had the data in Claire been intact. And their portals were incapable of traveling forward in time. It was time to face the inevitable: She wasn't going home. But that didn't mean she would give up her search for Chance. She'd use the resources at hand, Tesuvian technology, to find her brother. And she *would* find him.

Her eyes caressed the sleeping man at her side again. But while she sought her brother, perhaps she'd be foolish to deny herself one more shot at finding the man who would be her soulmate. Perhaps it wasn't so impossible to imagine herself building a new life, here, among these people. Perhaps she should take that chance with Gildon. As she observed the gentle rise and fall of his chest, admired the dark crescent created by his lashes, and longed to brush her fingertips over the soft fullness of his lips, emotion—thick and unidentifiable—rose in her throat. She felt the most absurd inclination to cry. And she realized what a fool she'd been. Her heart was already involved. It might not be love . . . yet— she really didn't know him well enough for it to be love—but there was something there. Something more than the mere physical attraction she'd thought it to be. How naive she'd been to believe that, as long as she didn't become sexually involved, she'd shield her heart.

No, all things considered, Cadence decided she'd be even more of a fool if she continued to deny herself the opportunity for happiness. It was time to deepen her relationship with Gildon, to let life and love take her where they would.

The only obstacle to that course of action was Gildon himself. It had been he who had so commendably put on the brakes last evening. Perhaps she would have to let him know, in subtle ways, that she was no longer averse to a sexual relationship. That she wanted, and needed, more than a friend.

Gently extricating herself from his arms, she rose and tiptoed across the room to the bathing chamber. It was time to prepare to face a new day . . . and a new future.

The massive, newly constructed, black-stone cathedral of the Vradir cult rose ominous and intimidating against the blood-red sky of a new morning. From within the summit of its central tower, Ish'Kara looked down on the surrounding Madaian lands as she gloried in the sensation of inhabiting a human body once again. One could not know the simple pleasure to be found within the human senses until one had been denied them.

She lifted the heavy weight of her luxurious blond hair away from her neck. She kept lifting her arms, as though in homage to the rising sun, until the thick tresses fell, caressing her naked back. Then, slowly lowering her arms, she ran her hands over the body that was now hers. The nipples of her small, pert breasts stood erect in the coolness of the morning air. Beneath her questing palms, the flesh of her flat abdomen felt silky soft. Her hands moved lower, brushing against the thatch of crisp gold curls at the junction of her thighs before moving around to explore the firmness of her high, tight buttocks.

Oh, yes. This body would do very well indeed. Her lover had chosen well.

She smirked. But then, of course, it had been in

his own best interests to choose a form for her that would please both of them.

Turning away from the high window and the glorious sunrise, she looked back toward the bed she'd just left. He lay sprawled upon the coverlets there, satiated and wonderfully handsome in his nakedness. Of all the men she had chosen over the years, she thought perhaps he suited her best.

She had no illusions where he was concerned, and he none of her. As well as either of them was able, they loved each other. But her lover was as coldly calculating and as self-serving as a man could be. They shared only one consuming passion: a love of life.

Ish'Kara narrowed her ice-blue eyes. And this time life eternal would be hers. She would defeat her nemesis. Even now she could sense her rival's presence on his world; indeed, each of her incarnations had been plagued by Ali'Yah's concurrent existence. The fact that she had long ago abandoned the genetic technologies that Ali'Yah so abhorred in favor of more arcane methodology mattered not at all; Ali'Yah considered all her methods equally immoral. Ish'Kara shrugged inwardly. Ali'Yah did not concern her at the moment.

Baltharak did. This time she would hold the Daemod being to their bargain.

Glancing over her shoulder at the rising sun, she gauged the hour. Yes, she had time to speak with him before everyone arose for the day. Reaching out with her mind, she nudged her lover deeper into sleep. She did not want him awakening before she was through. It was one thing to share one's power, quite another to reveal all of one's secrets.

Assured that her lover was safely asleep, Ish'Kara donned a crimson silk robe and moved to the other side of the enormous circular chamber. She closed her eyes and immediately felt the convergence of the ribbons of energy that banded this world. The architects and builders had done well in their construction. She'd designed this huge dark edifice with one purpose: to draw and augment the non-aligned energies of this planet for her use.

Now she drew on those energies and began the incantation. Using her amplified mental power and the command of sound, she began to manipulate the laws of nature. As the boundaries between this world and another weakened, the air before her began to shimmer and expand, like the surface of an enormous soap bubble. Carefully she placed into effect the force field which would prevent entry into her world from the next. Then, with an abrupt word, Ish'Kara waved her arms, and the periphery of the bubble became a fiery frame, its center a rippling gate.

The threshold was open.

Chapter Eleven

Moving to a window, Tailen Goryne stared down on the city that had been his home for his entire life. Soon he might have to leave it. Thousands from all over the continent were already preparing for evacuation.

Tailen glanced at the ancient star chart on a nearby wall. The representation of his home world drew his eyes like a magnet.

Tesuvia.

He had never seen it with his own eyes but, if he concentrated, he could dredge the inherited ancestral memory of its beauty from the depths of his mind. The evacuation committee's plan revolved around a return to Tesuvia, he knew. They believed that the problems that had plagued their ancestral world had been solved in the preceding centuries. He hoped they were right. But there would be no way to know without going home. Governed by the need to protect themselves, the colonies that had once worked together, sharing information and plans, had long ago lost contact with each other and their home world.

Did other colonies survive out there in the vast reaches of space? Or, like his own, had they been found by the Vradir and destroyed one by one?

He remembered his history lessons. His colony had survived the initial Vradir incursion precisely because of communication between the colonies. They had been warned in advance and had managed to apprehend the perpetrators of evil and dispense with them before it was too late.

Using the knowledge they'd gained during that initial infiltration, the surviving colonies had focused on finding the means to protect themselves from further such invasions. They had developed the three-ringed cities. Incapacitated the interplanetary portals which were their only means of travel and communication between colonies. And sealed the perimeter of the physical plane from those of the alter-realms where the Vradir priests obtained much of their power. Thus they had been able to prevent the entry of entities like the Gou'jiin and the Daemod.

Until now. Until someone had been fool enough to remove the safeguards and create a new link from the physical plane to the other-dimensional realms. Despite the hard-fought and hard-won battle so long ago, it had all begun anew.

He wondered again if all of the other colonies had fallen. Was this settlement alone in its battle? His hands knotted into fists at his side. Why had they waited so long to consider terminating their isolation? By the time anyone had thought it worth the risk of re-establishing contact with their sister colonies, the knowledge concerning interplanetary portal programming had already faded into obscurity. Over the years, a few curious priests had continued to seek the answer to the puzzle in their spare time, but—believing that it was their very isolation that protected them—no one had thought it important enough to focus on.

Tailen shook his head sadly as he stared down at the bright and beautiful city below. It was already too late for his people on this world. The dimensional thresholds and alter-realm entities had long since escaped the boundaries of Madaia to creep across the continent like the diseases they were. Had that been the only problem, perhaps there would still have been hope. But the evil infected many people too. Daily, their greed and ambition grew. And the Vradir would escape the boundaries of Madaia, growing and spreading like a plague.

Although returning to Tesuvia was a bit of a gamble in itself, the odds of their survival seemed better on Tesuvia than on a world that was slowly and surely being confiscated and enslaved by the evil Vradir—aided in their advancement by the alter-realm beings with whom they invariably aligned themselves. It had been ten millennia since the first Tesuvians had left their home world. And at least half that long since they'd last heard from other Tesuvians. But it was during one of those final communications that the colony had been informed that the Vradir had been expulsed from Tesuvia. That their home planet was now peaceful and regenerating itself. They had to believe that things would be better there. Besides, they had no place else to go.

Perhaps the greatest irony of all was that, even forewarned by a prophecy, they'd been able to do nothing to prevent its unfolding. Everyone had known that the dimension thresholds had been sealed for years, that protections were in place that prevented the creation of a threshold by an entity from another plane. No one really believed that a Tesuvian would be fool enough to undo the protection that had taken a century and thousands of lives to install. As a result, no one had done anything, ignoring the prophecy and going about their daily lives . . . until they had been forced to acknowledge that something was wrong. Until word of the first cases of possession, of disappearance, corruption and of violent death had begun to come out of Madaia. Until it was already too late. And Tailen was as much at fault in that as everyone else on this world.

Now he craved only one thing, to catch and punish those responsible for this disaster.

Frowning thoughtfully, he asked the question that had been asked countless times in the years just past: Who had disobeyed the tenets of the Eidan by creating the gates that granted the entities access? Who was the woman who would aid the Vradir priests in their bid for power?

Through the opening, Ish'Kara studied the world on the other side. Baltharak's world was a parallel one, as corporeal as this, though any hint of the beauty it might once have had was long since gone. It was a world in upheaval. Molten lava and flames leapt from ever-changing fissures that seemed to move along the planet's crust like giant crimson worms. Heat scorched the very atmosphere, creating shimmering waves unbearable to human flesh. In fact, nothing that maintained a corporeal form could live in that environment for more than a few moments.

Closing her eyes but refusing to leave her newly acquired body just yet, Ish'Kara sent a psychic inquiry through the threshold.

A moment later, the response came. *Who seeks me?*

Baltharak, it is Ish'Kara.

And what do you wish of me?

Anger, abrupt and potent, stiffened Ish'Kara's spine. *Don't play games with me, Baltharak. I have kept my end of the bargain. For over three years now, the thresholds have been open to the other realms. Many of your kind have found corporeal form. Now I await the answers I requested of you.*

Instantly a physical form, ugly and repulsive, materialized on the other side of the gate. The immortal Daemod were not limited to any one physical form.

Rather, they could choose from a repertoire of images and materialize at will—but only for a few moments at a time. For some reason that Ish'Kara had never understood, they seemed to enjoy mixing and matching favorite attributes from a variety of creatures. The result was invariably hideous.

Baltharak had chosen to wear the hind legs of some type of cloven-hoofed grazing animal. His hip area was clothed and appeared to be human. His torso was enormous, thickly muscled and black with two rubbery-looking male breasts. A primate source, Ish'Kara surmised. And his head . . . well, it was impossible to classify. Each feature seemed to have a separate derivation. The nose seemed distinctly snout-like. The eyes pale blue but not human. Equine perhaps. The top of his head seemed covered with glossy black feathers rather than hair. There were no visible ears. Only the shape of the mouth he'd chosen seemed almost human, but his smile negated even that impression, for his teeth were definitely carnivorous.

"So," the creature said. "You still wish to learn the secret of eternal corporeal existence."

Ish'Kara's eyes narrowed. "Of course."

Baltharak grinned evilly and studied her slyly from beneath his feathered brows. "You know that the Daemod are incapable of reproduction unless we breed with willing beings outside our own species?"

Ish'Kara frowned. What was he after now? "I am aware of that. Yes."

"You have chosen a very pleasing form, Ish'Kara. I will give the secret to you if you will bear me a descendant to inherit my kingdom."

Ish'Kara barked a short, discordant laugh. "And you, no doubt, would assume a suitably pleasing form."

"Of course." He leered.

Ish'Kara returned his grin although the expression

did not reach her icy eyes. "Don't be absurd, Baltharak. I do not make deals on top of deals. I have kept my end of the bargain. Now you will keep yours."

Baltharak continued to ogle her. "And if I don't?"

Ish'Kara smiled as though in anticipation. "If you don't, I will enjoy sealing all the gates to the alter-realms and then exorcising your kind from their hosts. With no place to go, trapped between worlds, your immortal kind will be sentenced to hell. *My* kind of hell." Ish'Kara had made it her business to learn much about the Daemod over the centuries. Although the Daemod cared little for anyone or anything—including their own kind—and were among the vilest creatures to populate any dimension, they did have a certain code among themselves. As the being responsible for such mass annihilation among the immortal Daemod, Baltharak would be answerable to the current Daemod dictator and his minions.

Throwing his hands up in rage, Baltharak opened his mouth and began to heap the vilest vituperation upon her as he stalked around in a small circle. The words and sounds he uttered were enough to make even Ish'Kara's skin crawl with revulsion. Yet she held her ground easily. She had been dealing with Baltharak and his kind for too long to be affected. In this meeting, she had the control; she did not fear him.

Finally, when he had vented his rage and anger, he stood and faced her again. "Very well," he said, eyeing her with intense dislike. "But you may not like the answer."

Ish'Kara shrugged. "I certainly don't like waiting for the answer. I have already waited far too long. What is it, Baltharak?"

He watched her closely. "The only means for a species which is not naturally immortal to achieve immortality is to steal the regenerative qualities they need from other beings. This method does, of course, kill the . . . ah, donor. Sometimes very slowly, depending on the feeding method." His beastly eyes twinkled wickedly. "In short, you must become a vampire."

Ish'Kara narrowed her eyes and took a threatening step toward the portal. "You sent me on that vampirism quest before, Baltharak. It didn't work. I want the truth this time."

"Did I?" He seemed legitimately surprised that he might have forgotten something. "Which method?"

"What do you mean, which method?"

"There are many forms of vampirism, my pet. What source of regeneration did I recommend to you?"

"Blood. Preferably human blood, you said."

"Ah, yes." He smirked. "Well, in any case, I didn't lie, Ish'Kara. I rarely lie." He shrugged. "I merely failed to give you all of the necessary details. You see, the blood of corporeal beings *does* contain all that is necessary for another corporeal body to regenerate, and thus live forever. *But,* before the ingestion of the blood takes place, the receiving body must be able to differentiate the regenerative qualities from . . . ordinary food. You did not undergo the process that would have enabled your body to synthesize and use the nourishment you gave it."

Ish'Kara silently cursed him to seven different hells. "What process?" she demanded.

"It's a very painful process of genetic alteration. One which can, I'm told, make your life an eternal living hell depending on the nature and severity of the side effects brought on by the physical transformation."

"You still haven't told me what this process involves," Ish'Kara pointed out with growing impatience. This was taking too long. Soon her lover would wake, and she was no further ahead now than she had been when she began this conversation. "And what are the side effects?"

He waved his strange primate-like hands as though to negate the importance of her query. "I can give you the details on conducting the ritual which initiates the transformation later. As for side effects, by far the most common one is an extreme sensitivity to the purity of sunlight. It can kill."

"The truth, Baltharak," Ish'Kara reminded him. "I know that the aspect of sensitivity to light is merely a component of ancient legends."

Baltharak met her eyes directly for the first time in their conversation. "All legends, no matter what world they come from, have some basis in fact. Ignore that at your peril."

Behind Ish'Kara, bedding rustled as her lover stirred. Baltharak's gaze moved beyond her. He grinned. "He is a stud, Ish'Kara. Your tastes are so predictable. I'm certain that I could assume a form that would be even more pleasing to you." His eyes moved back to her. "And I could pleasure you in ways that no human ever could."

For an instant, Ish'Kara felt a faint stirring in her loins. Anticipation wrought by the husky promise of delicious decadence in his voice. And then she remembered Baltharak's purpose in wanting to bed her. Under no circumstances would she ever bear a non-human child. She'd never even wanted a human one. "Never!"

Baltharak laughed, revealing more of his yellowed carnivorous teeth than Ish'Kara cared to view. "So vehement, my pet? You were tempted, then, weren't you? Just for a moment you longed to experience something new. That's what I love about you, Ish'Kara, your sense of adventure."

She heard the bedding rustle again and sensed awareness returning to her lover's mind. Ignoring Baltharak's taunt, Ish'Kara spoke. "I must go now. I will contact you again soon to conclude this discussion."

Baltharak stopped smiling. "Perhaps I will be available." He shrugged. "Perhaps not."

"You owe me, Baltharak," she hissed.

Baltharak lowered his head in acknowledgment of her statement. "That does not mean that you *own* me, my pet. I am not available to be summoned and dismissed upon your whim."

Every time Cadence glanced at Gildon across the breakfast table, she was reminded of their night together . . . and what they had *not* done. The sight of his large, strong hands selecting some fruit to add to his porridge brought to mind the sensation of them on her body as they kissed. The glimpse of his chest between the folds of his robe reminded her of the sound of his heartbeat and the warm security she'd felt when enfolded in his arms. His eyes, bluer and less shadowed in the light of day, contrasted sharply with her memory of them the night before, glittering with mystery and elusive promise in the moonlight. Just thinking about it made her wish she could roll back time and relive the excitement and anticipation she'd felt the previous evening.

Was he, too, thinking of last night and what might have been, she wondered. He appeared to be deep in thought, but his expression gave no clue as to the direction of his musings. Were her chaotic emotions mirrored in any way? Did she invade his thoughts when he would rather focus on other things? Did thoughts of making love to her, however ill-advised, flash torturously in his mind?

Gildon spoke into the heavy silence, startling her. "I must go to my mother's this morning," he said. "I would like you to come."

So much for mirrored emotions, Cadence thought wryly. She was contemplating seduction, and he was thinking about his mother. Oh well, at least his thoughts had included an invitation for her.

However, if the intense, thoughtful expression on his face was any indication, there was much more on his mind than a simple visit. Nodding slowly, she said, "All right." Then, as she scrutinized his set features she knew she needed more information. "Is there anything in particular I should do to prepare?"

He shook his head. "No, you look fine. However—"

"However?" Cadence prompted.

He cleared his throat. "You should be warned that my mother is a very . . . eccentric woman. Just be yourself and don't worry about offending her. It's almost impossible not to. Simply address her by name: Shaylon. Any attempt to grant her respect by calling her *kaitana* she will merely see as an attempt to flatter and she'll wonder at your purpose."

Cadence observed him. There was still something he wasn't saying, but he'd probably said as much as he intended. "I see. Well, I think I can manage to be myself."

Since Shaylon lived in another apartment within the Temple of the Avatar, they had no need to use one of the transfer portals that Cadence so disliked. As she and Gildon walked the corridors and courtyards, her host remained silent and thoughtful, and Cadence was left free to observe her surroundings undistracted. Not for the first time, she noticed that very few people mixed the colors of their clothing. If they wore green, their entire outfit was green. And here, within the confines of the huge Temple of the Avatar where Gildon made his home, the predominate clothing color was white. She gave the phenomenon a moment of consideration, but no explanation came to her.

"Gildon—"

He looked down at her. "Yes?"

"Is there a reason why so many people wear only one color? Either all green or all white?"

"Here within the inner city, all people wear the color representative of their chosen Order. Green is the color of the Sadhue Order, the healers and medical researchers. Scarlet is the color worn by the Prelates. The Kami warriors wear indigo, the Shido historians orange, and the priests and priestesses of the Avatar white. Each Order, of which there are many, has an indicative color."

"Does the color have any particular significance?"

Gildon shook his head. "Not that I'm aware of, although it may have at one time." It was obvious from the absent manner in which he responded to her query that his mind was elsewhere. Yet Cadence felt she had been inordinately patient in awaiting explanations for all of her questions, and now was as good a time as any.

"All of these Orders are branches within the Temple of the Eidan, correct?"

"Yes. Although the Order of the Avatar also has its own governing body, which permits it to act independently when necessary."

"Why?"

He looked down at her with a slightly startled expression as though he was just becoming aware of the nature of the conversation. "The Order deals with many of the negative aspects of existence, and we investigate the mysteries surrounding them until we gain an understanding of them. An Order with such a purpose cannot exist entirely under the auspices of the Temple of the Eidan, where all energy is aligned with the One and the Light. Our work is sensitive and can lead to misunderstanding. We have been known to make contact with all but the most powerful of dark entities, and we must continue to do so in order to learn about them. We cannot protect our people from entities we don't understand."

Cadence's mouth dropped open and she stopped dead. "You're an Order of witches! Aren't you?"

He frowned. "What are witches?"

Cadence waved her hands in agitation as she sought a description for people she herself had never learned much about. "It's a kind of religion, I guess. Some of them are bad and some are good, just like anybody else. But, from what I understand, some of them affiliate with spirits or entities—some good apparently, but many evil—in an attempt to gain personal power. They use herbs and things a lot, I think. And spells, I believe."

Obviously scandalized and more than a little insulted, Gildon met her gaze. "The priests and priestesses of the Avatar never seek personal power. We seek only to commune with the One. Any affiliation we have with alter-realm entities is in the interest of gaining knowledge and understanding. Nothing more. As a High Priest of the Avatar, I am assigned the task of protecting my people from all things arcane. To do that, I must understand the threat. Do you understand?"

Cadence nodded. "Of course. I didn't mean to offend you."

Gildon shrugged. "You didn't know." They walked on in silence for a short distance. Gildon was once again frowning thoughtfully. Abruptly, he looked down at her and spoke. "What's a spell?"

Cadence grinned wryly. "I think I should just get my computer to translate the entire English dictionary for you. My translations may not be very precise."

"Precision is not always necessary for understanding."

She nodded. "All right. I believe that a spell is an incantation of some kind, an almost nonsensical chant that has no clear meaning but which is supposed to have some kind of power."

Gildon's brows lifted as though she'd made a surprising revelation. "That's very interesting."

"How so?"

"How did the Tesuvian language sound to you when you first heard it?"

"Tranquil and melodic, very chant-like."

"Yes. And we have learned to manipulate the laws of nature with the sounds we produce. Our small children can spark illumination in a dark room. Our builders levitate huge stones into place by combining their psychic abilities with the power of sound." He looked down at her. "Perhaps some remnant of this knowledge remains among your people, misunderstood and powerless now, but reminiscent of times past." He guided her down a corridor to the left. "It's an interesting hypothesis."

Gildon fell silent again, and Cadence's thoughts turned to her own situation. No matter what these people believed, she still could not accept their assertion that she was the answer to some prophecy. Yet Tailen had said they had to determine which of the two women in the prophecy she represented before they'd help her find Chance. She had accepted his edict at the time because she'd had no choice. But she was determined to find some way to convince these people that she had no importance to them. The question was: How?

Gildon drew her to a halt before a carved white door. With a practiced hand, he brushed his fingers over two of the curling embellishments. Two sweeping choruses of notes sounded. But nothing happened to the door; Gildon just stood there.

Cadence looked from him to the door and back again. "Is something wrong?"

He shook his head. "No. It is a courtesy when visiting another's apartment to allow them to complete the sequence authorizing entry. I am waiting for my mother to respond."

"Oh." This was the first time she'd seen a door actually work the way doors did where she came from. A moment later, a note sounded and the door swung open. Placing his hand on the small of her back, Gildon ushered her inside.

Of all the places Cadence had been since arriving on this world, this apartment was the darkest. The walls were still white and the floor tiled, but the lighting was muted.

"I see you've brought the alien." The voice, as strident as the softly inflected Tesuvian language would permit, emanated from a dim corner.

"Yes, Mother." Gildon stepped forward, drawing Cadence with him. "Her name is Cadence. Cadence, I'd like you to meet my mother, Shaylon."

Now that her eyes had adjusted to the dimness, Cadence could see the woman more clearly. Clad in a white robe and trousers similar to those worn by Gildon, she sat on a low cushion with a book resting on her lap. She appeared quite tall and a bit too thin. Her silvery blond hair had been twisted into an elaborate coronet atop her head. Despite the color of her hair, though, had Gildon not introduced her as his mother, Cadence might have been hard-pressed to determine her age. Shaylon's skin remained smooth and unwrinkled. Cadence met her eyes and almost shuddered at the iceberg coldness reflected there.

"I'm pleased to meet you, Shaylon."

Shaylon's lips twisted in a cold imitation of a smile. "You don't know me well enough to know if you'll be pleased you met me yet." Rising, she came toward them. Ignoring her son, she stood in front of Cadence and stared. Cadence was about to look away, to glance at Gildon for an explanation, when Shaylon reached out with both hands. Grasping Cadence's cheeks, she held her still as she stared deeply into her eyes.

The silence stretched. Cadence found herself immobilized by the eye contact, unable to break the invisible link. Finally Shaylon released her. Cadence felt anger stirring within her. She was not some specimen to be examined without her consent. Studying this woman whom she was fast beginning to dislike, Cadence found that displeasure erased all thoughts of protocol. "Did you see something interesting in my eyes?"

Shaylon blinked as though emerging from a trance and, ignoring Cadence's question, looked at her son. "She is not alien. She has a Tesuvian soul." With a disappointed shrug, she turned and walked away.

Cadence looked at Gildon. A frown drew his dark brows together as he stared after his mother. "Did you see anything else?"

Shaylon turned to her son with a smug, spiteful smile. "Find out for yourself." And then her eyes narrowed suspiciously. "What have you come here for?"

"I need to see Father's and Jakial's journals."

She shrugged. "Perhaps Jakial kept none. He knew that others might interpret his work incorrectly or try to use it improperly."

"He never spoke so to me."

Shaylon made no further comment as she turned to search a shelf for something.

Gildon shook his head slightly as if to negate his brief moment of worry. "I'm sure Jakial would have continued to make regular journal entries, no matter how sensitive the nature of his work. He is my father's son, after all."

Shaylon whirled. "He is not your father's son!" The sudden, disharmonious pronouncement hung in the air, stunning them with its venom.

As though instantly regretting her words, Shaylon seated herself and began reorganizing the books and papers on the low table before her.

"What did you say, Mother?" Gildon asked, his

tone—even to Cadence's relatively untrained ear—sounded uncommonly smooth.

Shaylon looked at him with cold, hate-filled eyes. How could a mother look at her son that way, Cadence wondered. She was extremely uncomfortable. "Nothing," Shaylon said. "I misspoke. I will not repeat myself."

"But you will explain." It was not a question, but a statement of fact as Gildon moved forward to stand looking down at his mother.

Shaylon stared at him a moment. Cadence had the distinct and disturbing impression she was trying to decide which would hurt her son most, speaking or staying silent. And she *wanted* to hurt him. Cadence was certain of it.

The woman was a viper. How could she possibly reside in the inner city? According to what Shahra had told her, no one this malicious should have been able to pass through the inner gates. Or was Shaylon's spitefulness directed solely at her second child and thus not truly characteristic of the woman?

Shaylon turned her eyes to Cadence, studied her as though seeking something. "Perhaps it is time for the secretiveness to end," she mused almost absently. Abruptly, she smiled. The expression sent a shiver up Cadence's spine. "I will explain."

Chapter Twelve

Gildon and Cadence took seats on cushions opposite his mother and waited for her to begin. True to Tesuvian custom, but incongruous considering her attitude, she'd insisted on putting out a small repast of cheese and fruit and a decanter of flavored spring water when it became obvious that her guests would be staying more than a few moments. Gildon camouflaged his impatience behind a bland mask. Finally Shaylon seated herself and fixed her zealous gaze upon Cadence and Gildon, in turn.

She studied Gildon as she poured herself a glass of water. "You know that my first love has always been the work of the Avatar," she began. She looked at Cadence, explaining her statement. "The esoteric mysteries of alter-realms and other-dimensional beings fascinated me almost from the time I could speak. I was an adept before I'd reached maturity thanks to the private teachings of my mother. So the possibility of leaving the Temple of the Avatar not only never occurred to me, but was impossible for me.

"Yet when I fell in love with a man of whom the Order didn't approve—a skillful Kami warrior—I was told that was exactly what I would have to do should I accept him as my companion." Her lips twisted with remembered rancor and she intensified her study of Gildon's face. "Are you shocked, my son?"

"Nothing you can say will shock me, Mother." Gildon poured himself a glass of water in an effort to still the trembling anticipation in his gut. He hated her for stirring an emotion he'd thought long dead. Not the hope for a kind or loving gesture, for that hope had died long ago, but the dread. After all these years, she still had the ability to hurt him and, through the anticipation of that pain, induce uneasiness. But he would never let her know she held such power. Never.

Shaylon smiled and glanced at Cadence as though to share a joke with her. "Don't be so sure, my son."

"Continue, Mother."

Shaylon nodded. "The only choice the paranoid old men and women allowed me was to have all knowledge of my career erased, to sacrifice my calling—which was my life—or to give up my love for the man who was my soul. I decided I would do neither.

"In order to keep my career, I agreed to take as companion the man they chose for me, but I knew that I had to taste love in the arms of my lover first. We shared two glorious weeks together before I took Torak to wed. We planned to share more time—circumspectly of course—after a decent interval had passed, but . . . it was not to be."

Deep within himself, Gildon felt his tension growing. He knew what his mother was going to say. Felt it in every fiber of his being; it would explain so much. Yet he didn't want to believe it. Couldn't allow himself to believe it. So he could do nothing but continue to listen to her in silence and pray that his instincts were wrong.

Shaylon met his gaze and he saw amusement in the depths of her eyes—eyes so much like his own. He hated her for the enjoyment she took in stunning him, in destroying the foundation of his world. Remaining outwardly composed and unruffled, he merely raised a brow to encourage her to finish the tale. "And why was it not to be?" he asked quietly.

Her eyes narrowed on his face. "Because on his next campaign, Dahlell was killed." She looked at Cadence, speaking her next words to her. "I was devastated, of course, but had to hide my feelings from Torak, for he knew nothing about Dahlell and would not have understood." She paused and popped a strawberry-like fruit into her mouth. "Then I discovered that Dahlell had left me the greatest gift of all, a part of himself. His child."

His worst fears confirmed, Gildon felt the bottom fall out of his stomach. But before he could voice a thought, Cadence spoke in a softly accented voice, her tone revealing nothing but genuine curiosity. "How did you know the child was Dahlell's and not your companion's?"

Shaylon's suspicious gaze studied her a moment, seeking a possible threat before answering. "I had not yet taken Torak to my bed," she answered bluntly. "After Dahlell, I found the thought of another man touching me repulsive. So I had feigned ill health, hoping that my feelings would change before he grew suspicious."

Although she appeared somewhat surprised, Cadence nodded. "I see."

Shaylon continued. "However, after I discovered my condition, I could delay no longer. Despite my feelings about him, I took Torak to my bed. I could not afford to endanger my position or my child's security by having his paternity in question."

"How could you?" The question, the accusatory exclamation, burst from Gildon's lips despite his intentions.

Shaylon looked at him, a smile of satisfaction upon her lips. "How could I what, my son?"

Gildon ignored her expression. "How could you allow a child of impure bloodlines to be trained in the ways of the Avatar? How could you have taken that risk? Did it not matter to you that he might be too weak to withstand the allure of the dark forces?"

"Jakial is my son." She leaned forward, eyes narrowed. "I am one of the most accomplished Avatarian priestesses that training and bloodlines have ever produced. His father was a Master-Adept of the Kami. Jakial is not weak. His abilities may very well exceed your own, my son." Sighing, Shaylon released some of her tension. "Had I ever doubted the security of our tenets in his hands, I would have turned myself in and driven him from the Temple."

Gildon stared at her. He had no doubt that she meant what she said, for there was nothing she valued more than her vocation. He desperately wanted to share her faith in Jakial, but the very idea went against everything he'd been taught. "And you were certain enough of his strength to risk the principles of a tradition tens of thousands of years old?" Gildon asked in disbelief. "Have you not considered the horror now taking place that began in Madaia, a province under Jakial's jurisdiction? What if the mutterings and rumors have basis in truth?"

"You've always wanted him to fail. Don't think I didn't see your jealousy."

"Have you heard from him? Just once in the four years since the breakdown of order in Madaia, has he contacted you?"

"No." Uncertainty flashed briefly across her features. Suddenly her eyes narrowed maliciously; her lips stretched into a cold smile. "Perhaps you should not be so quick to disclaim him. Can you be so certain of your own paternity, my son?"

Gildon stared at her, unable to contemplate any more. The thought that he, too, might be at risk for alter-realm temptation every time he conducted his work distressed him. And fear, any kind of fear, was lethal for a priest or priestess of the Avatar dealing with powerful other-dimensional beings. They would sense it immediately and use it.

To Gildon's surprise, Cadence spoke into the heated silence, her tone not betraying by the slightest inflection that she was bothered by Shaylon's venom. Did she not fear his mother? But then, she had never betrayed any fear of him either. "I don't believe that Gildon's paternity is truly in question, is it, Shaylon?"

His mother looked at her. "And why do you say that, Cadence?" she asked after a moment's suspicious consideration.

Cadence smiled, a gesture that mimicked Shaylon's for its lack of warmth. "You dislike Gildon too much for him to be anyone but Torak's son."

There was a moment of stunned silence. A hesitation that hinted that perhaps Shaylon would attempt to refute Cadence's statement. Then she laughed. "Very perceptive, Cadence." And she flashed a loathing-filled glance at Gildon. "Every time I look at him, I see . . ."

"Torak?" Cadence prompted.

Shaylon started and surfaced from some distant place. "Yes," she said quickly, solemnly. "Torak." Had her response been too swift? Shaylon was an enigma that defied solution.

"Enough," Gildon said. "I have never had any illusions about your feelings for me, Mother." He rose and stood looking down at her. "And now, more than ever, I need to see the library of Jakial's journals . . . and Father's as well."

"He may have taken them with him."

Gildon looked at her in astonishment. "You would have permitted that?" Traditionally, all journals stayed with the Temple of origin, the place where the research was conducted. If the priest or priestess involved moved on and required the notes, copies were made.

Shaylon merely smiled in answer to his question, and Gildon realized she would have permitted Jakial anything that did not directly threaten the Temple of the Avatar or their people. He could only hope that their father's teachings—correction: *his* father's teachings—had been strong enough that Jakial had observed the principles involved.

Gildon looked down at Cadence. "I will be back shortly, and then we will take our leave." She nodded, and he turned toward the library, which occupied a circular chamber in the center of the apartment in which he'd been raised.

As soon as Gildon had left the room, Shaylon looked at Cadence. "Do you love my son?"

Cadence stared at her. What motivation did Shaylon have for asking such a question? "I care for Gildon," she responded cautiously.

Shaylon studied her through narrowed eyes, as though seeking something more. Finally she murmured, "Then I will continue to hope."

Hope for what, Cadence wondered. Shaylon didn't care for Gildon, so why did she seem concerned with his love life? "I haven't known Gildon long enough to fall in love with him," Cadence remarked, hoping to spark a response that would give her some clue as to Shaylon's true feelings.

"Nonsense! Love can happen in a minute or a decade. It can last a few months or a few centuries. It depends upon the people involved."

Cadence frowned slightly, wondering at the undercurrent in Shaylon's conversation. What did she know? "And you think Gildon and I could have fallen in love so quickly?"

Shaylon shrugged. "Many women seem to find my son attractive." Her tone was dismissive.

In an odd way, Cadence felt she was beginning to

understand Shaylon. She was a woman who had allowed bitterness to poison her life. She wasn't the first person to do so, and wouldn't be the last. How different might she be today if she'd been permitted to take the man she loved as a companion? It was a question that would never have an answer. And because of that, three people's lives had been miserable: Shaylon's own, her husband's, and her son's.

"May I ask you a question?" Cadence asked abruptly.

Shaylon eyed her suspiciously for a moment. Finally she nodded. "Perhaps I will answer."

"Why do you consistently call Gildon *my son* in such a derisive manner?"

The older woman smiled. "Because he is my son in every way. He is hard and cold, brilliant and determined. He may not be the son of my heart, but he is more my son than Torak's. There is great irony in that." Her lips twisted. "I always appreciate irony."

Cadence's heart lurched with pity for the little boy that Gildon had been. What must it have done to him emotionally to grow up with the awareness that his mother didn't love him?

Suddenly it was Cadence who turned suspicious eyes on her hostess. Why had she chosen today to break thirty years of silence? Why do so in front of a stranger? Cadence was certain that she'd had a reason. But what was it? Shaylon struck her as the type of person who rarely acted on impulse. Suddenly the implication struck her.

"You're afraid you're wrong, aren't you? Afraid that something has gone wrong with Jakial? You chose this way to warn Gildon."

Her face frozen in a mask that revealed nothing, Shaylon held her silence.

"Why did you choose today to break your silence? Why in my presence?"

"Assurance, perhaps." Shaylon shrugged. "Warning."

Her statement made absolutely no sense. Why would Cadence need either assurance or warning? Shaylon must have meant something else, but there was no time to ask, for just then Gildon returned to the chamber with an armload of books.

He looked at his mother. "I found a number of Jakial's journals," he said. "I'll take them home to study and return them when I have finished."

His mother lowered her head in a sharp nod. "As you wish." As though dismissing them, she picked up her book and returned to her reading.

Although Cadence walked at Gildon's side through the corridors as they returned to his home, her mind stayed in the apartment they'd just left. "Gildon—"

He looked down at her, his storm-hued eyes shuttered and wary. As if he expected her to ask him questions he had no desire to answer. "Yes?"

Cadence forged ahead. "What did Shaylon mean when she said I had a Tesuvian soul?"

He shrugged and continued walking. "She believes you are the reincarnation of a Tesuvian. My mother swears she has always had the ability to see into a person's soul." He hesitated and then shrugged again. "There is no way to verify her claim, but she seems to have been correct on a number of occasions."

Cadence frowned. Reincarnation again.

As soon as the door was secured behind Gildon and Cadence, Shaylon rose and made her way into her bedchamber. Crossing the mosaic floor, she entered her dressing room and moved directly to the back, to a blank wall of white brick. After glancing once over her shoulder to ensure that she remained alone in this solitary apartment, she began pulling on one of the bricks. When it finally came free in her hand, she dropped it to the floor as she peered into the small dark hole created by its removal. Slowly, uncertainly, she reached into the small chasm and groped around. Her fingers touched something. She went absolutely still—hesitating.

It had been so many years.

Closing her eyes and holding her breath, she carefully removed the small book from its place of concealment. Holding it reverently in her hands, she moved toward her bed and ascended the two steps to sit upon it. Laying the small volume in her lap, she caressed it with gentle hands.

It was the only thing she had left of Dahlell. Its red satin binding was worn, frayed at the edges and faded with age, yet she fancied it still carried his scent. The journal was a piece of him, carrying on its aged pages his most private thoughts. The rainbow-hued verse revealed his character in his choice of wording and description. And yet his poet's soul had found the modern color blocks confining and he'd regularly slipped into usage of the symbols and runes that formed the more ancient, but still viable, Tesuvian handwritten script.

She sought strength, and opened the small book at random. Her eyes found the page. The words inscribed upon its surface spoke of a young warrior's hopeless love for a young woman forbidden to care for him.

Tears held in abeyance for nearly two decades seared her eyes. No! She hadn't cried in too many years to count. She would not waste energy on tears now.

Lowering her head in sudden determination, she flipped pages, searching for a particular entry. The entry which she'd allowed to guide so much of her life. What if she'd been wrong to let it influence her so? What if she'd interpreted it incorrectly? How could she live with herself?

The mere thought was so agonizing that she shoved it away, unable to face it.

Ah, there it was. Shortly before their first physical union, Dahlell had gone to the Lidai Order to have his future foretold. Although he'd never told her of it, he'd recorded the results in his journal. Only after his death, when she'd read the account of the predictions made for him, had she learned that he'd known that a long-term association between them was doomed.

She scanned the page until she came to the portion that had changed her own life. *And you shall love only one woman in your life. Though she is not for you, she will bear a son of your loins, and the son of another. The brothers will grow to be strong and powerful men, giving the appearance of shared purpose. This will not be so, for both play a part in the destiny of our people. He that is noble of heart and is best loved will be the savior's strength. And he that is plagued by envy and ambition, and is weak of heart will be the demon's tool.*

Dahlell had paused here in his recording of the prophecy to inscribe a personal note. *At this point in the foretelling,* he wrote, *the priest seemed very anxious to discover the name of the woman I loved. I could not bear the thought of gentle Shaylon being subjected to interrogation, and thus lied, telling them I had not met her yet. I feel certain the One will forgive such a small mistruth.*

Shaylon sighed. *Gentle Shaylon,* he'd written. She'd forgotten his view of her. Had she ever been gentle? Or was it simply that Dahlell's love had prevented him from seeing her as she was? She suspected it was the latter. If they had become companions, would time and familiarity eventually have killed their passionate young love?

It was possible, she conceded. Time had dulled her own passion. She had even grown to respect Torak over time, although she had always disliked the physical side of their relationship. But he had not been a demonstrative man, and his physical needs were often outweighed by his passion for his work, so he had seldom initiated sex. In fact, for years it had seemed that they had been more strangers to each other than companions, often going days at a time without sharing more than a few words. Yet he had been an admirable and commanding man and a good father. His death had affected her more than she'd imagined possible. In hindsight, she realized that she had lost a friend.

She shook her head, dispelling the memories and focusing again on the small portion of Dahlell's prophecy that pertained to her and her sons. When she had read it originally, she'd done so from a mother's perspective, with love and bitterness clouding her judgment. But the prophecy had been written for Dahlell, who would have been hindered by no such emotion. And since the prophet had undoubtedly seen Dahlell's death, neither would it have been foretold with Dahlell as a participant, for he did not live long enough to love his child.

It was that realization that, just recently, had begun to frighten Shaylon. Only now that time had dulled her pain and bitterness was she capable of looking beyond her own feelings. If the prophecy had spoken in generalities, as she now suspected, then the *best loved* of her two sons was Gildon.

He had been a terribly introverted child, standing on the outside . . . alone, looking on. But when other children did seek him out, it was because they genuinely liked him. In contrast, Jakial would march into a group of children and take control, force them to accept him into their games. He had never lacked playmates, but he had been feared and respected more than loved. Even her mother's eyes had recognized that.

She had often seen Jakial paving the way for a more hesitant Gildon to join a group of children, and

196

thought him such a selfless child. Had she been wrong? Had he had less altruistic motives for his actions? Had he merely sought to experience vicariously the emotions that were always directed at Gildon and never at him: liking and acceptance?

By the One! What if she had made a terrible mistake? What if her distaste for a child who would succumb to the call of darkness had been visited upon the wrong son? Even now, her heart swore that Jakial was all she could have asked for in a son, but her intellect was no longer so convinced.

She stared sightlessly across the room. Very soon now, she would know for certain. And she was terrified of that knowledge. With worry for the future bowing her proud shoulders, Shaylon rose and placed the small journal on her dressing table. There was no need to hide it anymore. The prophecy was in motion.

As they approached the door to his apartment, Gildon, still laden with an armload of books, entreated Cadence to open the door.

"What do I do?" she asked. Although she'd seen Gildon open the door a number of times, she'd never bothered to memorize the precise sweep of his fingers on the ornate design. Now she followed his directions and felt a small sense of triumph as the alien door disappeared.

Gildon stepped into the apartment and strode toward the table, where he deposited his burden. "I have much to do today."

Turning, he seemed surprised to see her just behind him. Now he stared down at her with a hint of confusion in his expression, as though he couldn't remember what he'd been about to say. His eyes swept her features. Blue flame flared in his irises. The hint of disorientation, if it had really been there, faded from his expression.

Christine Michels

Suddenly there were only the two of them, a male and a female. Passion arced between them with potent magnetic force, drawing them inexorably together, holding them within its powerful grasp. Gildon's lips closed over hers, and the floor swung away beneath her feet.

Yes! This is what she wanted. What she had wanted ever since last evening.

It was wonderful! Exhilarating! And very addictive.

And yet, even as Cadence succumbed wholeheartedly to the drugging intensity of his embrace, she felt him putting the brakes on, drawing away. Opening her eyes, she looked up. His storm-hued eyes were once again shuttered and distant.

Damn him! How could he be so in control when she felt as though her blood had turned to liquid fire? It wasn't fair. She wanted to scream in disappointment. Indignation clawed at her and hovered on the tip of her tongue. She refused to speak the words, refused to add to his power over her by letting him know how much he affected her. With pride stiffening her spine, she backed away as though his withdrawal meant nothing.

"I need to begin studying these journals immediately," he remarked into the silence. Was there a trace of strain in his voice? Stars, she hoped so, she dearly hoped so. "I will need to postpone further lessons for a while."

Further lessons? Was that what this had been? A lesson? "I see." It couldn't be true, could it? But the suspicion wouldn't go away. She had to know. "And are these kisses we share—the ones that you immediately pretend haven't happened—a part of my education?" She stalked away from him as she spoke, distancing herself. Pivoting, she faced him again and continued without missing a beat. "What are you trying to do? Determine just how much sexual frustra-

tion I can endure?" She immediately regretted that
last sentence; it revealed too much, but she couldn't
call it back, so she merely raised her chin and waited
for his response.

"Sexual frustra—" Mouth open, he stared at her.
And then, suddenly, he seemed engrossed in the details of the raised carving on the wall. He cleared his
throat. "I don't understand what has made you suspect such a thing, Cadence. The . . . kisses have nothing to do with your lessons."

He sounded as though the words were strangling
him. Why? Was he lying? "Then why do you keep
stopping? What is going on?"

His gaze returned to her almost challengingly. "I
can remember one instance when it was you who
broke off the kiss."

"Don't try to change the subject. I want an explanation."

He sighed, obviously extremely uncomfortable.
"What exactly do you want to know?"

"I've already told you. Tell me why you kiss me if
you have no desire to . . . go beyond that."

He turned away from her and strode to the window overlooking the city. "I kiss you because . . . I
desire you very much. You are a beautiful woman."

She took up a position at his side and touched his
arm, drawing his eyes down to hers. "So what's the
problem? And don't hand me that noble platitude
about my needing a friend."

For the first time, the shutters completely disappeared from his eyes. She saw pain in their depths.
"I am a priest of the Avatar, Cadence. As you heard
earlier today, I am not permitted to take a companion outside the temple. I will not break the tenets
with which I've been raised." He looked away again,
staring out over the city.

Cadence frowned, trying to understand his explanation, trying to equate Tesuvian customs with her

own life experience. "So you've never been with a woman outside your own temple?"

Surprise widened his eyes. "Your questions are becoming very personal."

Cadence remained unrepentant. "I'm not Tesuvian, remember. I'm trying to understand."

He considered her silently for a moment. "I have had partners outside the temple occasionally," he conceded finally, "but since I am not permitted to take a companion among them, I make certain that the relationship remains casual. Now do you understand?"

Yes, she understood. She understood that because of his tenets, no matter how she felt about him, they could have no future. She understood that he was trying to protect her, to keep her from developing deep feelings for him which could only cause her pain. She understood that it was already too late, and she felt absurdly close to tears. But she voiced none of this. Nodding, she merely said, "Yes."

Some of the tension eased from his features. "Later, when I have completed some of my research, I will introduce you to the Order of the Shajati."

"What's that?"

A peculiar expression lit his eyes. "It is best shown." He cleared his throat. "And now I really must attend to some things. Do you require some reading to occupy your time?"

She contemplated him, caressing his handsome features with her eyes. It was amazing how much more you wanted something after you'd been told you couldn't have it, she mused. "No," she responded aloud. "I still have a couple of books that Shahra left me."

He nodded without comment and, retrieving the volumes he'd put on the low table, made his way toward the stairs to his lower-level study. Cadence observed his exit with a wry twist of her lips. Life was certainly perverse.

After making her way to her suite, she lay down to labor her way through one of the books Shahra had left. However, the dry historical reading combined with her weak reading skills, which lagged far behind her aural skills, soon killed her interest. Finally she rose and, taking her duffel bag from the closet, began to sort through its contents. Where was that Fortunan report on Chance's disappearance? Surely there'd be some hint as to where she should begin her own investigation.

It was mid-afternoon. Gildon had not bothered to break for lunch for two reasons: One, he needed to find the information about the ancient Tesuvian name *Ish'Kara* as quickly as possible. And two, he wanted to avoid Cadence. It had been difficult enough to keep her from his thoughts when he hadn't been altogether certain of her feelings toward him. Now that he knew she would welcome him into her bed, the task was virtually impossible. Seeing her over lunch would only have intensified the torment.

He decided that he, too, would take advantage of the sensual skills of the Shajati when he escorted Cadence to the temple this evening.

Shaking his head as though to dispel the thoughts that consistently disrupted his concentration, Gildon focused on the book before him and turned a page of his father's journal. *Ish'Kara*. The name fairly jumped out at him. He leaned forward, eagerly scanning the reference. It didn't say much, just that Ish'Kara was an ancient Tesuvian soul who had been born into many incarnations. Unlike most souls, she appeared to retain useful memory of her previous lives.

Gildon read ahead, hoping for more details. Nothing. But a footnote directed him to another reference, and that led to another volume, until throughout the afternoon he devoured all of the cross-referenced notes left by his father mentioning Ish'Kara.

An hour later, Gildon sat back to stare sightlessly at the wall. Torak had first heard the name Ish'Kara while in contact with a Daemod being from whom he'd hoped to learn more about parallel planes. He had recognized the appellation immediately as a Tesuvian name and had thought that perhaps the Daemod had been in contact with a colleague within the Order. The Daemod being was extremely reticent about disclosing more information, but a little persistence did reveal one very interesting and heretofore unheard-of detail: Ish'Kara had joined the Daemod on their plane in spiritual form. Faced with a puzzle beyond the scope of his learning, Torak visited the Lidai Order. It was there that he'd learned about Ish'Kara.

Not all souls were recognizable or traceable; in fact, the majority were not. But in each generation a few people destined for greatness, or notoriety, are born. Many of these strong souls carry their distinct potential, whether for good or evil, into the next incarnation. The ten High Priests of the Lidai Order—whose education included the tracing of such souls as an integral part of infant-naming ceremonies—were fairly proficient at recognizing many of these ancient souls. Ish'Kara was one such being.

Over time, it had become apparent to the Lidai High Priests that this soul consistently worked against the will of the One, aligning herself with evil entities and dark forces in the eternal pursuit of her own plans. Resurgence of the Vradir cult often coincided with her existence. When this was brought to the attention of the Tridon—the three most enlightened High Priests within the Temple of the Eidan—her name had been struck from the naming books, ensuring that no child would ever again be burdened with the inauspicious name Ish'Kara.

Eventually, it seemed, Ish'Kara's soul had ceased to be reincarnated, for she had not been heard from or identified in some time—until his father's discovery.

Who was Ish'Kara? And why was Cadence dreaming of her? Was it a warning from the Empyrean guardians? Was Ish'Kara the female who would be instrumental in their destruction? The prophecy had predicted two *alien* women. Could Ish'Kara be considered alien? So many questions. And another query, even more important to him on a personal level: Why was there still an association in his mind between the name Ish'Kara and Jakial?

The tower windows had been shuttered against the waning light of day. Ish'Kara sat in the darkness, enfolded by it, as comfortable in its black anonymity as a child in the womb. Not usually given to introspection, she now forced herself to look back over her existence. She sought out the errors she had made in her quest for physical immortality, analyzed them, castigated herself mercilessly. Underestimating her opponent had been her biggest mistake.

Ali'Yah. She narrowed her eyes in remembrance.

They had been sisters in one long-ago incarnation. When it became apparent that her sister would not join her in her quest and was, in fact, working to destroy her, Ish'Kara had struck back. Luring Ali-'Yah's lover to her quarters, she had drugged him, recorded his seduction for Ali'Yah to savor at her leisure—Ish'Kara's white teeth flashed in the darkness in appreciation of her own sarcasm—and then she had killed him. Regretfully, of course. Kadar was a handsome man. But his nauseatingly principled and incorruptible character had made it necessary.

However, she had miscalculated. Her action,

rather than cowing her soft-hearted and virtuous sister, as she had believed it would, had spurred Ali'Yah to new lengths. Her darling little sister and her so-righteous followers had destroyed, not only themselves, but an entire continent to prevent Ish'Kara from achieving her goals. Such sacrifice was beyond Ish'Kara's comprehension. Why would anyone go to such effort when it was so much easier to join her?

In each incarnation where they had met in opposition, it had been that same lack of comprehension which had defeated her, she realized. Her only consolation came from the knowledge that neither had Ali'Yah ever won one of their confrontations. It appeared that the Fates had paired them well for this eternal contest: So evenly matched were they that they invariably perished together.

This time, in the event that her plans for assassination failed—as they had in the past—she must know her opponent well. Surprisingly, Ali'Yah's soul apparently inhabited a non-Tesuvian for this confrontation. What did the Empyrean guardians have to gain by such an unusual maneuver?

A moment later, she shook her head. The convoluted reasoning of such beings eluded her. Any doubts she had had about Ali'Yah's form in this existence, however, had been appeased by Jakial's description of the result of his attempt to probe the alien woman's mind. She had to be Ali'Yah.

Ish'Kara intoned a note, and the darkness in the chamber retreated before the sudden flaring of phosphorescent crystals. She had made her decision.

As always, it would be most prudent of her to attempt the assassination of her nemesis before Ali-'Yah regained the full memory of her past lives and the nature of her association with Ish'Kara. Or was that the guardian's purpose behind the alien incarnation? Perhaps, in this foreign woman, Ali'Yah's memories had not come to her slowly over a lifetime of experience as they would have in a Tesuvian re-incarnation. Perhaps this woman already possessed complete knowledge of their past—as did Ish'Kara herself.

The possibility annoyed her. She really must investigate Ali'Yah, come to know her in this incarnation. Discover her weaknesses and failings. She would watch her. Closely.

Chapter Thirteen

It was early evening when Gildon led Cadence across the huge central square toward a low, sprawling building. Its entrance, unlike those of most of the other buildings, was barely above ground level. Hanging baskets brimming with colorful flowers adorned its gleaming white facade, but there were no symbols or signs to indicate that this edifice housed a branch of the Temple of the Eidan calling itself the Order of the Shajati. In fact, Cadence discovered, none of the buildings in the square displayed any recognizable form of identification.

Gildon strode silently at her side. All through the evening meal he'd remained silently thoughtful, and perhaps a bit troubled. Although now she could only see his face in profile, the tense set of his jaw hinted that he was no further ahead for all his thought. That being the case, she felt no compunction about intruding on his reflections.

"How do you know which buildings belong to which Order?" she asked.

He surfaced from some distant place. "Pardon me?" The shadows in his eyes darkened his storm-hued irises to the color of night.

Cadence wished that he would talk to her, share whatever burden he carried. But she knew he still didn't trust her completely, so she merely repeated her query.

"The layout of the Temple of the Eidan is something we simply know," he responded. "For our entire recorded history, the smaller temples have been constructed according to the same design." He waved in the direction of the stone wall separating the inner city from the rest of Jafna. "However, buildings in the central and outer areas of the city are differentiated by the sculpting on their facades. For example, a public lodging will have a scene of an oasis sculpted to the right of the door, a personal domicile will have a kitchen scene, and so on."

"Why wouldn't a personal residence have a scene of a family? You'd think that would be more obvious."

He shrugged. "Perhaps, but very few Tesuvians are audacious enough to create images of themselves, even in abstract."

Cadence looked around with newly opened eyes. That was what was so different. Why hadn't she seen it before? There were no images of people anywhere. Inanimate objects aplenty, a few animals and birds, but no paintings or sculptures or statues of people. "How much audacity does someone need to have a picture of himself?"

Gildon grasped her arm to lead her up the few steps to the double doors of the building. "Considerable. Particularly in these times. For a while, a sense of security allowed some families to begin keeping images of each other, but I believe that most of those have now been destroyed."

"Why?"

He looked directly at her, impressing upon her the importance of his next statement. "Each reproduction captures something inherent to that person and no other. Our history tells us that it is possible for certain alter-realm entities to seek out and possibly control a person through such visual representations. With alter-realm contact, like your experience with the Gou'jiin, increasing on a daily basis, despite all efforts to the contrary, it is not wise to take chances." He halted before the double doors of the building and ran his hands over a pair of designs on the left door. Following the invariable musical notes, the doors opened inward.

They entered another world.

Delicate wind chimes overhead lilted softly, echoing throughout the large foyer. Immediately before them were a small waterfall and pond that appeared to have been transplanted intact from some pristine mountain glade. Clinging to the wet stones, blooming plants perfumed the air with the subtle fragrance of their waxy white flowers.

Cadence sniffed appreciatively. "This is beautiful." She flicked her gaze toward her escort. "So what is the prime purpose of the Order of the Shajati?" she asked. "Gardening?"

Gildon's teeth flashed. "That is a part of what they do. The Shajati are dedicated to the sensual arts. Music, massage, aromas, art, and many other things, including certain types of gardening. All things that appeal to the senses. The priests and priestesses of the Shajati believe that when the physical body has achieved sensual bliss, we are only one step away from spiritual enlightenment."

"I see." Cadence looked around. Two wide, roughly circular corridors that looked as though they'd been carved from gray stone by ancient glacial streams led off to the right and left. No one was in sight. "And what are we doing here?"

"We are here to relax."

At that moment a young woman emerged from the corridor on their right. She flashed Gildon a wary glance before smiling and dipping her head respectfully. "My name is Lantah. Come with me." She had the most tranquil and musical voice that Cadence had yet heard. She wondered if the Shajati trained its members in fashioning their voices into instruments of sensuous pleasure as well. Probably.

"The baths are wonderful tonight," Lantah said as Cadence and Gildon followed her down the corridor. "The *zatina* are in full bloom this night."

Cadence raised a questioning brow. Lantah must have caught the gesture, for she immediately spoke. "I apologize, kaitana. I forgot that you are a stranger to our world. The fragrance of the *zatina* has a mild sedative influence that works to release physical and mental tension. They only bloom five nights a month."

A moment later she halted before an ornately carved luminous mauve door and turned to Cadence. "This bathing chamber is free, kaitana. Would you like someone to assist you with your bath?" She ran her hand over a couple of the scrolling ornamentations, unlocking the door. It immediately disappeared.

"No. Thank you."

Lantah dipped her head in acknowledgment. "Enjoy the mineral waters, kaitana. I'll come to take you to your masseuse in an hour."

"I'll see you later," Gildon murmured, his expression curiously intent. "Enjoy yourself."

Cadence smiled. A warm mineral bath and a massage? She'd never been so pampered. It sounded heavenly. "I will. Thank you."

Cadence entered the chamber and, a moment later, the door reappeared behind her. Slowly she moved forward. Here too the designers had sought to replicate nature. The lighting simulated the diffused illumination of sunlight permeating a glade through a forest of leafy trees. Centrally located and set in the center of a thick green carpet crafted to mimic the most delicate grass, the bath itself was a huge, rough-hewn, stone bowl. Steam rose from its surface, and Cadence could just make out a set of stone steps that led down into its bubbling depths.

She didn't have to look for the *zatina*. The small mauve-colored flowers on their lush green vines seemed to cloak almost every surface of the stone walls. Their fragrance, subtle and enchanting, permeated the room. It was indeed soothing.

Stepping nearer the pool, Cadence noticed that a bright emerald robe had been laid out for her to use when she left the small pool. Its fabric shimmered with the luster of satin. A number of ornate glass dishes along the perimeter of the bath held soap crystals of varying colors and scents.

Smiling in anticipation, Cadence removed her gown and underclothing, folded them and placed them on shelves apparently designed for that purpose, and then stepped down into the pool. The warm water crept up her thighs and stomach with an almost tranquilizing caress. Finding a small seat carved into the stone along the wall of the pool, Cadence reclined and immersed herself neck deep.

Heaven! She'd just lie there and enjoy it for a few moments.

She awoke with a start some time later. What had awakened her so suddenly when she'd been so relaxed? Low, sensuous music that hadn't been playing when she'd drifted into a half-waking doze filled the chamber with its delicate, soothing strains, but she knew instinctively that the music was not the reason she sought.

Her Stellar Legion-honed senses told her that all was not as it should be.

She reached for a container of soap crystals, using the maneuver as a pretext for scrutinizing the entire room. Nothing. Her scalp tingled, the small hairs on the nape of her neck rose.

She was being watched. But from where? On a world where the extraordinary was common, the idea of a peephole in the wall seemed almost too mundane. Here it was accepted that you might meet up with a smokey entity who would take possession of your body, or a see-through human form who took perverse pleasure in scaring you to death. That awareness left her at a loss to determine what form of prying tactics might be in use.

Stars! Listen to her. Listen to what she had come to accept. Why wasn't she stark, raving mad?

Slowly soaping her body, she scanned the room again. As she did, she felt a gradual reduction in the tension. Whoever the voyeur had been, he or she was gone now. "I hope you enjoyed yourself," Cadence called out quietly but sarcastically in English.

She had barely completed her bath when Lantah returned. "Your masseuse is ready for you, kaitana."

Moments later, in a room decorated exclusively in white and sea-green, Cadence lay on her stomach on a comfortable table while the masseuse, Lynor, massaged aromatic oils into her skin. Soft, relaxing music filled the chamber and low, blue-tinted lighting soothed the senses. Soon there was not an ounce of tension in her. Her eyes drifted closed; it was simply too much effort to keep them open. She had never felt more completely serene.

Suddenly there was a subtle change in the soft flow of the air currents in the room. Had somebody come in? Despite her languor, her combat-honed senses refused to allow her to ignore the intimated change. She pried her eyes open and . . . screamed.

"Stars above!" Frantically reaching behind herself, almost bowling over Lynor in the process, she grabbed the silky green robe and draped it over her naked body as well as possible. Once she realized what Cadence was attempting, the masseuse aided her in her endeavors.

A little less exposed now, Cadence felt marginally more comfortable in facing the five G-string-clad men who stood before her, although she was hard-pressed not to gape. "Can somebody please tell me what is going on here?" she managed to ask.

Lynor moved forward to stand looking down at Cadence with puzzlement in her eyes. "Do you not wish to chose a lover for the evening, kaitana?"

"You're joking!"

Lynor frowned slightly. "No, kaitana. We have found that certain tensions can only be satisfied completely by taking a lover. Are you not aware of this?"

Cadence's mind remained fastened on a single concept. "A lover!"

She gaped; she couldn't help it. The men standing before her ranged from rather ordinary in appearance to downright spectacular. And the G-strings left no doubt as to their qualifications for the position in question.

"Yes, kaitana." Lynor patiently repeated her explanation. "One of the final steps in releasing the tension from the body is the achievement of sexual fulfillment. Any one of these brothers of Shajati would be happy to aid you in this endeavor. You need only choose."

Cadence grinned. This entire episode was taking on the aspect of a farce. "Just one?" she asked, injecting as much drollery into her tone as the Tesuvian language would allow. It was wasted.

Lynor's eyes widened. "You would wish more than one?"

Cadence grimaced and flicked another glance at the most spectacular representative of the Shajati before her. In her opinion, even he didn't measure up to Gildon.

Gildon! This visit had been his idea. *This* had been his solution to her untimely proclamation of sexual frustration earlier today. Damn him! She waffled between acute embarrassment, righteous anger, and self-deprecatory amusement.

"No, actually," Cadence responded finally. "I don't wish any of them."

"You find none of my brothers pleasing?"

Cadence met Lynor's troubled gaze and realized that she could not hold these people at fault for her predicament—not even Gildon. The Temple of the Shajati was simply a component of their world, much as erotica booths were a part of hers. And although she had never deigned to make use of an erotica booth, she knew many people who had and she had never faulted them for finding sexual release in a manner that was safe and hurt nobody. "It's not that I don't find your colleagues . . . um, pleasing, Lynor. It's just that, where I come from, we only seek sexual release with our companions." The statement was only a partial mistruth: It was true for her, even if it wasn't true for every member of her society.

"This is so for us as well, if we have companions. But you have no companion here," Lynor argued logically.

"True." Cadence shrugged. "I guess I'll just have to wait until I do."

In that moment, with Lynor staring at her as though she had two heads, Cadence felt more alien than she had at any other time since her arrival. Did everyone here avail themselves of the sexual release to be found in the Temple of the Shajati?

Did Gildon? Was Gildon even now finding release in the arms of some lissome, shapely Shajati priestess? The thought hurt more than she would have thought possible; jealousy rose within her, naked and spiteful. She choked it back. She had no right to be jealous. In fact, she had no rights at all where he was concerned.

Gildon lay beneath the ministering hands of his own masseur, thinking of Cadence. He'd never wanted to be a priest of the Shajati so badly in his life. Or, failing that, an aromatic oil. Anything to be with Cadence, touching her, listening to her breathing quicken with passion, watching the pulse pounding in her delicate throat. He wanted to caress her soft, wild-honey skin. Plunge his tongue into her mouth and hear her moan in surrender.

A cry split the air, startling him from his tormenting daydream. It had to be Cadence. Nobody else in this temple of pleasure would scream. What was wrong?

"Where is Cadence?" he demanded anxiously of the masseur he knew as Kenlon.

The young priest, his own eyes reflecting curiosity, didn't bother pretending he didn't know of whom Gildon spoke. "She is two chambers ahead on the right, kaitan."

Dismissing Kenlon, Gildon hastily donned his trousers and raced down the corridor, praying that he was not too late to protect her from whatever horror had found her in this place. By the One! He'd been certain she would be safe here.

He reached the chamber door just as five young men began exiting the chamber. By their expressions, they looked a bit confused but not alarmed in any way. Gildon looked past them into the chamber. Cadence sat upon the massage table with her back to him. She was just plunging her arms into an emerald satin robe.

Puzzled, he stepped into the room. Seeing no cause for alarm, he fastened his gaze on Cadence, who had not noticed his presence although the masseuse nodded faintly in his direction. "I'm sorry, Lynor," Cadence was saying. "It is not your fault, nor the fault of . . . your brothers, but I just can't. . . ." She waved one hand expressively, although Gildon had a moment's difficulty in interpreting the gesture. "Not with a man I don't know."

Gildon felt a curious lightness flare to life somewhere in the region of his heart. Despite her sexual frustration, she did not wish to avail herself of the release available to her. But why had she screamed?

"Cadence—"

She started and looked over her shoulder. "Oh, Gildon." A flush rose to her face.

"You screamed."

Her color deepened even more. "Actually, I thought it was more of a yell than a scream."

Gildon raised a questioning brow.

Cadence shrugged. "I'm sorry. I was just startled."

"By what?"

Cadence looked to Lynor for help. "The kaitana was alarmed when she opened her eyes and saw five men in the room, kaitan. That's all."

"I see." In the guise of assuring himself as to her health, his eyes swept Cadence again, but deep within himself he knew that he merely wanted to memorize her as she was now. The shimmering emerald robe clung to her lithe body in all the right places and intensified the green of her eyes. Her light ash brown hair, still damp from her bath, framed her face in riotous little curls. The fragrance of the oils on her skin, released by her body heat, reached out to him, coiled around him and sought to draw him closer. He resisted. "You wish to leave, then?"

Her eyes clung to his face for a moment. "If you don't mind. Yes."

"I don't mind. I will meet you in the outer foyer when I've dressed."

Ish'Kara sat naked—her preferred state—watching the setting sun. Ali'Yah was different this time. She couldn't quite put her finger on *how* she differed, but she knew it was so. A result of this alien incarnation, no doubt.

From the woman's relaxed attitude, Ish'Kara was almost certain she was not yet cognizant of her more ancient identity. Now would be the best time to arrange an assassination. If she could do it quickly, before Ali'Yah gained awareness, the battle would be easily won and she'd extinguish Ali'Yah's opposition before it began.

If only she dared go herself into the enemy camp, but she could not. There was too much at stake. And not even she, with a few millennia of experience to draw upon, was invincible.

She would need to make her plans quickly, yet she lacked sufficient knowledge to do so. She needed to know Ali'Yah's schedule or, lacking that, habits. Who and what had meaning to her? With whom did she associate? Was there any place she went alone?

Ish'Kara compressed her lips. She would make another psychic visit tonight. It would have to be thorough, for she didn't intend to make another.

Sensing movement across the room, she knew without looking that Jakial had risen from his desk to approach her. He worked so diligently, poring over ancient tomes in an attempt to garner all the knowledge she already possessed. Yet Jakial felt compelled to learn these things for himself. She had no quarrel with his purpose as long as he didn't attempt to turn his increasing knowledge against her.

Jakial's hands alighted gently on her shoulders and began massaging the tension from the muscles. "You look worried, my darling. Is there anything I can do to help?"

She shook her head. "Not unless you know of a way to isolate Ali'Yah before she gains the full knowledge of her identity. I want her assassinated. Soon."

Jakial moved around to face her. His longish, dark brown hair, having escaped the queue at the nape of his neck, curled attractively around his aggressive masculine features. His granite eyes were as hard as the stone whose color they mimicked. She had never been able to read him as well as she would have liked. Not without going to the effort of a mental scan. However, when she had scanned him, his thoughts had never disappointed her. In fact, at times she almost believed that he felt more strongly about her than she about him.

"I'll think about it and see if I can come up with something," he said. He trailed his hands down from her shoulders over her naked breasts, and Ish'Kara felt a quickening in her loins. A delightfully wicked glint flared in his eyes as he moved around her and gently spread her legs so he could kneel between them. "And if there's anything I can do for you, you have only to ask. I am your humble servant. You know that." He plucked gently at her erect nipples. "Anything coming to mind?"

Ish'Kara laughed. Jakial could always make her laugh; she loved that about him. "Show me what you have in mind," she directed. "Perhaps it will prove to be a shared vision."

Some time later, Jakial cradled Ish'Kara on his lap. "Have you been able to obtain the rest of the information you needed?" Jakial asked into the silence.

Ish'Kara didn't have to ask which information he was referring to. She had yet to receive the particulars they needed from the Daemod to complete their quest for physical life eternal. Baltharak, still angry with her, and true to the arrogance of his kind, had refused to respond to her summons. She shook her head in response to Jakial's query. "My informant is angry with me at the moment."

"He is Daemod, correct?"

She stared at her lover. She'd underestimated him. "Yes."

"They are particularly susceptible to bribes, are they not?"

Ish'Kara's jaw twitched as she clenched her teeth

in anger. "I have already paid for this information three times over."

Jakial shrugged. "So use a bribe that has no personal value to you—a woman perhaps. The Daemod love human females, do they not?"

Ish'Kara's eyes narrowed thoughtfully. Jakial was right. The last time they'd met, Baltharak had been seeking a woman. Of course, any woman she furnished might not be willing to bear his offspring—which was apparently his primary concern. But, if she supplied a female, that aspect would simply have to be up to him. With all his abilities, if he could not seduce a mere human female, he did not deserve offspring.

Not for the first time she wondered why the immortal, one-sex Daemod had been created with a sex drive and the ability to procreate with other species. Another of the omnipotent One's mistakes, no doubt. Oh, well, it was not her concern.

"What are you thinking?" Jakial interrupted her thoughts.

"That it's worth a shot." She smiled and kissed the tip of his nose before rising. Another thought occurred to her. "Are the fighters staying in top condition, as I ordered?"

"Of course, darling. Nobody would dare disobey your orders."

"Good. Once we have the information we desire, we must have the ability to protect it. I will also need the fighter's skills to . . . lay in a few ingredients."

Jakial laughed. "Slaves, my darling. Fodder for our use. When did you learn such tact? Ingredients indeed!"

She frowned. He was right. She had never been quite so coy in stating the obvious before. "It must be a remnant of this body's previous personality." Shrugging, she turned away; it was of no consequence. "And now I have some business to attend to.

I want this entire continent under my dominion within a week."

It was dark and cold. Not the cold that was the result of the absence of sunlight, but the soul-deep cold that was the result of fear and desperation. She was running, running endlessly. Evil hovered all around her. There was no escape. Yet she couldn't let it win. If she let it drive her away, who would remain to fight? Somehow, some way, she had to defeat it. She stopped and turned to confront it.

Suddenly the absolute darkness grayed and lightened and she could see. She faced a crowd of a thousand people. All were ordinary of face and form. Yet the evil was here, looking at her, enjoying her confusion. She sensed it.

Where was it? How could she find it? Evil was supposed to be twisted and ugly; she had not been prepared to confront a human face. If she looked into their eyes, could she see it? Recognize it?

Slowly, warily, she began to move through the crowd, looking into the eyes of the people confronting her. They laughed and joked and talked as she walked, as though they didn't even see her. Wait. Was it this man? His eyes were shifty and cruel. Evil?

"You!" she cried, pointing at him. "It's you. Be gone."

Even as she spoke the words, the flesh of his features began to dissolve, running down his body like melted wax, revealing the soul within. It was shadowed and tainted, impure, but not evil. She'd slain the wrong person. "No!" She cringed with the load of guilt she bore. "No more innocent people. Please"

Continue, a voice whispered, emanating from the walls around her without definable source. *Find her*.

Her! Of course, now she remembered. Evil had many names, but she sought only one of its most ardent disciples: Ish'Kara!

"Ali'Yah," a voice called from the throng of people, taunting in a childish sing-song voice. "It's time to die . . . again."

"Ish'Kara?" She looked around, unable to find her. She was frightened. "I'm not prepared for you."

Laughter began building, getting louder until it echoed all around her. "Too bad. You were warned and you ignored it. Now you are mine."

In that instant, the crowd of people disappeared and she was in a long dark tunnel. *Time to die. Time to die.* The words echoed over and over all around her. She sensed Ish'Kara on her heels, tasting her fear, enjoying it. *Time to die,* the voice whispered in her ear with maniacal pleasure.

"No!" she shouted in defiance. The sound startled Cadence awake and she bolted upright in bed.

Another nightmare! And this time she remembered it. Every frightening bit of it.

Shuddering, she looked around the familiar confines of her bedroom suite. The shadows seemed to breathe. The only illumination was provided by the distant pair of moons. Could she get the right note that would activate the fluorescent crystals? Opening her mouth, she intoned the note. Nothing. She'd been off key. Sighing, she tried again. A faint mauve glow began to brighten the crystals, and as it grew the darkness retreated.

She examined the room and shuddered. She felt as though she was being watched again, but she was afraid to trust her nightmare-clouded senses. Hell's universe! She couldn't remember being this frightened since she was a child facing a huge, unfriendly world after her parents had died. And she didn't like it. Things were going to change. Immediately, if she could exercise any control whatsoever over the situation.

Rising, she grabbed the silky peach-colored robe she'd placed near the bed and donned it over a new nightgown. Although this one too reminded her of a spider web, especially in the torso area, it was fashioned from enough shimmering gold satin to at least approximate a real nightgown.

Tying the belt of her robe, she began to pace the room, checking for signs of intrusion. Nothing. All her fear appeared to have been generated by a simple nightmare.

No, she took that back. Nightmare it was, but there was nothing simple about it or the way it made her feel. So the question facing her was: What was she going to do to eradicate this fear? She frowned thoughtfully. What would Chance advise?

Face it. The words appeared in her mind as rapidly as though Chance had been there to say them. Chance had never run from anything. He would advise her to face her fear.

In the dream, Ish'Kara had told her she'd been warned, but Cadence had received only one warning. One that, at the time, she had thought was meant for Gildon. It had come from Shaylon. What had she intended by her cryptic words? Cadence needed to see her again.

The hair at the base of Cadence's neck prickled. She spun around. Dammit! She *knew* she was being watched.

Lifting her eyes to the ceiling, she recalled the name that haunted her dreams. "Stay out of my dreams, Ish'Kara or whatever the hell your name is. Do you hear me, you bitch? Stay away from me or you'll wish you'd never met Cadence Barrington."

A flicker of movement at the doorway flashed in the corner of her eye, and she spun to face a new threat. "Who are you speaking to, Cadence?" Gildon asked softly.

She flushed and shrugged deprecatingly. "Nobody. Just exorcising a personal demon." When he only looked puzzled, she shrugged again and explained as well as she could. "I feel I'm being watched. I felt it earlier too."

He frowned. "A scry, possibly. They are extremely difficult to guard against."

"A scry?"

He nodded. "It's a means whereby a person separates his consciousness from his body and sends it to another place to make observations."

"It sounds dangerous."

He leaned against the door frame. "It is. Particularly in these times when any entity that comes along can take over the physical body, isolating the consciousness. Also, even when completed successfully, a scry is very taxing for the scryer. However, there are those who deem the rewards worth the risk and effort. And, as with all things, practice, however painful, gradually decreases the amount of effort expended."

Cadence cast another nervous glance toward the ceiling. "Why would anyone want to spy on me?"

Gildon's lips twisted wryly. "With all you have been told, do you really have to ask that?"

Cadence avoided his gaze. The prophecy again! Stars, she was getting tired of their notions about her importance in their war against this cult they called the Vradir. Whoa! A war had two sides. If one side considered her an important asset, mightn't the other consider her a liability.

Gildon interrupted her sudden silence. "I heard you cry out. You had another nightmare?"

She nodded, her thoughts still on the possibility that she might be a target. Why hadn't she considered that possibility before? Because she'd hidden it from herself, unwilling to face it?

"Do you remember anything about this one?"

She dragged her thoughts into the present, considered Gildon's query and shuddered. "This dream? Yes. Too much."

He studied her for a moment. "Come." He held one arm out to her in a welcoming gesture. "We'll have some hot *cai* and talk."

Gildon listened to Cadence as she finished imparting her dream. Her voice was calm, her manner composed, yet he sensed that the situation was taking more of a toll on her than she herself realized.

She was a trained fighter. That being so, her instincts were honed for combat and self-preservation. He was certain that her training demanded that she confront anyone who posed a threat. Yet she couldn't fight what she couldn't see or understand.

Her biggest problem in understanding the significance of her dream and what was required of her was that she still didn't grasp, or believe, her connection to this world. And yet, conversely, he'd seen her wave her fist at the ceiling and threaten Ish'Kara, confronting the source of fear in her nightmare.

Should he tell her that Ish'Kara was real? He negated the thought immediately. It was not his place to do so. Besides, she had not believed either himself or Tailen when they'd told her of the prophecy. She needed to hear these things from someone she could trust.

Gildon sighed mentally. Who? She had no friends here. Her Empyrean guardians were communicating with her through her dreams because no more direct method was available. The warning they delivered was very real even if part of it had represented itself symbolically in her mind. Could he tell her that much? Would she accept it?

If only she were Tesuvian. If only her mind were not so intensely shielded. Then he could take her to the Communion chamber and allow her to attempt to make contact with the guardians by utilizing the augmenting power of the crystal.

Wait! He was assuming that, because neither he nor Tailen had been able to contact her mind, she would be unable to make contact with the Empyrean guardians. Perhaps he assumed too much.

Cadence had directed her eyes pensively toward the large bank of windows behind him while she sipped her *cai*. "Would it be possible for me to see your mother again?" she asked.

He frowned thoughtfully. What could Cadence possibly want with Shaylon? "I believe so. I'll contact her soon to see what I can arrange. All right?"

She nodded. "Yes. Thank you." Almost absently, she returned her introspective gaze to the window.

She was so beautiful. The bodice of her robe gaped slightly, giving him a tantalizing view of the gentle curve of one small breast cloaked in delicately embroidered, diaphanous gold thread. His loins stirred with desire. By the One! Was this constant temptation, this torment, penance for his many failings? Resistance was getting more and more difficult.

Perhaps he would be able to indulge his physical senses without risking his heart. *Fool!* a voice cried in his mind. *Did you really think that just by avoiding her you could protect your heart? You already love her.* The voice was so clear and so unexpected that he actually sought the thread of contact that would have indicated a telepathic connection. It wasn't there. The thought had come from his own mind.

No! It couldn't be true. He had to get out of here. "Gildon—?"

"Go back to bed, Cadence." He was blunt, but he couldn't help it. Escape was the only thing on his mind.

Chapter Fourteen

Entering the coolness of his lower-level study, Gildon moved to the far end, an area he kept clear for the performance of rituals and ceremonies that required elaborate preparations and space. The entire study had a twelve-foot ceiling, and this area alone was at least twenty-five feet in diameter. Occasionally, however, he used his study to perform the disciplined exercises of the Kami warrior, although he preferred the spacious Temple of the Kami, and that was what he intended to do now. Not even this ungovernable passion would be able to withstand the intense concentration of the Kami drill.

He hoped.

Whipping off his robe, he threw it unceremoniously into a corner and, clad only in his white trousers, began the maneuvers.

He couldn't be in love with Cadence. It was impossible! He hardly knew her.

He pivoted, lunged, and blocked an imaginary opponent with his arm. The cloth of his trousers, not designed for such exaggerated movement, strained to the point of tearing.

By the One! He didn't want to return to his chambers for warrior garb. With a frustrated grimace, he released the fastening on his trousers, removed and discarded them as carelessly as the robe. The drill did not require clothing.

225

Returning to the maneuvers, he stretched one arm skyward and leapt over an envisioned adversary.

After all, if Cadence left tomorrow, he would simply return to the lifestyle he'd maintained before her arrival.

Somehow that picture looked very bleak and lonely now.

No! he cried silently and sliced violently at the air before him with a series of controlled downward arm movements as he stalked forward with firm, measured steps, pressing his foe into retreat. He would not love Cadence. He would not make the same mistake his mother had made. Tomorrow, when he took Cadence to the Communion Chamber, he too would seek guidance from the One.

That decision made, he immersed himself completely in the demands of the Kami training, finally putting from his mind the torment of ill-fated love and blazing passion. He was oblivious to all but the precision movement of muscles and tendons in response to his demands. Oblivious, too, to the woman making her way down the stairs.

As she caught sight of Gildon, Cadence hastily averted her eyes and lowered herself to sit on the cool stone steps in stunned confusion. She had wanted to speak with him, but she obviously couldn't interrupt him in his current state of nakedness. Yet she couldn't bring herself to go back upstairs alone either.

She hated herself for her newly discovered cowardice. She was a fighter by nature as well as training and she wanted to battle . . . something. Had the source of her fear been something tangible, she would gladly have faced it, fought it until it bothered her no more—whether by winning or losing. But here on this world, she didn't understand the nature of the campaign. Unable to sleep for the thoughts whirling in her head and plagued by the continuing sensation of being watched, she'd decided that solitude was not her preferred state at the moment. But it appeared that Gildon was occupied.

Cadence despised voyeurs, and she tried to keep her eyes turned away—she really did—but this was the man she had admired and desired almost from the first moment they'd met, despite her determination otherwise. As relentless as gravity, the sight of Gildon drew her eyes.

He was performing some type of fighting technique, very like a martial art in some aspects, very different in others. His intense concentration and the level of energy expended suggested that Gildon himself might have a demon to exorcise. He was poetry in motion. Male beauty personified. She admired the rippling muscles in his strong, tapered back. Followed with her eyes the indentation of his backbone to his narrow hips. Admired the solid strength of his powerful thighs and calves. And wished with all her heart that he would forget about the strictures imposed by the Temple of the Avatar long enough to give them a chance. They could face the problem of spending their lives together later . . . if there was a later for them.

But Cadence understood the concept of duty very well and could not bring herself to attempt to undermine one of his most admirable character traits: his intense sense of honor. With a sigh, she rose and silently moved back up the stairs, resolved to face the nebulous fears that hid in the shadows of her room and get some sleep.

The next morning at breakfast, Gildon looked as tired and drawn as Cadence felt. Not surprising, since Cadence had heard him still moving about at dawn.

"I was up most of the night intensifying the warding on the apartment," he said as though he had read her mind. "It should help to prevent further scrying, although not even the most elaborate warding is affective against an accomplished operator."

Cadence took another bite of breakfast and looked across the table at him. "What exactly is warding? Have I heard you use that term before?"

He considered. "I'm not sure. Warding is the process by which we shield entrances from unauthorized admission. The process requires a combination of specially programmed crystals, vocalization, and telekinetic ability in order to manipulate the energy produced."

"Does it use a force field, like the doors?"

He shook his head. "No. It's quite different. Warding can prove to be quite painful to unauthorized psychic entrants, and it serves the double function of immediately alerting the occupants to an attempt at physical entry."

"The equivalent of an electric fence," Cadence said, substituting English terminology as she nodded with understanding.

"A what?" Gildon asked.

"Electric fence." She saw the question in his eyes and knew she could not possibly explain the concept of electricity. "Never mind, it's not important."

He allowed her to dismiss the analogy and returned to his thoughts. When he had come upstairs last night after his workout with the intention of seeking his bed, he had decided to check on Cadence first. Upon listening at the door to her bedchamber, he had been satisfied by the sound of her even breathing, yet alarmed when he felt his scalp prickle in faint warning. Extending his much more attuned senses, he investigated the subtle sensation. Cadence was right. She was being observed. He could barely discern the presence on the periphery of his senses, but it was there.

This could mean only one thing. The Vradir cult

had found her and her life was in danger. Whether she accepted it or not, the Vradir, too, believed she was the one destined to play the role of savior foretold in the prophecy. Now, more than ever, it was important to aid Cadence in recognizing her position. "Cadence—" She lifted her eyes to his. "I know your beliefs are vastly different from ours, but I would like to make a suggestion."

"All right."

"This nightmare of yours seems to contain a recurring theme." She nodded in acceptance, and he continued. "I still believe that this dream may be the Empyrean guardians' means of attempting contact. It could even be a warning." He sensed her beginning to withdraw. "Wait!" He held up a hand to forestall the argument hovering on her lips. "As Tesuvians, we invariably confirm or alleviate any such suspicion through communion. That is all I'm suggesting, that you attempt communion. It is not painful and costs you nothing. If I'm wrong, nothing will happen."

She eyed him warily. "What do I have to do?"

"The Communion Chamber is in the main temple. It's a small room which contains a very large crystal that has been programmed with the unique capacity to augment mental capacity, be it thought or prayer. It permits the consciousness to take flight, joining the guardians in their realm . . . if they permit it. And on very rare occasions a few have even touched the One."

Cadence frowned. "You're sure it's not dangerous? You said last night that scrying involved the consciousness leaving the body, and that *that* was dangerous."

Gildon smiled slightly. She forgot nothing. "Rest assured, this is an entirely different process. For one thing, in communion only the questing Mind leaves the body, rather than the entire consciousness. You remain aware of your body and what's happening to it at all times. Second, this procedure takes place within the protected environs of the main building of the Temple of the Eidan itself. Should something untoward enter there, a thousand priests would know it at once."

Cadence considered him. "You really think this might help?"

"I do."

"All right then, I guess."

He smiled. "We'll leave within the hour." At that moment a tickle in his mind informed him of telepathic contact. The distinctive psychic knock belonged to Tailen. "Excuse me," Gildon said to Cadence as he withdrew his *falar* stone, placed it over his forehead, and closed his eyes to block out distraction. *I am here, Counselor.*

Gildon, my friend, time is drawing ever shorter. How go things with Cadence?

Gildon sighed. *The same, Tailen, although she has had a nightmare, which may be significant. I am taking her to the Communion Chamber this morning.*

There was a pause and then Tailen continued. *Good.* Another pause. *We have detected forces amassing in Madaia. The invasion is progressing, my brother. The central cities in all of the provinces are now under siege by alter-realm entities. The number of possessions and disappearances climbs by the hour.*

Gildon frowned. *The shields?* he asked. He and his brethren of the Avatar had shielded the central cities against the formation of alter-realm thresholds months ago. Although their preparations were a less extensive version of the century-long construction of planetary shielding put into place by his ancestors, it should have continued to protect the central cities until removed from within.

Disappearing, Tailen responded. *We don't know how. Perhaps they have accomplices within, although*

I hate to imagine that. Or, perhaps they have found some means of disabling the shields from outside. Your brethren are even now attempting to fortify them, but I have little faith that the augmentation will hold. The damage has already been done: The entities are within. He paused. *We must reach Cadence soon if she is to help us, my brother. It will not be long before the invasion of the inner cities begins. Once that happens, based on historical experience, it will only be a matter of days until the battle is lost.*

Gildon swallowed. Time was running out. Time! If only they knew for certain who had caused this. . . . If they knew what could be done to stop it. . . . He would gladly have petitioned the Tridon for permission and volunteered to travel back in time to undo the damage despite the disruption of the time line. But it wasn't possible. He still had no idea what could be done to prevent the unfolding of events. Would they gain that knowledge before it was too late? *The evacuation portals, are they nearing completion?* he asked.

The physical construction of some interplanetary portals is now complete; however, they have yet to be properly programmed because we still lack information. A number of panicked central-city residents are beginning to demand an explanation.

Gildon remained focused on his previous thought. *These interplanetary portals have the capability of temporal displacement, do they not?*

There was a moment of silence during which Gildon sensed a certain surprise from Tailen. *Yes,* he responded a little hesitantly. *What do you have in mind, Gildon?*

Gildon explained his idea and waited anxiously for Tailen's response.

You could not be the one to go back, Gildon. Execution of the perpetrator would be required. Only a Kami can be authorized to execute a citizen. You know that.

Gildon grimaced mentally. By the One! He was Kami at heart.

He sighed. But he was also a priest of the Avatar.

Still, Tailen continued, *I will put your proposal before the Council of Prelates. There is enormous merit in being prepared. Perhaps, if we know the necessary details soon enough, a Kami can be found who would be willing to make the sacrifice.*

An hour later, Gildon escorted Cadence through the Temple of the Eidan and halted before a pair of doors carved from a light and lustrous wood. No holograms here. These were very real doors with a remarkable patina that was indescribably lovely. He opened the doors and observed Cadence, waiting for her reaction. She did not disappoint him.

When she was a few steps within, subliminal instinct prompted her to halt, as it prompted all visitors to this room to pause and assimilate the unique ambience of its beauty—a tribute to the legacy of the One Universal Consciousness. She was barely aware of Gildon's presence. Heeding the subliminal call himself, Gildon opened his senses to the glory of the One. The atmosphere was one of profound peace.

Gold carvings and raised motifs embellished the luminous white walls. A tinted-glass skylight in the domed ceiling cast splendid, multihued reflections upon the rich mosaic flooring. The depiction seemed to shift, undergoing a metamorphosis of its significance to the beholder at each transformation in the pattern of light and cloud outside.

Yet the hall's most striking feature rested in the chamber on the right, a giant crystal carved into a pyramidal shape that reached almost to the center of another domed skylight. Alive with shifting patterns of light, it was one of the focal points of the energies banding this world. Perhaps it was from the crystal that the hall absorbed its atmosphere of peace and purity. Gildon allowed the ambience to flood his soul, healing him.

Then, as the reverence inspired by the magnificent room gradually relinquished its grasp on his senses, Gildon turned his attention to Cadence, who continued to stare about with the awe of the uninitiated. "Come," he said, guiding her with a hand to the small of her back. "This way."

They entered the much smaller Communion Chamber. The giant prismatic crystal dominated the room. Cadence continued to stare, silently in awe of a power even the inexperienced could sense. Twelve vaguely person-shaped depressions in the marble-tiled floor radiated outward in a star-like pattern from the crystal. Gildon directed her to one of these.

"Lie here with your head touching the crystal. I will lie here." He indicated a position once removed from hers. "Watch me, and position yourself as I do."

Taking his position with his head in contact with the crystal, Gildon placed his hands over his midsection in the traditional pyramidal posture: fingertips touching, palms distanced, and thumbs folded inward. He checked to ensure that Cadence had mimicked his position. "All right?"

"Yes," she murmured. He sensed her nervousness.

"Good. Now breathe deeply and exhale slowly; focus on the relaxation of your body. Your mind is a black curtain, devoid of thought. Visualize it." He allowed her a few moments. "Are you relaxed?"

She nodded; her eyes remained closed.

"Now focus your mind on one thought: that you seek guidance from your Empyrean guardians, and imagine yourself drawing power from the crystal to project that need into the heavens. Can you do that?"

She frowned slightly. "I think so."

"Relax," he cautioned. "Don't try too hard. Let it

happen."

A short time later, his attuned senses perceived a change in the energy of the crystal. It had worked! So far, anyway. And it was time for Gildon to form a nexus. Despite their inability to establish telepathic contact, he should be able to aid Cadence in directing her externalized Mind.

His disciplined intellect focused, drawing upon and converging the forces of the pyramid. The swirling patterns of light confined within it seemed to break free, bathing them with prismatic energy. The scintillating luminosity danced upon the immaculate surfaces of the walls as though passing through rippling water.

Gildon's Mind began to merge with Cadence's; utilizing the augmenting power of the crystal, they became one Mind—joined and yet separate, with differing objectives. Gradually the eddy of light within the pyramid began to pulsate, echoing the beat of an immense heart. Gildon felt the power of the Mind of which he was a part grow to awesome proportions. Slowly it extended its senses beyond the temple toward the heavens, and with sudden sureness the Mind projected itself into the vast blackness of space.

Cadence felt herself compelled upward through a maelstrom of light. The sensation seemed to last forever and she almost fought it. But in that instant, a tremendous sense of peace pervaded her being. She was like a child in the womb, safe and warm, with only the vaguest thoughts hovering on the edge of her consciousness. She never wanted it to end.

But abruptly it did end.

As the sense of motion ceased, she floated, suspended within a timeless abyss of color more brilliant than could be perceived with the human eye. She sensed Gildon with her, a part of her and yet detached. Once more the Mind extended itself, discerned its direction, and willed advance.

Cadence saw what looked like a huge immaculate white cloud stretching off forever. And then a pair of doors opened in the cloud. So enormous were they that Cadence felt as small as a child in relation to them. What was this place? She slowed, hesitating, but felt Gildon's assurance and moved forward.

A floor of white cloud stretched endlessly before her. She could see no walls. And yet the cavernous place eddied with mist that consistently transmuted itself, forming corridors and enclosures. Not knowing where she was supposed to go, or even if she was supposed to be here, Cadence moved forward cautiously. It was then that two gossamer columns of mist appeared before them. One indicated that Gildon should follow it into a corridor that appeared magically on their right. Cadence immediately missed his presence, and sought to follow him, but the other mist-like being halted her and bade her follow it.

Before long, she entered a space that had the feeling of being a separate chamber, although she had seen no walls or doors to indicate this was so. The column of mist disappeared. Before her stood three luminous beings. She didn't know whether they were clothed in mist or whether the brilliant white of their clothing merely blended into the mist surrounding them, but the only facets of them that she could perceive clearly were their faces. The mist swirled, making the faces before her seem disembodied.

Come. The word resounded all around her and yet it was not loud, merely . . . diffused. One of the beings waved a mist-like arm, beckoning her to stand before them. *Why have you come before us?*

"I . . ." Cadence struggled to remember her purpose in coming here, remembered Gildon's insistence that her nightmares had a purpose. "I've been having a dream I don't understand."

Come closer. As Cadence drew nearer, a small white table appeared before her. She could see that it contained a huge book, its pages edged in gold. The script on the pages appeared to be some type of foreign symbology.

Read.

Cadence looked at the beings, feeling awed and reverent, wanting very badly to do as they asked. "I can't. I don't understand the language."

Another of the beings waved a hand over the tome. *Read, Cadence.*

Cadence returned her eyes to the page. To her astonishment, she could now read the words written there. Had the beings done something to change the book? Or had the transformation been enacted within herself? She didn't know, but began reading the words inscribed there. *Recorded here are the passages of the original soul designated Csilla, born Ali-'Yah, then Lay'Lah, then Na'Sine, then Athena, then Devona, then. . . .* The list went on for pages.

Cadence lifted her eyes to the beings. "What is it you want me to see here?"

Slowly the pages began to turn as though guided by an unseen hand. When they stopped, one of the beings reached forward and, with a misty finger, indicated the bottom of the page. . . . *then Shadi, then Nathara, then Cadence.*

Cadence stared at the page, knowing what it meant without asking for an explanation. This person who had lived so many lives was the Ali'Yah in her dreams. Cadence and Ali'Yah were one, the same soul, separated only by a few millennia of other existences.

How did she know? Because she'd heard the name Ali'Yah in her dreams and recognized it as her own name? Or because on some level of her being she had always known that there was more to her than one life could account for? *This* was why Gildon's people accepted reincarnation so readily: They'd obtained proof.

Come. The three glorious beings began moving to the right, and Cadence followed. *Watch,* the center one said. Cadence categorized this being as female, for she seemed more fragile, more . . . empathetic than her counterparts. Cadence turned, following the gesticulation of a delicate arm of mist.

What you are about to see may be difficult for you. Even as she concluded her warning, the wall of mist before Cadence began to shimmer with colorful images, like a projection from a camera. The first scene, viewed as though from far above, revealed an enormous island continent. The gigantic mountains on its northern coast descended into timber-rich foothills and grassy plains upon which animals roamed freely, undisturbed by hunters. Further south, huge orchards of fruit marched in clearly defined columns. Tropical beaches lined the southern shores of the great continent, and Cadence recognized it. There had never been a more magnificent place on Earth than the island continent of Atlantis. Even its cities were marvels of architecture attuned to the world they'd colonized.

And then the scenes began to flash more quickly, imparting the mundane as well as the significant. It seemed that every moment of her life as Ali'Yah flashed before her, but perhaps that was only her perception. And then the end drew near. The Darkness came, propagated by her sister, and the beauty of her world began to fade. She, and others like her, fought the Vradir, but they were too late and not strong enough. The result of their battle was an explosion of incomparable destructive power! The black waves roiled around her, vicious and hungry, swallowing everything and everyone without bias.

Cadence looked at the beings, wondering at their

purpose in showing her this. As though they'd read her mind, they responded, three voices in unison in her mind, *We do not manipulate time without purpose, Cadence. Since the moment of your birth, you have been destined to come to this world. Now you must fulfill your destiny.*

Gildon and Tailen were right! Her coming here was no accident! "But how?" Cadence asked. "I don't understand."

You will. Watch. One of the beings raised an arm, gesturing again in the direction of the curtain of mist.

And there was another life. Another set of images, flashing faster and faster upon the canvas of mist. Cadence grappled to understand the flood of images; she felt certain that she would descend into a world of madness as the images crowded into her thoughts, tearing their way out of her subconscious mind with jagged nails.

Another life. The images moving past her mind's eye at lightning speed. Her consciousness descending into a maelstrom of strobe-like recollections. Agony, as a thousand lifetimes of memories and knowledge flared into focus, an inferno in her mind. Madness hovered like a bird of prey on the periphery of her mind as the emotions associated with each remembrance burst the confines of containment and ripped through her heart with all of their original strength: The height of joy as a child was born; the depths of despair as a husband died; profound sorrow over an evil act committed by one human against another; pity for an old woman whose life ended in a gutter on a city street, wasted. They were all there, every emotion she had ever felt.

Then that life ended, and there was another, and another. And, in each, she waged a battle against evil in one form or another. In many she again faced Ish'Kara. For it was her destiny to defeat her sister, and she could not move on to an untried existence until she fulfilled it.

Another life. Another, until she lost count. Until she knew she couldn't take it anymore. The agony became unbearable. The madness crept nearer, waiting, sharp talons outstretched to snatch her.

No!

And then it was over. The pictures ceased so abruptly that she felt dazed and unsteady. She looked around for the three beings who had led her here, but they had disappeared. All the walls and corridors faded away, and she stood in a chamber that seemed to be tens of miles long and equally as wide.

"Wait!" she cried. "What is it you want me to do?"

You will know.

Cadence sensed Gildon approaching in the distance. Just before she turned to meet him, the beings contacted her, once again communicating through a harmony of the three minds speaking in unison.

You now have all the knowledge you held before and more, for you have learned much in your current life. We caution you: There is no mind save your own, which has been specially shielded, that Ish'Kara cannot read upon contact. For that reason, you must be cautious in the information you share. And be warned: We may maintain this shielding on your mind only as long as Ish'Kara herself exists. No longer.

We have been with you since the beginning. We will be with you always. The voices ceased, and Cadence knew she was alone.

Gildon was puzzled. He had spoken with his guardians, requested their advice in delivering himself from the forbidden love he felt for Cadence, and their response had been completely ambiguous: *In this matter, the future takes care of itself. You are only as you have been before. There is no wrong in that.* And they'd declined to say more. His request for clarification had fallen upon an empty chamber.

What did it mean?

Sensing Cadence ahead, he moved to join her. Had her journey here been successful, he wondered. Since the primary hurdle for her to overcome had been establishing contact with the crystal in order to project, he had to assume that she had obtained at least some satisfaction in coming here. Had she been given a reason for her nightmares? More importantly, had she been given guidance that would allow her to aid his people in their battle?

They did not communicate as they began their voyage back. The trip duplicated their ascension, in reverse. A few moments later, Gildon stirred and blinked, feeling rested and vibrant as always after a communion session. Looking over at Cadence, he saw that she too was rousing.

He waited until she rose to a sitting position and then asked, "How did it go?"

Cadence snapped a look at him as though she'd forgotten his presence. Her eyes were wide and slightly glazed as she met his gaze and held it, her complexion as pale as he'd ever seen it. "I'm not quite certain." Her voice trembled a bit. "It was very strange."

He frowned. He'd never heard of anybody having quite that reaction to communion. "Strange? How?"

Cadence shook her head. Images of other people and other lives still ran rampant through her mind. What she had accepted so easily while . . . in communion once again seemed illogical. The entire episode had a dreamlike quality that made it difficult to accept her perceptions. And yet, what other explanation could there be for the images in her mind, the knowledge stored in there for her to draw upon?

She had lost the sense of being a foreigner that she had carried into this room, for she now felt as Tesuvian as Gildon. She understood perfectly what he did within the Temple of the Avatar, for the memory that Ali'Yah had been a priestess within the Temple of the Avatar flashed through her mind. Cadence understood the purpose behind the Lidai Order, and the Shajati Order, and the Shido Order and all the others, for she had once lived in a society just like this one. She understood that her arrival had been foretold in a prophecy.

"Cadence—" Her mind swam through a murky river of disjointed thought to focus on Gildon. He stood before her, his hand extended to aid her in rising. She placed her hand in his, felt the electric jolt that such contact with him always generated. Unable to deal with more emotion at this point, she immediately stepped away. "How was it strange, Cadence?" Gildon asked again, and she realized she had not answered him. "What did you learn?"

She looked at him, knew that of all the people here, she should confide in him . . . to some degree, at least. He had a right to know. But she wasn't ready yet. It was all too fantastic. Unbelievable, really. And she needed to get it straight in her own mind before she tried to communicate, even the basics, to someone else. "I'm sorry. I just can't talk about it yet."

Even Ish'Kara, who was accustomed to dealing with the Daemod, had to struggle to conceal her revulsion at the form Baltharak had chosen for their meeting. A huge, black, pulsing globule of flesh formed his lower body; from it sprouted at least eight thick, long, grasping tentacles which served as legs. His torso looked vaguely insectoid, and four pincer-brandishing arms flailed about without any apparent control. He'd chosen a humanoid head perched precariously atop a thin, almost graceful neck of indeterminate source.

Christine Michels

"You said you had something to offer me if I came," Baltharak began without preamble. "What is it?"

"A woman." Ish'Kara observed the interest flare in his slitted bright blue eyes. "I am going to attempt to have her brought here for you."

"Show me," he demanded.

Having anticipated his interest, Ish'Kara had prepared a projection crystal. The large blue crystal was now suspended over her forehead, much as a *falar* stone would be. Intoning a note, she activated it and projected the memory of Ali'Yah as she existed in this incarnation. Immediately a miniaturized replica of one of the visions she had obtained through her scrys formed on the floor between herself and the threshold in which Baltharak stood.

She had chosen to begin with the vision of Ali'Yah preparing for the baths. As she'd foreseen, Baltharak's lecherous and avaricious nature ensured that his attention was immediate and intense. When she had played that scry in its entirety, she moved to the one of Ali'Yah asleep in bed. A black forked tongue flicked out of Baltharak's mouth, leaving a glistening sheen of saliva on his humanoid lips. Ish'Kara had accomplished her goal of whetting Baltharak's appetite. She discontinued the projection.

Baltharak's eyes flashed up to hers. "Where is she?" he asked.

Ish'Kara shrugged. "At the moment, I believe she is in the inner city of Jafna."

"Ah, the nucleus of the enemy camp. Correct?"

She nodded. "Which is why I said I would attempt to have her brought here for you. We are still working out the details for the abduction, and as with any such venture, things can go wrong. If we succeed, I want your word that she will never return to this plane." Although she knew that as a Daemod, Bal-

242

tharak's word was not completely reliable, it was better than nothing. And she needed the information only he could provide.

"You have my word." Baltharak looked back to the place on the floor where he had seen the image of Ali'Yah as though he could still see it. And perhaps he could, through his own mind. The physiology of the Daemod was a mystery to her. When he returned his gaze to her, he said, "If you fail, I may take her myself."

Ish'Kara bit back a smile, concealing her satisfaction, for that was exactly the reaction she had hoped for. "The sonic grenades I gave the Daemod are working well, then?" She really had no need to ask, for her intelligence had revealed the grenades as extremely effective in disrupting the substandard shielding initiated by the Avatar in protecting their central and inner cities. She scorned their abilities. In millennia of isolation and peace, they had allowed themselves to lose much of the knowledge that had defeated her before. That would be their downfall.

"Yes. They are." The Daemod focused on her with his brilliant alien eyes. "You have more questions?" Finally, his mood was more accommodating.

Ish'Kara nodded. "During our last conversation, you suggested that blood vampirism was not the only form of vampirism capable of granting eternal life. What other forms are there?"

"That question really requires no answer, my pet. If you put your devious little mind to work, you'd realize that you already know the answer. However, I will explain." The precision of Daemod speech, when they kept a rein on their love of foul language, always surprised Ish'Kara. Then again, she supposed that eternal life granted them plenty of opportunities for education.

"There is soul vampirism," Baltharak began,

"which, like blood vampirism, involves metamorphosis on the part of the would-be vampire. The vampirism of the soul in most cases kills the donor immediately. There is life-force vampirism, which, rather than a metamorphosis, requires a syphoning device to gradually draw off the donor's energy and transmit it to a feeding device worn by the vampire. Death of the donor, depending on the health of the vampire, can take years. And there is vampirism of intense emotional energy. This again requires a feeding device on the part of the vampire, something to absorb and transmit the passionate energies. This form of vampirism is, of course, inexact. It requires a crowd of people all sharing the same intense emotion, and most vampires have found they have been unable to find a catalyst to produce the energies for a sufficient period of time to be effective." Baltharak shrugged. "There are many lesser forms of vampirism too, my pet. But none have the means to accomplish your goal. I'm afraid you will be limited to a choice among those I've given you."

Ish'Kara had begun pacing back and forth in front of the threshold as he spoke. Now she paused and looked at him. "You can tell me how to construct the device for life-force vampirism?"

"Of course." With a sudden gesture, one of his flailing arms threw a huge data crystal toward her. There was a brief flash of light as it burst through the bubble-like surface of the shielded threshold, and then, reflexively, Ish'Kara caught it. "It's all there."

"You knew I would ask this and what I would choose?" Ish'Kara asked, holding the crystal up to the light to ensure that it did indeed contain data.

"I know you better than you know yourself, my pet." Baltharak's eyes began to glow with lurid fire. "And now my debt to you is paid in full, and it is you who owes me. Don't disappoint me. Bring me the woman."

Ish'Kara's gaze snapped to his. "I warned you that I could make no promises in that regard."

"Ah, but you lured me here with the bribe." He smiled, flicking his forked tongue at her. "If the bribe is unpaid, it becomes a debt. Bring her to me." And with a wave of his hand he dispersed the threshold.

Chapter Fifteen

They returned to Gildon's apartment in silence. Gildon was angry with her; Cadence could see it in the set of his jaw and his thunder-cloud eyes, but she ignored it. There were just too many pictures floating through her mind at the moment, too many emotions, for her to be concerned with Gildon's feelings. Later, when she had come to terms with all the flotsam in her mind and relegated it to storage according to its significance, then she could focus on the important details . . . and Gildon.

Gildon opened the door to his apartment and silently ushered her in. The moment the door materialized behind them, he spoke. "Is there nothing you can tell me, Cadence?"

She met his stormy gaze, saw puzzlement combined with the anger reflected there. "I just need some time to sort it all out."

"Time!" He stalked forward until there was barely a handsbreadth between them. "Time is something we're running out of, Cadence. More people are losing their lives every day. I need to know the answer to just one question." He paused.

Oh, Stars, she was confused. All she could think of was how much she wanted to feel his arms around her. How badly she wanted to rest her head against his chest and listen to the solid beat of his heart. "What's that?" she managed to ask.

"Will you be able to help us?"

Cadence blinked and forced herself to think. "I believe so, yes. But I don't know how much yet." Her eyes flicked down to his full-lipped mouth. Why didn't he kiss her? "And there are still some things I have to work out. Things I need to understand."

He blinked. His gaze traveled over her face. The expression in his eyes changed. He made a strange growling noise deep in his throat, half moan, half something else. She watched a battle being waged in the depths of his storm-hued eyes, recognized it, and—Lord help her—she hoped that this time his strong sense of honor would lose.

"Cadence—" His hands made an aborted movement toward her.

"Yes?"

"Move away from me." His voice sounded almost strangled.

Cadence swallowed. She found herself mesmerized by the sudden blaze of blue flame in his eyes and couldn't have moved if she wanted to. Couldn't even speak. She merely shook her head.

He groaned again, deep and feral, as he caught her to him in a fierce embrace. His lips snared hers in a searing kiss that she felt all the way down to her toes. She felt the brush of his tongue against her lips and opened to him without hesitation, welcoming his invasion. Yes! This was what she wanted. This incredible unequaled excitement. This man.

His large, warm hands caressed her bare back, exposed by the cut of her gown, soothingly, sensually, and she moaned in surrender. He crushed her against his hard chest, and her breath caught in her throat as sensation tingled sharply in her nipples. His hands moved lower, kneading the soft flesh of her bottom, pressing her gently against his erection, and the last vestige of rationality deserted her. Reduced to a trembling mass of super-sensitized nerves, she could only feel.

As Gildon's mouth left her lips to trail over her cheek and temple and into her hair, she pressed her face against his chest, feeling the texture of his robe against her cheek. And then he was lifting her in his arms, carrying her into the nearest bedchamber: his own. Cadence saw little beyond the bed, which was neatly made and covered in a green satin spread.

He stood her upon the first step of the dais that held the bed so that she was at eye level with him. His eyes glittered with a savage passion that made her knees buckle again and she grasped his arms to steady herself.

He gripped her chin gently in his fingers, looked deeply into her eyes. "Cadence—" And then he groaned. "May the One help me, I cannot stop." Before she could open her mouth to tell him how pleased she was by that, he covered her lips with his in a soul-searing, devouring kiss the likes of which she had never experienced. Then, backing away from her briefly, he grasped the fabric of her gown, pulled it over her head in a single, expert move, and discarded it on the floor.

She was clad now only in her underclothing. His eyes feasted on her near-nakedness, devouring the sight of her in a manner that made her feel a little self-conscious. She extended her hands toward the fastening on his uniquely cut robe. "Your turn," she whispered. As the robe fell away from his handsome chest, her own gaze was no less ardent. She ran her fingers admiringly through the silky hair that formed a V between his flat male breasts, followed its trail as it arrowed down to the waistband of his trousers. As her fingers worked at the fastening, his hands found and removed the strapless cups that supported her breasts, discarding them carelessly. And then one of his large, warm hands closed over her left breast while he bent his head to lavish attention on the turgid peak of the other.

Cadence gasped as sensation shot through her. She was aware of nothing but the tingling in her breasts as they swelled eagerly in response to his attention. His mouth left her breast to trail a path of fire up her neck until he captured her lips once again. Still kissing her, he lifted her to lay her on the bed. The coolness of the satin against her heated flesh came as a shock; she gasped. And then, for a moment that seemed like an eternity, he left her while he removed his already unfastened trousers. Feeling bereft, she watched him, her fingers curling into impatient fists on the bedding while her eyes drank in the sight of him. He kicked the trousers away, and his manhood, jutting, enormous and pulsing, from a thick thatch of black hair at his groin, drew her gaze. She felt a rush of answering heat flood her nether regions and she eagerly reached out to welcome him as he rejoined her on the bed. Her hands drifted over his smoothly muscled body, exploring the contours, discovering the planes, as he stretched out beside her and began, once again, to lavish attention on her aching breasts. His lips closed over the sensitive tip of one breast, tugging at it, raking the responsive nub with his tongue. His hand moved down her body slowly, pausing to torment her navel briefly before moving on, leaving a trail of fire in its wake. Then he was stroking the insides of her thighs, stoking the coals of desire, igniting an almost volcanic heat. Cadence moaned and lifted her hips in involuntary invitation.

He lifted his head from her breast to look into her face with smoldering eyes, and watched her as he slowly pressed one finger into the moist crevice of her body. She gasped, and her pelvis lunged uncontrollably against his palm. A lingering, satisfied, heart-stopping smile curved his lips, and then he bent his head to her breast while he plunged his finger into her body again.

"Gild—ah!" Cadence was unable to suppress her cry of longing. Stars! She'd wanted him for so long. Looked for him her entire life. And she needed him *now*. But he ignored her impassioned plea.

Trailing her hands over his body, Cadence found his swollen sex and wrapped her fingers gently around it, caressing him. He pulsed twice in her grasp, then he gasped and moved his hips beyond her reach. Cadence moaned in frustration. "Now, Gildon," she urged. Her hand traced slowly down his arm in silent supplication.

Before she could blink, he was over her, nudging her knees apart to kneel between them. Yes! She lifted her hips in unconscious invitation, but he merely leaned forward, supporting himself on his forearms, to rain kisses over her breasts and torso, as his sex pressed against her. Slowly he trailed his kisses upward until he found her lips once again. His chest hair became an erotic torment as it brushed against her hard, super-sensitive nipples. His mouth was an instrument of tyrannical seduction as he consumed her with his passion, while withholding himself. His erection, butted so unsatisfyingly against the heart of her womanhood, incited a carnal madness that stole her equilibrium. She was spinning in a whirlpool of primitive and untamed lust. Gildon became her anchor. She clung to him, writhed beneath him.

Finally, while she was in the grip of this cyclonic storm of passion, he entered her. Fiery hot, enormous, and as hard as rock, he filled her. Her hands clutched frantically at the smooth, hard flesh of his back as the intensity of sensation increased and miniature starbursts exploded behind her eyelids. She thought that she could not possibly stand any more, could not climb any higher, but she was wrong. As he withdrew and slowly pressed back into her body, finding the rhythm as ancient as humankind itself, Cadence raised her hips in spontaneous anticipation of each erotic thrust. His movement stoked the fiery storm of passion until it became a raging inferno. She climbed higher and higher upon the hot winds of the firestorm raging through her blood . . . until, finally, she burst the bounds of earth and soared above it all. Bliss. Supernatural bliss, shared with a lover like no other, *her* lover.

"Kadar," she cried.

Still pulsing within her, he clutched her close, groaning her name. "Ali'Yah."

Only when she came down from the incredible high induced by the most transcendent lovemaking experience of her life did she realize that it wasn't *her* name. The name was that of the woman who had been her soul's first incarnation. How had Gildon known it?

And Cadence, too, had called out a name, she remembered. But the name on her tongue hadn't been Gildon. What had it been?

Gildon raised his head and, gently smoothing her hair, looked down into her face. "Who is Kadar?" he asked.

Yes, *that* was the name. It sounded familiar. She began searching her new memories. Yet, meeting Gildon's gentle eyes, she could only shake her head and answer him honestly. "I've never known anyone by that name."

"Then why did you call me by it?"

She stared at him. "I'm not sure." She lied now. Her memory told her that Kadar had been Ali'Yah's lover, but she didn't want to tell Gildon that. Not yet. "Why did you call me Ali'Yah?"

He frowned thoughtfully. "I did, didn't I? And yet, neither do I know anyone by *that* name. It's an ancient name, no longer in use." Rolling to one side, he cradled her against him. "What is happening here, Cadence?"

"I don't know for certain, but I'm beginning to think that maybe your Empyrean guardians had a hand in bringing us together."

He shook his head. "That's not possible. The guardians know that as a priest of the Avatar, I cannot take you as companion." Then, apparently realizing how his words would sound to her, he winced. "I apologize, Cadence. I am sorry that I have allowed a physical relationship to begin between us when there can be no hope of anything deeper. It isn't fair to you."

Cadence, still resting her head on his shoulder, moved it slightly to look up at him. "I'm not worried about that. At least not yet." When he looked down at her, surprise in his eyes, she raised herself up on one elbow and elaborated. "Look. Why don't we just give this relationship a chance without worrying about outside factors? For all we know, after being together for a while like this, we might get to hate each other. Then all your guilt and worry will be for nothing." She thought about her belief that she was now targeted by the other side, and as bits and pieces of the communion experience presented themselves, she remembered the guardians' purpose in bringing her here. They had said they did not manipulate time without purpose. Would she live to have a future? She'd never survived a confrontation with Ish'Kara.

"It's possible, you know, that neither of us will survive this war your people are engaged in. Or perhaps only one of us will."

He gripped her arms, suddenly, urgently. "What do you know?"

Cadence shook her head and laid two fingers across his lips. "Nothing. I was merely stating a possibility." When he relaxed slightly, although still retaining a hint of suspicion in his eyes, she continued.

"When all of this is dealt with, if we're still alive and these feelings we have for each other are still strong, then we can look at the factors for or against our getting together. Lovers usually find some way of overcoming their problems, even ones that seem insurmountable." She studied his face, saw the hesitation there. "All right?"

"You're sure that is what you want? What if there is no solution?"

She caressed his whisker-roughened cheek and countered with a question. "Do you want to deny us the chance of experiencing something wonderful together when the future is so uncertain?"

His storm-hued eyes searched her face. "No," he murmured finally and then drew her down to him for a hear-stopping kiss. "And I intend to work very hard to make certain that what we share *is* wonderful." He proceeded to do just that.

Gildon looked down upon Cadence's sleeping form. She was so beautiful, and her beauty was made greater by the fact that she herself did not recognize it. She stirred slightly, restless beneath his gaze.

Or was it his gaze that bothered her? He looked suspiciously around, but a careful scan revealed no sign of a scryer.

He looked back at Cadence. He disliked leaving her alone, even for so short a time as he would be gone, but unless he placed a guard at the door again—a measure that Cadence had disliked immensely—he had no choice. He knew he should wake her and discuss the matter, but he didn't have the heart to rouse her when she slept so peacefully. Rather, he would check the already intense warding and leave Cadence a message telling her he would be back shortly and not to leave the apartment. If luck was with him, he would be back before she awoke.

The confusion engendered by their strange familiarity with each other continued to plague him. He knew only one person who might be able to confirm his suspicion: his mother, Shaylon. So he would use the excuse that Cadence wanted a private visit with her as a pretext to visit her himself. He hoped that she would humor him and read his soul as she had professed to do for so many others.

A short time later, he left the apartment. As he walked the corridors of the temple, his thoughts returned to Cadence and their lovemaking. He had never experienced anything quite like it, not even on his visits to the Temple of the Shajati. What could possibly have made their lovemaking so unique, so special, if not the emotion *love?* Thoughts of her filled his mind more now than before. He pictured her in a hundred different poses he'd seen and memorized, and another hundred that he only fantasized. He pictured her as his companion, as the mother of his children, as his lover for life, and welcomed the depiction. How could this be wrong? Or, as Cadence had suggested, how could they grow to hate each other? It simply wasn't possible.

So intense were his thoughts that when he realized he was standing before his mother's apartment, he did not quite remember having traversed the corridors that took him there. He rang, and waited for her to unlock the door. It took so long for her to grant him entry that he'd been on the verge of attempting a telepathic knock to confirm whether she was at home or not. Finally, the door disappeared and he stepped inside.

"So the time span between your visits is getting shorter," Shaylon said. She stood at the food fabricator in the center of her kitchen, removing a tray of vegetables freshly transported from the growers in the central city. "Am I getting more popular in my old age?"

Gildon ignored her sarcasm, coming right to the

point as she had demanded of him throughout his life. "I have a couple of questions to ask you, Mother."

She looked up, studied him closely with eyes too much like his own ever to be fooled by his expression, no matter how shuttered. "It's important to you. Very well, sit. I'll join you shortly."

Gildon seated himself and waited impatiently—although he thought he concealed it well—for Shaylon to join him. She came to the table with a pitcher of fruit juice and two glasses. "Since it is near the evening meal and you have not brought Cadence with you, I assume that you don't want a snack. Correct?"

Gildon nodded and extended his glass to accept her silent offer of juice. "Yes. But thank you."

Shaylon nodded. "You're very preoccupied. What's on your mind?"

Gildon hesitated. "Cadence wanted me to ask you if it would be all right for her to visit you."

Shaylon's eyes snapped up to his. "Do you know why?"

He shook his head. "No. However, I noticed that she made the request after having had a nightmare, so perhaps she feels that you may be able help her with something to do with that."

"Tell her she may come tomorrow afternoon just after the midday meal."

Gildon dipped his head. "All right."

"Now, why are you really here?" Shaylon asked. "You could have asked telepathically if I'd be willing to see Cadence."

Gildon grimaced mentally. He should have known his mother would see through his pretext for coming. There wasn't much she missed. He cleared his throat and sipped his juice. Finally he met her gaze and plunged into the question. "Have you ever read my soul?"

Shaylon studied him for endless moments, then

turned her eyes to her glass and examined it with equal intensity. Eventually she responded. "Yes, of course I have. Why do you ask?"

"Something happened today that made me suspect that I possess a reincarnated soul." He pinned her with his gaze. "Do I?"

She nodded. "Yes."

"Can you tell me anything else about it?"

"What do you want to know?"

He shrugged. "Anything. Everything. How old is it? Where did it come from? Do you know the names of some of the incarnations?"

Shaylon shook her head. "You credit me with more talent than I have, my son." Gildon noted that there was less derision in those last two words than there had been at any time in his life, and wondered why. "You possess an ancient Tesuvian soul, one very experienced in many things. I know nothing more."

He nodded, believing her. "Thank you, Mother."

Cadence woke, found a note instead of Gildon, and read it as she returned to her own chamber. *You were sleeping so peacefully, I couldn't bear to wake you. I have gone to visit my mother and, while I'm there, I will ask if you may call on her. I will return soon. Gildon.* There was no mention of their lovemaking, or of love, even in closing the note, but Cadence had expected none. Their situation was still confusing . . . to both of them.

Content, Cadence decided to take a long bath. She'd always found that there was nothing better for sorting out her thoughts than a soak in a tub of warm water. As she entered her chamber, she had a strong desire to activate the computer in her helmet and talk to Claire. She actually paused before the shelf. But the helmet seemed almost strange to her now, a part of another life. And though she would still have enjoyed talking to Claire because it would have helped her to organize her thoughts, the memory of the scry gave her pause. If Ish'Kara was watching her, or someone else who worked for the Vradir cult, Cadence did not want them to know how much she, herself, now knew.

Bypassing the computer, she continued on to the opulent bathroom alone. While she was soaking in the perfumed water, she realized she was beginning to come to terms with the memories belonging to Ali'Yah. They no longer ran rampant through her mind, but had relegated themselves to the status of actual memories: there for access and remembrance when something triggered them, but dormant at other times.

She did feel different, though. Still Cadence, so it was not as though her body had been taken over by another personality . . . her own remained dominant. Rather, it was as if something had been added.

She frowned, trying to pinpoint and understand the change. She was charged with energy and a strong sense of purpose, the sense of purpose that always before had been lacking in her life. Now her destiny lay clearly defined before her: defeat Ish'Kara, and protect the innocent from her evil designs. Yet exactly how she was supposed to do that she still didn't know.

Why didn't she question her sudden acceptance of destiny? She had never been the type of person to accept the idea of destiny or fate controlling lives.

She searched her memories. The protection of the innocent had always been her intent. In every incarnation, she'd chosen a career or calling that allowed her to meet that goal in some way. Even as a Legionnaire, she had wanted to protect the innocent. However, within the Legion, her purpose had not been so obvious; right and wrong had not always been clearly defined. And she had felt . . . lost, as though she were missing something. That something was now found: The factions in this conflict were distinct, and she was on the side of right.

Yet, through all of this, she did not lose sight of who she was and the one purpose she still held as Cadence. She had to find her brother. Tailen would authorize someone to help her find the portal that had taken Chance now that it was clear that she was the person whose arrival had been foretold. The *savior*.

Stars, she wished they hadn't called her that, even in a prophecy. The implications were frightening. How could she, an ordinary woman, defeat an army of Vradir and their alter-realm allies to save a race of people and a world of innocent creatures? She certainly could not shoulder the entire responsibility herself. The mere thought made her want to run and hide. No, much of the outcome would be dependent on the measures the Tesuvians themselves had prepared, and, about that, little as yet had been discussed with her. She dearly hoped they had not placed too much emphasis on the abilities of their so-called savior.

But she would not think about that now, she decided as she lathered soap shavings over her body. For the moment, she was going to enjoy her bath and contemplate the pleasure of finally being able to do something to actively seek Chance.

Gildon had already returned and had set out the evening meal by the time Cadence completed her bath and came out of her bedchamber. He studied her face for a moment, seeking a sign that she regretted the altered status of their relationship. There was none. With a smile, he wrapped his arms around her and felt her arms encircle his waist.

"I ordered a new dish for you to try," he said. "I think you'll like it."

"What is it?"

"It's a delicate pastry dish containing three vegetables and a fruit which together create a unique
taste. We call it *fozlek*."

A few moments later, when they had finished their
meal, and Cadence had assured him that she did indeed like the *fozlek* very much, Gildon knew it was
time to return to the business at hand. As much as
he would like to pretend that the world outside his
apartment, along with all of its problems, did not
exist, he could not.

"Cadence—" He waited until she looked up at him.
"I know from your reaction that the communion was
successful, but I need to know how successful. Can
you tell me what you learned during contact?"

Cadence sighed, wiped her mouth with her napkin. "I think you have probably guessed some of it
by now." Then she nodded. "Yes, the communion
was successful. Much more successful than I had anticipated." She paused, looking about the chamber.
"Can you tell if we're being observed?"

Gildon nodded. "Usually, if I look for the signs."

"Can you check now, please?"

He closed his eyes and extended his senses, slowly
sweeping the room. He sensed no psychic imprint.
Opening his eyes, he said, "I'm almost certain that
we are alone."

"Good." Cadence poured herself a glass of fruit
juice.

"So, since the communion was so successful, do
you now know how to help us in combatting the alter-realm entities?" he asked. "They appear to be the
greatest threat at the moment."

Cadence shook her head. "No, in fact there's much
I don't know yet. But I do know that the entities gain
much of their power and abilities through the Vradir
queen, Ish'Kara, including their access to this world.
Once she's been defeated, most of the thresholds—

with the exception of those few actually created from this plane—will be sealed. Those that remain can be sealed by priests of the Avatar without too much difficulty. The entities still here at that time will begin to lose power, for they draw their strength from their own realms. It can take many years to dissipate completely, though, and during that time they will still be a threat."

Gildon stared at her. "How do you know this?"

"During the communion I learned that I am the reincarnation of a woman named Ali'Yah, who lived in ancient Atlantis. She and Ish'Kara have always been enemies, and have fought each other in many incarnations since Atlantis. That is how I know Ish'Kara so well."

"So, then, you know how to defeat her?"

Cadence swallowed and rose from the table to move across the room. Standing at the balcony door, she stared off into the distance . . . toward Madaia . . . and Ish'Kara. "Not exactly," she responded finally.

Gildon set down the glass from which he'd been about to drink. "What does that mean?"

Cadence whirled, her attitude defensive. "It means that I have been given Ali'Yah's knowledge and memories, but I still have to learn how to access what I need when I wish it. *And,* when I can do that, I need to be able to convert that knowledge to something usable by me, Cadence." She jabbed a thumb at her chest to emphasize. "A Stellar Legionnaire from Earth space. It's my knowledge combined with Ali-'Yah's that will destroy Ish'Kara." She managed to stop just short of telling him that, in any battle between Ali'Yah and Ish'Kara, there had never been a winner, that they had invariably killed each other. Cadence intended to change that. She had no desire to die—even for a good cause.

Gildon stood facing her. A troubled, thoughtful expression drew his brows together. "So how are you going to access the information you need?"

Cadence shrugged. "You tell me. For some reason, you too seem to have been granted a glimpse of your reincarnated soul, or you would not have recognized me as Ali'Yah during"—she waved one hand in the direction of his bedchamber—"earlier," she concluded. "And if Ali'Yah's memory is reliable, then I think your name was Kadar."

His eyes were suddenly intense on her face. "Who was Kadar to Ali'Yah?"

Cadence blinked, assailed by painful memories and emotions that were not her own. "Kadar was a warrior-trained priest of the Avatar. He was Ali'Yah's lover and companion. Ish'Kara killed him." Cadence's face twisted with pain at the visions that plagued her.

"I remember!" Gildon strode forward to grasp Cadence by the shoulders. "I remember," he said again. "Ish'Kara was your sister then, but she hated you."

Cadence nodded. "Yes."

He turned away, paced excitedly across the room, then pivoted to face her again. "We must tell Tailen about this. Perhaps he will know a method for you to access the knowledge you need."

Remembering her earlier thoughts, Cadence held up her hand. "There's something I need from you and Tailen first."

He frowned. "What's that?"

"Your help in finding the portal my brother was examining when he disappeared."

"Of course," Gildon said, his confused expression disappearing. "Do you have some record of the location of the portal?"

Cadence nodded and hurried from the room to retrieve the investigator's report completed by the Fortunan Guardian. Having perused it earlier, she knew exactly what she was looking for. Returning, she read from it, automatically translating in the process. " 'The disappearance of one Chance Barrington occurred during an archaeological expedition at a site approximately two hundred miles west of the Gemini mountains on the continent of Sendiri. It—.' "

Gildon held up his hand, and she halted. "It's a good thing we only have one range of mountains," he said. "The only city located west of a mountain range is Lagos, in the province of Chabia. Chabia borders on both Shemeir and Madaia. So we can be pretty certain which city they were in. What other details does it give?"

Cadence began reading again. " 'Barrington is alleged to have disappeared from before the eyes of his companions at approximately two in the afternoon while the group was working in a large building that the archaeologists refer to as the *castle* due to the ten crystalline towers that rise from its roof. This edifice is located at the center of the city being examined. At the time of his disappearance, Barrington was exploring the carvings on a pedestal-like artifact that held a golden winged figurine. When he had finished examining the carvings, he removed the figurine from the crown of the pedestal, cried out, and began to fade away. Logan Swan, a colleague who had been standing very near, is alleged to have rushed to Barrington's aid. However, by this time Barrington had completely disappeared. Swan, too, upon entering the area surrounding the pedestal faded but, according to colleagues, rematerialized seconds later.' " The document was signed by a number of witnesses as to accuracy, including Logan Swan.

Cadence looked up. "That's basically it. There are a few drawings and things, a bit more data concerning the Guardian's investigation of the area, but this is the information that can help us." She didn't like

Gildon's puzzled expression. "Right?"

He shook his head. "I'm not sure, Cadence. Unless some of your information is incorrect. . . . But the building you have described is the Temple of the Eidan in Lagos. The Eidanian temples do not have long-distance portals."

"But . . . how do you know it was a long-distance portal? And what do you mean by *long distance?*"

"The golden color of the winged figurine signifies a portal capable of interplanetary travel. We do not at this time have any such portals—at least no completed ones. And, as far as I know, none have been constructed within the Temples of the Eidan themselves."

Cadence stared at him in disbelief. "So what you're telling me is that Chance is not on this world? That he was pulled somewhere by a portal designed for interplanetary travel—which as of yet has not been built?"

Gildon, looking a little uncomfortable, nodded. "Yes."

Her eyes clung to his face. "You said these portals haven't been completed yet. That means you're aware of their construction. Right?" He nodded again and she continued. "So where will these portals be programmed to take people upon completion?"

"Tesuvia."

"Tesuvia!" Swallowing, she studied the abstract mosaic tiling on the floor, seeking a solution. Abruptly she looked up. "Can we at least ask Tailen about the portals? Hint that they may need to construct a portal within the temple?"

Gildon shook his head. "If we do that, we will be altering the course of events based on future knowledge."

"How do you know that's not the way it's supposed to be?"

Gildon hesitated. Cadence heard the faint rasp of his hand on his whiskered jaw as he rubbed it thoughtfully, and then he shook his head. "No, I think we must wait to speak with Tailen about the portal your brother used until we discover that such portals are being constructed."

Cadence clenched her fists in frustration. An instant later, her eyes narrowed with a sudden suspicion. "Why is it that every time I ask for your help in finding my brother, you always have some excuse for not doing so?"

"You know why I haven't been able to help you."

Cadence nodded and paced. "I know what you've told me, but I'm beginning to wonder if I'm not being manipulated." She stopped and looked at him. "Maybe you're afraid that if I find him, I'll leave before helping your people with the Vradir. Maybe I should just refuse to help you until I get some help in return."

Gildon's eyes hardened and a muscle twitched in his jaw. "You can't do that."

He was right, but she didn't have to let him know that. "Oh, yes, I can."

Stalking forward, he gripped her upper arms, raising her onto her toes as he spoke directly into her face. "There's nothing I can do to help you find your brother yet."

She stared defiantly up into his stormy eyes and ignored the traitorous warmth that raced through her body whenever he came near. "Prove it," she said.

Chapter Sixteen

A short time later, Tailen showed Cadence and Gildon to seats in his personal apartment, adjoining his office. It was the first time Cadence had seen it, and she examined it curiously. Although it was slightly larger than Gildon's apartment, there was not much to distinguish it from any other lodging she'd seen. The Tesuvians did not appear to flaunt their station in life with the acquisition of possessions.

Looking at the two men, Cadence had an attack of impatience and smothered it ruthlessly. Gildon had finally agreed to inform Tailen of the details of Chance's disappearance, but only *after* a normal, casual visit in which they would update Tailen about the results of Cadence's communion.

Since the evening meal had just passed, the snack that Tailen's novice transcriber placed before them consisted of cookies, *cai*, and a light wine.

"So then," Tailen looked at Cadence as he seated himself and began the conversation, "did the attempt at communion help in explaining the nature of your nightmares?"

Cadence's brow arched in surprise. "You know about that?"

Tailen nodded and, as host, poured *cai* for them. "Gildon mentioned it earlier."

Cadence nodded, wondering what other discussions Gildon and his superior had had concerning her. "Yes, actually the communion was much more successful than either Gildon or I had expected." With Gildon interjecting occasional comments, Cadence informed Tailen of everything she had told Gildon.

Tailen studied her. "That at least is progress, but we must find a means for you to begin to utilize Ali-'Yah's knowledge as though it is your own. We need to begin planning." He looked at Gildon. "After I spoke with you today, I was informed that a priest of the Geduin Order finally has recovered the knowledge necessary to complete the programming of the interplanetary portals. The work on them is even now being finished, so our people should be able to begin an exodus to safety tomorrow. But"—he looked back at Cadence—"escape is an option our people have that the creatures of this world do not. Indirectly, we are responsible for unleashing this devastation here, and we must do all we can to repair the damage."

Cadence nodded, understanding his desperation, and at the same time relieved to discover that the Tesuvians had made some effort to plan for the preservation of their people that did not hinge on the prophecy. She looked at Gildon. The subject of the portals had been broached; surely now was the time to talk about Chance's disappearance. She arched a brow in his direction.

He caught her glance, gave a slight nod, and looked at Tailen. "Where exactly are these portals located? Is access relatively restricted? Have alarms been incorporated to detect possessed individuals?"

Tailen, slightly startled by the deluge of questions, held up his hand. "Yes, alarms have been incorporated. No one not purely human will be transported. Yes, access is relatively restricted. In each city, we have placed four portals in the central city and four in the inner city. Due to the uncontrolled aspect of the outer cities, we did not place portals there. However, the wide range of acceptance programmed into the central city gates will grant access to all but the most dark alignments. This should ensure that nobody will be left behind."

Gildon nodded. "And where exactly in the inner city are the four portals located?"

"Let's see, I haven't been to see them myself as yet, but I believe there is one in the Temple of the Sadhue for the healers and the infirm, one just inside both the south gate and the north gate from the central city, and one in the main building of the temple proper."

"There is one in the Temple of the Eidan? In each city?"

"Yes. We felt the temple might be one of the last bastions of defense. Why do you seem so surprised?"

Gildon gestured with his chin in Cadence's direction, and she proceeded to describe for Tailen the nature of the portal from which Chance had disappeared, as reported in the account of his disappearance.

"Amazing! So your brother has gone to Tesuvia."

"It sounds that way, yes." She glanced at Gildon, remembering the argument they'd had before coming here. "Is there any way to confirm that?"

Tailen frowned. "You mean to go there, confirm his presence, and return here?"

Cadence shrugged. "If that's the only way, yes."

He shook his head. "I'm sorry. The portals have all been programmed for one-way travel."

"Why?" Cadence asked.

"As a safeguard for this world, so that once it is clean, it will remain so. And for ease in completing the portals themselves, which has been difficult enough as it is. A two-way portal takes double the length of time to program, and our people are anxious. But why do you want confirmation? Do you have reason to doubt the validity of the report you spoke of?"

Cadence slowly shook her head. "No."

"Then I'm afraid I don't understand the problem. The portals are all designed to take you to a specific time as well as place, subject to an incremental variance of a few minutes that is a programmed safeguard. This ensures that no two people will arrive at a location at precisely the same time. So, depending on the number of people who use the portal, I would estimate that no more than a few days will separate your arrival on Tesuvia from that of your brother."

"And this time can't be altered?"

"Well, of course, it can be altered, but the alteration requires specific knowledge of how to do so."

"So Chance could not have inadvertently changed the settings when he was examining the carvings on the pedestal just prior to his disappearance?"

Tailen studied her thoughtfully for a moment. Finally he responded. "It is extremely unlikely. The strokes and contact points necessary to reprogram an arrival time are very precise. If they are not followed exactly, the program remains unchanged. I'm certain your brother will be on Tesuvia in *this* time, when we arrive."

"And if you are wrong and he did manage to change the settings, or if something else happens to keep me from finding him . . . what then?"

Tailen, slightly taken aback, looked to Gildon for an explanation.

Gildon cleared his throat. "Cadence apparently feels that . . . we are asking more of her than we are prepared to give in return."

Tailen held his silence for a moment as though examining the statement from all angles. Then he said, "I see." He returned his gaze to Cadence. "If, when you arrive on Tesuvia, your brother is not there, you have my personal guarantee and promise that I will do everything within my power to help you find him. All right?"

Cadence studied him. "And what if something happens that I am not able to leave here? Will you find him anyway, and tell him about me?"

Tailen studied her with concern. "Yes," he said solemnly. "You have my word."

Cadence nodded. "All right then."

Tailen smiled. "Good." He looked at Gildon. "Now, I think we should return to the problem of how we can help Cadence in accessing the knowledge she needs." Gildon nodded, and Tailen continued. "Memory, including knowledge, most often seems to surface when drawn by association." He transferred his gaze to Cadence. "Do you think something like that might help you?"

She frowned. "I don't think so," she responded hesitantly. "It's like I've been given someone else's data crystal. I know there's information there, but I don't know what it relates to."

Both men stared at her. "I understand," Tailen said after a moment of silence, "but we must find a way around this problem. As much as I wish it were otherwise, we need your help. You are the only one familiar with this Vradir queen."

Gildon nodded, drawing Tailen's eyes to him. "Ish'Kara. I remembered the name and researched it after Cadence first spoke it. The name has been stricken from the naming books. Hers is an ancient soul, and very powerful."

"She cannot be killed." Cadence's quiet words fell like stones into the placid surface of a pond, creating rippling waves of uneasiness.

"What do you mean?" Gildon asked.

Cadence blinked, as though returning from some distant place. "Her soul doesn't forget, like most. Killing her only releases it to be born again. If she is fully aligned with the Daemod at the time of her death, she can escape into their plane. From there, she needs only to be granted access to this world in order to possess a body of her choosing."

"The demoness," Tailen murmured. "Now I understand the reason for the prophecy's terminology. How can you defeat her, then?"

Cadence searched her mind. "I don't know. The memory of Ish'Kara surfaced just for a moment, and then was gone."

Gildon cleared his throat, drawing Cadence's eyes. "When I first explained the process we use for communion to you, didn't you tell me that your people had a similar process? You said that instead of helping you get in touch with a superior being, the process helped you to get in touch with the hidden aspects of yourself."

Cadence's brow cleared. "Of course! Meditation. It might work. I haven't done it in a couple of years, but I'm pretty certain I can still achieve the deep relaxation I'd need." At one time she had meditated regularly and had had to keep a computer on, silently in the background, to record the wonderful ideas that came to her during this time of introspection.

Since no more could be accomplished just then, their meeting with Tailen wound down to a normal visit, and they left a short time later.

The suns were setting as Cadence and Gildon crossed the cobbled square heading back to the Avatarian temple that housed his apartment. The distant yellow star was little more than a small bright ball perched atop the glorious splash of color on the horizon. The mauve daytime glow of the nearer red sun deepened now, its crimson radiance striking fire to the crystalline spires that speared the sky from the inner-city edifices. Cadence caught her breath. She'd never seen anything so beautiful. She caught Gildon's arm. "Look," she said, drawing him to a halt beside her. "They're like pillars of fire."

She saw his gaze darken with an appreciation that mirrored her own. "Nature's beauty can never be surpassed," she murmured.

"No, it can't." But Gildon's gaze was no longer on the spires, and his eyes glittered with a heat that rivaled that reflected by the suns. "Are you ready to go home?"

Meeting his eyes, Cadence could only nod as her abdomen did strange things in response to the expression in his eyes. He grinned—a tender, sexy smile that had her heart doing flip-flops—and wrapped his arm around her waist to escort her home.

The moment Gildon ushered Cadence into the apartment, he swept her into his arms, crushing her against his chest. His full-lipped mouth claimed hers, and Cadence's heart leapt in response. As his hot tongue invaded, Cadence's senses exploded. The room spun, and she raised her arms to wrap them around his neck. His hands slid down to cup her bottom, to press her against his surging erection, and molten liquid flooded her nether regions. She moaned with sudden fierce want. And then the horizon tilted as he lifted her in his strong arms and carried her into the bedroom.

Once again, their lovemaking took them to that place that neither of them had ever been with another lover. That place where their souls touched and they became one in a way few people could ever hope to understand. That place for lovers who share a love so powerful it endures for eternity. But Cadence and Gildon were still only beginning to understand that themselves.

Some time later, he plucked her from the bed and carried her in the direction of the bathroom. "What are you doing?" she asked.

He looked down at her, his eyes lit by a tenderness

that stole her breath. "I'm going to bathe you and massage you."

Cadence hated to allow the outside world and her responsibilities into the room, but she had no choice. "I really should go and try meditating."

"You need to be relaxed for that, don't you?"

"Yes."

"Then I will relax you. I took some training from the Shajati, you know. My brother felt it was something all young men should do." He grinned. "Who knows, maybe you will even touch the One as the Shajati say is possible."

Cadence met his eyes. "I thought we already did that."

A spark flared in his eyes and his gaze dipped to her bare breasts and back to her face. "They say that all things are a part of the One," he murmured as he set her on her feet in the bathing chamber. "If someone can be more so than another, then that person is you, Cadence." He brushed her cheek with his fingers. "And in touching the heart of you, I have touched the One."

As her heart fluttered strangely in her chest, Cadence stared. The men of her acquaintance, all hard men's-men, would have slit their own throats before allowing such romantic sentiments to pass their lips. She didn't know what to say to such an earnest declaration of his feelings, so, like Gildon, she spoke her heart. "I love you." It wasn't as poetic, but he didn't seem to mind.

Sweeping her into his arms, he kissed the top of her head. "We will find a way to be together always," he promised. "Somehow."

Then, holding her away from him, he smiled, lightening the atmosphere. "And now it is time to show you how well I learned my lessons from the Shajati."

Cadence was inclined to think he'd learned his lessons very well indeed. She lay absolutely still in the water, as ordered, while Gildon soaped and massaged every inch of her body, but it wasn't easy. Every slick caress of his hands on her body incited the hunger that had been so recently sated, and she wanted nothing more than to run her hands over his sleek, wet body in turn. Finally she could stand it no more. "I thought this was supposed to be relaxing." She was startled by the breathlessness of her tone.

He looked at her and smiled. "The strain you are now under is only *one* source of tension. All the other tensions and stresses have been released from the muscles of your body and crowded from your mind."

"And when exactly are you going to relieve *this* tension?" Cadence managed to gasp as his hands worked their magic on her upper thighs.

"Soon," he promised. His fingers brushed the soft curls at the junction of her thighs, and she arched uncontrollably against his hand. "Don't move," he reminded her.

"I can't help it." She moaned in frustration.

Then he lifted her and turned so that he lay beneath her in the warm water. She felt his enormous erection against her stomach and was pleased to discover that she wasn't the only one affected by his ministrations. "Now?" she asked.

"Now," he confirmed with a tense smile.

With release imminent, Cadence decided to repay him a small measure of frustration. Rearing back on her heels, she studied him consideringly. "I think that perhaps I should massage you for a while. You know, to be fair."

Gildon's gaze scorched her with its glittering heat. "I don't think that would be a good idea."

"Why?" she asked, eyes wide with feigned innocence, though she was unable to keep the teasing smile from her lips.

Rather than responding, he grasped her waist and lifted her, positioning her over his erection. As he slowly slid his thick staff into her body, all thought of further baiting dissipated.

Gildon was right, Cadence mused. She had never been more relaxed. Having returned to her own bed-chamber for the privacy she needed, she sat with her back propped against the wall and her legs stretched out comfortably before her. She had never managed to get herself into the lotus position without experiencing at least some degree of pain. Since meditation required comfort, not pain, she had long ago given up trying to sit in that traditional posture.

Before she sought a deep trance state, she focused her mind on the one question she needed answered above all: *How can I combat and defeat Ish'Kara?* With that question firmly embedded in her mind, she wiped all directed thought away and just let her mind flow. Thoughts came to her, random and disjointed. She examined them casually, as one might a bed of flowers along a walkway, but granted them no importance. Then, as her trance deepened, she became aware that the thoughts she was examining were no longer her own.

The part of her that had been a woman named Nathara remembered the sun rising over her husband's grave. *How could the world continue so unchanged, so beautiful, when her personal world, now lonely and shadowed, had changed forever?*

And then one of Ali'Yah's memories flitted across her mind—a recollection of Kadar. Although she didn't believe it would be what she sought, curiosity compelled Cadence to focus on this one. Kadar was a handsome man about the same build as Gildon, although his features were harsher and more angular. Their coloring was almost identical with the exception that Kadar had ebony-dark eyes. He stood before some type of metal furnace, naked except for a loincloth, and seemed to be almost reaching into the flaming depths as he worked. Sweat ran in rivulets over his muscled physique and down his forehead, pooling in the creases of his eyes until he dashed it away. Cadence was about to move on, to discard the memory as unimportant, when she heard a voice, hers and yet not hers: Ali'Yah's.

"Are you sure it will work?" And Cadence realized that since she was seeing this memory through Ali'Yah's eyes, she would not, of course, see Ali'Yah. It was a strange sensation.

Kadar turned to face her. "Once we imbue the metal with the soul-entrapping quality it will work against anyone. Even Ish'Kara."

"You have the details of the rite?"

Kadar nodded. "I have worked out even the smallest details. There is nothing that can go wrong. Once the blade of the sword undergoes the transformation I have worked out, we need only bring it into contact with Ish'Kara's body and blood for it to perform its purpose. And she will be trapped within it."

"Forever?"

He shook his head and looked a little worried. "No. There is a weakness. The first person to grasp the hilt of the sword—after it's been released by the wielder who entraps the soul—becomes a receptacle for the trapped soul."

"So it's possible that Ish'Kara will again escape."

Cadence remembered the warmth of Kadar's hands on Ali'Yah's upper arms as he grasped them and looked earnestly down into her face. "No. It will work. We simply have to come up with a means to safeguard the sword, to ensure that no one ever touches it again after Ish'kara's soul is captured."

The memory ended, and Cadence moved on, accessing and discarding disconnected recollections that belonged to other people, other lives. Nothing more surfaced. She began to get frustrated and took a deep breath in an effort to calm herself.

All right, her initial question had been answered; she now knew *how* she was to defeat Ish'Kara: with the specially imbued soul-entrapping sword. She would have preferred something that didn't entail such proximity, like a laser or blaster, but, as a trained fighter, she could deal with it. The question that remained was, how was she to go about creating the weapon? Surely Kadar must have shared his knowledge with Ali'Yah at some point.

Focusing on this new query, she deepened her trance. Scenes flashed and were as quickly gone. A number of times, her mind returned to the scene with Kadar before the huge fiery furnace, but no new information came to her. Then, finally, there was one more scene which held significance for her.

Kadar lay in his finest clothing upon a healer's table. His eyes were closed and he didn't breathe. Slowly the table moved on its wheels into a chamber filled with white light. There was a brief flash, and his body was gone. What had happened?

Cadence accessed an ancient memory and recognized the glass-walled room as the disintegration chamber for the dead. And she remembered Gildon's explanation that the Tesuvians believed in leaving no physical remains behind. Now she knew what they did with their dead. But what did this scene mean to her?

Had Kadar died before passing on the knowledge Ali'Yah needed to complete the weapon?

Of course. If he had not, she would not have been compelled to destroy Atlantis to put a stop to Ish'Kara and her cult, to keep them from spreading unchecked among an innocent and primitive people.

Cadence opened her eyes and sighed, discouraged. What now?

A few moments later, she entered the kitchen in search of a drink and a larger space in which to pace.

Gildon was already seated at the table, drinking a deep purple beverage that looked like wine. Cadence halted in surprise. "I thought you had gone to bed."

He shrugged. "I couldn't sleep. How did it go?"

"I'm not sure." Seating herself, she poured herself a glass of wine from the bottle on the table and sipped it before returning her gaze to Gildon. With an arched brow and a glance that found the ceiling, she asked, *Is it safe to talk?*

Gildon closed his eyes for a moment, extending his senses in search of the psychic footprint that would betray someone scrying. He was about to pronounce them in the clear when something shimmered on the edge of his cerebral vision. Whoever it was was very good at obscuring the signs of his presence. Gildon had almost missed the signs. Gildon opened his eyes and gave a slight negative shake of his head.

"So," he said. "I don't believe you have yet seen my office. Would you like to?" Once in his office, he could activate the same type of shielding that he used when in contact with alter-realm entities to prevent their escape. Not even the most expert scryer could penetrate that.

Cadence nodded and smiled, although the gesture looked a little forced. "Yes. I'd like that."

Gildon rose, wineglass in hand, and extended his free hand to Cadence. "Come then."

Downstairs, he seated Cadence in a comfortable chair near his desk and intoned the note which activated his protections. Then, as a glistening rainbow-hued bubble appeared in a 12-foot-diameter area around them, he sat at his desk. "What is it?" he asked without preamble. "What did you learn?"

As Cadence told him the results of her meditation process, Gildon began to get a strange feeling. He had begun to suspect that he might be the most recent incarnation of Kadar. If he was right, and Cadence needed the knowledge Kadar had held to craft

the weapon that would entrap Ish'Kara, then . . .
then Cadence had been correct when she'd surmised
that the guardians had had a hand in bringing them
together. But what did that mean for *them?* For Cadence and Gildon?

Would the feelings they felt so powerfully now
fade when Ali'Yah and Kadar were no longer so man-
ifest in their subconscious minds?

He recalled how he had begun to feel his personality changing almost the moment he had met Cadence. Had that change been wrought by his own
interest in her? Or by the emergence of Kadar's soul
in response to the nearness of Ali'Yah's? Would he
and Cadence become strangers to each other when
this was over? The thought distressed him. He liked
this feeling of togetherness, of belonging and being
part of another person. He didn't want to lose it.

"Gildon—" He met her quizzical inspection. "What
are you thinking?"

He sighed, shoving aside his own insecurities.
They were being carried along in Destiny's arms, and
there was nothing they could do about that until her
purpose for them had been met and fulfilled.

He told Cadence of his intuition concerning the
identity of his soul.

She frowned. "I had begun to consider the same
possibility. If you *are* Kadar, the most recent incarnation of the same soul, does that mean you can seek
out his memories?"

"Typically such memories are suppressed so that
each person can live out his or her life untainted by
the transgressions and guilt of previous existences.
However, in this instance, I would bet that the guardians have removed those barriers. Like you, I probably merely need to learn how to access the
memories and make them a part of my own remembrances."

Cadence considered him thoughtfully. "My meditation process is very like the process you use for communion, with the exception that, at the moment when you would usually launch your consciousness outward, you turn inward, into your own mind. If the question you want answered is uppermost in your thoughts just prior to going into trance, your mind should automatically seek the answers."

"Show me."

She demonstrated the position she found most comfortable and detailed her process for achieving a trance-like state.

Gildon at times found his attention wandering from her words to the movement of her lips, to the line of her cheek, or to the curve of her breast, but determinedly wrenched his concentration back where it belonged. "I understand," he said when she concluded. "I think I'd like to be alone to attempt this. Solitude often aids concentration. Why don't you go on up and I'll see what I can accomplish."

"All right." Cadence rose, and he rose with her, stopping her as she neared him to kiss her goodnight. He did so with no small regret, for he had hoped to spend the night holding her in his arms.

"I'll see you later," he murmured, letting her go reluctantly.

It was almost dawn by the time Gildon climbed the stairs to join Cadence in bed, but he had the answers they needed. Wrapping his arms around her, he sank into a welcome sleep.

Just past midday, Cadence and Gildon left the apartment. "Unlike Kadar," Gildon continued the conversation they'd been having over lunch, "I don't have a personal mastery of metal working, but I believe I know a very talented young man who will be willing to assist us. After I leave you with my mother, I'll go and see him."

Cadence nodded. "And you're certain that everything else concerning Kadar's process you can duplicate yourself?"

"Yes. I'm positive of it."

Cadence sighed. "That's a relief."

They walked in companionable silence for some moments. Then Cadence decided it was time to ask a question that had been haunting her ever since she'd accepted her destiny here. "Gildon—?" She brushed his arm with her fingertips, drawing his eyes down to hers. "When we're ready, how do we find Ish'Kara?"

He considered her silently a moment before speaking. "We'll seek her out in Madaia."

"That's what I thought." Cadence looked at the novices scurrying through the corridors and waited until there was no one in earshot. "Getting to her won't be easy, will it?"

Gildon shook his head. "No. She has an army of ex-Kami warriors at her disposal, along with all of her allies, human and non. No," he said again, "getting to her won't be easy." He looked at Cadence. "But we'll do it because we have to. Although my people have finally found a means of escape, the species of this world have not. It is our responsibility to deal with the poison produced by our own kind."

Cadence searched her memory for reference to this cardinal sense of responsibility and found it within Ali'Yah's remembrances. *We are Tesuvians; we are one people sharing one creed. If one of our brethen commits a crime, it is the responsibility of that person to make restitution. If he or she will not or cannot do so, then the responsibility for restitution falls to all Tesuvians.*

Cadence marveled at the incredible sense of morality that would prompt the adoption of such a philosophy. Very few civilizations would have been capable of it. Certainly not her own, where the idea of one creed serving all peoples would have been considered preposterous. Religions and governments clashed constantly, and would probably continue to do so. Yet she couldn't help imagining what Earth might have been like today if her people had accepted responsibility for their behavior. Would it have been more like this world, with its open skies and fresh air? Would fruit and vegetables grown outside vast, controlled greenhouses be fit to eat?

They halted outside Shaylon's apartment door, and Gildon ran his hand over the chimes in the prescribed pattern. A moment later, the melody was completed from within the apartment, and the door disappeared. Shaylon waited to greet them, looking uncharacteristically anxious. "Come in," she invited.

"I am on my way to another appointment," Gildon advised her. "I will stop back in about an hour." He looked at Cadence. "All right?"

She nodded. "Yes. Thank you."

As Gildon left and the door reappeared behind him, Cadence heeded Shaylon's invitation and sat down on the plump green cushion at the table. Shaylon placed a small plate of cookies on the table, seated herself, and poured them each fruit juice before meeting Cadence's eyes. She came directly to the point.

"Why have you asked to see me, Cadence?"

Cadence sipped her juice, giving herself time to try to formulate the answer in a way that would not offend Shaylon in some way. "I was remembering our last conversation, and your mention of a warning. That warning was not meant for Gildon as I'd first supposed, was it?"

"What makes you say that?"

"I don't know . . . a feeling that I missed something I was supposed to have grasped. I assumed that you had begun to have doubts concerning Jakial's strength of purpose. Was I correct?"

Shaylon considered her thoughtfully. Then she nodded.

"But why did you tell *me?* What does Jakial have to do with me? I've never even met him."

"You will," Shaylon murmured. "Either way, you will."

Cadence's brows snapped together in consternation. "Either way? What do you mean by that?"

Once again, Shaylon considered her for a long time in silence. Cadence began to get uncomfortable beneath her penetrating regard. Finally Shaylon spoke. "You have now accepted your place among us." It was a statement, yet Cadence felt compelled to respond.

"Yes. How did you know?"

Shaylon shrugged. "Your posture and your mannerisms have changed slightly. You have direction, an air of purpose."

"I see." So Shaylon was an accomplished reader of body language. "Can we please return to my earlier question? What did you mean when you said that either way I would meet Jakial? Your comment sounded . . . like a warning."

"Perhaps it was."

"Why?" Cadence reached across the table and placed her hand over Shaylon's. "Please, I need you to help me understand."

Shaylon looked at their touching hands for a moment, apparently surprised by the contact. And then, as though suddenly coming to a decision, she rose. "I will return shortly."

Two minutes later, she reappeared carrying a small, red-bound book. Opening it to a page, she handed it to Cadence and indicated a handwritten paragraph. "This is a foretelling my lover received from the Lidai before he died. Read it."

"But I can't read Tesuvian characters! I'm barely

gaining familiarity with your modern color-barred language."

"Yes, I believe you can, if you try. Read it."

Cadence turned her eyes to the page and searched her memory for knowledge of the symbols she saw there. And she did read it, once and then again. "Oh, stars!" she breathed a moment later and reread the last two sentences. *He that is noble of heart and is best loved will be the savior's strength. And he that is plagued by envy and ambition and is weak of heart will be the demon's tool.* Suddenly things began to become clear. Tragically clear.

For a young mother to know that both of her sons would figure prominently in the destiny of their people would be difficult enough, but to know that one would be a tool in the destruction of their civilization would be frightening and devastating. Such a young woman, guided only by instinct and a mother's perceptions, might have tried to protect the son she believed good. And she might have detested and vilified the son she believed destined to be the instrument of evil.

Lifting her gaze to Shaylon's, Cadence observed a sheen of moisture in the other woman's eyes. "Age has given me the benefit of insight," Shaylon said. "Did I love the wrong son, Cadence?"

Cadence felt the other woman's pain across the table. She wanted to say that Shaylon should have loved both her sons equally and simply let the prophecy play itself out as it would, but such words would do nothing but add to the burden of pain and guilt the other woman already felt. "I don't know, Shaylon," she lied. She laid her hand over the other woman's again, offering what comfort she could. "I don't know."

And now, at last, she understood the too-subtle warning that Shaylon had tried to give her: If Cadence loved one son, then she must fear the other.

That was why Shaylon had been so interested in Cadence's feelings for Gildon. And when Cadence had said she was merely fond of Gildon, Shaylon had said, *Then I will continue to hope*. She had been hoping that it was Jakial that Cadence was destined to love. Hoping that she had not spent a lifetime despising the wrong son.

Cadence sipped her fruit juice and wished fervently that she had not fallen into this alien world of prophecies and strange beliefs. But then she remembered the matron at the orphanage saying, If wishes were credits we'd all be rich.

At that moment a slight noise to her right attracted her attention. A man stood there. A novice being educated by Shaylon, perhaps? He was of medium height for a Tesuvian, probably six foot six or so. He had dark brown hair and a tanned complexion which contrasted attractively with his white trousers and robe. But it was his eyes that arrested her. They were a dark blue-gray that constantly changed hue like roiling storm clouds. Eyes like Shaylon's . . . and Gildon's.

As though to confirm her sudden horrified suspicion, he spoke. "Hello, Mother."

"Jakial!" Shaylon gasped.

Chapter Seventeen

Gildon met with Traic of the line of Suda in the central city. The young man's nervousness in being confronted by a white-robed priest of the Avatar was obvious. "I'll be with you shortly, kaitan." He avoided looking directly at Gildon.

Gildon nodded and studied the enclosure. They were in the rear courtyard of Traic's parents' home where he was working at his forge. Although a master metalworker in his own right, and of an age to have his own domicile, Traic had chosen to stay with his parents until he'd registered enough excess service to earn a larger home for himself and the young woman he'd chosen as companion. Now, with the evacuation in progress, he didn't know what would happen to their plans. Gildon knew this from speaking with another priest of the Avatar, Ashur Ventarc, whom he'd asked for a recommendation in his search for a metalworker. Traic's work had received Ashur's most glowing endorsement.

Gildon observed as Traic removed an item from the forge, hammered a couple of imperfections, and then replaced it to be heated again.

At that moment a loud popping noise sounded and both men pivoted, seeking its source. A threshold! Subconsciously Gildon had recognized the sound of its inception, but he'd hoped he was wrong. The large oblong gateway, ringed by a coruscation of flame-hued light, stood barely twelve feet away. And within the threshold a Gou'jiin's glowing yellow eyes stared back at them.

Gildon's heart began to pound. He had to close the threshold. Now! Before the Gou'jiin entered!

Raising his hands to direct the energy, he began the intonation of syllables which, when combined with his mental will, would collapse the gate. He prayed he was quick enough. As Traic moved to stand behind him, Gildon became conscious of the young man's fear. He heard the sounds of the many passersby in the street just beyond the courtyard wall and knew they too were in jeopardy if he failed. And he recognized the determination in the face of the Gou'jiin. It wanted corporeal existence, badly. It wanted to feel and taste and hear through human senses. It wanted to indulge itself.

But even as its smoky form moved toward the threshold, the bubble-like surface of the gate was fortified. A Daemod would have had no trouble breaking through, but the Gou'jiin with its insubstantial form was thwarted. Relaxing slightly now, Gildon narrowed his eyes to slits and completed the incantation. A second later, with the whooshing sound of a hungry blaze, the threshold collapsed inward.

Traic's relief was palpable. He moved out from behind Gildon and turned to face him. "You saved my life!"

Gildon nodded, a small smile curving his lips. "My own, too."

As though he'd suddenly realized that the priest of the Avatar meant him no harm, Traic's natural loquaciousness came to the fore. "I'll be glad to escape this place! They say that Tesuvia is much like it is here," he said as he moved back to his forge to check on the unfinished work there. "Is that right?"

"I don't know, Traic."

In Destiny's Arms

"My family is scheduled for access to a portal within three days."

Gildon wasn't surprised. He had expected the evacuations to begin the moment the portals were completed. "Have you heard an estimate on how long it will take to complete the evacuation?"

Traic shrugged. "I've heard a week, but I'm not certain that's correct." He removed the item from the forge, hammered and scraped the imperceptible imperfections again, and placed it on a polished stone table before wiping his hands. Then, turning to Gildon, he said, "Now, what can I do for you, kaitan?"

Gildon wasted no more time. "I need a very ancient style of weapon forged. A short sword, about this long." He held his hands a little more than two feet apart. "Are you familiar with it?"

Traic frowned thoughtfully. "Not personally, but I have records of such weapons."

Gildon nodded and continued. "The metal composition must be at least ten percent gold, fifteen percent meteoric iron, and five percent nickel. The balance of the composition is not of great importance, as long as the weapon is strong." He paused and studied Traic's somber face. "Is that a problem?"

The boy's eyes flew up to meet his. "The meteoric iron may be a problem. I will need to check my inventory. One moment."

Gildon nodded and waited as Traic walked to the rear of the courtyard and opened the door of a small stone building. As soon as the door was open, Traic descended some stairs, revealing that the structure was merely the entrance to an underground storage space of indeterminate size. He returned moments later. "You said the percentage of meteoric iron necessary was fifteen percent?"

"Yes."

"Then I should have just enough. It's a good thing you requested a small weapon." He stuck his hands

287

in the pockets of his dark blue trousers. "What kind of ornamentation do you require?"

"None!" Horrified by the idea that the attractiveness of the weapon might induce someone to pick it up, Gildon responded more vehemently than he'd intended. He altered his tone. "The sword should be plain in the extreme. Only a single name should be engraved upon the hilt: Ish'Kara."

Traic nodded. "All right. Anything else?"

"Yes." Gildon studied the young man's clear blue eyes, fair complexion, and blond hair; he looked so young, so . . . trusting. Gildon hoped he wasn't endangering him. "The forging of this weapon should be kept absolutely secret. Tell no one. When you have completed it, while it is still very warm from the forge, I require it delivered to my apartment in the Temple of the Avatar." A thoughtful frown drew his brows together. "Do you need help in moving through the inner-city gate?"

"No, kaitan. I have done so often."

Gildon nodded. "Good. Then all is in order?"

"Yes, kaitan. All will be done as you wish," Traic responded as though he received such unusual requests from inner-city priests every day. "When is the weapon required?"

"Tomorrow evening, just before moon rise."

At this, Traic raised a brow slightly but said only, "Certainly."

"I also need a small casket constructed. The base should be constructed of a strong but fairly light metal. Its top must be transparent, and I need a copper plate suitable for an inscription affixed to the cover."

"I will have to commission the cover from a crystal or glass worker. Do you need the casket tomorrow evening as well?"

Gildon shook his head. "No." He stared to one side, wondering who best to have the casket delivered to so that it would be available when he needed it. "As long as it is completed by the next evening. Since I will be gone by then, have it delivered to Prelate Tailen."

"It will be done as you wish, kaitan," Traic said.

As Gildon left the portal and was walking across the inner-city square to the Temple of the Avatar he heard his mother's telepathic call. There was no psychic knock, no warning signal to the contact whatsoever. *Gildon! Come quickly!* she said. And then the contact was broken.

Mother, what is wrong? he sent, but there was no response.

Breaking into a run, he groped in his pocket for the *falar* stone, hoping that his inability to make contact was due simply to a lack of power. *Falar* stone in hand, he barely slowed as he placed the chain firmly over his head so that the stone lay on his forehead.

Mother, what's wrong? he sent. No answer. He kept running.

And then he felt the faintest stirring of her psychic energy. *Quickly* . . . The contact was so faint he almost believed he'd imagined it. Why was his mother so weak? What had happened to her?

When he reached Shaylon's apartment, he swiftly ran his hands over the door carvings. The instant the door disappeared he raced into the apartment.

"Mother—?" A quick glance told him that neither Shaylon nor Cadence were in sight; he ran toward the rear of the apartment. "Cadence—?"

He was racing past the closed door of his father's study on his way to his mother's bedchamber when he heard a faint cry.

He stopped, stared at the door for a fraction of a second in incomprehension. His mother never went in there.

He hurried through the insubstantial barrier before it had even faded in response to his physical contact. His mother lay on the floor before a personal portal that had been so expertly concealed within the wall of the study that he had never known of its existence.

Cadence was nowhere in sight.

He knelt at Shaylon's side, visually checking her body for harm. "Mother, what happened?". He could see no injury. "Where is Cadence?"

She grasped the fabric of his robe, her grip surprisingly strong, and pulled him closer. "Jakial," she murmured. "He is Vradir. I tried to stop him." She gasped and swallowed. "He . . . he turned my psionic blast back on me with quadrupled force. He is . . . very powerful now. Cadence is . . . He took her, my son. I'm sorry."

Panic rose in his throat, choking him, but he forced it back. "It's all right, Mother," he said as he straightened her legs to ease her into a more comfortable position. "I'll call the healers to care for you, and then I'll go after her."

She tightened her grasp on his robe again. "It is too late for a healer, Gildon; the life is leaving my body." She tugged, drawing him closer as the strength of her voice failed. "Listen to me. Take Cadence as your companion, it was meant to be."

"All right, Mother." He agreed only to soothe her agitation, for it became obvious in that moment that his mother's life truly was fading. He felt . . . numb.

Where was his dislike for the woman who had been a mother in name only all of his life? Where was his compassion for a dying person? Where was his grief for what might have been? It wasn't there. He felt nothing, and that frightened him. And so he pretended he felt something.

He looked down on Shaylon's still attractive features and met the dark blue eyes so like his own. They were a bit dazed now, fogged with the coming of death. He smoothed back Shaylon's silver-streaked blond hair and gripped her hand in his. "Mother, let me call the healers. Maybe you're wrong. Perhaps they can help."

She merely shook her head without speaking, and even that effort seemed to tire her. And then, with one last effort of will, she beckoned him. As he bent near, she spoke softly, breathlessly. "The red book . . . on the table . . . read it."

"I will, Mother," he promised.

"Forgive me, my son." There was no rancor or dislike in her tone . . . only regret. "I loved . . . the wrong son." Her hand fell away from his robe, the slack fingers falling across her body. "Forgive me, Gildon."

He nodded. "Of course, Mother."

She tried to smile, softly, gently, the kind of smile he had always wanted from her but never received. And then the breath left her lungs for the last time and the light faded from her eyes.

For a moment he could only stare, unable to come to terms with the reality that this woman, who had always been so strong, had died.

But as the meaning behind Shaylon's death penetrated his numb mind, grief tightened his chest. Not grief for the mother who lay dead before him, but grief for the brother he had always loved so dearly. There was no chance now that Jakial would return to Shemeir. No chance that they would recover the relationship they'd once had. In one afternoon, he had lost his mother and his brother forever. And the woman he loved had been stolen from him.

Cadence. His heart cried out in agony, demanding that he follow immediately. His mind overruled it. He would do Cadence no good if he went plunging into the enemy camp without preparation, for they would both die.

Sitting back on his heels, he closed his eyes and

Christine Michels

called Rion of the line of Pilyr, a priest of the Sadhue Order who specialized in valediction preparations.

Brother Gildon. How may I help you?

My mother is dead, Brother. I would ask that you make arrangements.

There was a pause. *Of course, Brother.* A wave of sympathy came through the contact, but Gildon shook it off. He needed his grief and anger to sustain him through what must be done. *She is in her apartment?* Rion asked.

Yes.

I will be there within moments.

Even here, in the inner city, it was no longer safe to leave a body alone for long, so Gildon used the time until Rion arrived to search the apartment for clues as to what had happened. A plate rested unbroken against one wall, the cookies that it had held scattered across the seating area just off the kitchen. A sure sign that Cadence had fought her captor. But there were no other signs of resistance.

A small red book on the table caught his eye. *Read it.* His mother's words replayed in his mind. Subduing his curiosity, he placed it in an inner pocket of his robe. He would read it when Cadence was safely back in Shemeir.

Moving back into the study, he avoided looking too closely at his mother's body, except to ascertain that she still rested peacefully, and then proceeded to examine the portal. Why had his father had a secret portal constructed? Although personal portals weren't unheard of, they were unnecessary for the most part. Very few people possessed them. If one had been constructed here, there must have been a good reason. He just couldn't think of one. Unless . . . his father had not been the one to commission the portal's construction.

Had Jakial's nefarious plans begun that long ago? Although Jakial had had his own apartment, he had taken over their father's study after Torak's death.

But why not have the portal constructed in his own apartment?

Even as he asked the question, Gildon knew the answer. Jakial had known he would eventually leave his apartment for a post elsewhere; that had always been in his plans. Rather than have his portal within an apartment whose future occupants he couldn't hope to be familiar with, he had decided to construct it within an apartment whose occupant he would always know: their mother.

In another apartment, the risk of someone discovering the portal and closing it to traffic from Madaia, as all other portals on the continent had been closed, would be greater. Jakial had known that their mother rarely entered Torak's study and so was highly unlikely to discover the hidden portal. He also would have placed a certain amount of trust in the fact that, when he did choose to use the portal, his mother would not immediately consider him an intruder as the owners of another apartment would.

Gildon sighed. Speculation served no purpose; the portal was here now.

He set about examining its settings. It was set for a destination somewhere in the city of Eston in Madaia. Since the source portal settings could not be changed by the traveler, all Gildon had to do was step into the portal, activate it, and he knew he would arrive at the same portal in Madaia which had been Jakial's destination in his abduction of Cadence. There was one major problem: Jakial would have set a trap.

Before he had time to consider his best plan of action, Rion Pilyr arrived. They gripped forearms. "I will leave you to prepare her for passage; there are some things I must do," Gildon said. "Delay the valediction for two days at most. If I have not returned, proceed without me."

Although Rion seemed confused, he did not question Gildon's intentions. "As you wish, my brother."

The moment Gildon was able to leave his mother's apartment, he hurried to his own to make the necessary preparations. The first thing he would do was inform Tailen of Cadence's abduction and his intent to pursue her. Then he would become Kami again. Although he would carry many of the safeguards of the Avatarian priesthood with him, it was the warrior within him who would go after Cadence.

It took little time for him to change into the indigo warrior garb and arm himself with dislocator and knives. That done, he left his bedchamber and raced down to his study. It took considerably more time to try to anticipate the types of arcane dangers he might encounter.

And too, there was the nature of his mission. What if he didn't return? No one would know the secret of the soul-entrapping sword. Yet he dared not tell anyone. Ultimately, he decided that the only thing he could do was record the details of the sword's imbuement in his journal. He hoped that, if he did not return, this information would leave the priests who came after him enough to work with.

That done, he filled his pockets and a bag with crystals modified to produce varying results, from explosions to impenetrable walls. Finally, fingering the crystals and wondering if he'd forgotten anything, he climbed the stairs. Upon reaching the kitchen, he packed a small sack with dried fruits, nuts, and flat breads ordered from the fabricator. Although he wasn't hungry yet, it was nearing time for the evening meal and he had no idea how long he'd be gone.

As he walked the corridors back to his mother's apartment, he considered the problem of the portal. How could he avoid the guards at the other end?

He still had not arrived at an answer when he reentered Shaylon's apartment. No, *his* apartment now, he supposed—if he wanted it.

Rion and whatever assistants had followed him had removed Shaylon's body, and the apartment was empty. As Gildon moved slowly through it, a sudden feeling of emptiness struck him, and he went directly to the study. For a moment, he could only stare at the place where his mother had lain, the place where she had spoken the last words she would ever speak in this incarnation. And he suddenly realized what her final moments must have cost her.

Jakial, the son she'd loved best, was Vradir. Like any good priestess of the Avatar, when she had discovered that, she had used all the arcane knowledge at her disposal in an attempt to stop him. Had she had warning, time to prepare crystals to augment her natural powers, Gildon had no doubt that she would have triumphed, for his mother had been among the most talented within the Temple of the Avatar. Still, she had turned her not inconsiderable mental power against the son she had loved, and had, in turn, been killed by him. The pain of that in itself must have been terrible.

He found his heart stirring in unfamiliar sympathy for the woman who had been his mother, and wondered from whence the compassion had come. Kadar? Had Kadar been a gentler man than he? Or had he, Gildon, always had the capacity for such consideration of others but merely needed the catalyst of love to liberate it?

He shook his head. He must think of Cadence, and the battle that was to come.

Forcing his brooding thoughts aside, he strode forward—unconsciously sidestepping the spot where his mother had lain as though she still rested there—to examine the portal again. If he changed the settings on the portal to designate another portal in the city of Eston as his destination—even *if* he could find one still receiving—he stood a chance of finding himself outside whatever place Cadence was being held, unable to help her. If he didn't alter the settings, he would probably be captured, and equally unable to help her.

Although he chafed at the seemingly too rapid passage of time, Gildon took a minute to download the destination coordinates that had been programmed into the portal. Then, reading the coordinates into one of his father's old data processors, he requested a map of Eston. When the three-dimensional diagram shimmered in the air before him and he directed the processor to overlap the portal coordinates, a red dot appeared on the map. He studied it. It represented the portal destination as a hillside overlooking the valley in which the city had been constructed.

"That's not possible," Gildon muttered, raking his fingers through his hair in agitation. "Recalculate coordinates," he directed the processor. The red dot signifying portal destination disappeared momentarily and then reappeared in the same location.

He paced back and forth. Why would Jakial have constructed a portal on a hill in the middle of nowhere?

He wouldn't! With sudden insight, Gildon stared at the map. There had to be a new edifice there, something not in the records, constructed in the months since contact had been lost with Madaia.

By the One! Now what? He definitely couldn't take the chance of attempting to program a known portal in the city as a destination when he had no idea what type of building had been constructed there on the hill. It could be an impenetrable fortress. He sat down at his father's desk and clenched his fingers in his hair. Somehow, he had to gain access to a portal *within* the new edifice without using the portal through which they would expect him to arrive.

How?

A few moments later, he rose to pace the study. He could alter the coordinates of the portal slightly, program a location close enough to Jakial's original coordinates so that they would have to be within the same building, and see if he received a match. If this portal perceived a receiving portal on the other end of whatever coordinates he programmed, it would accept the coordinates. If not . . . well, he'd be back at the beginning again. The process would involve a lot of trial and error, and endless moments of wasted time as he programmed the portal's data crystal to search coordinate locations at random. Even a small apartment like this one possessed hundreds of possible coordinates. Depending on its size, the building in Madaia could possess thousands, yet he could think of no other method that wouldn't place him directly into the hands of Vradir warriors.

He began.

Running his hands over the coiled designs set into the walls of the portal, he initiated the search. The moment it stopped at a possible portal coordinate, he placed the *falar* stone over his forehead, and attempted to trigger the coordinate location.

Nothing. If indeed a portal did exist at the location, which was likely based on the expertise of the data crystals, then it had been deactivated and was no longer receiving.

He tried again, and again. An hour later, his weapons and the crystals began to weigh heavily on his person. Yet he dared not set them down. If he did, when one of the sets of coordinates finally worked, he would be transported without the gear he needed.

Sighing, he adjusted the weight and tried another set of coordinates. Then, without bothering to close his eyes for concentration anymore, he sent the signal to the portal that would activate the transfer *if* the destination portal at the programmed coordinates was receiving. In the next instant, his father's study faded from view and he spun in a vortical universe of gray-white mist. *It worked.* Now, if only he hadn't inadvertently activated a portal that would place him in even worse peril.

Cadence swallowed, trying to dredge some moisture from her mouth to soothe her dry throat. It was an exercise in futility. Jakial working at a desk across the room, glanced over at her once in a while with spiteful, vengeful eyes as his fingers drifted up to test the bruise on his right cheek where she'd struck him with the plate she'd thrown. At least she'd been able to deliver some small reminder of his contact with her. He hadn't come close enough to her, without his dislocator in hand, for her to be able to use any of her Legionnaire combat techniques. If he had, he'd have a lot more than a small bruise on his cheekbone to worry about, she assured herself.

She tested the bonds on her wrists and ankles for the thousandth time. Her feet tingled painfully in response, but the knots weren't any looser. In fact, the ropes around her ankles seemed to be getting tighter. Was her flesh swelling around the constriction? She hoped not. When the opportunity came for escape, she needed to be able to run.

The moment she'd been ushered into the chamber, she'd been directed to lie face down upon a small pallet in one corner. Her hands had then been bound behind her back, and her legs bent to fasten her ankles with the same length of rope that secured her wrists. Knowing that the blood would quickly drain from her elevated legs if she remained in that position, she'd rolled onto her side the moment Jakial had moved away. Even so, it seemed that her feet were falling asleep. She prayed that an opportunity to escape would come soon.

She looked around the enormous circular chamber to which she'd been brought. Actually, it was more octagonal than circular, she realized now. The only light came from two high, narrow windows, hardly more than slits in the stone, and three luminescent crystals set on furnishings throughout the chamber. The walls were all of black stone, a color abhorrent to most Tesuvians because of its propensity to absorb all light without giving any back. Adjacent to her, a shadowed alcove was barely visible in the gloom. She wondered briefly what was in it, but quickly turned her thoughts from the contemplation of the unknown to the consideration of escape. The chamber proper only had one door that she knew of—the one through which she'd been ushered a few hours ago—but even it had merged invisibly into the wall. Still, she could guess pretty accurately where it was in relation to the furnishings in the chamber.

Even as she was trying to distinguish the door from the surrounding walls, it flickered out of existence and a woman strode into the room. She was quite beautiful—tall, slender, and blond with eyes the translucent color of ice. Cadence had never seen her before, and yet there was something about the haughty tilt of her head and the smooth arrogance of her stride that was familiar. Ish'Kara!

"Ah, my darling sister, I see you recognize me." She stood, hands on hips, smirking down at Cadence. "Which means that, unfortunately, we were not swift enough in abducting you to prevent your memory from returning."

Cadence accessed Ali'Yah's memories and superimposed her memory of the dark-haired Ish'Kara over the image of this one before her. Yes, the carriage was identical. She smiled, studying her opponent. "I could never forget you, Ish'Kara."

Ish'Kara shrugged. "This time your memory will do you no good." She smiled with all the sadistic satisfaction of a feline eyeing a bird. "I have some very interesting plans for you."

"Really?" Cadence mocked, squelching the urge to squirm beneath the other woman's avid gaze. She remembered her Stellar Legion training: Fear was only useful insofar as it prevented a person from placing herself recklessly or unnecessarily in danger. Here it was of no use to her. "And what might they be?"

Ish'Kara's eyes narrowed. "You are more . . . assured than I remember. I don't think I like that. But no matter, I know many methods for destroying misplaced self-confidence."

Cadence stared up at her and felt a hatred that was not her own crowd her mind. She forced it back. She would face this woman as herself until it became necessary for her to draw on Ali'Yah's knowledge. "I have no doubt that you do, Ish'Kara. As do I." She forced a cold smile to her lips.

Ish'Kara laughed humorlessly. "I see you have finally learned the art of bravado. That should make our time together more interesting." With that, she turned dismissingly away from Cadence and strode across the room to Jakial. They spoke in a low-voiced conversation that Cadence couldn't hear, but she watched them together.

Even an untutored observer could have seen that they were more than passingly familiar with each other. The manner in which Ish'Kara ran her fingers through his hair as they spoke left no doubt in Cadence's mind that they were lovers. But Cadence wanted to know more than that. Using the knowledge of body language taught by the Legion to all of its Internal Affairs investigators, she observed them closely, reducing their mannerisms to individual gestures that spoke in silence.

Ish'Kara ran her hands over his shoulders. He leaned toward her slightly, saying something.

Ish'Kara laughed quietly. Jakial reached to place a hand on her waist, and she tapped it gently with her own as though consoling him.

Cadence inspected the tilt of their heads and the positioning of their arms. She analyzed their posture and expressions. And she came to a conclusion: For the first time in Ali'Yah's memory, Ish'Kara was truly fond of another human being. Cadence would not attribute the emotion of love to her, for she was certain that Ish'Kara was inherently incapable of love. No, Ish'Kara viewed this man as one might a beloved pet. Which meant that he was not irreplaceable, but valued nonetheless.

Jakial on the other hand appeared a little more adoring, perhaps a little more in love than Ish'Kara. Then again, how much love could a man capable of harming his mother, as he had done, be capable of feeling?

Ish'Kara ran her hand over his brow and he smiled, closing his eyes. Cadence began to feel almost like a voyeur, yet in that same instant something began to bother her about the relationship she was seeing. What was it?

And then she realized what it was: Jakial, like Gildon, appeared to be a strong, capable man. Something about him screamed *leader*, which, since he had been the Prelate of this province prior to the resurgence of the Vradir cult, made sense. Yet, with Ish'Kara he seemed very . . . acquiescent, almost submissive. Why? Had Ish'Kara found a means of psychic dominance?

Cadence searched Ali'Yah's memories. There had always been a certain amount of conjecture about the possibility of control and beguilement by alter-realm creatures. That was why so many safeguards were used in maintaining barriers whenever contact with them was made. Was the conjecture fact? And had Ish'Kara somehow learned to utilize the other-dimensional proficiency? According to the tenets, which Shaylon had violated in raising Jakial as a priest of the Avatar, he would have been vulnerable to just such an attempt. But how had Ish'Kara bound him to her?

Cadence eyed the couple speculatively. With the illusion of love perhaps. Ish'Kara had always been an accomplished seductress, and even before her powers had matured she had stopped at nothing to possess whomever or whatever she wanted.

At that moment, Ish'Kara turned to look at her. "What are you thinking, Ali'Yah? I sense that it's directed at me; I can feel it."

Cadence concealed her surprise. It seemed that not even the shielding provided by her Empyrean protectors granted complete security from Ish'Kara's powerful, probing mind. "I was wondering how much you've changed," Cadence said, not lying exactly, but not telling the complete truth either.

Ish'Kara came forward to stand grinning down at her. "More than you can know, sister dear. More than you'll *ever* know."

Abruptly Ish'Kara looked over her shoulder at the man still seated across the room. "Jakial, her feet are turning blue. I think you may have been a bit overly enthusiastic in securing her. Untie her, and then bind her in a standing position over there." She pointed to one of the four stone pillars in the large chamber. "I'll return in a while." With that, she headed for the wall.

Cadence comprehended rather absently that there must be another door to the room since Ish'Kara was not heading in the direction of the access with which she was familiar. But that was not the thought uppermost in her mind. Somehow she had to effect an escape, and doing so was going to be extremely difficult if she was bound. "Are you afraid I'll overpower him?" she called after Ish'Kara's retreating back, injecting nonchalance into her tone.

Ish'Kara turned and smiled, her ice-blue eyes drilling into Cadence. "Remember that excess confidence of yours we spoke of?" she asked rhetorically. "I've found that clothing is often one of the major sources of self-confidence." Her eyes widened with malicious glee. She looked over at Jakial. "Strip her," she ordered. "But don't enjoy yourself too much, darling."

Chapter Eighteen

Gildon emerged from the portal and sent a fervent prayer of thanks to the One that the corridor into which he'd emerged was empty. And then he reeled. The perception of evil assailed his psychic senses like an overpowering stench of putrefaction. Every instinct he possessed screamed for him to leave this place. But he couldn't. He took a deep, calming breath, and another, until he became accustomed to the psionic signature of corruption.

He had to find Cadence quickly, and get away from here.

According to his calculations, the coordinates placed this portal a level above and approximately thirty yards east of the portal Jakial had used. However, the location of the portal really had told him nothing about Cadence's present whereabouts. She could be anywhere by now. He might have found her with a scry, if he had the time and a secure position from which to perform it, but he did not. And he simply could not leave his physical body unattended in this den of corruption. As a starting point, the portal that had brought her here was the best he was apt to get. From there, if the One was with him, he might be able to psychically discern some trace of the path she'd taken. He would seek it out.

He looked to his left. The hall ended in a blank wall no more than twenty feet away. He quickly checked in that direction for a flight of stairs that might have been concealed. Nothing. He moved silently and cautiously down the corridor to his right. The hall seemed like the access to a tenebrous void, for within a few feet the light faded and blackness stretched endlessly before him. The black stone from which the building had been constructed seemed to absorb what little light was provided by the luminescent crystals that lined the hall.

There was something else about this place that unnerved him, something more than the constant impression of being surrounded by dark forces. He warily reached out to touch the black stone face of the wall nearest him. It was cold, colder than any natural stone. He frowned, extending his senses to explore the sensation.

A powerful energy radiated around him, familiar and yet unlike anything he knew. Despite his reticence, he explored it with his mind, touching it, knowing it was necessary for him to understand it. He felt the energy coil around him, become one with him as it absorbed his vibratory rate and took it as its own. He felt it there available as an augmentation to his psychic strength.

Non-aligned energy!

There was always a certain amount of non-aligned energy on any world, but it normally was available only in quantities insufficient for practical use. The force that he perceived here was unheard of. Somehow the Vradir had found a means of drawing it to one location, of harnessing it. And this black stone, which looked as if it had been carved from the barren cliff faces in the province of Shadish, had something to do with it.

The implications were frightening.

He moved on, his caution unabated. Why was it so quiet? Where were the people? The guards?

A few steps on, he poked his head carefully around

a corner. No stairwell. He paused in indecision. Should he take this new corridor in the hope that it would lead him to a flight of stairs, or continue on?

He decided not to turn. This hall ran in the direction he wanted to go, and he had no idea where the other would end. Finally, at the end of the corridor, he came upon a flight of stairs. As well as descending, they rose past him for at least three levels above the one on which he'd emerged.

He listened carefully for the sound of voices before moving into the stairwell. Once he was in it, there would be nowhere to go if someone came upon him. Distantly, from below, he heard the low drone of many voices in conversation, but he was certain they were farther than the one level he wanted to descend. With every sense alert to the possibility of danger, he moved into the stairwell. Ten quick silent steps. He paused and listened. Quiet, except for the slightly louder drone of the voices from below. He continued, swiftly and silently.

Without realizing it, he almost moved beyond the level he sought. The stairs were designed to focus on the floor two stories below his point of entry. A small landing in mid-descent provided the only indication of another floor, and the one narrow, unadorned door inset in the wall afforded the only visible access. A public entrance obviously, since there was no ornamentation to provide a combination lock.

He sighed thankfully. He wouldn't have wanted to risk looking for a lock combination here. Although he could have disabled the chimes, standing too long in one place would have definitely increased the odds of being discovered.

Using the wall to conceal himself from any occupants that might be in the chamber beyond, he sidled up to the recess and touched the door. It disappeared, and Gildon cautiously looked within. Rather than a room, it appeared to be some type of balcony.

Constructed of gray stone, the floor and railing contrasted subtly with the unrelieved black of the walls. He could hear the murmur of voices much more clearly now, but the balcony appeared to be empty. He slid through the door and, as it reappeared behind him, quickly perused the parts of the gallery that he'd been unable to see from without.

He was alone.

Abruptly the babble of voices from below ceased. Silence screamed, enveloping everything. He was afraid to move.

Why was everything suddenly so quiet? Had somebody sensed his presence? He wished he could see the room below. Slowly he slid nearer to the railing despite the awareness that, in such intense silence, even the soft sound of his footfall might attract attention. He had to see what was going on.

Cautiously he craned his neck to peer over the balcony railing. By the One! The Vradir were in assembly. He hardly dared to breathe. The occasion could prove to be extremely useful to him, *if* he was careful.

He studied the crowd in the massive room below. Although the throng represented only a small sampling of the number of Vradir throughout the province, there had to be at least 500 people down there, all clothed in the black garments of their cult. Each had the strange rune of a looped cross—the symbol the Vradir had adopted as emblematic of their quest for eternal life—emblazoned upon their backs in luminous red fabric.

His eyes passed slowly over the crowd, drawn to a woman who moved from the left side of the raised dais at the front of the room. Her blond hair flowed about her shoulders as her regal walk carried her to center stage. Exuding authority, she raised her arms high over her head. The silence stretched as the entire chamber waited. Gildon held his breath.

Abruptly she lowered her arms in synchronization

with a single drum beat that echoed eerily throughout the hall. The moment the echo faded, she shouted to the gathering, "We are Vradir!"

"We are Vradir," the crowd repeated enthusiastically. "Hail Ish'Kara, our queen," they shouted.

Gildon's eyes moved back to the woman. So . . . this then was Ish'Kara. She shouted her next words: "We are eternal!"

"We are eternal," the crowd responded.

Gildon could feel the anticipation in the air. He should move on, but he was afraid any activity on his part would draw eyes to the balcony. Ish'Kara's senses were acute. At the moment, she seemed concerned with whipping her followers into some type of euphoric abandon, but he couldn't discount the strength of her abilities.

Gildon clenched his fists as he observed the cult in action. Every instinct within him told him to do something to end this obscenity against the One. He need only slip his dislocator through the railing, fire it at Ish'Kara, and the Vradir's queen would be gone. Only his recollection of Cadence's assertion that Ish'Kara could not be killed stayed his hand. He would not release the demoness's soul from physical existence just to begin the horror again.

And so he restrained his natural impulse and waited. Soon, he hoped, he would be able to safely cross the balcony to the other door and continue on his way.

Half an hour later the throng below had degenerated into a celebration of excesses which, characteristic of the Vradir, expressed itself in drunkenness and sexual abandon. Men and women were passed from group to group without thought for love or the transcending experience of true sensual pleasure. Here, pain seemed almost as integral a component of their hedonistic ecstasy as a caress. Sickened, Gildon turned his eyes away from the orgy and observed the woman who was the queen of this cult of corruption and perversion.

Ish'Kara raised her arms, and the drum boomed, drawing her cult members' attention if not their total silence. Those in the act of copulation did not bother to stop, merely turning their heads to listen to their queen's words.

"And now," she said, "for those of you who do not have mates, or who are tired of those you have, I present a gift." She waved her arm expansively to the side and a corpulent Vradir warrior herded ten nubile young women onto the stage. Naked except for the diaphanous black gauze that floated around them from a fastening at their necks, they halted facing the lecherous crowd and stared out over their heads with glazed eyes.

Drugged, Gildon concluded. His stomach churned with the need to do something, to protect these children of the One. Yet he could do nothing. The Vradir warrior who had directed them onto the stage picked the young women up, one by one, and threw them into the lecherous crowd. Their screams where barely heard above the animalistic, gleeful howls of the Vradir.

Gildon hung his head, unable to watch. He had to escape this place.

With a quick glance through the rails, he saw that Ish'Kara was leaving. Before she'd completed her exit, he was working his way across the gallery to the door on the far side. The door that, according to his calculations, would lead to the portal through which Jakial had brought Cadence. He hoped that Cadence was being held near it, for he didn't know how long he could wander in this place without betraying himself.

Cadence shuddered inwardly as Jakial's avid gaze groped her naked body for the thousandth time. He had rarely taken his eyes from her in the last hour, probing and judging, attempting to undermine her self-confidence. And it had worked, but she refused to show that. Despite being secured to the pillar like an animal, she stood proudly, refusing to succumb to the urge to hunch her shoulders in an effort to hide her breasts from his zealous eyes.

The uncertainty of her fate weighed heavily upon her, and she wished for Ish'Kara's return if only to put an end to the terrible anticipation. She didn't have long to wait. Scarcely five minutes later, Ish'Kara strolled into the room garbed in a black ceremonial robe. Cadence noted the change and wondered at its portent.

Ignoring her, Ish'Kara strode across the room to Jakial, lifted his face, and kissed him deeply, with a carnal hunger that should have been reserved for privacy. "That's a promise for later, my darling," she said. Then she looked over her shoulder at Cadence. "Did she give you any trouble?"

"Of course not," he said, and Cadence had the impression that his masculine pride was affronted. Had there been the slightest chance of escaping him, she would have fought him when he'd removed her clothing. But since he'd kept her feet and her hands bound, pride had demanded that she not give him the pleasure of watching her struggle.

"Good." Ish'Kara patted his cheek. "And now I must ask you to leave so that I may take care of that other matter we discussed."

Jakial's brows drew together. "I would prefer to stay."

"I know you would, darling, but you must understand that I must maintain some secrets even from you. At least for a time." He scowled, and Ish'Kara bent to brush his lips with hers and then murmured something Cadence couldn't hear into his ear.

Jakial rose and left the room.

Without a glance in her direction, Ish'Kara set about making preparations. Preparations which Ali-'Yah's memories told Cadence were involved in threshold creation. Ish'Kara was accessing an alterrealm! Stars! Exactly what fate did she have in mind for her?

The narrow passageway that opened off the balcony formed a squared-off U shape around the upper level of the assembly chamber. Gildon followed the first branch to a right-angled corner without coming across any portals and was forced to turn down a hall that ran behind the huge chamber. Finally, about halfway down the hall, he came to a door that opened in the direction he wished to go. Opening it, he peered into the corridor beyond and quickly jerked his head back.

Two Vradir warriors were walking slowly toward him. Luckily, their engrossed conversation had prevented them from seeing him. But what if they came through the door? They would surely sense his presence, and there was no place to conceal himself.

He breathed slowly, girding himself for the moment of battle.

The moment never came. The men's conversation had just grown clear when their voices began to recede. Cautiously he looked around the corner. The corridor was empty, yet he could still hear them. Where had they gone? He leaned a fraction farther around the corner and caught sight of them descending a narrow set of stairs that stretched from the gallery level down to the rear of the assembly chamber. Once again, fate was on his side.

Dismissing the stairs, he examined this new corridor before moving out from behind the relative security of the wall. Like the hall in which he now stood, the walls were of black stone and the floors gray. The corridor did not have any obvious doors

311

along it, which meant it was unlikely that he would find the portal he was looking for. The lack of doors also suggested that if someone chanced to come along, he would have no option but to silence them quickly. Taking a breath, he moved out, ever conscious of the amount of time that had passed since Cadence had been abducted.

Where was the portal?

He reached the end of the corridor, which once again forced him to take an unplanned turn. A mere ten steps into the new corridor, the hall jogged back in the direction he wished to go, and he paused to consider the new territory. This corridor was wider and had a more traveled look to it. There were four doors along it, and . . . two guards leaning against the wall, carrying on a muted conversation.

This was it. It had to be. What other explanation could there be for the guards? The portal Jakial had used to bring Cadence here had to lie beyond one of those four doors. But Gildon wouldn't be able to tell which one until he got close enough to see the depictions on their surfaces, and before he could do that, he had to get rid of the guards. At least he had the element of surprise on his side: They expected him to emerge from the portal.

He studied the guards and considered. Their stance led him to conclude that they were not Kami trained. However, when he took into consideration the slovenliness of the Kami-trained Madaian warriors he had encountered previously, he couldn't be absolutely certain of that. Suddenly one of the men moved to pace up and down the corridor. The other, watching him, raised his voice slightly to continue their conversation—they appeared to be discussing the merits of a woman of their mutual acquaintance—then moved away from the wall to fall into step beside his companion.

Gildon shook his head. Definitely not Kami

trained, he concluded. If they were going to walk the corridor, they should pace in opposite directions so that the entire corridor remained constantly in view. Their stupidity would work in his favor.

Checking behind himself to ensure that he had not been discovered, he waited until the Madaian fighters came near his end of the corridor. Then, as they turned and headed back the other way, he altered his vibratory rate to veil his presence as much as possible, and moved silently in their wake. If all went well, he intended to draw upon the power of *halal*. It was quiet and very effective.

As he neared the men, all of his senses became instinctive with the exception of the telekinetic sense upon which he intended to draw. *Halal* took tremendous concentration, which was why it was almost impossible to employ in the heat of a battle. He no longer heard the men's crude comparisons of the woman. He no longer felt the soul-numbing coldness of the black walls around him. And he no longer saw the men before him . . . not as physical bodies, at any rate. Now he saw them as two distinct patterns of energy.

He moved closer. Closer. One of them seemed to sense something, for he glanced nervously over his shoulder. It was too late.

Gildon struck with the swiftness of a water viper. His touch, like the sensation of being struck by a flying insect, barely registered. But its effect was immediate, disrupting the flow of the life force within the fighter's body. His heart convulsed. His lungs collapsed. And with a single, almost silent gasp he sank dead to the floor. His confused partner hastily backed away as he scanned the corridor. Almost immediately, his eyes settled on the shifting heat-wave haze that was Gildon, but his identification of the threat came too late. A minute later, he too lay dead on the floor.

Gildon stared down at their bodies, briefly wondering who they had been before the Vradir had seduced them into its folds. He considered using the dislocator to get rid of their bodies, but decided against it. The power of the weapon could quite easily be sensed, and he didn't want to reveal his presence unnecessarily.

Instead, he turned his attention to the doors lining the corridors. The second door he tried opened onto a small storage room, and he hastily dragged the bodies into it. That done, he turned his attention to locating the portal. There were still two doors he hadn't checked.

The third of the four was the one he sought. A pair of wings carved into the door proclaimed the location of a portal, and it was at the correct coordinates. Gildon was certain that this was the portal through which Jakial had brought Cadence. With a careful glance in either direction to ensure that he remained alone, he sank down on his haunches and closed his eyes. The psychic resonance method of tracing somebody was much less certain than a search committed through a scry, but it was all he had.

Relaxing himself physically, he extended his psychic senses in search of some extrasensory indication that would tell him, not only that Cadence had been here, but in what direction she'd been taken from this point. Such exercises did not always work; the revelations were dependent upon the One, who knew all things. Success was contingent upon absolute faith. Once an indication was afforded, it must be accepted immediately. Any tendency to deny the accuracy of the knowledge granted often resulted in its being withdrawn, and the seeker was left groping for the thought that eluded him.

The revelation came suddenly: Cadence had indeed come through this portal, and she'd been taken down the hall to his left.

In Destiny's Arms

Gildon opened his eyes and rose. The One was with him. His mind's eye could see the course, like a faint trail of stardust, along which Cadence had walked. He moved swiftly in its wake, determined to find her before the effect dissipated. The path led him to a flight of stairs near the front of the building. And that was where his luck ran out.

He had begun to follow the trail up the stairs when two men stepped out onto a landing directly in front of him. Gildon, acting with the trained reflexes of a Kami, dispatched one almost instantly with a blow to the throat, but the other turned to face him.

He was probably of about Gildon's height, but had accorded himself the benefit of additional height and maneuverability by taking a stance on the stairs slightly above Gildon. Time slowed. Gildon analyzed his opponent. This man did not have Kami training, he was certain. Still, he obviously had some combat training and it would be a mistake to discount him too readily. As the Vradir studied Gildon in turn, he glanced at least three times in the direction of the door through which he and his fallen comrade had come. That could mean only one thing: There were more Vradir beyond that door.

The Vradir fighter leapt, kicking at Gildon's head in an attempt to finish the contest quickly. Gildon dodged and struck the man in the chest as he landed a couple of stairs lower. The Madaian flashed Gildon a venomous glance and reached into the front of his tunic. Instinct told Gildon the fighter reached for a dislocator. With the rapid response provided by his warrior training, Gildon withdrew his own weapon and fired just as the Vradir's dislocator discharged.

The blasts came off almost simultaneously, but Gildon's had been properly targeted and thus proved more effective. He avoided the Madaian's shot, and watched as the fighter dispersed into a vaguely man-shaped pattern of effervescent energy without co-

315

hesion and then disappeared. Without compunction, Gildon turned the dislocator on the Madaian he'd slain earlier and disposed of his body as well. Now there were no physical remains to indicate that a battle had taken place.

Wasting no more time, he raced up the stairs. Although the dislocator was an almost silent weapon, it might still have been heard, and if it had not, the vibratory disturbance surely had been felt by somebody. He didn't want to be in the area should either possibility be investigated.

An instant later, he was glad that he'd fled with such alacrity for he heard voices behind him and turned to see at least four men emerging from the door through which his previous two opponents had come. Luckily, he was at the top of the second flight of stairs. He ducked hastily to the side.

He found himself confronting a spiral staircase. His gaze tracked upward. He was in a tower. Was Cadence up there somewhere?

The tower rose high above him. There would be no escape from it except back down these stairs. At least none that he knew of. He swallowed. Somehow he had to find Cadence and guide her to an operational portal without being apprehended. Since the whole of this huge black edifice could very well be alerted to his presence, the task loomed before him like a sheer-faced cliff that must be climbed. He would not fail.

He began to ascend the stairs, his awareness of Cadence's presence growing with every step. He could feel her. And yet his senses told him that something was dreadfully wrong. Urgency clawed at him. He had to reach her . . . *now*.

He ran up the steps, pausing at each door he came across only long enough to sense whether Cadence was beyond. It wasn't until he reached a floor only two stories beneath the pinnacle of the tower that he sensed her presence.

The door he confronted was elaborately scrolled, and did not grant access upon contact. He gritted his teeth, struggling to contain the urge to batter it down with his physical strength, aware that such an exercise would only serve to alert anyone else in the chamber to his presence. Pressing upon the tip of the uppermost vine-like design, he muted the chimes. Then, removing a thin, rectangular data-processing crystal from one of his pockets, he held it near the door and transmitted the thought that activated it. He watched anxiously as small flame-colored lights flashed on its surface, seeking the pattern that matched the one programmed into the door's locking mechanism. Finally the flashing of the lights slowed as a pattern began to take shape, and an instant later the flickering stopped altogether. Gildon studied the intricate configuration displayed and then began to duplicate the pattern, tracing his fingertips over particular segments of the scrolling design on the door. Before completing the last touch, he positioned the bag containing his collection of combat crystals for easy access. His fingertips made one last sweep over the design, and the door faded from existence.

A single glance told him that he was looking at an alcove attached to a much larger chamber. Although he sensed more than one presence within, he saw no one. Automatically shielding his thoughts to conceal his presence, he stepped quickly through the door and slipped to one side.

By the One! There was a threshold open in here! He could feel it, and that meant that safeguards were at an absolute minimum, if any were in place at all. But then, he should have expected as much from a woman who would unleash alter-realm beings on an innocent world to serve her own selfish designs.

Voices! Straining to make them out, he breathed as shallowly as possible as he moved silently along the alcove wall to get a look at what transpired within.

"She's yours. Take her." A woman's voice, cold and unfeeling. Ish'Kara?

"I can't believe that even you would do this, Ish'Kara."

Cadence! Confirmation of her presence sent his pulse soaring, but did not prevent him from hearing the underlying note of terror in her strong, controlled tone. What was happening? Who was Ish'Kara telling to take her? Take her where? He slipped more quickly along the wall until he could peer into the larger room.

There were only three in the room: Cadence, naked and bound and yet managing to somehow exude a regal aura that he'd never before seen in her. Ish'Kara, looking down her nose at Cadence, her lips curved with the pleasure her machinations afforded her. And a man, tall and well-formed, with hair the color of night and eyes of lurid blue. A Daemod! Even without the lurid eyes, Gildon would have recognized the psychic stench of a Daemod. And yet the being walked freely about the room, no safeguards in place, as the threshold that gave him access to his plane shimmered beyond him.

The Daemod were immortal. Equally content in a corporeal or a spiritual existence, they could not be killed. And their tremendous shape-shifting abilities prevented an opponent from disabling them for more than a few seconds even while in a physical form. About the only thing the Daemod were susceptible to was cold, and it merely slowed them down.

And neither could he kill Ish'Kara, not without the sword that was even now being forged.

He fingered the briar crystal. When thrown and shattered, it would grow within seconds into a huge, impenetrable wall of thorny crystal. He could program it to absorb heat in direct proportion to the rate of its growth, which would cool the chamber to the point of freezing within seconds. It would work for a short time to imprison Ish'Kara, until she found the special intonation of sound which would shatter the wall. And it might work for the Daemod. The alter-realm being could, of course, leave his body and slip through the crystalline thorns with no problem, but the cold would deter him. It was the best plan Gildon could think of.

There was only one problem: Cadence needed to be standing at his side *before* he threw the crystal, or she would be as trapped as the others.

He observed the occupants of the chamber. Cadence was speaking to the Daemod. "I won't willingly bear your offspring, Baltharak. And I will be useless to you."

The Daemod, Baltharak, scowled and whirled to face Ish'Kara, foul language dripping from his tongue like venom. Finally his speech became understandable. "How does the whore know so much about my kind? Did you tell her that we cannot take an unwilling female?"

Ish'Kara smiled, unperturbed. "Actually, Ali'Yah was herself a priestess of the Avatar in a previous incarnation. As a result, she is reasonably familiar with your kind. But she would never have demeaned herself by an affiliation with you, as I have. She considers herself . . . too good, too righteous."

"A priestess!" the Daemod barked. "Then your bribe is useless to me. I demand another."

Ish'Kara's smile faded, and she turned her back on the Daemod, stalking across the room.

Yes! Now if only the Daemod would follow.

Ish'Kara stopped in front of the shimmering threshold and turned. Gildon hastily ducked back. "Perhaps I can give you another," she said. "But first

I want you to get rid of this one. Permanently. If you take her to your plane, she will not be reborn and she will never again be a bother to me."

Gildon risked another glance around the edge of the wall. The Daemod stood scarcely three feet from Cadence, his back to her, scowling fiercely at Ish'Kara, and saying nothing as he considered her words. Gildon's eyes flicked to Cadence. She waited silently, in apparent calm, as her fate was decided. He wished he felt so calm. The briar crystal in his hand grew warm as he watched the Daemod, willed him to walk toward Ish'Kara.

And then as though in answer to a prayer, the Daemod moved. Gildon waited no longer. Throwing the briar crystal in the wake of the Daemod's steps, he intoned the note that would program it to absorb the heat of the chamber, and raced to Cadence's side.

As the unique crackle of the rapidly growing crystal permeated the chamber, an almost inhuman howl of rage resounded in the air around them. Gildon ignored it, his eyes only for Cadence. Flashing a quick smile at the expression of welcome in her eyes, he pulled a knife from a sheath beneath his shirt and sliced her bonds. "Your gown?" The fine hair on her naked body was already rising in response to the swiftly dropping temperature.

"Over there." She pointed at a pallet against the wall. Retrieving the gown, he hastily dropped it over her head, allowing the voluminous folds to fall into place where they would, and turned to usher her from the chamber. She was limping slightly. His eyes sought the source of her hurt and saw the bruises on her ankles. Lips tight with an anger he couldn't express, he swung her up into his arms. As he strode from the tower chamber, he looked back to assess the briar crystal's effectiveness.

He couldn't see through it anymore, although he could still hear Ish'Kara venting her rage and the

Daemod shouting obscenities. The crystal was quite beautiful actually, despite its deadly properties, the way it caught and reflected the light in the chamber, brightening it. In reality, the wall of crystal looked like nothing so much as a barrier of extremely thorny, interwoven plant stalks, devoid of foliage and cloaked in ice. Yet its rapier-sharp thorns could cut human flesh to ribbons in seconds. Even more dreadful was the thought of what occurred when one of those crystalline thorns left a splinter inside human flesh. The only way to halt the growth of a briar crystal was to intone a vibratory tone the exact opposite of that produced by the crystal itself, shattering it. If that note did not sound, the tiny crystal shard would continue to grow, delving its way into the body, causing excruciating pain until death loomed like a welcome gift.

The barrier was holding for the moment, but it wouldn't take Ish'Kara long to find the key to its destruction, and he wanted to be out of the building before she did. He looked down at Cadence. "Let's get out of here."

"My thought exactly."

They attained the bottom of the tower without incident. When they reached the entrance to the large stairwell where he'd fought the two Vradir, Gildon set Cadence on her feet so that he could peer around the corner.

It was crawling with Vradir!

He looked at Cadence. "I don't suppose you happen to know another way out of this tower?"

She swallowed and shook her head. "But a lot of the doors have been designed to blend into the walls so that they don't interrupt the flow of power." She looked at the circular walls of the tower base. "Do you think there might be something on the other side?"

"I'll check." While he walked around the base of

the tower examining the walls, he noted that Cadence moved to the edge of the stairwell entrance to keep an eye on the Vradir.

The walls seemed solid, but he kept his hopes high. They had to find another means out of here, and quickly. They couldn't use the stairway without being seen. The Vradir seemed to be filing in and out of the chamber below as though it was a dining hall. And Ish'Kara had probably already telepathically summoned fighters.

By the One! He'd known that getting out would probably be more difficult than getting in, but it couldn't be impossible. He continued to grope along the wall. He almost moved on and then realized that he felt an indentation where none existed visually. There was *something* here. But what?

Exploring the area more carefully with his fingers, he attempted to determine the size and shape of the aberration in the wall. It was a door! But it was more than concealed, it was a secret one. It did not disappear upon contact, and anyone unlocking it would have to know precisely where the scrolls were in order to decode the locking mechanism.

He snatched the decoder from his pocket and held it next to the door. He was about to activate it when Cadence came hurrying toward him.

"Someone's coming," she warned in a low voice.

He glanced in the direction of the entrance, realized that it was concealed at the moment by the spiral staircase that rose up into the tower. His nerves humming with tension, he hastily sent the mental command that would activate the crystal and watched anxiously as the lights began to flash. *Hurry! Hurry!* The words became a litany in his mind as he pulled Cadence close to his side.

He heard men's voices raised in excitement. Footsteps entered the tower. Within seconds, as they began to climb the stairs, the men would see Gildon and Cadence.

No! They hadn't come this far to be caught now.

Chapter Nineteen

At that moment, the flashing lights slowed as the decoder began to distinguish the pattern. Without waiting for it to complete the decoding, Gildon ran his hands over the door, finding by touch the uppermost section of the scrolled design, and began to trace the portion of the configuration that had been deciphered. Ignoring the threat at his back, Gildon concentrated on tracing the pattern exactly. He felt the sweat bead on his brow, sensed the tension holding Cadence rigid at his side.

A shout of "Intruders!" echoed in the stone tower. Cadence's fingers dug into his arm.

The door disappeared. Too late?

Not sparing a glance in the direction of the footsteps pounding toward them, he ducked through the doorway, pulling Cadence with him. Only when the door had reappeared behind them did he allow himself a small sigh of relief as he studied the chamber in which they found themselves.

It was a small circular room that was obviously some type of workshop. Two tables near a short pillar in the center of the room held metalwork in varying stages of completion. Shelves containing finished items lined the walls. Gildon moved forward to inspect the rows and rows of identical objects that rested there. What were they?

The circular bands of gold metal were very like

bracelets, but too large for that purpose. Each had a single luminous black stone embedded in the center of a design carved into the metal. Or was it a design? The markings resembled runes, and runes could be very powerful. Yet he couldn't identify them. Alien runes, then?

A gasp at his side drew his attention. There was horror in Cadence's eyes as she looked at the strange bands. "What is it?" he asked.

She shook her head slowly, uncertainly. "I'm not sure. But I don't like this. I don't like this at all."

"Do you know what they are?"

She swallowed. "They look like collars to me."

Gildon swung his gaze back to the shelf. She was right! They did look like collars. Collars to fit a human neck.

A sound from the other side of the door drew his attention. "I think we'd better find a way out of here." The prospect did not look promising. There were shelves along every wall.

Cadence followed his gaze, read his discouragement. "Ish'Kara would never create a room with only one access," Cadence murmured. "There has to be a hidden exit somewhere, or"—she looked at Gildon with hope shining in her eyes—"or a portal."

The noise at the door continued unabated. "Well, if it's here, we'd better find it quickly," Gildon said. "It may not take them long to decode the lock."

They hastily began circling the chamber, pushing and pulling on each section of shelves in search of the exit they knew existed. Nothing. Halting in frustration, Cadence leaned on the truncated pillar in the center of the chamber and stared around the room. "What are we missing?" Her gaze tracked upward, searching the cornices and ceiling. Then she froze. Gildon looked up.

Directly overhead, in the center of the ceiling, was a large round crystal. His eyes quickly turned to the cornices. Yes! There was a crystal concealed in the design at each of the four directions.

Their eyes met. "It's a portal!" Gildon said.

Cadence spoke simultaneously. "The entire room is a portal!" She turned to explore the pillar against which she leaned. "The settings are concealed like those on the door. Can you operate them?"

Gildon stepped to her side and began running his hands over the pillar. "Yes," he murmured, even as he altered the setting, programming into it the coordinates of the hidden portal in his mother's apartment. It was the only portal that he knew of that hadn't been closed to access from Madaia.

He completed the reprogramming and wrapped his arm around Cadence as he closed his eyes and sent the command that would initiate transport. Vaguely, he heard a shout and opened his eyes; he thought he saw Madaian fighters enter the chamber. And then there were only himself and Cadence spinning through a gray mist.

When the world materialized around them again, or rather they materialized into the world again, they were back in Shaylon's apartment. Gildon immediately turned and removed a crystal inset in the programming design.

"Why did you do that?"

"To discontinue reception. Now no one can follow."

She nodded. "Of course." Wrapping her arms around him, she hugged him fiercely. "Thank you for coming for me."

Enfolding her in his own embrace, he looked down into her beautiful face. "I had no choice," he answered. "Losing you would have been like losing a part of myself." And then, with the threat of danger not so immediate, he bent his head to capture her soft lips in a searing kiss. Drinking in her scent and her warmth, he gloried in the reality that she still lived.

Slowly they returned to themselves, and awareness. "If only we didn't have to go back to Madaia," Cadence murmured.

Gildon nodded agreement. "The weapon will be ready tomorrow night, as we planned."

Cadence turned to look around the chamber. "Where is Shaylon? How is she?"

Gildon realized that Cadence had not been aware of the extent of Shaylon's psychic injury. He gripped Cadence gently by the shoulder, turning her back to him. "Shaylon died, Cadence." She stared up at him without comment, paralyzed by shock. "There was nothing you could have done." Pulling her into his arms again, he caressed her back, comforting her with his touch.

The next morning they rose late. Although Cadence's ankles still sported bruises from the tight ropes, they were no longer painful and she could walk without limping, so she refused Gildon's suggestion that she see a healer. He nodded curtly, accepting her decision, and began donning his clothes.

Sitting on the bed, still wrapped in a blanket, she observed him as he once again donned the pristine white garb of his Order. He was unusually tense, his expression severe. She suspected that, in his own way, he was grieving for his mother but that, because of the nature of the relationship they'd had, he felt compelled to deny his feelings. Being a man, however, he wouldn't appreciate it if she pointed that out to him. And he certainly wouldn't be open to a conversation about Shaylon's motivations. How could she tell him what Shaylon had told her?

But Shaylon hadn't told her. She had shown her!

"Gildon—" He turned to face her questioningly. "Your mother had a small red book in her apartment

327

when I was visiting with her. Do you know where it is?"

He frowned slightly. "Yes. Why?"

"Because it's important that you read it. Where is it?"

"How do you know it's important?"

Cadence smiled softly. "Your mother asked me to read part of it."

Gildon nodded, slid open a drawer in the closet, removed the little book and held it up. "Here." Replacing it, he closed the drawer. "But I don't have time to read it now. Later. My mother's valediction is just after the midday meal this afternoon, and I have much to do to prepare."

Cadence rose, wrapping the sheet around herself, and walked toward the closet. "I'll show you what section to read. It won't take long."

"Cadence, I—"

She interrupted, "You *need* to take the time, Gildon."

He scowled, and for the first time she saw the fierceness in his countenance that she'd only suspected in his character. But, unlike the novices, young priests and priestesses who scurried from his path whenever he entered the hallowed halls of the Temple of the Eidan, Cadence had no fear of either him or his calling.

Ignoring his expression, she removed the book from the drawer, found the page she had read earlier, and passed him the volume. "Read it." That said, she walked into the bathing chamber, leaving him alone to learn of the terrible secret that had shaped his mother's life.

She bathed and dressed in a jade-colored dress, the darkest color she had in her closet. Even though the Tesuvians did not appear to dress for mourning, Cadence felt compelled to dress as appropriately as she could for the valediction. She tried to dredge up a memory of a valediction, wondering how it differed from a funeral, but the only picture she received was of Kadar lying in state in his crystal sepulcher in the disintegration chamber.

When she emerged from the bathing chamber some time later, Gildon was gone. She eventually found him sitting thoughtfully at the kitchen table, his meal untouched before him. He looked up at her entrance.

"She knew this and yet she did nothing?" His tone was accusatory, demanding.

Cadence seated herself and poured a cup of *cai* before answering. "What would you have done in her place, Gildon?" she asked. "You have two sons, one of whom may succumb to an evil influence, and the other may figure prominently in the safeguarding of his people. You have no idea which is which. So, what would you have done?"

Gildon stared at her in silence.

"Would you have put them both to death in order to prevent the prophecy from unfolding?" she demanded.

He frowned. "No. Of course not."

"Well, then, what is it exactly that you think she should have done?"

He rose in one swift, smooth movement. "I don't know. Something. Anything." He turned and stalked toward the window.

Cadence sipped her *cai* in silence.

Abruptly Gildon whirled. "She could have told someone else about the prophecy. Had an expert in the Lidai Order aid her in interpreting it."

Cadence nodded. "Perhaps. But what would she have risked in doing so?"

"What do you mean?"

Cadence shook her head in exasperation. "She would have had to reveal her affair and the circumstances of Jakial's birth, which might have resulted in her expulsion from the Temple of the Avatar, and certainly would have resulted in Jakial being denied training as a priest of the Avatar."

"Exactly. Jakial *should* have been denied training."

"But the way your mother interpreted the prophecy, Jakial was the one who would need the training most."

Gildon stared at her in confusion and then dawning astonishment. "You mean she thought *I* was the one who would betray our people? Impossible! How could she have believed such a thing when it was Jakial who lacked the full birthright?"

Cadence shrugged. "She interpreted the prophecy literally, Gildon. And from the moment of his birth, Jakial was the son she loved best because he was the child of the *man* she loved. It was only recently that she began to doubt her interpretation."

Gildon's eyes took on a distant, musing expression. "So that's what she meant," he murmured.

"What who meant? What are you talking about?"

Gildon blinked and looked at her. "My mother. Just before she died, she said she'd *loved the wrong son*. I had no idea what she meant beyond the fact that Jakial had turned on her."

Cadence sighed. "Your mother was a person who allowed a terrible secret—the prophecy—to affect the way she lived her life. I think on some level she feared you, or at least what she felt you would become, and she protected herself by denying her natural feelings for you."

Gildon stared at her, his face an expressionless mask. And then he threw up his hands. "Enough! I have no more time for this. I must prepare my address for the valediction." He left the room, heading down the stairs to his study, without having eaten a thing.

Cadence let him go. He had a lot to think about. Whether what he had learned would help him to forgive his mother and view her differently, she didn't know. It was much easier for Cadence, who had never endured Shaylon's emotional coldness, to accept the woman's motivation. But she hoped the knowledge would aid Gildon in establishing a more discerning view of his mother, if nothing else.

A couple of hours later, Cadence walked at Gildon's side as they entered the Sadhue Temple where the healers had prepared Shaylon's body for the valediction. Despite herself, she was nervous. "What will happen?" she asked.

Gildon looked down at her, his gaze focusing from far away. "It's not an elaborate or intricate ceremony, but there will be a good number of people in attendance. Although she had no close friends that I'm aware of, my mother was a well-respected priestess. Initially, we will all converse and share our memories of her if we wish, or speak of other things. After a time, each person will file past my mother and say a sentence of farewell. As her son, I am expected to say slightly more. Then Shaylon's physical remains will be discharged."

Cadence nodded. "I see."

They entered the temple, and Gildon led her through a maze of halls to a large chamber. A number of people already conversed within. He halted at the entrance, wishing dearly that he did not have to take part in this. The next couple of hours would be difficult as he accepted condolences on the death of a mother he had never had the chance to learn to love. Since she had never been an integral part of his life, it was difficult to feel loss at her passing. He felt loss only for the things that might have been and now never would be.

With a sigh, he guided Cadence into the room. Shaylon, her blond beauty as yet unaffected by death, lay garbed in the pristine white robes of her calling at the far end of the chamber. Pulling his eyes away from her, he extended his hands in greeting to the first person he encountered, Taveir Mitai, High Priestess of the Avatar in the mountainous province of Chabia. "We are one with the One," he intoned, conveying the ritual greeting before introducing her to Cadence.

Taveir returned their greeting with a compassionate smile and, after a moment of polite conversation, Gildon and Cadence moved on. They met Rion Pilyr, High Priest of the Shido Temple in the desert land of Tamoa, Nolan Suda of the province of Mesyn, Kailea Rys of Artan, and others, until finally they reached a man Gildon had met only once before, and knew only vaguely: Ven Antera, central member of the Tridon.

The Tridon consisted of three people who had attained the level of High Priest within each and every discipline or Order under the auspices of the Temple of the Eidan. Of the three members of the Tridon, only Ven Antera had chosen to also remain Prelate to his people in the province of Kyri. He was the sole person within the chamber who appeared old, and he was of such venerable age that no one knew his exact age except, perhaps, himself.

As Cadence and Gildon approached him, Gildon felt the presence of the One more keenly than at any time other than in direct communion. To gaze into the gentle, lined face of Counselor Antera was to feel the touch of the One. Gildon extended his hands and felt the warm grasp of the aging High Priest infuse his soul with serenity.

"I am honored to make your acquaintance again, kaitan."

"As am I, Brother Gildon Kysnjan." Antera's deep, rich voice rolled over him as his penetrating azure gaze looked deep into Gildon's own unique eyes. Then he transferred his gaze to Cadence. "And you are the alien woman who will aid us in the trials to come. Welcome, child."

"Thank you, kaitan."

Antera smiled and directed a telepathic query to Gildon. *I sense discord in you, young brother. May I help?*

Thank you, kaitan Antera, Gildon responded, *but there is nothing you can do.*

Ven Antera inclined his head in acknowledgment. "Be at peace. Remember you are one with the One." As the powerful tonal vibrations of the words sang in Gildon's ears, he felt a tremendous weight lift from him that he had not consciously known existed. He stared briefly into Ven Antera's eyes and felt the meaning of the term *brotherhood* more keenly than ever before. Perhaps it was only fitting that he should. Although his robes were now gold, at one time Antera, too, had worn white. Nodding again, Ven Antera excused himself and moved on to speak with another.

Tailen approached from the other side of the room. "Gildon, my friend," he said in greeting as they gripped forearms. Since Tailen, of all the people here, was the only one besides Cadence who knew how lacking Gildon's relationship with his mother had been, he did not offer condolences. "It is terrible that we are forced to speak of business on such an occasion, but I'm afraid I must ask your indulgence. May I speak with you?" His eyes flicked to Cadence. "Both of you?"

"Of course," Gildon said.

Cadence merely nodded and studied Tailen curiously.

"Walk with me as we speak." Tailen gestured toward an alcove that opened onto an interior courtyard and began strolling. "Our most recent scrys of Madaia have been fruitful. We've just received word that the Madaian troops are on the move. They could well reach the provincial borders of Chabia, Shemeir, and Ascalon within twelve hours."

Cadence looked up at Gildon. "Ish'Kara must be trying to force the battle before we're ready for her. We have to move quickly. Will we be able to leave for Madaia in the morning?" she asked, knowing he would understand her meaning. They could tell no one, not even someone as trusted as Tailen, about the means they hoped would prove successful in defeating Ish'Kara. She must not learn about the existence of the sword.

Gildon began to nod, but Tailen interjected, "You may not find getting into Madaia so easy."

Gildon pinned the taller man with the probing intensity of his gaze. "If you're referring to a complete deactivation of portal reception in Madaia, I had expected that after my successful incursion into their territory to retrieve Cadence."

Tailen shook his head. "They *have* now discontinued all portal access, but that was not what I was referring to."

Gildon frowned. "Then what is the problem? Cadence and I can travel over land by kuma, avoiding Madaian troops until we reach a Madaian town. Once we are far enough into the province, who is to differentiate us from other Madaians? The most dangerous segment of the journey will be penetrating Ish'Kara's stronghold."

Tailen shook his head. "Our Kami scouts discovered a few hours ago that the Madaian borders are also sealed . . . from inside. How they managed to generate a force field of such magnitude, I don't know. It is probably alignment-regulated because it must be designed to allow their troops out. Yet no one from this side has been able to penetrate it."

Gildon stared at him uncomprehendingly for a moment. Then, scowling thoughtfully, he looked down at Cadence. "If that is so, you should be able to pass through it as you did the city gates. Shouldn't you?"

Cadence remembered the sensations she'd encountered when moving through the gates that Gildon had reprogrammed to test her. It seemed like a lifetime ago. "I don't know. I don't understand how I accomplished that."

Tailen frowned. "Cadence cannot go alone into Madaia. It is too dangerous. We had planned to send Kami and priests of the Avatar to support her."

Gildon looked at him. "A large group would never have worked. It would be too easily detected. My plans do not change, I will go with her."

"Just the two of you? How do you plan to penetrate the barrier?" Tailen demanded.

"I don't know yet. We'll think of something."

Tailen still didn't look convinced.

"Gildon is right, Tailen," Cadence said. "No matter what barrier Ish'Kara has thrown in our paths, I have to go into Madaia. She must be dealt with before she further consolidates her power base."

Worry furrowed Tailen's brow as he slowly shook his head. "Barely one-tenth of our population has been evacuated through the new interplanetary portals." He halted and swung to face Cadence. "How long until she moves at full strength, do you think?"

Cadence shrugged. "I don't know. A couple of days perhaps. Not long. Ish'Kara is always well organized."

Tailen sighed. "Then we must find a means of increasing the number of evacuees so that all but a few necessary people are gone from here in two days. And of course you must do whatever you can to slow her down until our people have an opportunity to escape. The Kami of each province are naturally prepared to do battle to defend the population, so they will buy us some time as well, but they cannot stand for long against an army that by this time may well be only half human. Even with the priests of the Avatar to provide support, the alter-realm incursion will eventually simply overwhelm them."

Cadence nodded as Ali'Yah's memory provided horrific images that brought Tailen's words vividly to life. "I know," she murmured. "I'll do all I can to stop the violation of this world." It had gotten to the point where she could seldom differentiate Ali'Yah's emotions from her own. But perhaps they were not so different after all. As a Stellar Legionnaire, she had been taught to put her life on the line to save the innocent. Here she was being asked to do no more than what she was trained to do . . . but on an unusual world with extraordinary weapons.

Tailen, his expression pensive, began to turn away. And then, as though in afterthought, he turned back and said, "Let me know when you are leaving."

Cadence and Gildon nodded in unison, and a very grave Tailen gripped Gildon's forearm again before taking his leave of them. The discussion over, Cadence took a moment to absorb the unspoiled beauty of the courtyard into which Tailen had led them. A fountain in its center added a carefree tinkling music to the melancholy atmosphere. A profusion of flowers in planters scented the air with their delicate perfumes. And a flock of small, colorful songbirds serenaded them, unaware of the problems affecting the human beings. Oh, to be a little bird right now.

"Come," Gildon said, guiding her back inside with a hand on the small of her back. "It is almost time for the valediction to begin."

Cadence was about to step into the building when she noticed a strange creature sitting on the high courtyard wall looking down at them. "What is that?"

Gildon turned to follow her pointing finger with his gaze. "A Morar. Or at least that's what they call themselves. They normally go out of their way to avoid people."

Cadence studied the winged creature. It was about the size of a large domestic cat. Definitely reptilian, it looked like a miniaturized version of the portrayals she'd seen of mythical dragons. Its scales shone in beautiful metallic shades of copper, gold, and silver in the sunlight. "What do you mean, *they* call themselves Morars?"

Gildon shrugged. "We have communicated with them on rare occasions. They are highly intelligent, telepathic creatures who want only to be left alone. We abide by their wishes."

"Do you know why this one is here?"

Gildon stared at the beautiful winged reptile for a long moment. Finally he shook his head. "It refuses to communicate anything beyond the fact that it is observing."

"Observing what?"

"I don't know. Come, we must go in." With one last glance over her shoulder at the fascinating creature, she followed Gildon into the temple.

As Shaylon's nearest living relative, Gildon was first to speak. He cleared his throat and slowly studied the people in attendance. "As most of you know," he began, "Shaylon of the line of Kysnjan was a wife and the mother of two sons, but she was a priestess of the Avatar before anything else. Her duties within the temple were her world, and her passion." He paused, and met Cadence's gaze briefly before continuing. "My mother was a person who felt nothing in half measures. Her loves and her hates were a product of the intensely passionate nature given her by the One that fueled her loyalties and her convictions. Although occasionally the smaller pictures, the things that touched her personally, were fogged for her, Shaylon never lost sight of the larger picture, of where her duties lay for the good of her people.

"Only once in her entire life did she allow herself

to deviate from the path she'd set for herself. And in the end I believe she held herself accountable for even that failing. I will miss Shaylon, my mother, but I believe we all share the greatest loss: the loss of a priestess of incomparable talent." He looked at Shaylon's body lying before him in the crystal sepulcher. "Be at peace, Mother. You are one with the One."

With that, Gildon moved away to stand at Cadence's side, and another man strode forward. "That is Lacleer of the line of Rhystan," Gildon murmured. "He is a High Priest of the Avatar in the province of Kensi."

Lacleer looked out over the assembly. "Shaylon was my counselor. I will always think of her as a mentor and a friend. She will be missed." Lacleer stepped aside to make way for the next attendee.

"Neran of the line of Calyrr," Gildon whispered. "Priest of the Avatar from the province of Zhao."

And so it continued for over half an hour, as Gildon identified each attendee that stepped forward to say something about their personal connection with Shaylon. Finally Ven Antera took his place behind Shaylon's sepulcher and faced the assemblage. The expression in his eyes grew distant as he stared out over the congregation for a number of moments. The silence stretched, becoming uncomfortable, and a few people began to look at each other questioningly. Then, as though waking, Ven Antera blinked and began to speak. "I learned of Shaylon's importance to us as a people many years ago when I was High Priest among the Lidai Order. Although I never came to know Shaylon herself very well, I did know the man she loved. And I am acquainted with her sons. Shaylon was a dedicated woman who possessed the unique talent of seeing into the depths of almost any person she met." He opened his mouth as though to say more, but something stilled his tongue. He sighed and concluded, "She will be missed." Leaning forward as though speaking to Shaylon, he murmured something too low for anyone to hear and then moved away.

Rion Pilyr came forward with an assistant and slid the sepulcher toward a doorway accessing what Cadence had assumed to be a glass-enclosed alcove. As the assemblage moved forward, some into hallways along either side of the glass alcove, Cadence realized that this was the disintegration chamber. At Gildon's side as he took up the position left for him, she saw that the chamber was octagonal and that it was completely encased in glass. She could see the attendees who had moved into the hallways standing on the opposite side looking in.

When the people were settled, as though rehearsed, they broke into song. It was the first time Cadence had heard anyone in this civilization sing, and she couldn't make out the words. Yet the song imparted a haunting, soulful quality that stirred ancient memories. Tears burned the backs of her eyelids, and without consciously being aware of it, she joined in the singing, her memories supplying her with the words to the song of farewell. It communicated the loss always felt by the living who were left behind, their grief that they must now live without the presence of the other in their lives, and their joy that the one they loved was now with the One.

When the melody was over, Cadence was not the only one to wipe surreptitiously at an escaping tear.

"I wish she had let me know her," Gildon murmured at her side, and Cadence looked up to see that his eyes glistened suspiciously. She understood the nature of his grief, too, the sorrow for what might have been.

Suddenly a brilliant light filled the disintegration chamber, and Cadence looked back to see Shaylon's body shimmering in a cocoon of scintillating embers. Directly over the body, a skylight opened. And

Christine Michels

then Shaylon was gone, her physical remains reduced to a cluster of atomic particles scattered to the four winds.

Cadence stared at the empty sepulcher, trying to reconcile in her mind the swiftness of Shaylon's demise with the vibrant if bitter woman she had known for so short a time. If only . . .

"The bitch has eluded me again!" Ish'Kara stormed wrathfully, rounding on the three men who stood just inside the doorway of her tower study. "Tell me how that happened. How was a stranger able to work his way into this . . . this fortress without being stopped? How were they able to escape?"

No one spoke. Ish'Kara walked slowly past each one, staring into their faces. "What, no answers?" she demanded of the last one, the head of her personal security force.

He cleared his throat. "We have none, kaitana."

Ish'Kara smiled. It was not a pleasant smile. "You have none," she echoed in a falsely nonchalant tone. She grabbed him by the throat. "And I'm supposed to accept that? Reward your incompetence by taking you into a new age with me?"

He struggled against the grasp of her hand. "No, kaitana," he choked.

"I'm glad to hear it." And she reached out with her mind, delving into his consciousness. She could smell his fear, taste it. Drawing only slightly on the augmenting non-aligned energies, she found the area of his brain that controlled his heartbeat. And with a slight twist she shut it off.

As the man dropped to his knees and fell forward onto his face, she turned to his two compatriots. "You." She indicated the center one. "You are now in charge of security. See that you do a better job than your predecessor."

The man swallowed. "Yes, kaitana."

Ish'Kara, who had begun to walk away, swung to face him. "I want to know the instant Ali'Yah approaches. If she gains access to this building without my being forewarned, you will all die, slowly and painfully. Is that understood?"

"Yes, kaitana. But—"

Ish'Kara's eyes narrowed. "But what?"

"The borders have all been sealed, have they not? Surely this woman will not even get into the province."

Stalking forward, Ish'Kara stabbed a long-nailed finger into his chest. "Do not underestimate her. She has always found or been granted the means to find me in the past. This time will be no different. Expect her. Watch for her." She lowered her voice to little more than a discordant whisper. "Because this time, if I don't kill her, you'll *all* die."

Chapter Twenty

Dusk had fallen, and they had not quite an hour until moonrise when Gildon opened the door to admit Traic Suda. The young man held a long wooden box in his arms. "Am I too early, kaitan?" he asked as he stepped into the apartment.

Gildon shook his head and grasped the proferred box. It was warm, radiating the heat of the newly forged sword. "No. Just on time, I think."

"I wrapped the metal in an insulated material so that it would not cool too quickly. And"—he reached into a sack hanging from his shoulder—"I've brought you a scabbard to carry the weapon." He paused. "Just in case."

Gildon eyed the intelligent young man, wondering just how much he'd guessed about Gildon's unusual request. "Thank you." He set the box containing the sword on a table, opened it, and made a brief inspection of the warm weapon. Satisfied, he took the younger man's data crystal and recorded the transaction for him. Then he escorted Traic back to the door. "Perhaps, if all goes well, we can do business again sometime. On Tesuvia."

Traic turned and smiled. "I'd like that, kaitan. Walk with the One."

Gildon dipped his head. "Walk with the One."

He turned back to the table to find that Cadence had emerged from the bedchamber where she'd been

342

changing, and was now bent over the box, inspecting the sword. Unable to help himself, he stared. For the first time since he'd met her, she was dressed in some of the clothing she'd brought with her. Sand-colored trousers of some sturdy fabric hugged her hips and thighs like a second skin while thick-soled boots encased her feet. The only Tesuvian article she wore was a dark indigo tunic that had to have come from a novice in the Temple of the Kami.

He cleared his throat. "What are you wearing?"

She looked over her shoulder at him. "Traveling clothes. We're leaving as soon as the sword is ready, aren't we?"

Gildon shook his head. "Actually, I hadn't planned on leaving until dawn." He walked forward to look down at her. She looked so . . . desirable. His eyes dipped to the V neck of her tunic and he reached to finger the fabric. "Where did you get this?"

"A young woman named Marina. It's a good color to wear for night traveling. And I really think we should cross the Madaian border at night."

Gildon studied her curiously. "Why?"

Cadence shrugged. "A feeling, that's all."

Gildon eyed her a moment more before nodding abruptly in acquiescence. "If you believe it will be better, then that's what we'll do."

A few minutes later, he led her through his study to a lower-level courtyard she had not known existed. Apartments rose on either side for a full two stories, but stairs ascended to street level on both the east and west boundaries. Cadence turned in a slow circle, studying the enclosure. It was quite large for a courtyard, probably at least thirty feet square. The soft mauve glow of luminary crystals set into the stone walls bathed the atrium-like area in a subtle radiance of enchantment, endowing the white stone beneath their feet with an almost fluorescent glow, even as it darkened the foliage of the plants to near black. A number of benches rested in asymmetrical positions throughout so that people could sit and enjoy the exotic scent of the flowers and the trilling songs of the birds. Overhead the night sky glittered with millions of diamond-like stars. The moon had not yet risen.

She turned to Gildon. "How long?"

Kneeling on the stone floor, Gildon had opened a satchel and was in the process of removing items. He glanced up at her briefly. "A few minutes. No more."

"Is there anything I can do to help?"

Without lifting his eyes from what he was doing, he shook his head. "No."

"What do you have to do?" Gildon had never told her exactly what was involved in preparing the weapon.

Continuing with his preparations, he again responded without looking at her. "There is an entity that binds itself to the souls of others. That is how it lives. I intend to lure one through a threshold into the weapon."

Cadence frowned. "You won't hurt it, will you? By trapping it, I mean?"

That brought Gildon's head up and he looked at her in surprise. "With all that is at stake, you are worried about the well-being of one alter-realm entity?"

Cadence raised her chin. "I don't like the idea of using another intelligent being as a tool without concern for its feelings."

Gildon nodded shortly and went back to his preparations. "Neither do I. However, you can rest assured that the Gervin are not concerned in the least about where they reside as long as they are afforded the opportunity of binding with another soul."

"They are not highly intelligent, then?"

Gildon shook his head. "No. That's why, as soon as they come into contract with a new soul, they release the one they have. That will be the one drawback to the weapon. After the initial entrapment, as soon as somebody picks it up, the Gervin will sense the presence of a new soul and release Ish'Kara. Her soul will undoubtedly find its way quickly into the body of that unlucky person."

"And the Gervin entraps the new soul?"

Gildon glanced at her. "No. The weapon is designed to allow the entry of a soul only through the tip of the blade, so it can release an entrapped soul without capturing a new one. I've commissioned the preparation of a casket for the safekeeping of the sword. I plan to leave a carefully worded warning inscribed on the cover." He sat back on his haunches and looked at her. "That's one thing you can do, prepare the English wording for the warning on the casket containing the weapon."

"We're leaving it here when we leave?" Cadence asked incredulously. "Isn't that a little dangerous?" She knew the curiosity of the scientific types of her day.

"Yes, but we can't risk transporting it. We don't know how the portal would affect the entrapped soul. It may release it, and we can't take that chance."

Cadence considered him thoughtfully. He was right. After all they had gone through and had yet to go through, they couldn't take the chance of freeing Ish'Kara on a new unsuspecting population. She was too cunning, too practiced at deceit. Cadence nodded. "All right, I'll see what I can come up with."

"I'm almost ready here." Gildon rose and checked the sky. "The timing should be just right."

"Why does moonlight figure so prominently in this?"

Gildon shrugged. "According to the memories I accessed, it's something to do with the ambience being attractive to the Gervin. Also, sound is often more resonant at night. There are fewer diffusive tones floating around." He gestured to a bench a little removed from where he'd begun his preparations. "You may sit there if you like."

Cadence moved to the seat he'd indicated, instinctively knowing that he needed absolute quiet for the remainder of his preparation. Or was it instinctive? Perhaps the knowledge came from Ali'Yah. It had become difficult to differentiate some things.

She watched as Gildon used some type of luminous yellow-green powder to create a large circle on the stone floor. Then, stepping outside the ring, he placed four uniquely colored, cube-shaped crystals at each point of the compass. That done, he made a slow circuit, chanting the tones that triggered each crystal. As each was activated, the cube emitted a colored radiance that seemed focused exclusively within the circle.

Gildon removed the newly forged, still-warm weapon from the insulating material in which it had been wrapped and carried it to the center of the protective ring. Standing over it for a moment, he raised his eyes to the sky, checking the position of the moons. Only one would have risen in time for the imbuement of the weapon, but it would be enough to bathe the courtyard in moonlight.

After placing his *falar* stone over his forehead, he raised his arms to direct the power of his mind as he began the intonation of sounds which would open a threshold to the dimension inhabited by the Gervin. The rise and fall of his voice, the strange cadence of the recitation, were vaguely familiar to her and yet not. At the conclusion of one dirge-like refrain, a shimmering bubble-like enclosure appeared over the circle, completely enclosing it.

Cadence frowned. She realized that this was a particularly potent protection. Was this imbuement of the weapon dangerous? Was Gildon in danger? She continued to watch his actions very carefully.

In Destiny's Arms

Time passed. The incantation grew more complex, and her newly trained ear had difficulty perceiving all of its intricacies. A threshold flared into existence, tearing an entry in the fabric protecting this world from that. Its flaming periphery drew Cadence's eyes like a magnet, but she forced her gaze to the opening itself, to the world beyond the threshold. At first she couldn't see much. The plane beyond the gate was in darkness. Then her eyes adjusted to the sheen of silver moonlight bathing an alien landscape. It appeared to be a cold world. Frost glittered on everything, the grass, the skeletal branches of a bush; it even sparkled in the air.

And still Gildon stood, arms upraised, eyes on the heavens as he chanted the powerful sounds. The *falar* stone on his forehead gleamed with incandescent brilliance in the near darkness of the courtyard. Gradually the silvery brilliance of a full moon bathed the enclosure. The moon had risen. Cadence felt the hair on her arms rise as the sound of Gildon's invocation swept over her, potent, commanding, and . . . enthralling.

Shaking her head, Cadence cleared her mind and focused on what was happening within the circle. Was there something at the gate? Something looking back at her? She had the strong impression that there was, but whenever she tried to concentrate on it, it wasn't there.

She frowned and transferred her gaze to Gildon. His eyes were now on the threshold itself. She could see his breath emerging in small puffs as the cold of the world beyond the threshold penetrated the protective circle. Slowly, never losing the cadence of his chant, Gildon backed away from the entrance. His tone sounded almost entreating now, and he lowered his arms, gesturing to the weapon at his feet as though in invitation. That was when Cadence saw the entity.

It was nothing more than a hazy outline, and she could find no comparison to describe it. It wasn't even as substantial as the smoky Gou'jiin. Rather, it was like a delicate finger of mist that constantly changed shape yet never assumed any recognizable configuration. It emerged from the threshold so slowly that Cadence had the impression that it was exercising extreme caution. Then, gradually, it began to move in the direction of the weapon.

Reaching the sword, it paused, hovering over it as though considering. Although Cadence could barely discern the creature, let alone any particular characteristics, she had the peculiar sensation that it was contemplating Gildon. The tone of Gildon's chant altered again, once again becoming commanding and powerful. The entity seemed to shrink away a bit, then slowly, as a person might lie upon a bed, it sank into the metal of the weapon.

Gildon intoned a sharper pattern of three notes, and the threshold closed inward with a soft whooshing noise. Then he began to disperse the other protections.

Cadence heaved a sigh of relief. The shield protection that Gildon had installed had worried her, but everything seemed to have gone as planned. She noted the tired slump of Gildon's shoulders and, rising to her feet, drifted toward the circle. Everything *had* gone as planned, hadn't it?

A moment later, Gildon emerged from the circle and gave her a weary smile. As though he'd read the question in her eyes, he said, "Everything is fine."

Cadence sighed and felt the tension leave her shoulders. "Good." She moved forward to aid him in erasing the signs of the night's work. She could see the lines of strain around his eyes. This particular threshold creation had taken much more out of him than she'd anticipated. "You'll need to rest for a couple of hours before we leave."

He paused in his work to look at her. "I thought you wanted to cross the Madaian border before daylight."

"I do. We can spare two hours."

It was dark—so dark she could barely see Gildon in front of her as they drew near the Madaian border. The moons had set and the sun was not yet lighting the sky. Although she now rode her own kuma, dubbed Leiri, Cadence relied heavily on the fact that the creature eagerly followed Lofen, its mate and Gildon's mount. Abruptly the animal halted beneath her, and she peered ahead to discern that Gildon too had halted. She nudged Leiri forward until she was alongside Gildon.

"What is it?" she whispered.

She sensed more than saw Gildon shake his head. "Something's not right," he responded so quietly she barely caught the words. "I'm going to scout ahead." Fitting action to words, he dismounted and faded into the darkness within three steps.

Cadence dismounted and stayed with the two kuma, which stood silently in the darkness as though understanding a need for quiet. The minutes dragged on, and Gildon did not return. Where was he?

For the tenth time, she made a slow study of what she could see of the surrounding landscape. It wasn't much. If she concentrated, she found she could discern the horizon, and that led to an ability to see that Gildon had disappeared over a rise of land in front of them. But damn! Where was he?

Deciding that her combat training was well up to a clandestine foray into the unknown, she left the two kuma and began to move in the direction Gildon had gone. Near the top of the rise, she dropped onto her belly, palmed her laser, and slowly snaked her way up until she could see over the hill. At first glance, she saw nothing but more blackness. Then slowly she perceived a dark shape in the grass not far in front of her. Gildon?

With infinite caution, she moved forward. As she crawled nearer, Gildon glanced over his shoulder at her. His eyes glittered like dark stones in the faint light of the waning stars. Holding his finger to his lips, he signaled that she should say nothing. Then, with a gesture of his chin, he nodded ahead as though to say, *look.*

Cadence followed his gaze and saw . . . nothing. Absolutely nothing. As though sensing her confusion, Gildon grasped her forearm in one warm hand and pointed forward with the other. Obligingly, she kept her eyes focused forward. Then she saw it. A flash of eyes in the darkness. Glowing eyes. Fiery eyes. Inhuman eyes.

Gildon's pointing finger made a sweeping motion, and Cadence began to scan the perimeter of the Madaian border. More eyes, flashing in the darkness so briefly they could easily be missed. Some red. Some yellow. Some blue-green. All devoid of pupils. Daemod eyes.

Cadence breathed an almost inaudible sigh. Thank the stars for Gildon's acute perceptions. Had he not sensed the Daemod presence, they would have ridden right into them and their mission would have been over before it was begun. They could not hope to defeat an army of the shape-shifting Daemod.

As Gildon slowly and cautiously began to back away from his position of observation, Cadence followed him. Quarks! What were they going to do now?

Once over the rise and safely down the hill, they rose silently to their feet. "Your instincts about traveling at night were correct," Gildon murmured. "While in a non-corporeal form, they cannot conceal the fire of their eyes for more than a few moments.

The night makes each change visible. In daylight, the Daemod camouflage would have been complete. We might have sensed something wrong, but we wouldn't have been able to discern their presence."

Cadence swallowed. She didn't understand how he could speak so nonchalantly about the presence of an army of beings that terrified her. She frowned, realizing that the emotion had not come from her own experience. No, the Daemod terrified Ali'Yah. Cadence they just made nervous. Very nervous. She didn't bother seeking the memory that might explain Ali'Yah's terror. She didn't want to know. "How are we going to get past them?" she murmured in an undertone.

He shrugged and mounted Lofen. "Travel along the border until we find a place where they're not so concentrated, and slip between them."

"Can we do that? I thought they had extremely acute senses."

"They do." He paused and looked over his shoulder at her, waiting until she'd settled herself in Leiri's saddle. "But so do I. As long as I'm concentrating, I can *feel* them whenever they're near." In the next instant, he goaded Lofen forward and all opportunity for conversation ceased.

Fifteen minutes later, Gildon again halted, left his mount, and worked his way forward to investigate the border. Cadence waited impatiently. Was the sky beginning to lighten just a bit? Was it a bit easier to see? "Please hurry," she whispered silently.

A few moments later he returned. With a quick nod and a half-smile, he said, "This is it."

"Gildon—" He turned back to look at her. "We don't even know if we can penetrate the shield they have at the border. Won't the Daemod be alerted to our presence when we try to pass through it?"

He met her gaze solemnly. "I honestly don't know, Cadence. But we're out of options. We'll just have to deal with whatever comes our way."

Cadence studied his grave expression, and then nodded. "All right." As they rode over the rise and descended toward the Madaian border, however, her tension increased exponentially with its nearness. At this moment she wanted nothing more than to forget every memory of every past life she'd ever lived, forsake her destiny, and run away with the man she loved. But he couldn't do that, and neither could she. Nervously she looked to right and left, watching for the fiery flash of Daemod eyes.

Gildon drew to a halt ahead of her. Turning, he waited for her to approach. "I think the shield is fairly close," he murmured. "I can feel some kind of power emanation. We should lead the kuma from here on."

Cadence nodded and dismounted. They'd taken no more than a few steps when they began a sharp descent. They both placed their feet carefully on the grassy slope, but the dew had made it slippery and they took more than one skidding step. The kuma, unburdened by riders, didn't seem to have much difficulty. After a few nightmarish moments during which Cadence had been certain that the Daemod would hear them, they reached the bottom of the steep slope.

"I'm glad that's over," she whispered.

Gildon nodded. "I think we should be thankful for that hill. I doubt that they would have left this area unguarded if the steepness of that slope hadn't convinced them that nobody would cross the border here."

Cadence looked back the way they had come, and realized she could definitely see much more clearly than she could earlier. "We have to hurry. It's almost dawn. There could be a patrol."

They started walking. "Can you sense where the border is?" Gildon asked.

She looked at him in surprise. "Don't you know?"

His lips twisted with a wry expression. "I know it's within a few yards of here. And I can feel some kind of power that's probably the shield. But we don't exactly have a line drawn on the ground representing the borders, if that's what you mean."

She shook her head. "Well, I can't feel a thing. And if it's the same type of barrier you used in your gates, I probably won't until I come into contact with it."

He nodded sharply and quickened his pace. Lofen followed at his heels while Leiri trailed behind her. A moment later Gildon halted. Cadence drew abreast of him. "There's definitely a barrier here," he said. "And I don't think it's a nice one." He stretched his hands out tentatively. With a sharp indrawn breath, he jerked them back almost immediately.

"What is it?"

"Painful," he said. "Very painful."

"I meant what kind of barrier is it? Is it the alignment barrier like you thought?"

He nodded. "Yes. It's programmed to resonate in harmony with pure evil. If I tried to force my way through the barrier, I would die."

Cadence reached out her hands. Gildon had to wrestle with the urge to yank her away, to protect her from the pain of contact. But she gave no sign of suffering pain.

She frowned. "It's cold," she said with a shiver. "Like icy cold gelatin."

"Can you move through it?"

Without a change in expression, she stepped forward, one step, two. Her aura did that strange kaleidoscopic thing which made him pray that no one was near enough to see the display of color. Then she turned and moved back toward him. "It's just like the gate."

He nodded. "All right. Now see if you can take a kuma through."

Cadence grasped Leiri by the halter and moved forward. The kuma balked a little as it came into contact with the unseen barrier, but was able to pass through without experiencing pain. Gildon smiled in relief. It worked! With a hasty look around to ensure that they were still alone, he beckoned Cadence back.

A moment later they were both mounted and holding hands, believing that, in that position, whatever transformation that allowed Cadence through the barrier would encompass both Gildon and their kuma. It didn't work. The kuma halted at the barrier and either would not or could not move forward.

Gildon frowned. "Maybe you have to come into contact with the shield first."

With a quick nod and a muttered expression that Gildon couldn't hear, Cadence dismounted again and moved to her kuma's head. Gildon followed suit. Cadence wrapped her right hand around Leiri's halter and grasped Gildon's hand with her left. Gildon likewise held Lofen's halter, and together they moved forward.

Gildon could feel the rippling wall of pain-inducing energy ahead of him and had to exercise every bit of willpower he possessed to put one foot in front of the other. Cadence pulled a little ahead of him, ensuring that she came into contact with the barrier first. And then they were moving through it. He felt its icy coldness, had difficulty taking a breath in the thick gelatin-like atmosphere, but felt no pain.

On the other side, they didn't even bother to pause to relish their success. The sky had grayed considerably at the edges, and the stars were winking out in ever greater numbers. They had to be away from the border before the Daemod patrols came upon them, for the non-corporeal Daemod could overtake them without warning.

Some time later, safely away from the border, they

slowed their mounts and began to assess the country through which they traveled. It was even worse than it had been when Gildon had first found her. The dry grass beneath their feet literally disintegrated to powder with each step their mounts took. The land was so parched that huge cracks had opened in soil already dead from lack of moisture. Animal skeletons littered the plains, their bones picked clean by scavengers and bleached white by the suns.

"I can't believe this!" Cadence exclaimed after a few moments. "How did this happen?"

Gildon's body was rigid with tension as he fought to control the rage that swept through him. "The thresholds," he muttered. "And the alter-realm entities."

"I don't understand."

He looked at her, the anger hardening his eyes, and he knew even as he spoke that his rage would be obvious in his tone. "Do you think if we had only a human enemy to fight, no matter how evil, we would be abandoning our homes, our lives here? It is the Vradir alliance with sinister and corrupt other-dimensional beings that we cannot fight. The powerful diseases that come from their worlds we cannot combat. The disruption of our weather patterns caused by the constant opening and closing of thresholds can't be reversed. How do you combat drought or flooding?"

Cadence ignored his anger, knowing by the bleakness in his eyes that she was not its focus. "I remember," was all she said. And she did suddenly remember it all as though she'd lived through it before. And, of course, she had, as Ali'Yah. The only way to destroy the random thresholds was to obliterate the source of the power they fed upon. But what was it this time? In Atlantis, Ish'Kara had used a huge specially programmed crystal.

Cadence knew from Ali'Yah's memory that she should have been able to sense power sources in much the same way Gildon did, but she couldn't. That was probably why she'd been able to move through the gates and the barrier shielding Madaia. But it also left her at a disadvantage. "Gildon—" She waited until his eyes focused on her. "When you came to find me, did you sense any unusual core of energy?"

He frowned. "What kind of energy?"

"I don't know. Something strong. Something that the thresholds could be drawing upon."

His expression cleared. "The building where I found you draws and stores non-aligned energy. I felt it. It's a very powerful source."

"Then that's it. That's what has to be destroyed in order to seal the thresholds."

"We have to destroy her fortress?" Cadence merely nodded in reply. "That may prove difficult."

"But it's possible isn't it?"

Gildon nodded. "Yes, I think it's possible. I just have to determine where to set some explosive crystals in a manner that will weaken the foundation." He looked at her. "And we can't set them off until you're safely back out of the building."

Cadence shook her head. "The repercussions of loosing all the power stored in that massive edifice could be . . ." Her voice faded away as she remembered Atlantis. Remembered that the shattering of that powerful crystal had ruptured Earth's crust. Remembered the years of darkness that had followed as the ash from a thousand volcanoes spewed into the air.

"Could be what?" Gildon's voice startled her back to the present.

She swallowed. "They could be catastrophic."

He stared at her until she met his gaze. "You're telling me again that we may not survive this, aren't you?"

She shrugged and looked away from the piercing

perception of his storm-hued eyes. "If we succeed as planned, a lot of Madaian people won't survive. If we don't succeed, an even greater number all over the continent won't survive."

Suddenly, Gildon drew his mount to a halt and sat staring straight ahead. Cadence halted Leiri and looked to see what had immobilized him. The creature that stood before them was unlike anything she'd ever seen or imagined.

"What is it?" she asked in a hoarse whisper.

Chapter Twenty-one

Gildon shook his head. "I've never seen anything like it, but from a description I read once, I *think* it's a Morar queen."

Cadence stared at the enormous creature. Over six feet tall, it looked like a giant, scaly seahorse on two short, squat legs. Its iridescent scales seemed to encompass almost every conceivable hue, with the major colors being metallic: gold, copper, and silver. It had two enormous wings folded behind its shoulders, and two small arm-like appendages sprouting from beneath the wing-joints. A bevy of smaller Morars, like the one Cadence had seen in the Sadhue Temple courtyard, rested on the ground in a semicircle around the queen. "What's it doing here?"

"I have no idea. It's extremely rare to see one. They almost never leave their colonies."

Come closer. The words resounded in Cadence's mind, yet she recognized that the source was not an auditory one. She looked at Gildon. "Did you hear that?"

He met her eyes in surprise. "You heard?" When Cadence nodded, he looked back at the Morar. "I wonder how she penetrated your shields."

"I don't know."

Come closer. The words were more demanding this time. *Do not fear me.*

Gildon dismounted and slowly began to lead Lofen

forward. Cadence followed, never taking her eyes from the Morar queen. She was beautiful in an alien way, with her scales glittering richly in the light of the first risen morning sun. But what did she want with them?

The queen studied them for endless, silent moments as they drew to a stop before her. Finally she spoke. *I should not be here. It is unwise to interfere in human affairs. However, in this instance, I believe it would be unwise not to.*

Cadence and Gildon glanced at each other, but remained silent, waiting, for there was nothing they could say to that.

The queen centered her golden eyes upon Gildon. *As you know, the future has many paths. They are dependent upon the choices made by those who live in this time.*

Gildon nodded. "Yes."

You will each have choices to make in the hours ahead. You must choose the life of one who was once loved rather than the death of one who is now despised. She looked at Cadence. *And you must choose the death of an enemy over the life of a loved one.* She glanced from one to the other. *If you do this, all will be well for you.*

"I don't understand what you're suggesting, Queen," Gildon murmured.

I can say no more. Think about it, and you will understand when the choice is upon you.

"But what happens if we don't understand in time? What happens if we make the wrong choice?"

Cadence stared at him, wondering once again how he could accept these mysterious revelations so easily. But she had only to access Ali'Yah's memories to know how integral to the Tesuvian culture was the belief in being able to predict the future . . . and alter it.

Then this time will end for us and many other spe-

cies on this world, and a time of shadows will begin.

"A time of shadows?" Cadence repeated. Why did those who foretold the future invariably speak in riddles?

The Morar stared at her with those all-too-human golden eyes. She felt a tickling in her mind, and then the queen spoke. *You know of what I speak. You must not deny your knowledge.* Pausing, she looked at both of them. *Remember what I have said.* And then, with a flap of her huge wings the ungainly-looking Morar queen rose gracefully into the air, her guard of smaller Morars in her wake.

Cadence glanced at Gildon, noted that he was already remounting his kuma, and decided that now was not the time to try to interpret the nuances of the Morar's guidance. She made a quick survey of the surrounding countryside, saw that it remained clear of threat, and hastily remounted Leiri.

For the remainder of the day they carefully avoided approaching anything that even looked like a town, and they saw no one. Rather than stopping for meals, they ate from the supplies they carried with them as they rode. As it neared time for the evening meal, fatigue began to plague them. Having had little sleep the previous night, they needed to replenish their store of energy. Cadence slumped exhausted in her saddle, but at least she was only tired. Her excellent physical condition seemed to have prevented her from getting the extreme saddle soreness that Gildon had predicted she might.

"We are near the city of Rabar," Gildon said into the silence that had enveloped them over the last few miles. "We should be safe enough among the outer city's crowds to risk seeking lodgings."

Cadence lifted her eyes to his and nodded. "All right."

Within the hour they came upon a trail of hard-packed earth that led into the city of Rabar. In an attempt to be as presentable as possible, Cadence slapped some dust from her cognac-colored suede leather trousers. She froze in mid-slap as a thought occurred to her. "Gildon, will I stand out in these?" She pinched a fold of her slacks.

He shook his head. "Not in the outer city. Animal skins are worn there. There are many . . . uncultured areas in the outer cities."

Deciding she was too tired to take offense at the allusion to her uncultured civilization, Cadence merely nodded.

Gildon led her into the sprawling outer city of Rabar. It was a wild, ungoverned place full of sounds of all kinds, even discordant ones. More than once, Cadence saw Gildon's mouth tighten in reaction to some particularly raucous noise. But she felt strangely at home. It was rather like the noise and confusion at the space docks on Space Station Apollo where arriving crews continually jostled for space with departing personnel weighted down with purchases. She gazed around with interest.

The sound of rousing, energetic music caught her attention and she looked to her left to see a quartet playing stringed instruments and carefully tuned bells. A group of voluptuous women wearing little more than cleverly fastened diaphanous veils danced upon a raised platform before a crowd of grinning men.

As Cadence and Gildon rode on, another vendor caught her eye. This one had a number of beautiful young women modeling clothing. His neighbor was selling finely crafted knives. Looking to her right and left, Cadence took it all in as they moved through the streets. There were vendors trading virtually everything: exotic birds in dainty gold cages, cosmetics and perfumes in elaborate crystal containers, fabrics, foods, drinks, and weapons.

"This should do," Gildon said as they finally

reached a structure that provided lodging. "The stables for the kuma will be in the rear." He headed down a narrow alley between two buildings. After settling the kuma in the stables with an abundant supply of grain, they slung their belongings over their shoulders and walked around to the front. The sword was safely concealed at the bottom of Cadence's duffel bag, which would not leave their sight even for a moment.

The interior of the lodge was the most dimly lit place Cadence had yet encountered—probably to hide the dirt, she mused. Her keen eyes had quickly picked out the layer of dust that covered the floor in any spot where the passage of feet had not polished it away. A wide wooden staircase to the right of the large lobby led to a second floor. Gildon moved toward a broad stone counter on their left that had once been polished and beautiful, but was now marred by the grime of contact with scores of unclean clients. Reaching it, he extracted some crystals from his pockets and rapped them slightly on the counter to attract the attention of the lodge keeper. Since Madaia was no longer connected to the data processor system of exchange primarily used to record transactions, Gildon had brought specially programmed crystals with which to barter for their needs.

Cadence watched Gildon deal with the swarthy, rather rotund lodge keeper. Soon they concluded their negotiations and, for the first time since they'd entered the establishment, the lodge keeper looked at her. His oily eyes slid over her in shrewd evaluation as he turned to get something from the wall behind him, and Cadence was hard-pressed not to shudder. Her immediate instinct was to leave, to get as far away from that slimy piece of humanity as she could, but a bargain had been struck and to leave now would only draw attention. Battling back the potent instinct, she turned and followed Gildon up the stairs.

A few steps down the second-floor corridor, Gildon said, "This is it." He held up the small square that the lodge keeper had given him, and Cadence saw that it contained the model of a lock pattern. He traced the design with his fingertips. There were no chimes to accompany his actions. A moment later, the door swung inward.

The chamber was neither as large nor as pristine as the bedrooms in Gildon's apartment, Cadence noted as she set her duffel bag on the floor next to the bed. But the bedding was crisp and clean, which was her primary concern at the moment.

"I ordered a chamber with a fabricator so we won't have to try to find an eatery." Gildon indicated the small, waist-high, circular device in one corner. "Its selection will be limited, though."

Cadence shrugged. "I don't mind. I'm too tired to think about food anyway." She spun a slow circle in the center of the room. "Is that the washroom?" She pointed to the only other door in the room.

Gildon nodded. "Yes. I must warn you that it will be little more than functional."

Cadence eyed him. "Will it have a tub or a shower, and hot water?"

"Of course."

"Then it'll be wonderful."

Gildon gave her a tired smile. "You go first. I'll check the fabricator menu."

After a shower and a light meal, too tired even to make love, they simply fell into bed content to curl up in each other's arms. It was still dark when, some time later, Gildon's eyes flew open. Moving his hand slowly, he grasped Cadence's arm and shook her slightly. When she stirred, he whispered in her ear, "Wake. Something is wrong." Though his words were barely audible, he felt her nod almost imperceptibly.

He pulled his dislocator from beneath his pillow where he'd concealed it and sat up to stare into the tenebrous void that was their room. Unable to see anything in the pitch blackness, he strained his other senses, listening for a scrape in the darkness or the faint sound of breathing that would signal an intruder. Nothing. He sniffed. What was that odd odor?

Cadence moved closer to him. "Something's burning," she murmured into his ear. He felt the fabric of the Kami shirt she wore as a nightshirt brush against his bare arm.

She was right, the odor was of pungent smoke. But why didn't they find it difficult to breath? Concluding that if there had been an intruder in the room, he would have made a move by now, Gildon intoned the note that activated the light crystals in the chamber.

He was wrong! The intruder, dressed in the black robes of the Vradir, stood across the room, holding a smoking brazier. His onyx eyes glittered with . . . anticipation, and he grinned. "The lodge keeper informed me that two of his guests had not yet joined our fold." He shook his head in mock dismay. "Always there are those who think they can live among us without our becoming aware of them. It just doesn't work. Today, you will join the Vradir and share in our purpose."

"How do you know we have not already joined?" Cadence demanded. And once again Gildon marveled at her warrior's skill, for her voice didn't betray the slightest trace of fear even to someone trained in detecting it, as he was. Watching the Vradir, enjoying his quickly masked expression of confusion, Gildon brought his dislocator to bear behind the folds of the bedding.

"The door to this chamber records the individual

vibratory resonance of everyone entering this room. One of you definitely is not in harmony with us."

"And the other?" Gildon prompted, still holding the dislocator, reluctant to use it too soon in the event that the Vradir possessed information they needed.

The man frowned. "The other did not register at all. You will tell us how you accomplished that."

"Perhaps your recorder was malfunctioning," Cadence said, as she slipped one hand beneath the pillow at her back. Had she hidden her weapon, too, Gildon wondered. While he was in the bath, perhaps?

Ignoring her, the Vradir looked at Gildon and smiled again. Unpleasantly. "I know you're holding a dislocator. You cannot hurt me with your weapon." He lifted the brazier in his hand, swinging it back and forth a bit, and Gildon noted that the smoke formed a strange grayish wall around the Vradir priest. "We are protected from the phase-action."

"We?"

"Those who will aid me in convincing you to join our cause. Quickly now, rise and dress before they arrive." He looked at Cadence in a manner that would have been apologetic had it not been for the avid gleam in his eyes. "I'm sorry I cannot offer to turn my back. You understand."

"Of course." Cadence swung the blankets aside and, while the Vradir's eyes were on her shapely legs, she aimed the laser that had been concealed in her palm unerringly at his chest. In an almost conversational tone, she asked, "Are you protected against this, too?" The beam of cutting light shot across the room, striking the Vradir in the chest, freezing forever the surprised expression on his face. His hand made an aborted movement toward the wound, and then, as the strange wall of smoke around him dissipated, he fell to the floor.

Cadence squeezed her eyes closed for a second and swallowed, betraying for just that instant that she was not as strong as she led everyone to believe. Then, glancing at Gildon with a falsely bright smile on her lips, she said, "You see. My laser may not be as thorough as your dislocator, but it does have its advantages."

"Yes." Gildon moved quickly across the room to right the fallen brazier before it could start a fire. When he turned toward the chair where he'd left his clothing, he saw Cadence peering through a small gap in the curtains into the alley behind the lodge.

"It's almost dawn."

He nodded. "Good. We have to get out of here before his colleagues arrive." He gestured with his chin in the direction of the corpse.

Cadence avoided looking at the fallen Vradir as she hastily began to dress and repack her belongings. A scant three minutes later, they climbed out the second-story window of their room, preferring to take their chances with the height rather than with the owners of the stealthy footsteps they heard in the hallway.

"Come on," Gildon whispered to Cadence, who was hanging by her fingertips from the window ledge in the predawn darkness. "I'll catch you."

A second later, she dropped. He broke her fall, but not quite in the way he'd intended; her buttocks struck him rather forcefully in the chest. "Thank you," she said quietly as he set her gently on the ground.

"You're welcome," he gasped, thankful that his whispered words concealed his momentary breathlessness. Grasping Cadence's hand, they ran off in the direction of the stable.

If there was any pursuit out of Rabar, they didn't see it, and an hour later they slowed their mounts, setting a more comfortable pace. The day passed uneventfully as they gradually ascended the low mountains that stretched all the way to the Madaian coastline. They were forced by fatigue to camp for a portion of the night despite their awareness that time was wasting. The Tesuvian evacuation, according to Tailen's stepped-up plan, would be near completion with the exception of those priests of the Avatar and Kami warriors who had stayed to hold back the Madaians and their alter-realm allies. They slept only long enough to ensure that their senses remained sharp before moving on in the darkness of early morning.

It was almost midday when they neared their destination, the city of Eston . . . and Ish'Kara. Gildon halted on the summit of a hill looking down into the huge valley where the city rested. Cadence dismounted and moved to stand beside him. Eston, like every other city on the continent, had been built of gleaming white and gold. Yet there was something dark about it, as though the shadow they now faced hung over the city in a visible pall. Perhaps it was only her perception, but Cadence shuddered.

Gildon, with binoculars pressed to his eyes, studied the town below.

"What do you see?" she asked.

It took him a second to respond, and when he did, he sighed and shook his head before looking down at her. "Guards," he said. "As we expected. I can make out three of the entrances to the city, and there are four guards at each one. I think we can assume they'll be at the fourth entrance as well."

Cadence looked from the city to the huge, ugly black fortress on the summit of the steep hill opposite them. "And that is Ish'Kara's stronghold?"

Gildon nodded. "Yes."

"Maybe we don't have to go through the city to reach it. If we follow this ridge around"—she gestured with one arm—"it looks like it may take us very near."

"It's worth a try."

Some time later they came to the end of the trail. A 30-foot-wide chasm separated them from their destination. The huge black stone edifice seemed to cast a shadow three times its size even though it was only slightly past midday. Cadence suppressed a shiver. It looked almost like a huge, hulking predator. And yet she was thankful for one thing: There appeared to be no one on lookout duty. At least not in this direction. So she allowed herself to relax slightly and turned her attention to the problem at hand: crossing the chasm.

It didn't seem possible. "Now what?" Cadence asked in exasperation.

Gildon dismounted and began to survey the situation. At its narrowest, the chasm was still at least 20 feet across. He scrutinized one area critically, moved to another, shook his head, and walked back to the first. "I think I should be able to climb down here."

The slope he indicated was only slightly less than vertical. Cadence eyed him incredulously. "Are you crazy?"

He shook his head and pointed. "Look, I can follow that trail there down to that scrub tree, then move over to that boulder. From there I can cross the gorge at that narrow point, and climb back up that faint trail to the base of the fortress."

Cadence followed with her eyes the path he'd outlined and conceded that it just might be possible . . . for him. She wasn't nearly as optimistic about herself.

"I want you to stay here," he added, as though reading her mind. "If I can install the explosive crystals and find an entrance without being caught, I'll come back for you. If not, then you'll have to find your own way of confronting Ish'Kara."

The realization of what he'd just said froze Cadence's breath in her throat. This was it. The moment that could be their last together. *I may never see him again.* Her moss green eyes flew up to connect with his. "I love you," she murmured as she moved into his outstretched arms. Suddenly chilled, she hugged him to her, memorizing the feel of his body next to hers. Its heat and scent and contours.

"And I love you," he replied. He didn't offer her false assurances, and she appreciated that. They both knew that there were no guarantees in what they were about to attempt. Lifting her chin gently on the tip of one finger, he captured her lips in a kiss. And with that kiss, he said more than words ever could. He spoke of love and need and a promise for the future, if not in this life, then the next. For their two souls were destined to be together, and nothing, not even death, could keep them apart forever.

Then he gently set her from him and began to secure his supplies firmly to his shoulders. With one final poignant look and a kiss on the tip of her nose, he descended over the side of the precipice. "See you," Cadence called softly. She wouldn't say goodbye it was too final.

His only reply was a gentle smile. She closed her eyes, holding that last view of him next to her heart. *Don't let him die,* she prayed.

Gildon didn't know how long it took him to reach Ish'Kara's cold black fortress. It seemed like forever. His hands were cut and bleeding from the sharp stones he'd been forced to use as handholds in his descent. His warrior garb was torn and dirty beyond recognition, let alone repair. And he had a cut on one cheek just below his eye where one falling stone had struck him. He considered himself lucky. He'd made it without plunging to his death on the rocks at the bottom of the gorge.

Now, as he began to circumnavigate the edifice, he realized that it was very unlikely that he would find an entrance at ground level. The main entrance, which he could now see from his vantage point, had a long ramp of soil and gravel to grant access. Since that would undoubtedly be the first level, the level at which he now stood would be the basement. It was possible that a small entry or exit opened directly onto the basement level, but not likely. Still, he didn't need to get inside to set his explosive crystals, so he would do that before worrying about finding an access for Cadence to get into the building.

He heard occasional voices on the balconies just over his head as he moved cautiously around the base of the building, but he ignored them. Only after he'd set eight of the ten crystals he'd intended to detonate did he hear a voice he couldn't ignore. Jakial! By the One, he detested even his voice now. How could his brother have turned his back so completely on all that they'd been taught? How could he have furnished his knowledge to those who had no respect for life?

Moving slowly away from the building, he craned his neck, peering upward to try to pinpoint his brother's location. There! On the balcony two stories above. He was speaking with a man in warrior garb.

Remembering the two crystals that had yet to be set, Gildon hastily completed his task before palming his dislocator. Slowly he moved into a position where he had a clear view of the brother who'd betrayed his people and had killed his own mother. As a Kami warrior, it was Gildon's duty to dispense justice. He leveled the dislocator, fully intending to fire it, and froze as the words of the Morar queen replayed in his mind.

You must choose the life of one who was once loved

rather than the death of one who is now despised. Jakial! She'd been referring to Jakial. Gildon had barely begun to lower his weapon when his brother's eyes found him. They stared at each other, knowing one another so well that even the blurring of distance did not prevent Gildon from reading the expression on his brother's face. And then Jakial surprised him by favoring him with a wave and a salute. The fighter on the balcony with him followed the direction of his eyes, saw Gildon, and stiffened. But Jakial merely placed a hand on the man's shoulder in a calming gesture. Knowing that he could waste no further time in leaving this place if he hoped to escape with his life, Gildon decided to forgo the search for an entry. They would have to find another means to confront Ish'Kara. Within seconds she would know they were here at any rate; the element of surprise was gone. Perhaps they could somehow induce Ish'Kara to come to them.

As hastily as possible, considering the difficulty of the climb, Gildon retraced his path back to Cadence. Every time he found himself forced to pause for a moment, he examined the huge black edifice looming over him for any sign of activity that might signal pursuit. He was still about 30 feet below the summit where he'd left Cadence when a movement on the tower balcony caught his attention.

Jakial stood next to a woman with flowing blond hair. His arm was extended in Gildon's direction, pointing him out. Gildon tried to maneuver himself over to a position where a ridge of stone would offer some protection from whatever Ish'Kara might do. He didn't have long to wait.

Ish'Kara reached out her arm, fingers up, fist closed, and slowly opened her hand to free a crystal. The small orb began to cross the chasm toward him, levitated by Ish'Kara. What type of crystal was it? Would he have a defense?

Before he could make a determination, a voice rang out, echoing surreally through the gorge. "Ish'Kara! It's time to face *me* now." Gildon looked up to see Cadence perched on the edge of the abyss almost directly opposite Ish'Kara on her tower balcony. She wore the sword in its scabbard at her waist. What was she doing? She was too far away to attempt to use it.

As Isk'Kara turned to face her, a cold smile upon her lips, the crystal orb, no longer buoyed by her telekinetic power, plunged to the floor of the ravine below. It exploded upon contact into a hundred thousand needle-like shards, each no doubt programmed to burrow into the body and seek out the heart of its victim. There was no way he could have avoided all of them.

Gildon closed his eyes. Cadence had saved his life, but now how would she save her own?

Chapter Twenty-two

"It's so nice to see you again, Sister," Ish'Kara called. "If only for a few moments."

Cadence didn't reply. Rather, she raised her arms skyward and closed her eyes. Gildon's breath caught in his throat as she teetered dangerously on the edge of the huge crevice. *Move back!* he willed. And miraculously, she did take a single step back, but she didn't even open her eyes to do so.

He glanced at Ish'Kara. Alone on the balcony now, she too stood with arms raised and eyes closed. What were they doing? What kind of powers did these two women, once sisters, possess?

And where had Jakial gone? He risked a glance behind him, wondering if his brother now pursued him.

In the next instant the wind began to howl around him, clutching at his clothing with invisible fingers as though to pluck him from the cliff face. Clouds, black and threatening, came out of both the north and the south horizon, driven along by a supernatural force. Within seconds, they clashed overhead, churning and boiling and grumbling at tremendously escalated speeds.

Awed, he stopped and stared, only to find that the wind increased its intensity. If he didn't want to plunge to his death, he had to get to level ground. A stone turned unexpectedly beneath his hand, throw-

ing him off balance. Desperately he sought anothe
handhold. His fingers caught, slipped again, an
then seized a hold on a larger stone. It remaine
solid beneath his grasp. Thank the One!

A flash of light, blindingly bright, flickered to h
left. Before the flash had even faded, thunde
boomed so loudly that he felt the vibration in th
rocks beneath his body. A howl of rage sounded. H
turned to see what had happened and saw tha
Ish'Kara's black stone fortress now bore a smokin
hole where one corner of the edifice had been.

He prayed that the crystal charges he'd set had n
been activated by the blast, for when the charge
went off, the castle would crumble in great section
killing everybody in it . . . including Ish'Kara. An
she had to be stabbed with the specially constructe
sword *before* she died. He looked up at Cadence
wondering if she could now receive his thoughts. *R
member the sword*. And again, as though she had r
ceived his communication, she pulled the weapo
from the scabbard at her side.

"Such an ancient weapon, Ali'Yah. What are yo
planning?" Ish'Kara called across the 20-foot spa
separating her from Cadence.

Cadence smiled, but it was not the gentle smile h
was accustomed to seeing. The same fierce expre
sion she had worn during her fight with the Gou'jii
shone in her eyes. "You will find out very soo
Ish'Kara." She raised the weapon as though to thro
it across the expanse separating them.

"I don't think so." And in that instant Gildon fe
himself plucked from the cliff face in an unyieldir
grasp. Within seconds he hung suspended over th
gorge. He noted hundreds of Vradir now pourir
from the entrance of Ish'Kara's fortress. "Throw th
weapon, and your lover dies!" Ish'Kara taunted.

Gildon's gaze flew to Cadence. Or was it Ali'Ya
who stood there so boldly? For Gildon truly did n

recognize the carriage of the woman he saw. She hesitated; the arm holding the weapon dropped slightly. Ish'Kara's triumphant laughter echoed louder than the storm, became part of that primal fury.

And once again the words of the Morar queen came back to him. The words she had directed to Cadence: *You must choose the death of an enemy over the life of a loved one.* Cadence had to let him die or all would be for nothing.

Fear flared in his brain, attempting to crowd out rationality, but he forced it aside. Again he sent a message, hoping that she really could hear him and that the previous times had not been mere coincidence. *Cadence, remember the Morar queen. Remember what she told you?*

Yes. But I can't do it.

Even as he hung over the gorge, his life dependent upon the whim of a madwoman, he gloried in the knowledge that, for whatever reason, the Empyrean guardians had allowed him to communicate with Cadence as Tesuvian couples were meant to communicate. *You have to. Our love will not die. It has lived long already. Remember Kadar.*

In the next instant, Cadence squared her shoulders, raised the sword, and threw it as though throwing a knife at a target. Time slowed. Guided by unseen forces, the weapon flew end over end unerringly across the chasm. Even as he prepared himself to die, Gildon wondered at that. Did Cadence, too, possess the strong telekinetic abilities that Ish'Kara did? Such strength was very rare. Why had she said nothing?

Ish'Kara's face contorted into an inhuman mask of rage. The storm grew so violent that nothing could be heard beyond the scope of its fury. Clouds roiled. Lightning flashed. Thunder roared. And Ish'Kara screamed an incantation of protection, using sound and mental power to erect a barrier before her.

Just as quickly, Cadence, her face frozen in an expression of cold intent, reversed it.

But how? How could she have the strength of concentration to perform an incantation when she was still guiding the sword telekinetically?

Time seemed to stop. Gildon stared from one woman to the other and in that instant received a revelation—one he should have understood long ago. This was not an eternal contest between two women, two immortal souls destined to meet again and again. This was a contest between two diametrically opposed omnipotent consciousnesses: the One, and the Other. Light and Darkness. Little had been recorded about the Other—probably because most preferred to believe it did not exist—and what had been written was unclear. Was it truly another universal consciousness? Or only a part of the One, the darkest aspects of itself which it forever fought to purge?

Whatever the explanation, Gildon was as certain of his sudden belief as he was of his love for Cadence. Ish'Kara and Ali'Yah were mere conduits for the power of the two sides. Tools locked in a timeless battle of good versus evil. Ish'Kara's eternal self-indulgence and ambition had made her the perfect tool of Darkness. And Ali'Yah's unending need to protect the innocent had made her the consummate instrument of Light.

Rage boiled within him as he watched Cadence's delicate woman's body buffeted by the force of the storm, racked by the strength of the power wielded through her. "Enough!" he bellowed.

As though goaded by the sound of his voice, time began moving forward again. The sword reached Ish'Kara, embedded itself in her chest as if wielded by the strength of an invisible hand . . . or an omnipotent one.

Screams from below drew his attention. The Vradir!

Now! Now he could destroy the fortress. As he began to fall, no longer suspended in space by the unseen might of Ish'Kara's telekinesis, he half sang, half shouted the intonation that would activate the crystals.

Had it worked? Had the sound reached the crystals through the diffusive noise of the raging gale?

He would probably never know. He felt the wind rushing past his ears. Saw the ground rushing up to meet him at bone-crushing speed. Heard a shout of denial in a man's voice. His brother's voice. Jakial?

Suddenly the good times flashed in his mind. The times that his brother had made him laugh, made him feel . . . loved. Craning his neck, he attempted to see Jakial just one more time before he died. There! High above him. He was raising his arms, voicing an incantation.

And just when Gildon knew that death was imminent, his plunge into the huge crevasse halted. Once again in the clutch of a huge invisible fist, he felt himself lifted, quickly and safely, to the top of the gorge. The force released him a few feet from Cadence, who now appeared to be levitating the sword back across the gorge.

Gildon turned, seeking Jakial. The huge castle rumbled as the explosions took place at its base and slowly it began to crumble, the moans and groans of stressed stone a strange complement to the screams of dying Vradir. Where was Jakial? For the first time, Gildon dared to hope that, despite everything, his brother could return with him. When his eyes finally found him, he saw that Jakial now stood on the tower balcony. Even as Gildon watched, he stooped to pick up Ish'Kara's body in his arms, making no effort to escape the crumbling edifice.

"No!" Gildon shouted. He couldn't see his brother die. Not now!

As though sensing Gildon's gaze, Jakial looked across the chasm at him and smiled. It was the gentlest smile he had ever seen grace his brother's lips. And then Jakial calmly walked up onto the stone balcony rail. When the next explosion rumbled through the huge edifice, he serenely stepped from the balcony and plunged to his death with the body of the woman he'd loved in his arms.

Gildon reached toward him as though to forestall his death with the strength of his yearning. But his own telekinetic powers were much too limited. "Jakial!" He shouted his brother's name, and the agony of his loss echoed throughout the valley, merged with the tempest. The last sound he heard was the echo of his brother's laughter, carried on the winds of the storm, before he struck the bottom of the gorge. And the hope, so newly born, died.

Grief-stricken, Gildon turned his back on the canyon just in time to see Cadence crumble. He stared uncomprehendingly for an instant. She'd been so strong, so . . . indomitable. What had happened? The sword containing Ish'Kara's soul rested in the scabbard at her side, so the problem did not arise from that. It was as though someone had stolen every last vestige of her energy, as though the bolstering force that had sustained her had been withdrawn.

Of course, the contest was over.

Yet the storm raged on, pummeling the area with lightning and thunder. As the black castle continued to crumble slowly into rubble, it released the non-aligned energy that had been stored within it. Huge coruscations of prismatic energy streaked outward in gargantuan arcs, striking everything in their path. And the chaos escalated. A gigantic forked crevasse opened up, snaking down into the valley toward both the city of Eston and the storm-tossed sea that rampaged on the city's northern side. Enormous clouds of steam and smoke formed the instant the crevasse reached the ocean.

The contest was over, and for the first time Ali'Yah had survived the confrontation with her sister. Yet, if Gildon didn't get her out of there quickly, neither one of them would be alive for long. As the sea continued to churn and rise, sweeping inland, he shoved his grief behind the wall in his mind to be dealt with at another time and hurried to Cadence's side.

She was so pale, so fragile. As he lifted her into his arms and began running toward the nervous kuma a short distance away, he wondered if all people, all life, were just pieces on a gaming board to be moved about at the whim of supreme beings. Even as the irreverent thought took root in his mind, he recognized his indignation and anger over the danger to Cadence's life as its source, yet the idea would not go away.

It would take a long time for him to understand and accept what had happened here today . . . if he ever did.

Continuing to hold Cadence in his arms, he mounted Lofen and raced away. Leiri, with Cadence's belongings still secured to her saddle, was only too happy to follow her mate. Now, according to the plan, they had to get to the nearest operational interplanetary portal, which was in Chabia, where they would safeguard the sword in its specially constructed casket before transporting to Tesuvia. The most dangerous part of the journey would be getting out of Madaia. The power source for the random thresholds had been destroyed, preventing any increase in the number of alter-realm beings, here, but those already here would be battling for survival. Most threatening would be the Gou'jiin, which could not exist without a host, for many of their human hosts were dying in the city below. But he fully expected to have to avoid the occasional advance guard of Madaian fighters, too, for their invasion of the other provinces was believed to have been planned to begin today.

The kuma raced away as quickly as the mountainous terrain would allow, and Gildon allowed himself a moment to focus his attention on Cadence. He needed to understand the nature of her infirmity. Was it simply fatigue? Or something else? Remembering the brief communication they'd shared during her conflict with Ish'Kara, he gently probed her mind, hoping that her shields might continue to allow him contact. He reared back sharply, his physical recoil an expression of his mental surprise.

Her protective shields were gone! Completely. She had only the passive shield protection of a normal Tesuvian mind in slumber. Now, when she needed them most, the shields were gone. He stared at the heavens with bitter eyes. *Why?* he demanded of the Empyrean guardians, even though he knew they would not hear his call. *Why have you deserted her like a tool that has no further use? Why don't you protect her?*

She is protected. The words resounded in his mind, powerful and indignant.

Startled by the unexpected response to his query, for a moment Gildon could only stare at the unusually bright light that shone down through the thick cloud cover overhead. And then his mind began to work again. *How?* he asked. *Her shields are gone.*

We have brought you together. You are her protector. You are her shield. And we guide your steps toward the safe path.

Gildon fingered the contents of his drawstring satchel. Did he have on him the means to protect her? Perhaps, if they didn't meet too many threats.

As they rode on, the ground continued to rumble and shake beneath their feet. Earthquakes! They passed a small city where a quake had already struck, reducing the buildings to mounds of gravel.

They had traveled relatively uneventfully for more than an hour when Cadence finally opened her eyes. Gildon halted Lofen. "How are you feeling?" He gently brushed a strand of hair away from her face.

A small frown drew her brows together. "Like I've been run over by a docking bay drone."

"What?" Gildon stared at her. "What's a docking bay drone?"

"Never mind," she said. "It's not important." She twisted in his arms, looking around. "Where are we?"

"On the way to Chabia."

"Of course." She squirmed slightly, and he realized she was trying to get down.

"Are you sure you feel well enough to ride?"

She paused and considered. "No," she said. "But we'll be able to move more quickly, and I have a feeling that's important." Her eyes caught sight of a huge black column of smoke that had been rising into the sky from the south for the last half hour. "What's that?"

Gildon's eyes followed hers. "What's left of Rabar, I believe. The ground has been shaking in pretty much one continuous quake ever since Ish'Kara's fortress fell. I wouldn't have thought the non-aligned energy to be *that* powerful."

"If it wasn't, it was made more so," Cadence said as she turned sadly away from the enormous cloud of smoke.

"What do you mean?"

"Ali'Yah's memories tell me that the One forgives many things . . . except evil. I don't think more than a handful of Vradir will escape the wrath of the One today."

Gildon stared at her, saw the bleakness in her eyes. "This reminds you of Atlantis?"

She nodded. "A little, yes." She mounted Leiri, and they rode on.

In late afternoon they had almost reached the Chabian border and the city of Lagos near the Madaian boundary when the threat that Gildon had begun to believe might not appear ultimately did. Only it was not a Gou'jiin, but an immortal and virtually invincible shape-shifting Daemod.

The creature that appeared before them looked like something out of a nightmare. "Well, if it isn't the so pretty priestess and her heroic lover!" Sarcasm dripped like venom from the Daemod's forked tongue.

Cadence sighed in a bored fashion and met the Daemod's eyes. "Hello, Baltharak. So nice to see you again." She goaded the kuma forward as though to move around the Daemod, and Gildon followed her lead. It didn't work. Baltharak immediately placed himself in their path again. Cadence halted to stare at the creature with a wry twist of her lips. "Is there something we can do for you, Baltharak?"

The Daemod stalked forward until his lurid eyes glared into hers. "Yesss," he hissed. "You can undo what you have done. Open the thresholds."

"Why would I do that? We've just worked very hard and made a lot of sacrifices to close them, to protect this world from your kind so that it doesn't become a scorching hell like the other worlds you've taken."

"What do you know about the other worlds?" he demanded.

Cadence shrugged. "A lot of things have been revealed to me that I would've preferred not to know. I know that your kind consumes worlds, leaving nothing but devastation in your wake." She smiled slightly. "This world will eventually repair the damage that's been done; there aren't enough of you here to destroy it."

"Whore!" A spate of verbal sewage continued to

fall from his tongue in sickening waves. Cadence and Gildon merely sat upon their nervous kuma, eyeing the Daemod impassively until his tirade ended.

"Is there a point to this meeting?" Gildon demanded, painfully aware of the time slipping away.

Baltharak looked from one of them to the other. Finally his eyes settled on Gildon. "Just as there are not enough of us here to do permanent damage to this world, there are not enough of us here to survive."

Gildon frowned. What was this, some kind of Daemod trick? "You are immortal."

"Yesss," Baltharak hissed belligerently, shoving his face so close to Gildon's that he had to hold his breath to keep from gagging at the stench coming from the Daemod's mouth. "But our strength is linked to our world. When we are trapped on a world in insufficient numbers to make it our own, eventually we are condemned to permanent non-corporeal existence. We lose our vitality. Life becomes a living hell."

Gildon glanced at Cadence, saw that she was already looking at him. She nodded slightly, answering the question in his mind without his having to ask. He turned back to Baltharak. "How long would it take all the Daemod on this world to come to this location?"

Although the face the Daemod had chosen to wear was impossible to read, his eyes revealed a trace of confusion. "Mere minutes," he blustered in a manner that seemed a bit defensive. "Why do you ask, *human?*"

Gildon cleared his throat. Was he about to do the right thing? Or something very stupid? There was just no way to know. "If I open a threshold to your world"—he held up his hand at the sudden avid gleam in Baltharak's eyes—"a *single* threshold, would you and your kind take the opportunity to return home?"

The Daemod's eyes glistened as his inhuman lips curved in a satisfied smile. "Yes."

"No tricks, Baltharak," Cadence interjected. "Any attempt at deception, such as a concentrated invasion by your kind from the other side, and we'll disperse the threshold immediately, no matter who is in its grasp."

Baltharak eyed her with dislike. "You're beginning to sound more and more like your sister, little priestess."

"Enough!" Gildon said. "Call the others of your kind while I create the threshold. We haven't much time."

Forty-five minutes later, the last of the Daemod entered the threshold. Baltharak stood looking back at them from the other side, the fiery waste of his home world rippling and changing in the background. "Farewell, humans," he said, and with an insolent grin, he was gone.

Gildon dispersed the threshold. "You know," Cadence mused behind him, "it might almost be safe to stay here now."

He turned to face her. "With the exception of the Gou'jiin, which will continue to inhabit any living thing they can find, and the many powerful diseases and less dominant entities that came through the random thresholds, yes. But it will not be completely safe to live here for a very long time."

Cadence stared sadly toward the horizon and nodded. "I know. You're right. I guess I just wish it were otherwise."

"A number of priests of the Avatar will probably stay to cleanse the world as much as possible before leaving for Tesuvia. As you said earlier, the world will recover."

She nodded toward another nearby animal carcass, this one not yet skeletal. "I hope the animal species recover as well."

It was nearing evening when they approached the outer wall of the city of Lagos. The bodies of a few Madaian fighters, those killed by a less tidy means than the standard dislocators, littered the ground. It was quiet. Wary of possible Madaian stragglers, they entered the outer city. The portal they needed to access was in the Temple of the Eidan in the inner city. As they rode slowly through the almost deserted streets, they noted that the only people who remained were the Kami, a few Avatarian priests, and a number of Gou'jiin-possessed individuals who had been unable to transport because of the alien entities within them. These Gou'jiin-controlled people were bound to posts in a manner that prevented them from doing injury to themselves, or to the priests who were performing exorcisms.

Catching sight of Cadence and Gildon, one young priest approached them. "You are Brother Gildon?" he asked. When Gildon nodded in confirmation, he continued, "I am Dantik of the line of Rilare. Prelate Tailen warned us to expect you. He sent a small casket for your needs via portal. It is waiting in the assembly hall."

"Thank you." Gildon surveyed the streets around them. "How are things progressing?"

"All who could escape have gone. Only the possessed and the diseased remain."

"The diseased?" Gildon eyed the young Avatarian priest incredulously, certain that he'd heard incorrectly. His people had eradicated human disease centuries ago.

Dantik nodded. "Yes. A disease which we are not protected against came through one of the thresholds. So far, I believe it has been limited to this city. However, all that have contracted it have died and been disintegrated. We were not able to perform valedictions for them. I advise you to avoid the healing clinics in the central city and the Sadhue Temple."

Gildon nodded. "Of course. Thank you." He knew nothing about fighting disease, and the last thing he needed was to risk either his life or Cadence's now.

They traversed the rest of the city without incident and entered the deserted Temple of the Eidan. It took mere moments for them to find the casket. Gildon carried it across the assembly hall and set it in a camouflaged room just off the communion chamber. The secret chamber was generally used by high priests for secreting things not meant for the general populace, but it would serve admirably for the purpose they intended.

Wordlessly, Gildon watched as Cadence removed the scabbard containing the sword from her belt. Being extremely careful not to come into contact with the weapon itself, she lifted it by the leather scabbard and allowed it to slide out of the sheath onto the padded lining in the casket.

Gildon eyed her curiously. "You are keeping the scabbard?"

Cadence shrugged. "Yes, as a memento."

Saying no more, Gildon retrieved the lid they'd commissioned and read the inscription that Cadence had phrased.

This sword imprisons the soul of Ish'Kara. It is evil. Touch it and you imperil your race, for Ish'Kara will be freed. Be warned. Defeating her is not easy. Only when this specially constructed blade once again tastes her blood and contacts her soul may you be saved. And even that is not certain, for she gains strength with each incarnation. It was signed: C. Barrington.

As he placed it on the casket, Cadence smiled. "I hope I've worded it clearly enough, but knowing the skepticism of the people of my time, they wouldn't believe it anyway. I'm pinning my hopes on their never finding this room."

Gildon grasped her arm gently, drawing her eyes up to his. "It's over, Cadence. You can look toward your own future now . . . *our* future together as companions."

She stared up at him, hope and love shining from her eyes like a beacon in the night. "How?" It was the only word she could choke out past the sudden lump in her throat. She'd been afraid to contemplate their future, afraid that she would be forced to spend eternity living near but forbidden to touch the man she loved.

"You still retain Ali'Yah's memories, don't you? And Ali'Yah's soul is also yours?"

"Yes." What was he getting at?

"Ali'Yah was a priestess of the Avatar, Cadence. You have the knowledge already."

She shook her head. "But the lineage that is so important. I don't have that."

"I think the Tridon will allow us to work around that."

A worried frown drew her brows together. "And if they don't?" She couldn't bear the thought of getting her hopes up, of relaxing, thinking herself secure in his love, only to have her dreams torn to shreds.

He gripped her shoulders, pulling her against him, and rubbed her back soothingly with his large, warm hands. "If they don't, then I will leave the Temple of the Avatar and become Kami again." Placing his finger gently beneath her chin, he brought her eyes up to his. "I will not let you go, Cadence. No matter what." And his lips closed over hers in a kiss like no other. Her heart ached with love for this strong, noble man. She didn't know how long it was before he released her, slowly and with as much reluctance as she felt. "Come, Cadence. It is time for us to begin a new life together on a very old world. And in a few moments, perhaps you will finally be reunited with your brother. I hope all turns out well, for I'm looking forward to meeting him."

She placed her hand in his outstretched palm, determined not even to contemplate the possibility that Chance might not be at the other end of the portal. "What is Tesuvia like?"

He shrugged. "If my inherited memory is accurate, it's a very beautiful world."

Cadence shook her head in bemusement. She who had never had much of an adventurous streak was going to yet another world. Life was funny sometimes. At least, if she ever got homesick, she should have her brother there to tease her out of it, and Claire's extensive library to occupy her time.

"Claire!" She stopped in mid-step.

"Pardon me?" Gildon looked down at her quizzically.

"I forgot Claire."

Gildon shook his head. "I made arrangements with Tailen to transfer all of our personal belongings. Your Claire will be there waiting for you."

"You're sure?" The computer was suddenly very important to her. It was her last link to a home and a time she would never see again.

"I'm sure." He tugged her forward and they entered the room that had been converted into a large interplanetary portal. With his arm wrapped around her waist, they moved to stand before the pillar containing the portal controls. "Are you ready?" he asked, looking down at her with shining eyes.

"Hold on to me?" she murmured.

"Forever," he promised.

Secure in her lover's arms, Cadence closed her eyes as he activated the portal. There was a brief sensation of a million tiny needles piercing her skin, and then . . . nothing. Nothing beyond her intellectual awareness that Gildon remained next to her as she spiraled through an endless corridor of thick gray white mist. No sight. No sound. No smell. Yet, de spite the insular sensation that terrified her, she discovered that she now remembered this experience and understood it. Many times in the past she had endured the tingling misery of having every cohesive element in her body ripped apart as she was reduced to nothing more than an accumulation of molecules. The discomfort was momentary, and the reliability and benefit of such an efficient means of travel far outweighed any disadvantage. Somehow that knowledge, that understanding, blunted her fear.

Sound was the first sensation that returned. She could hear voices. Tesuvian language. And then, in an instant it all returned. The sensation of Gildon's arms around her, warm and reassuring. The unique smell of his warm flesh beneath her nose. And the sight of a large white room.

"Cadence!"

Everything within her went still. That voice! She was almost afraid to believe her ears, frightened of what disappointment would do to her.

"Cadence!"

"Chance?" she murmured hesitantly, turning slowly out of Gildon's embrace. And then she saw him coming toward her. Tall, dark, and as handsome as ever. In the next instant she was swept up in his powerful embrace.

"Oh, Cadence, I thought I'd never see you again. I couldn't believe it when this Tailen fellow sought me out to tell me you were coming."

Her eyes clouded with delirious tears of happiness, Cadence reared back to look into his handsome face. His ebony hair was a little long, and his face had grown leaner, but in her opinion he was still the most attractive hunk of male in the galaxy, with the possible exception of Gildon. As Chance's emerald eyes glowed down at her, made luminous by a sheen of moisture, a huge lump rose in her throat. "I thought

I'd never see you either," she echoed in a choked voice. And then, with an emotional smile trembling on her lips she added, "But even the Empyrean guardians knew better than to separate me from my twin for long."

"Huh?" Chance asked, as eloquent as ever.

She smiled and shrugged. "Never mind. It's a long story." And she hugged him fiercely once again.

"Welcome to our new home," he murmured thickly in her ear. "Welcome to Japura."

And she did feel as though she'd come home, for the two people she loved most in the universe were with her. It was all she needed.

As powerful emotion gradually relinquished its grip, Cadence became aware of the press of people surrounding them as other greetings and reunions took place. They were in a busy portal chamber.

Unable to bring herself to end the physical contact with her brother so soon, she locked one arm around his waist and turned with him to meet her lover. Gildon's eyes glowed with such satisfaction at her obvious happiness that one might have thought that he, personally, had arranged it. A soft, loving smile curved her lips in response. "Chance," she said, "I'd like you to meet my companion, Gildon Ksynjan."

Chance stepped forward to offer his hand as he studied this new man in his sister's life. After a brief hesitation wrought by his inexperience with the custom, Gildon accepted her brother's hand and said in his deep, melodious voice, "I think we will be good friends, Chance."

Chance considered Gildon for endless seconds before his expression softened and he nodded. "I believe we will." Then he frowned in mock severity and added, "As long as you're good to my sister."

Gildon smiled and reached out to take Cadence's hand in his. "I have waited a thousand lifetimes for her. Be assured, I will be good to her. She is my heart."

Futuristic Romance

Love in another time, another place.

In Fugitive Arms by Christine Michels. She is a Stellar Legionnaire, a defiant beauty who will prove she is dedicated and hardworking as any man. But when a mysterious explosion lands Corporal Shenda Ridell in the arms of an escaped prisoner, nothing can protect her from the unexpected perils—and dangerous desires—that follow.
_52029-X $4.99 US/$5.99 CAN

Banner's Bonus by Carole Ann Lee. Tressa Loring can think of much better ways to spend her time than traveling through space with an arrogant brute—especially one she has secretly adored for years. But unknown enemies force her to journey with Nick Banner, even as unending desire leads her to unexplored realms of passion.
_52027-3 $4.99 US/$5.99 CAN

Dorchester Publishing Co., Inc.
65 Commerce Road
Stamford, CT 06902

Please add $1.75 for shipping and handling for the first book and $.50 for each book thereafter. NY, NYC, PA and CT residents, please add appropriate sales tax. No cash, stamps, or C.O.D.s. All orders shipped within 6 weeks via postal service book rate. Canadian orders require $2.00 extra postage and must be paid in U.S. dollars through a U.S. banking facility.

Name _____
Address _____
City _____ State _____ Zip _____
 have enclosed $_____in payment for the checked book(s).
 ayment <u>must</u> accompany all orders.☐ Please send a free catalog.

Futuristic Romance

Love in another time, another place.

Don't miss these tempestuous futuristic romances set on faraway worlds where passion is the lifeblood of every man and woman.

Awakenings by Saranne Dawson. Fearless and bold, Justan rules his domain with an iron hand, but nothing short of magic will bring his warring people peace. He claims he needs Rozlynd for her sorcery alone, yet inside him stirs an unexpected yearning to sample her sweet innocence. And as her silken spell ensnares him, Justan battles to vanquish a power whose like he has never encountered—the power of Rozlynd's love.

_51921-6 $4.99 US/$5.99 CAN

Ascent to the Stars by Christine Michels. For Trace, the assignment is simple. All he has to do is take a helpless female to safety and he'll receive information about his cunning enemies. But no daring mission or reckless rescue has prepared him for the likes of Coventry Pearce. Even as he races across the galaxy to save his doomed world, Trace battles to deny a burning desire that will take him to the heavens and beyond.

_51933-X $4.99 US/$5.99 CAN

Dorchester Publishing Co., Inc.
65 Commerce Road
Stamford, CT 06902

Please add $1.75 for shipping and handling for the first book and $.50 for each book thereafter. NY, NYC, PA and CT residents, please add appropriate sales tax. No cash, stamps, or C.O.D.s All orders shipped within 6 weeks via postal service book rate. Canadian orders require $2.00 extra postage and must be paid in U.S. dollars through a U.S. banking facility.

Name _____

Address _____

City _____ State _____ Zip _____

I have enclosed $_____in payment for the checked book(s).

Payment <u>must</u> accompany all orders.☐ Please send a free catalog.

Futuristic Romance

Enjoy these futuristic romances set on faraway worlds where passion is the lifeblood of every man and woman.

Not Quite Paradise by Jan Zimlich. Single mom Laura Malek never expects to be held captive by a mysterious stranger in her own home. But she finds surprising solace in the broad-chested star traveler whose sure touch and strong embrace make her fear for the day he will return to his own galaxy. But Aayshen Rahs belongs among the stars, and only through the power of love can their passion survive in a world that is not quite paradise.

_52051-6 $4.99 US/$6.99 CAN

A World Away by Pam Rock. A privileged passenger on the skyliner *Moon Courier,* Alena Yor is waiting for the journey to end when she first meets virile officer Garner Rie. But any contact between the lowly officer and the highborn beauty is strictly off-limits in the rigid society. Then their ship crashes on a tropical, primitive planet, and Alena has to resist her own growing desire or fall captive to a forbidden passion that threatens to consume them both as it forever changes their lives.

_52043-5 $4.99 US/$6.99 CAN

Futuristic Romance

Keeper of the Rings

NANCY CANE

"A passionate romantic adventure!"
—Phoebe Conn, Bestselling Author Of
—*Ring Of Fire*

He is shrouded in black when Leena first lays eyes on him—his face shaded like the night. With a commanding presence and an impressive temper, Taurin is the obvious choice to be Leena's protector on her quest for a stolen sacred artifact. Curious about his mysterious background, and increasingly tempted by his tantalizing touch, Leena can only pray that their dangerous journey will be a success. If not, explosive secrets will be revealed and a passion unleashed that will forever change their world.

_52077-X $5.50 US/$7.50 CAN

Futuristic Romance

Star-Crossed

Saranne Dawson

Bestselling Author Of *Crystal Enchantment*

Rowena is a master artisan, a weaver of enchanted tapestries that whisper of past glories. Yet not even magic can help her foresee that she will be sent to assassinate an enemy leader. Her duty is clear—until the seductive beauty falls under the spell of the man she must kill.

His reputation says that he is a warmongering barbarian. But Zachary MacTavesh prefers conquering damsels' hearts over pillaging fallen cities. One look at Rowena tells him to gird his loins and prepare for the battle of his life. And if he has his way, his stunningly passionate rival will reign victorious as the mistress of his heart.

_51982-8 $4.99 US/$5.99 CAN

Dorchester Publishing Co., Inc.
65 Commerce Road
Stamford, CT 06902

Futuristic Romance

Ring of Fire

New York Times Bestselling Author
Phoebe Conn Writing As Cinnamon Burke!

When mine workers start disappearing from a distant asteroid, Ian St. Ives is sent undercover to discover who is responsible. But a fiery beauty imperils his mission, even as she inflames his desire.

Haven Wray's dedication to the space-age sport of Rocketball has destroyed her marriage, and she vows never again to let another man hurt her. Yet no matter how hard she fights, she can't deny her blazing attraction to Ian St. Ives.

Champion athlete and master spy, Haven and Ian yearn to share heated caresses and unite in fevered ecstasy. But mysterious enemies and hidden secrets threaten to extinguish the embers of their longing before they can ignite an inferno of love.

_52068-0 $5.99 US/$7.99 CAN

Dorchester Publishing Co., Inc.
65 Commerce Road
Stamford, CT 06902